KINGDOM OF SLUMBER

THE KINGDOM TALES BOOK TWO

DEBORAH GRACE WHITE

LUMINANT PUBLICATIONS

KINGDOM OF SLUMBER: A RETELLING OF SLEEPING BEAUTY

By Deborah Grace White

For Tamara
To our many adventures, past and future.

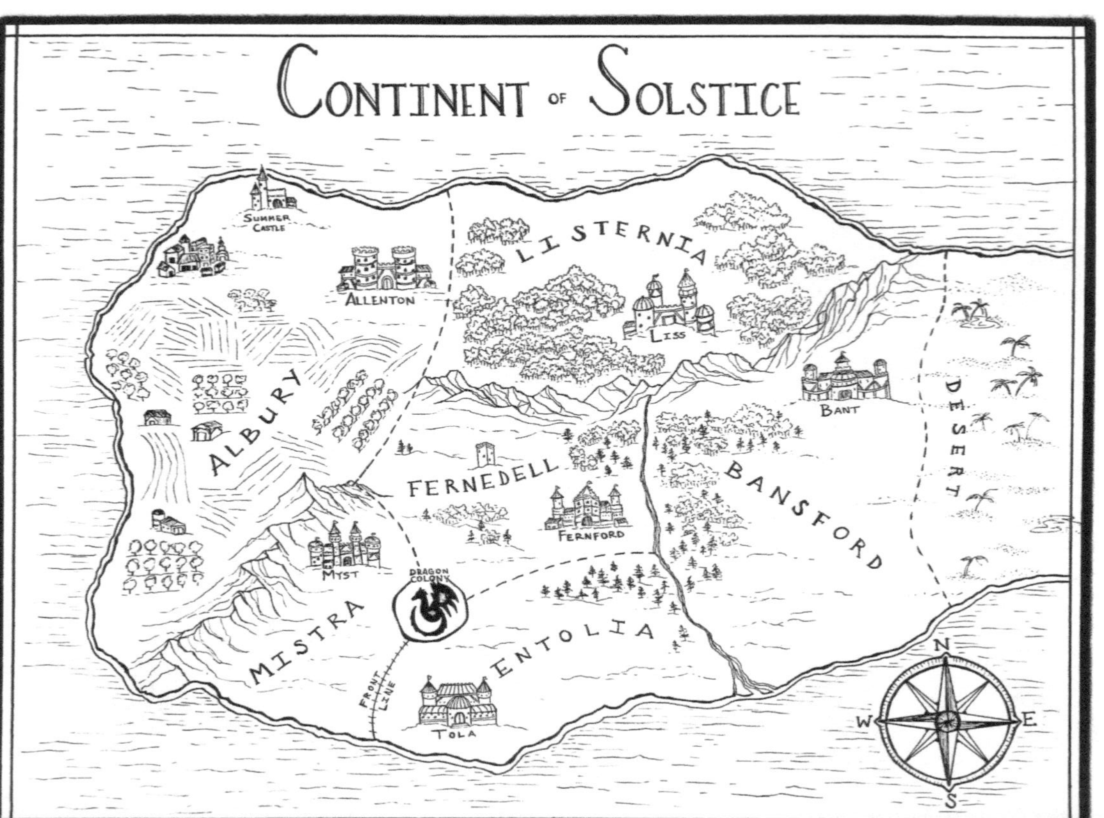

Continent of Solstice
Summer Castle
Allenton
LISTERNIA
Liss
Bant
DESERT
ALBURY
FERNEDELL
Fernford
BANSFORD
Myst
DRAGON COLONY
MISTRA
FRONT LINE
ENTOLIA
Tola
N
S
E
W

PROLOGUE

Lord Montgomery sighed, fixing his twin brother with an impatient look.

"Will you relax, Mortimer? You're clucking as much as the girls."

Mortimer followed Montgomery's gaze to see their sisters, also twins, sitting side by side on a settle and jiggling their legs in unison.

"Don't be so heartless, Monty," Mortimer protested. "Aren't you even a little worried for Victor and Ianthe? The physician said that after such a terrible pregnancy, he had grave concerns about how the birth would go."

Montgomery shrugged, only the tightness of his shoulders betraying any hint of anxiety. "We'll know soon enough."

"Really, Monty," Mortimer said, frowning. "I would have thought you'd have a little more sympathy for Victor. He is our cousin after all!"

"Sympathy?" Montgomery repeated incredulously. "That cousin happens to be the king, in case you've forgotten. He's got his crown, he's got his queen, he's about to have his heir. What could he possibly need sympathy for?"

Mortimer stared at him. "You think he wanted the crown so young?" he demanded. "He's only thirty-five! Aunt and Uncle's deaths were the last thing he wanted!" He dropped his voice. "And he confided in me that he and Ianthe had begun to despair of conceiving a child. It's been five years."

"I know how long it's been," said Montgomery with a snap. He knew that Mortimer wasn't trying to annoy him, but it didn't stop him from scowling. "And Ianthe is ten years younger than Victor, same as us. She probably has many children ahead of her. You know how dramatic Victor can be. I'm sure he overstated the physician's warnings."

Before Mortimer could retort, a page boy appeared in the doorway. The two sisters leaped to their feet, and Melodia hurried forward to relieve the page of the parchment he was holding out. Montgomery barely recognized the king's seal before she ripped it open, her eyes scanning the page rapidly.

"The baby is born!" she cried joyfully. "And the child and Ianthe are both well!"

In spite of his dismissive words, Montgomery let out a long breath, the same as his three siblings. His anxiety now cleared away, however, he felt the familiar resentment instantly creeping in to take its place. None of his siblings had any idea of his thoughts, of course. He'd made sure of that. Melodia turned to her sister, and Miranda embraced her tearfully. Mortimer slapped Montgomery on the back, beaming from ear to ear.

But Montgomery could see that there was almost a full page of writing, and he prompted his sister impatiently.

"What else does Victor say?"

She turned her attention back to the parchment. "So like Victor to send us word immediately," she said, wiping moisture from her eyes. "He knew how nervous we all were, bless him."

"Yes, yes, he's a paragon of virtue," Montgomery said impatiently. Anger flared in him, but he tamped it down. "What else does he say?"

Melodia's face dropped a little as she read on. "He says the birth was difficult, and at one stage the physician had grave fears for Ianthe. He says…" her voice was soft now, and she glanced at her sister sadly, "the physician has made it very clear there will be no more children."

Miranda put a hand to her heart. "Oh, the poor things. I know Ianthe wanted a large family. Still," she took on a bolstering tone, "this dear little mite is safely here, and no one can take that away from them."

"What's the boy's name?" Montgomery asked, showing interest in spite of himself.

Melodia looked back at the parchment, her eyebrows rising. "Actually…" she looked up at the other three, "it's a girl. And although it's not to be made public until the christening, her name is Azalea."

Montgomery froze, and he felt Mortimer do the same. Their eyes met, and as had once been so common, Montgomery knew his twin was thinking the same thing he was.

"And they'll have no more children," Mortimer said quietly. He gave a low whistle. "So no heir after all."

Montgomery was silent, his sharp mind instantly flying through the implications. A girl had never inherited the crown in all of Listernia's history. He glanced at Mortimer, who looked grave. Was he thinking of the accident of fate that had caused him to be born only a matter of minutes after Montgomery?

"Well," Montgomery said slowly, "that changes things."

"Precious little Azalea, she's very welcome," Miranda said briskly. "And since Victor mentioned the christening, we should finalize our plans."

Montgomery paid only cursory attention to the excited

chatter of the other three, his brooding thoughts on this new development. This changed things indeed.

"I'm so delighted you're here."

Victor's enthusiastic tone and beaming face made Montgomery raise an eyebrow. He was certainly taking his disappointment well.

"She'll call you all Aunt and Uncle, of course," the king babbled on. "You've been brothers and sisters to me all my life, after all."

"Oh Victor!" The girls converged on their cousin, embracing him with tears in their eyes.

Montgomery sighed. He knew they were five years younger than him, but they were still twenty. Too old to be behaving like sentimental children.

But Victor didn't seem to mind. He laughed with delight as he returned their hugs, then put a hand on the ornate door.

"Ianthe isn't yet well enough to get up," he said brightly, "but she's excited to see you all. We couldn't wait any longer. I can hardly believe Azalea is already two weeks old, and you haven't been able to meet her before now."

He pushed the door open and gestured them through. Montgomery felt uncomfortable about looking at the convalescing queen, but he couldn't help his eyes being drawn to the bed. She looked pale, her undeniable beauty marred by the shadows under her eyes, but her face was beaming with happiness.

"Welcome!" she said in her soft voice. She tilted her arms to show the bundle held there. "This is Azalea."

The girls rushed over, exclaiming with delight and making all the appropriate comments. Mortimer hung back, perhaps also, if to a lesser degree, feeling strange about approaching the queen in her bed.

"Come on Morty, Monty," Victor said jovially. "Don't you want to meet our daughter and heir?"

"Heir?" Montgomery repeated, startled. His eyes flew to Victor's. "What do you mean? She's a girl. She can't inherit the crown."

A shadow passed over Victor's face, and his shrewd gaze seemed to pierce Montgomery.

"Actually, Cousin, she can," he said calmly. His voice hardened ever so slightly. "And she will."

"Truly?" Mortimer looked cautious, but there was an excited note to his voice. Montgomery scowled at his twin.

"That's right." Victor nodded. "When the physician told us we couldn't have more children, I'll admit I was a little concerned about the future. But the law has been extensively checked since then. It's perfectly legitimate for a princess to inherit the crown if the monarch has no sons." He shrugged. "It's simply never happened before. Every other king has kept going until he had a son."

"Oh, how wonderful, Ianthe!" Miranda cried. She cooed down at the baby. "Our little future queen!"

"But that's preposterous!" Montgomery protested, unable to hold it in. "Listernia has never had a princess inherit. It can't be done!"

"As I've just explained," Victor said, his voice now as hard as granite, "it can be done."

"It's true, Monty," Ianthe said softly, and Montgomery's eyes were drawn reluctantly to the bed again. "It's all above board. Victor has made sure every relevant law was checked."

"It shouldn't be allowed," Montgomery growled. "It's absurd."

There was an uncomfortable silence, and even gentle Ianthe's face grew hard.

"Brother," Mortimer said, the rebuke quiet but firm. "Guard your tongue."

"It seems it's too late to guard your heart, Cousin," Victor said, from under lowered brows. "I take it the birth of our daughter made you covet what never was, and never will be yours."

His words ignited a spark of pure rage deep within Montgomery, the old wound flaring instantly to life. "This isn't about me," he spat. "It's about the good of the kingdom. Listernia will be the weakest kingdom in Solstice with only a princess to inherit."

"I disagree," said Queen Ianthe coldly. "I don't see any reason why Azalea can't be as strong a monarch as any of the other kingdoms boast."

She exchanged a look with her husband, and Montgomery followed her gaze. Victor was smiling, looking between his wife and his daughter with a fierce pride. The fool couldn't even see what a disaster this was.

"Of course you think that," said Montgomery dismissively. "You don't understand these things. You weren't born into the royal family, like the rest of us."

His rude comment sparked protests from all three of his siblings this time, and Victor took a menacing step forward.

But Queen Ianthe just let out a sigh. "I do understand these things, Montgomery," she said, her voice a little sad. "And we know some will be concerned about the prospect of our first crown princess." She again exchanged a glance with Victor. "But we've already got a plan to reassure them."

The king gave a brisk nod. "That's right." He cast his eyes around the group. "You know that the king and queen of Bansford have two princes now. The younger is not quite two years old."

"An heir and a spare," Montgomery drawled. "You must be green with jealousy, Cousin."

King Victor glared at him, although his voice was calm. "I would not trade Azalea for ten boys," he said. "But I do recognize my duty to the kingdom, and I agree that it is preferable to have a king as well as a queen." His eyes rested on his wife, a warmth in their depths that made Montgomery want to gag. "I know I am incredibly grateful that I didn't have to carry the burden of a crown alone for long."

He snapped himself out of it, looking at his cousins again. "It won't be formally announced until the christening, but the king and queen of Bansford have already expressed a willingness to form a betrothal between Azalea and their younger son, Bentleigh. The proposal is that he make substantial visits here throughout his childhood, and once he and Azalea are grown, they will marry, and he will live here permanently. One day, he and Azalea will rule Listernia as king and queen."

"That sounds like a very sensible solution," said Melodia approvingly. "Not only will it allay the concerns of the fastidious, but it will form an ironclad alliance with one of the most powerful kingdoms in Solstice."

The king nodded. "Precisely. Bansford and Listernia have danced around the idea of a formal alliance for years. This will solidify it beyond anything I could have hoped for."

"Yes," sighed Miranda, a little sentimentally. "I hope this Bentleigh grows to be a kind boy. And that Azalea isn't too disappointed not to get to choose her own husband."

"I hope so, too," said Queen Ianthe softly, her face a little troubled.

"Of course he'll be kind," said Melodia briskly. "Now, let's talk about this christening." She exchanged an excited look with her sister, the two of them turning to Ianthe. "We have a suggestion that we'd like to run by you."

"That's right," Miranda chimed in. Her glance encompassed King Victor as well. "We know that our father was the first royal to ever marry an enchantress," she said. "And that no magic-carrier has ever been so close to the royal family as we are." She drew a breath. "We've been talking, and we propose to give little Azalea magical christening gifts."

"You mean artifacts?" Queen Ianthe asked curiously.

Melodia shook her head. "Not objects, but actual magic," she said, her voice tinged with excitement. "We've been doing a great deal of research throughout your pregnancy, and apparently such gifts can actually help shape a person's life, if they are given soon enough after the birth."

"I can give her the gift of beauty, for example," Miranda said. "We would run our selections by you, of course. But we thought the christening might be a good opportunity to do it."

"I think it's a wonderful idea!" King Victor said.

Montgomery wasn't paying a great deal of attention to his sisters' foolish idea, but he did notice that Queen Ianthe looked a little hesitant. Ironic, he thought, her reluctance about the use of magic.

"If you're sure it's safe..."

"Of course, Ianthe," Melodia said earnestly. "You would be able to approve or disapprove every word we were to say over your precious girl."

The queen nodded, looking reassured. Montgomery narrowed his eyes. She was as foolish as the rest, unable to see anything but the good of her little brat.

"But wouldn't that take a great deal of magic?" the king asked suddenly. He frowned. "Would it be safe for *you*?"

Melodia nodded solemnly. "It would be more arduous than anything we've ever done," she acknowledged. "We would need to spend from now until the christening preparing, and I expect we would need to sort of...hibernate for some time afterward. But we are all agreed that it would be well worth the sacrifice."

"Are we?" Montgomery said acidly. "I don't remember ever agreeing to spend my strength on this little interloper."

"Interloper?" Victor stepped forward, fury radiating off him. "How dare you say that about my child, my own flesh and blood, the *only* rightful heir to my throne?"

"Shame on you, Montgomery," said Queen Ianthe, in a voice of choked emotion.

Her words sent a surge of anger through Montgomery, but they seemed to bolster Victor.

The king drew himself to his full height. "You don't need to worry about being asked to make any sacrifices for Azalea, Montgomery. You've made your feelings painfully clear. You will not be giving her any such gift. You are no longer welcome in this room, and you are certainly not welcome at Azalea's christening."

"How will I survive being excluded from this touching family moment?" Montgomery sneered.

His magic crackled in his anger, and for a moment he felt the urge to smite Victor, as he hadn't done since they were children and it was only play. He could feel the shock and disapproval emanating from his siblings, but he didn't look at them. Without a backward glance, he swept from the room, fury spurring him on.

They thought they could cut him out, did they? They would see what he was capable of.

∼

No one at the castle saw or heard from Montgomery again before the christening. He made sure of it. But he had his ways of knowing what was happening, and he was well aware of his siblings' plans. The baby was to be announced as King Victor's heir as soon as all the guests had arrived, and her betrothal to the Bansfordian prince was to be announced immediately after. Then the king's three enchanter cousins were to give their gifts, as a further display of the power of Listernia.

Montgomery, naturally, had plans of his own.

No one observed him as he made his way into the back of the throne room, concealed by magic more powerful than his own. It was a good thing he wasn't dependent on his own resources for concealment. Even with the external assistance, his own *gift* had cost him a great deal of power, and he needed to make it to the cradle before he was seen.

He watched, nauseated, as King Victor and Queen Ianthe presented their drooling infant to an adoring public. The mood of the room shifted as the child was named as King Victor's heir. But, to Montgomery's irritation, King Victor seemed to have read his populace correctly. The announcement of the betrothal to Prince Bentleigh of Bansford caused a palpable lift in tension. The foolish crowd even gave a collective sigh as the miniature prince toddled forward, prompted by a nursemaid, and laid a bright pink flower—an azalea, naturally—in the cradle.

Well, he was presumably supposed to lay it down. Being only two years of age, he didn't follow instructions as well as might have been hoped. He chucked the flower into the cradle with his chubby little arm, and from what Montgomery could see, it landed smack on the infant's face. The crowd tensed, and Montgomery knew a vindictive moment of satisfaction as he waited for her to cry. But instead, she broke the horrified silence with a gurgling, baby laugh which sent the whole room into transports. Montgomery rolled his eyes.

A short ceremony followed, in which the toddler was presented with a thick ring bearing the Listernian crest. It was a symbolic item traditionally worn by the crown prince of Listernia, and it made Montgomery's blood boil to see it given to a Bansfordian. That ring should be on his own finger. Of course it was much too large for the two-year-old's finger, so it was placed around his neck on a thick golden chain.

The pompous master of ceremonies explained to the crowd that the ring did not confer on young Prince Bentleigh the status of King Victor's heir. It was merely a symbolic gesture acknowledging the intended alliance, and the child's future role, as king to Azalea's queen. The master of ceremonies also explained, with the hint of a rare smile, that the ring, and its chain, had been strengthened with a simple enchantment that would ensure they were not lost, and could not be removed by anyone but the prince himself. Mortimer's work, most likely, Montgomery reflected darkly.

It was doubtful the toddler understood the import of all this, but he puffed his chest out proudly, clearly aware that he was for the moment at the center of attention.

"And now," King Victor said, stepping forward, "Crown Princess Azalea is honored to receive some very special gifts."

Montgomery slipped from the room. That was his cue. His siblings were nowhere to be seen, but that didn't trouble him. He knew their plan was to wait in an antechamber, and make a dramatic entrance. He hurried through the corridors, still invisible to onlookers, and reached the antechamber in time to see Melodia disappear into the throne room. Only Miranda remained.

They'd been quick then. He knew Mortimer was to go first, then the girls. He waited, silent and invisible, behind the youngest of his sisters. Miranda cast a couple of confused glances around the room, probably able to sense the magic that was keeping him concealed. But she must have decided it was creeping in from the throne room, because she shook her head slightly and stepped through the door after her sister.

Montgomery followed, waiting only until he had heard Miranda gift the brat with beauty, before throwing off the magic that kept him hidden. His sisters, slumped into chairs and utterly depleted from their exertion, stared at him in astonishment. The crowd gasped, but they looked excited rather than afraid, probably assuming his dramatics were part of the show.

Ianthe drew in a fearful breath, and Victor's hand flew to his sword, but they were powerless, just like their guards. With a muttered word, Montgomery threw magic over the room, freezing everyone present. For a moment he just stood there, smiling indulgently at the now silent and unmoving crowd. Then he strolled up to the cradle, and glanced down into it.

Crown Princess Azalea was frozen as well, but her eyes were still bright and inquisitive, and her mouth was curled into a half smile. Montgomery looked away.

"I must say, Cousin," he said, strolling up to King Victor, and flicking his shoulder disrespectfully. "I'm very offended not to have been invited to today's festivities. But fortunately," he dawdled back to the cradle, "I'm a generous person, and I've decided to give your *heir*," he turned the word into a sneer, "a gift anyway."

All right, enough playacting. He rolled up his sleeves, and his tone turned serious.

"People of Listernia." He lifted his hands over the infant. "You have heard the king's claim, that under the law this brat can supposedly be his heir. And he tries to smooth it over by uniting her with the Bansfordian child." He flicked a dismissive hand toward the frozen toddler. "But if we are to follow the *law*, we must remember that neither of these things can be formalized until she is sixteen years of age."

He gave a nasty smile. "But so many things can go wrong in

life. It's rare for our plans to go smoothly. We've all learned that, have we not? The littlest things can overset them. An unfortunately placed rabbit hole can cause a horse to stumble, and throw its rider against a rock." He named the way Victor's mother, the old queen, had died. "A freak summer storm can turn a simple voyage into a shipwreck." His sneer fell away for a moment at the memory of the disaster that had claimed not only Victor's father, but his own parents as well. He looked down at the baby. "And so very many dangers surround a child. A scraped knee, a sting from a wasp, a pricked finger."

His twisted smile returned. "Yes, I like that one. Time for my own gift, then. Instead of an anointing and a betrothal, here's what will happen on the princess's sixteenth birthday. She will prick her finger, and she won't live through the night." He turned to glare at his cousin. "And the whole kingdom will suffer with her."

"Montgomery, no!" The anguished cry made Montgomery start, pulling the dregs of his magic around him in a shield. Everyone in the room should still be frozen.

The sight of his twin brother's face, white and horrified, made him drop his defensive magic. Mortimer didn't have it in him to attack Montgomery, no matter what he'd done. Montgomery had been foolish not to check more carefully, but his brother must not have been in the room when he cast his freezing charm.

"What have you done, Monty?" Mortimer whispered. He knelt at the cradle, tears in his eyes.

"Little one, I haven't yet given my gift."

Montgomery bit back a curse. He thought he'd been the last, and that his siblings would have been all but catatonic by now. Mortimer closed his eyes, and Montgomery could feel him drawing magic around him. He wanted to stop his twin, but he had no strength to move. He'd already expended a great deal, and holding the freezing charm was taking everything he had.

"I have no time for fancy words, or careful preparation," Mortimer continued grimly. "But with every ounce of power I have, I reverse the dark magic that has been sent against you."

He threw his hands over the cradle, and a faint glow emanated from them. Montgomery could feel his control wavering, and he knew it was time to be gone. Let Mortimer do his worst. His fool brother might think their power was equal, but Montgomery had access to a magic Mortimer couldn't even imagine.

With a last malicious glance at Victor's frozen face, Montgomery sprinted for the door. Not until he had left the confines of the castle, utterly depleted, did he drop the freezing magic.

His work was done.

CHAPTER ONE

Azalea

"Will you stop fussing with my hair, Winifred?" Azalea batted her friend's hand away. "My maid has already done it, and it's good enough."

"Your maid is not gifted with hair," grunted Winnie, battling with an unruly strand. "And don't call me Winifred."

Azalea grinned, unrepentant. "What's the big deal, Winnie? It's just dinner."

"Just dinner?" Winnie demanded. "It's not just dinner! It's dinner with the king and queen of Bansford, not to mention Prince Bentleigh."

"Ben hasn't missed a single birthday of my life," said Azalea lightly. "If you're trying to convince me that his presence makes dinner a state event—"

"You know what a big deal this is, Princess," Winnie cut her off, her tone scolding. "You turn sixteen tomorrow. People have come from all over Solstice to attend your anointment and betrothal."

Azalea rolled her eyes. "Ben and I have been betrothed liter-ally since I was born, Winnie. It's not exactly big news. And that stuff isn't until tomorrow. Tonight it's just us." She gave a small shudder. "Plus Ben's serious and terrifying parents."

"So you should be at your best," said Winnie triumphantly. "And, you know as well as I do that the betrothal, like your anointment as heir, can't be legally formalized until you're sixteen. There." She stepped back, giving a satisfied nod at Azalea's dark hair. Her eyes transferred to her friend's, reflected in the mirror, and she leaned forward with a sly grin.

"Surely you want to look good for your handsome prince, Princess." Her face took on a dreamy look. "Because Prince Bentleigh certainly is handsome."

"Ugh!" Azalea groaned, covering her face with her hands. "Don't you start. It's bad enough that I'm going to be forced to marry my best friend, without having to hear every other girl in the court mooning over him every time our betrothal is mentioned."

"Well, I think you're extremely lucky," said Winnie frankly. Her eyes became unfocused. "And not just because he's a hand-some prince. If anyone looked at me the way Prince Bentleigh looks at you, I'd be well satisfied."

Azalea couldn't help laughing at the other girl's besotted look. "You're such a romantic, Winnie. Ben looks at me the way he always has. You're imagining things."

"I'm not," said Winnie forcefully. She gave Azalea a curious look. "Does it make me a romantic to want such things? Don't you want romance?"

Azalea shrugged, a slight edge beneath her cheerful smile. "Princesses can't afford to be romantic. Not the ones who are betrothed at birth, anyway."

Winnie's expression softened slightly. "You know, Princess Azalea," she said carefully, "whether I'm imagining things or not, Prince Bentleigh cares about you."

"I know he does," said Azalea quickly. "I care about him, too."

Winnie nodded. "Your parents care about you as well. And you know how nervous they are—how nervous we all are—about tomorrow."

Azalea sighed. "Yes, I know. And I wish they'd all stop fussing. Uncle Morty undid the curse the moment it was cast. There's absolutely nothing to worry about. I'll be completely fine."

"We don't know that, Your Highness," Winnie contradicted. "I've heard Lord Mortimer say it myself. He can't be sure how effective his intervention was. He doesn't know if it completely undid the curse, had no effect on the curse at all, or did something in between."

Azalea waved a careless hand. "Of course it undid the curse. He and this Montgomery are twins. Equal and opposite. The curse has had absolutely no ill effects on me in my entire life."

"It wasn't supposed to have any effect until your sixteenth birthday," Winnie started, but Azalea silenced her with a gesture.

"Please, Winnie," she said plaintively. "It's my birthday tomorrow. Can we please not have this conversation again?"

Winnie raised an eyebrow. "Well if you'd rather go back to talking about how handsome Prince Bentleigh is..."

"You fight dirty," Azalea complained. Her expression darkened. "I'm still cross with Ben, anyway. He used to sympathize with me about how overprotective my parents are. Now he's almost as bad! You should have read his last letter."

"No," said Winnie dryly, "I definitely *shouldn't* be reading your love letters from your prince."

"They're not love letters," Azalea scowled, feeling unreasonably defensive.

Ben had always been there, all her life, her closest friend and most reliable fellow troublemaker. He was supposed to be a safe haven when her parents' fears and expectations threatened to drive her insane. What was it about the approach of her sixteenth birthday that made everyone obsessed with how dreamy he apparently was, and how lucky she must feel to be betrothed to him? Not to mention Ben's growing obsessiveness about her safety. Was there no one left she could be carefree with?

A bell tinkled on the wall, and Winnie's tone turned businesslike. "It's time, Your Highness."

Azalea pushed herself to her feet, sighing. "Did you know, when I visited Ben's castle last year, I discovered that in most castles those bell pull things go the other way? So the royals can summon servants at will."

Her thoughts darkened as she remembered the trip, the one and only occasion her parents had ever allowed her to leave Listernia's capital, Liss. She had begged her parents to let her go for almost a year before they agreed. She'd never set foot outside the city before, and she'd been sure it would be a grand adventure. She'd been wrong. Only Ben's presence had kept it from being unbearably miserable. And even he couldn't soften how humiliating it had been to be followed by six Listernian guards, literally everywhere she went. To make matters worse, she had gotten the sense that Ben's parents had been offended by the excessive protection.

With a sigh, she turned her mind back to the conversation. "Apparently I'm the only royal in Solstice who needs the servants to use the bell to keep me on schedule."

Winnie laughed. "It's hard to imagine you pulling a bell to summon servants."

"Of course not," said Azalea brightly. "The servants' halls are the most interesting place in the castle! I'd never get to go there at all if I could summon anyone at the tug of a rope."

Winnie just chuckled, shooing her from her own room. Azalea made her way toward the small dining hall, flanked by the two-guard escort that always followed her everywhere, even in her own castle. Their presence was too familiar to trouble her, and she had a skip in her step. Despite everyone's edginess, she was determined to enjoy herself. It was her birthday tomorrow, after all.

Thanks to the prompt from the bell, she wasn't late, but she still wasn't the first to arrive at the private dinner. Her parents were already present, deep in conversation with Ben. They all turned when she opened the door, smiles lighting their faces as they took in her form in the doorway. Her heart lifted at sight of Ben's tousled chestnut hair and warm brown eyes, an answering smile leaping to her face. Then she remembered that he was in disgrace, and she lifted her chin slightly.

Ben clearly understood the gesture, because his smile turned rueful, although his eyes still twinkled at her. She sailed across the room with her habitual grace—*thank you, Aunt Miranda*—and sank into her appointed seat, across from Ben, and at her father's right hand.

"Welcome to our fair kingdom, Prince Bentleigh," she said with crushing formality.

He just chuckled. "Hello to you too, Zayla."

"Azalea," her mother sighed, her expression pained. "I don't even want to know why you're annoyed with Bentleigh this time, but please try to hold it in once his parents arrive."

"Oh, don't worry, Mother," said Azalea brightly, reaching for a steaming bread roll. "I'm far too terrified of King Rhinehart and Queen Eliza to say anything untoward in front of them."

She glanced mischievously at Ben across the table, and he grinned. She knew him well enough to read the answer in his eyes that he was far too well-trained to say in front of her parents. *Me too.* Despite her mixed emotions about their betrothal, she was genuinely glad that because of her, Ben would get to escape Bansford, which sounded like a grim and strict kingdom, and live a more relaxed life in Listernia.

"Well, that's a relief," her father said dryly.

"I'm sure." Azalea couldn't quite keep the edge from her voice. "It would be terrible for them to find out how irresponsible your heir is." Her father shot her a long-suffering look, and she brightened. "Not that you need me to be responsible, really, since you've got Bentleigh to be the son you never had. He's got your ring around his neck right now, and as of tomorrow, he'll be wearing it on his finger. He may as well be your heir, really."

A clinking noise drew her attention to Ben, fidgeting with his cutlery, and remorse washed over her. Things with her parents were a little tense lately—thanks to the approach of the fateful birthday—but she hadn't meant to make him uncomfortable. It was just that his presence was so familiar, it was easy to forget he was there.

"I'm sorry, Ben," she said quickly. "I know none of this is your choice, and I didn't mean to criticize you." She saw her father look between her and Ben, and she faced him. "I also owe you an apology, Father," she added, and the king's face softened slightly. "I was only joking."

"How are you feeling about tomorrow, Azalea?" asked her mother, deftly redirecting the conversation. Something about her timid expression as she asked the question chafed Azalea, as it had so often done.

She sighed. "I'm *trying* to feel excited, since I normally love birthdays. But it's a little difficult given how doom and gloom everyone is around here."

"Azalea," her father said, his sternness reappearing as rapidly as her impertinence had done.

"I know, I know," sighed Azalea. "It's such a shame Uncle Montgomery cursed me."

Her mother looked upset, and her father angry, as they did every time she casually mentioned the curse.

"That man is not your uncle," her father said, his brow stormy.

Even Ben shot her a reproachful look.

"I was only trying to lighten the mood!" she protested. "You didn't let me finish. I was going to say that it's a shame I got cursed, because Uncle Morty had to use his gift to undo it." She lifted her hands, counting on her fingers. "Beauty and grace from Aunt Miranda, health and wit from Aunt Melodia, and Uncle Mortimer told me once that he was *going* to give me good nature and sweetness." She flashed her parents a cheeky grin. "I probably would have been a very biddable girl if only he'd been able to follow through with the plan."

Ben choked on a laugh, and her mother had a wistful look, as if she was quite taken with the prospect. But apparently her father wasn't to be charmed out of his mood.

"If only we could be sure Mortimer's intervention really did undo the curse," he started sternly, "I might be more inclined to—"

Fortunately for everyone's temper, King Rhinehart and Queen Eliza were announced at that moment, and the conversation came to an abrupt end. True to her word, Azalea was on her best behavior through the meal, with one private exception.

"Salt, Azalea?" Bentleigh's casual question brought Azalea's eyes snapping to his face, and she raised an eyebrow. He knew she didn't like salt on her potatoes.

"Of course," she said, holding her hand out impatiently. He slid the salt across the table to her, and she gave a sneaky look at the two sets of monarchs. Satisfied that they weren't paying attention, she pulled the salt cellar onto her lap, sliding out the tiny piece of parchment wedged into the bottom. She smoothed it on her dress to see the message in Ben's familiar, even writing.

5 am. Royal fishpond.
Birthday surprise.

She raised her fork in her left hand, taking a leisurely bite of food as her right hand fished into a pocket. Pulling out a nub of lead, she scribbled quickly on the parchment. It now read:

5 am. ~~Royal fishpond.~~ Forest gate.
Birthday surprise. (It had better be good.)

She slid the parchment back into its hiding spot, returning the salt to the table. Ben reached for it in an unhurried way.

"Father?" He offered the salt, and Azalea had to admit he was good. If she hadn't been looking for it, she would never have seen the flash of movement that removed the parchment again.

A moment later Ben glanced nonchalantly at his lap. When he looked up at Azalea, his expression looked torn between amusement and exasperation. But she knew he wouldn't refuse. He never did.

Plus, it wasn't like he could complain to her. They weren't given any opportunity for private speech during the meal, and Azalea headed straight for her rooms afterward. She couldn't take her parents' increasing anxiety any longer. She would be relieved when her birthday was over, and everyone could stop worrying about a disaster that wasn't coming.

What she didn't count on, was her father following her to her rooms, to indulge in a little more anxiety.

"Father." She tried heroically to summon a smile. "Come in. If you're here to tell me again to be careful tomorrow, I promise you don't need to. I won't touch anything all day, if it makes you feel better. My maid knows not to use so much as a hair pin, and—"

"That's not why I'm here," her father cut her off. He sat

heavily on a seat, his eyes serious as they rested on her face. "I just..." He sighed, and Azalea sat as well. It was rare to see the king at a loss for words. "I know you sometimes find us a little overbearing," he tried again.

Azalea kept an admirably straight face at the understatement. Her father hadn't even allowed her to learn to ride a horse until she was fourteen, convinced she'd fall off and be killed, like his own mother had been. Mortification still gripped her whenever she remembered the incident when she was thirteen, and the royal family of Entolia were visiting. That was before Entolia became embroiled in a war with Mistra. The oldest Entolian princess, Zinnia, had only been ten, but she'd been extremely accomplished on a horse. She'd asked Azalea to ride with her, and it had been all Azalea could do not to burst into tears when her mother kindly explained to the younger princess that Azalea didn't ride.

Of course, she had known how to ride by then. She'd pestered Ben into teaching her a couple years before that, but she could hardy admit that to her parents, so the humiliation in front of Princess Zinnia wasn't lessened.

"The fact is, we worry about you," her father said, pulling her attention back to him.

"You mean, you worry that I'm going to drive you both into an early grave," said Azalea, with an attempt at lightheartedness.

Her father gave her a look. "I'm not exactly on my deathbed, Azalea."

"No," said Azalea, unable to help thinking of what he hadn't said. "You're not."

"Neither is your mother," the king said firmly, reading her better than she'd expected.

Azalea met his eyes. "I know she's not, but she always seems so..." She struggled to put words to the general sense of uncertainty, almost timidity, her mother had projected as long as she remembered. "Sometimes I wonder if I *am* driving her into an early grave," she muttered.

King Victor sighed, running a hand through his hair. "Of course you're not. Your mother wasn't always so…"

Afraid of her own shadow? Azalea thought, but her father measured his words a little more.

"…cautious." He met Azalea's eyes steadily. "I know it's hard for you to understand, Azalea."

She was silent, unable to deny it. She often struggled to relate to her mother. Azalea was, after all, as far from timid as she could be. She sometimes wondered how she had been born so different from her mother.

"Your mother wasn't so unlike you when she was your age," her father continued, as if sensing her thoughts. "But the first years of our marriage were difficult, as we waited for a child, with a whole kingdom waiting with us. Then it was such a difficult pregnancy, and your birth almost killed her. Physically, I'm not sure she ever fully recovered."

He sighed. "Even before that, she had become gradually less sure of herself. She told me once that she felt…adrift, inside her own mind." He was silent, then his gaze sprang quickly to his daughter's. An almost guilty look passed over his face, and Azalea had the distinct impression he hadn't intended to tell her such a personal detail. "And then, of course," he continued gruffly, "your christening happened…"

"So I really am the cause of all the trouble," Azalea said, her playful tone so forced it sounded painful even to her own ears.

"Of course not," her father said quickly. "You didn't cause any of this. That's the opposite of what I'm trying to say. I just want you to understand that we only make these rules because you're important to us, and to the kingdom, and we want to keep you safe." His eyes were on his hands. "You can't imagine the joy I felt the day you were born." He looked up with a tight smile.

"We'd waited so long for you." The smile melted away. "And you can't imagine the fear I felt the day of your christening, when my own cousin used his magic to freeze me in place, and I had to watch helplessly while he…"

The king trailed off, his voice uncharacteristically husky. Azalea looked away to give him some privacy. She couldn't help but be moved by his words, and by his emotion.

"I know, Father," she said softly.

He gave her a sad smile. "No you don't," he said, without rancor. "How could you? I hope one day you and Bentleigh will have children of your own, and then—"

"Ick, Father!" Azalea protested, the sentimental moment fleeing. "Can we please not talk about me and Ben having children? You promised tomorrow was just a formality, and we don't have to get married until I'm at least eighteen."

"And I meant it," her father said, his forehead furrowed. "But I don't understand your reaction, Azalea. You can't expect me to believe you dislike Bentleigh. The two of you have been as thick as thieves since you were children."

"Of course I don't dislike him," Azalea said wearily. She had no desire to discuss this topic with her father.

The king frowned. "I know it's not romantic, having your parents arrange your marriage, but monarchs do have to make decisions for their kingdom, you know. It can't always be about what you want." He leaned forward, capturing her gaze. "You will be queen one day, Azalea. You don't yet understand what a responsibility that is. How hard this life can be. Every rule, every restriction I've ever placed on you has been to help you, and to serve Listernia."

"I know, Father," Azalea said, more weary than ever. She wasn't sure what was worse—talking to her father about duty, or about romance. At least she had Ben's birthday surprise to look forward to.

"Well, I should let you sleep," her father said gruffly. "Tomorrow is a big day for us all." He stood, but made no move to leave. Azalea watched him warily.

"I just hope you know…" he started, again trailing off. He cleared his throat. "We think very highly of Bentleigh, and we couldn't be happier about the alliance he represents, but…" He met her eyes. "Your mother and I wouldn't exchange you for a son, Azalea, not for any consideration."

Azalea was momentarily speechless, her own emotion threatening to get the better of her. She stood quickly, enveloping her father in a hug.

"I love you too, Father," she said softly.

The king returned the pressure briefly, bestowing a soft smile on her.

"Father," Azalea said abruptly, as he turned to leave.

He raised a questioning eyebrow.

Azalea took a breath. "I know you want to prepare me for the future. I understand better than you think how hard this life can be." She paused. "But I also know that you've been afraid for me all my life." She gave him her most earnest expression. "Can you look me in the eye and tell me that, after tomorrow is passed, and nothing terrible has happened, you'll stop being so restrictive?"

"Azalea," her father said, sounding frustrated. "I know you want more freedom. But whatever happens tomorrow, Montgomery is still out there somewhere. And we have to assume he still wants you dead."

"So nothing will change," Azalea said tonelessly.

"A great deal will change," her father contradicted sternly. "Once your status as my heir is formalized, your responsibilities will increase. And with the betrothal to Bentleigh made official, you will have a greater role in our diplomatic relations with Bansford, as well as—"

"I know, Father," said Azalea wearily. There was a moment of uncomfortable silence, before she forced a smile onto her face. "As you said, it's a big day tomorrow. I'd better get some sleep."

Her father hesitated for a moment, then bid her goodnight and strode from the room. Azalea stood in silence for a long time after he'd left, watching the closed door.

She'd told Winnie that the curse hadn't had any effect on her life, but it wasn't true. Sometimes it felt like it defined every comment, every relationship, every breath she took.

CHAPTER TWO

Azalea

She was awake well before dawn, slipping into a practical dress and sturdy boots. She would have to be dressed very differently for the day's events, of course, so she fully intended to make the most of the free movement while she had it. She was well practiced at her silent preparations, and she had no fear of being overheard by the guards outside her door.

The sun still hadn't risen when she climbed out of her window, shimmying down a pipe and landing softly on her feet. Once again, Aunt Miranda's gift of grace was most welcome. She couldn't help but imagine how horrified her parents would be if they knew she was sneaking out on this of all mornings, but honestly, what did they expect? If they would give her a little more freedom, she wouldn't need to resort to subterfuge.

It wasn't yet five o'clock when she snuck out of the gate that led to the forest, but Ben was already there.

"Happy birthday," he said, stepping toward her with a bright smile.

She grinned. "Thanks. So where's my surprise?"

Bentleigh's laugh was a little self-conscious, which instantly roused Azalea's suspicions. He was normally very self-possessed.

"Slow down," he said. "I'm here, you've made your point. Can we go to the fishpond now?"

Azalea stared at him. "What's so special about the fishpond?"

"It's *inside* the walls," he said dryly.

Azalea made an impatient noise. "Don't start with this, Ben!" She gestured around at the innocuous forest clearing they were standing in. "What trouble am I going to get into here?"

"I don't know," said Ben frankly. "But I do know that you're not supposed to be outside the walls. And whatever trouble you'll find here, I think you'll find even less trouble standing by the fishpond."

Azalea folded her arms. "I'll also be watched by about twenty-five pairs of eyes. If you want to talk to me, talk here."

"Azalea, this isn't the morning to take risks," Ben started, and Azalea cut him off with a scowl.

"You're the one who taught me how to climb out a window, Ben. Every time I've snuck into the forest to explore, it's been with *you*. It's a little hypocritical of you to tell me to be careful." She glanced back toward the castle. "Besides, my parents are always willing to give me more leeway when I'm with you." She flashed him a grin. "Why do you think I put up with you?"

Her humor clearly missed the mark, because a flash of pain seemed to cross Ben's features at her words.

"That's because they trust me," he said gruffly, after a prolonged moment. "And I don't want to abuse their trust by leading you into danger."

"You're not leading me into danger," Azalea said, her voice more serious. "I know what morning this is just as well as you do. I'm not going to take any risks. I just want to talk where we won't be overheard. Then we can go straight back through the gate, and I'll be a model princess all day, I swear."

Ben hesitated for a moment, looking anxious, then let out a long breath. "Fine," he said, not very graciously. He eyed her in silence for a moment. "I know it's frustrating for you," he said seriously, "but you should consider your parents' feelings. The curse feels distant and unreal to us, because we were too young to remember. But to them it feels like yesterday. And this whole business with Prince Justin getting cursed and disappearing a few months ago must have brought it all back."

Azalea's expression grew grave at this mention of the disaster that had befallen the crown prince of their neighboring kingdom. "What happened in Albury made us all jumpy," she agreed. "But nothing like that is going to happen to Listernia. Honestly, although I feel sorry for him, it's not that surprising Prince Justin got cursed, is it? He was always a bit of a bear."

Ben's eyes searched her face, and for an unsettling moment she wondered if Winnie was right. Had he always looked at her like that?

"Magic doesn't work that way," he said softly. "It doesn't only affect the undeserving." He hesitated for a moment, then reached up to touch her cheek. "You were cursed, when you were only a baby. You hadn't done anything wrong."

Azalea's heart was hammering, and she was annoyed by how breathless she suddenly felt. Fortunately for her peace of mind, Ben dropped his hand quickly.

"Surely you didn't want to meet at dawn to talk about Prince Justin," she said, trying to speak lightly. "Where's this surprise?" She peered around, looking for a hidden package.

"It's not a physical gift," Ben said, once again sounding self-conscious. Azalea narrowed her eyes suspiciously, and he hurried on.

"I just wanted to...well, to wish you happy birthday, I guess. Before the festivities start."

"You already did that," Azalea pointed out.

Ben nodded, his gaze on the forest floor. "And happy anointing." His eyes slid to hers again. "And happy betrothal."

"Ugh, don't remind me," Azalea said, and Ben visibly deflated.

"I'm sorry," she said, with a laugh. "That sounded very rude, didn't it? I suppose I should be saying happy betrothal to you, too." He gave her a faint smile, and she sighed. "I don't mean to take it out on you. I know you had no more choice in all this than I did. You're wearing these chains too, so to speak."

She reached up and tapped a finger to the thick gold chain around Ben's neck. It disappeared under his tunic, but she knew that at the end dangled the emblazoned ring which was the symbol of their betrothal. He'd worn it around his neck as long as she could remember, and after the day's betrothal ceremony, he'd be wearing it on his finger, almost like a real crown prince.

She sighed. "It's just so strange, isn't it?"

"Actually," said Ben, not quite meeting her eyes, "that's what I wanted to talk to you about."

She frowned. "What do you mean?"

Ben took a breath. "I know this has been decided for as long as we remember. And I know that in one sense, today's ceremony changes nothing. But in another way..." He hesitated. "I just wanted to do this, before everything becomes official."

Azalea stared at him. "Do what?"

He blundered on, not answering her question. "I don't want you to feel like you have no choice, like this is something unpleasant that's forced on you. I want it to feel—"

"But I do have no choice," Azalea interrupted. "I don't mean to say it's unpleasant exactly, but that doesn't mean it's not forced on me. Well, on both of us. I mean, I know you're probably happy to escape Bansford, but—"

"Azalea!" Ben cut her off. "Will you stop talking, and let me say this?"

Azalea's lips twitched at the exasperated rebuke. She raised her hands in a sign of surrender, and Ben took another deep breath. Instead of speaking, he held out his hand. She took it without hesitation, long experience teaching her to associate the gesture with the call of adventure.

But although Ben tugged her forward, he didn't pull her into the woods for an unsanctioned exploration, not this time. Instead, he drew her toward him, so that they were standing mere inches apart. He kept his grip on her hand, but with his other hand, he reached up tentatively. His fingers hovered for a moment, not quite touching her hair.

"I don't think I've seen your hair down like this since we were children," he commented softly, and irrelevantly.

Azalea attempted a smile. "No hair pins allowed today."

Ben nodded, his eyes still on her hair. Then, abruptly, he slid his hand between her tresses, cupping the back of her neck.

By now, Azalea's heart was racing double time. Despite what she'd said to Winnie, she was extremely aware of Ben's strong, handsome frame, and of the unwavering kindness in his eyes. She was even aware, acutely so, of her own fondness for him, and how indispensable he was to her. If he'd been some unapproachable distant prince, she would probably have been as smitten with him as half of Liss seemed to be.

But he wasn't distant, or unapproachable. He was her best friend, and her betrothed. And she couldn't remember a time when that wasn't true. She'd never had the opportunity to look at him in an unbiased light.

"I know you've always pushed back against having your future written for you, Zayla," Ben said, his voice soft but steady. "And I know we've always been allies. But I need to be honest with you. It's...it's not the same for me as it is for you."

"Ben," Azalea whispered. Her eyes were locked on his, and she couldn't move even if she'd tried.

"Just..." Ben's thumb slid around from where his hand still rested on her neck, brushing with featherlight softness against her lips. A tingle spread out from his touch, half terrifying, half exhilarating. "Just let me get it out." He swallowed. "There are things I need to say, and I wish desperately there was some way I could give you the chance to hear them as just you, with me as just me. Without all," he tilted his head toward the nearby gate, and the castle beyond, "*this*."

He stepped even closer, and Azalea's breath caught in her throat. His familiar smell, like pine needles and woodsmoke, filled her awareness. His eyes were on her lips, and she could barely swallow. It seemed the approaching betrothal ceremony truly had sent everyone mad.

Was Ben, her Ben, going to kiss her?

And more importantly, did she want him to?

She felt like her world was spinning out of control. Ben was careening over a line they had never even come close to crossing. His eyes were searching hers, a spark in them she'd never seen—or never acknowledged—before. She suddenly realized he was waiting for her to speak, to give him some sign.

But her emotions regarding Ben and their betrothal were so convoluted and multilayered that she couldn't even unravel them herself, let alone articulate them to him.

She took a step backward, and he released her, the fire dying out of his eyes. The cold morning air rushed in, chilling her hand, her neck, the places his warmth had been. She took another step, her hand reaching behind her to look for support, although she knew it was an empty clearing.

Something sharp pierced her finger, and she gave a small cry. She brought her hand up before her face, staring in bemusement and irritation from the single drop of red blood to the thick, thorny vine she could have sworn wasn't there a minute ago.

She turned to Ben, momentarily forgetting the awkwardness between them, and ready to complain about the superficial injury. But the absolute horror in his eyes woke her up to the true situation.

It was her sixteenth birthday.

There was a vine where it shouldn't be.

She'd just pricked her finger on its thorns.

She seized her hand convulsively, her eyes locked on Ben's as tremors started to rock her whole body. She took a step toward him, but her legs gave out before she made it. She braced herself for the impact of her fall, but all she felt was Ben's strong arms as they closed around her, holding her up.

"Azalea! *Azalea!*" His anguished, choking cry was the worst sound she'd ever heard, but she couldn't seem to find her voice to respond. With a great effort, she focused on his face, strong and familiar and far more pale than she'd ever seen it.

"Ben," she whispered. "I'm so sorry."

She tried to keep her eyes on his terrified face, but the blackness at the edges of her sight was creeping in. She couldn't fight it. She could only succumb as the darkness claimed her.

CHAPTER THREE

Bentleigh

"AZALEA!"

Bentleigh's arms shook wildly, and not from the weight of Azalea's slight form.

This couldn't be happening. This couldn't be real.

"No, no, no, no, no, no, no." The word tumbled out of his mouth over and over again, panic clouding his mind as he clutched her unmoving form against him.

This couldn't be happening. She couldn't be dead. A surge of hot defiance raced through him. She couldn't die. He wouldn't let it happen. He gave her a gentle shake, one hand supporting her head, and the other wrapped around her waist.

But she remained silent and still, and anguish rose up, overpowering his defiance. There was nothing he could do against this enemy.

He gave a dry, gasping sob. This was all his fault. Why had he let her talk him into coming outside the gate? Why had he insisted on telling her how he felt, when she clearly wasn't ready to hear it? He'd driven her away, straight into the—

He looked up, anger again claiming him at sight of the thick, ugly vine. Unnoticed by either of them, it had snaked its way across the clearing toward them, ripping up the ground as it went.

His eyes dropped to Azalea's peaceful, excruciatingly beautiful face, and agony threatened to overwhelm him. The how of it didn't matter. All that mattered was the reality that she was gone, and he was to blame. He crumpled to the forest floor, burying his face in her dark, unfettered hair as silent sobs shook him.

But something warm tickled his ear, and his head sprang back up. He searched her face desperately, looking for the flush of life in her warm brown skin. Her face was paler than normal, and her features were unnaturally still. But now that he looked more closely, he realized her lips were parted slightly, and her chest rose and fell with each gentle breath.

She was alive.

He scooped her into his arms, lifting her from the ground and hugging her against him. He ran the few short steps to the gate and kicked it open with a splintering crunch.

He stumbled through, and heard a sharp cry from the guards whom he and Azalea had both easily evaded from long practice.

"The princess is hurt!" he gasped. "Call for the royal physician!"

One of the guards sprinted toward the castle. Another, a burly man two decades older than Bentleigh, hurried forward, reaching out as if to take Azalea from him. The man was undeniably stronger than Bentleigh, but the prince held him back with a glare.

"I'll carry her."

The guard hesitated, his eyes raking over Azalea's form, searching anxiously for her injury. Bentleigh saw the moment when his gaze fell on her finger, and his eyes widened with horror.

It was suddenly hard to breathe, and Bentleigh turned away, directing his steps toward the nearest entrance to the castle. Word inevitably spread, and by the time he reached the wing of the castle where the royal suites were located, absolute pandemonium was following in his wake.

He tuned it all out, focusing on the struggle of carrying his burden, and the reassuring feel of Azalea's breathing. The route to Azalea's suite was perfectly familiar, although it had been a long time since the days when they'd snuck around the royal wings pulling pranks. He'd become unwilling to actually go into her suite around the time she was fourteen, and he was sixteen. His continued refusal had irritated her, and she'd always seemed bemused by it. Had he really been so subtle? Could she really not know how long he'd been in love with her?

He'd acquired a sizable escort now, and one of the servants hastened to open the door for him. A maid was lighting a fire, apparently under the happy illusion that the princess was still asleep in the curtained four poster bed. At sight of Bentleigh and his unconscious passenger, she uttered a scream and collapsed in a dead faint.

Bentleigh ignored her completely, taking the last few steps toward the bed. The moment a helpful footman yanked the curtains back, he collapsed onto his knees, laying Azalea's still form down on her own coverlet.

A piercing cry of pure grief ripped through the room, and Bentleigh shuffled out of the way to allow Queen Ianthe to throw herself on her daughter's form.

"She's alive, Your Majesty," Bentleigh said quickly, and the queen turned her tear-stained face to him, looking like she hardly dared to hope. "She's breathing, look!" He nodded at the unconscious princess. "Lord Mortimer's magic must have saved her. But I can't rouse her."

The royal physician bustled into the room, brushing

everyone—even the queen—aside as he took charge of his patient. In watching his arrival, Bentleigh realized for the first time that the king stood behind his wife, his face frozen in horror. His eyes transferred slowly to Bentleigh, a storm of barely restrained fury growing in their depths.

"How?" King Victor's voice was awful in its calm, and Bentleigh felt a shiver go down his spine. But the last thing he cared about at this moment was consequences to himself.

"It was my fault," he said, wringing his hands. "She wanted to meet outside the gate, and I knew we shouldn't, but..." He took a shuddering breath. "We were talking, and she took a step back, and suddenly—" He gave a helpless shrug. "It was a vine, covered in thorns, but it wasn't there before, I swear. I checked the clearing thoroughly before she arrived, and there was nothing dangerous, nothing sharp. I even cleared all the sticks from the ground, in case..."

He covered his face with one strong hand. "I thought she was dead. I thought I'd lost her."

A firm grip on his shoulder startled him, and he dropped his hand. King Victor was looking down at him, his expression telling Bentleigh more clearly than words that it was time to pull himself together. He drew a shuddering breath and stood, nodding to the king.

King Victor cast a fulminating glance around the room. "All of you, out," he commanded the gathered audience. "Only Princess Azalea's maid and the physician's assistant should be here."

One glance at the king's face was enough to clear the room. Bentleigh's respect for the physician grew as the man calmly continued to examine Azalea, completely ignoring the chaos around him. The three conscious royals watched with palpable tension while he completed his assessment.

He had just looked up, his eyes finding the king, when there was a commotion at the door. Bentleigh hadn't paid any attention to the guards who were stationed in the corridor, but he saw now that they were trying to hold back some new arrivals.

"Let them through," King Victor said imperiously.

Two women in their mid-thirties tumbled through the doorway, followed more slowly by a man several years older. They were all well known to Bentleigh. Although they were of course no relation of his, for as long as he could remember, he'd followed Azalea's lead and called them uncle and aunt.

"No!" Miranda's horrified whisper was reflected in the eyes of her sister and brother. The gaze of all three was riveted on the bed, where Azalea lay peacefully.

"She's alive, Mortimer," Queen Ianthe gasped. She struggled to her feet, stumbling forward to seize Mortimer's hands. "You saved her."

Mortimer's eyes remained fixed on Azalea's form. "She's so still," he whispered. "What happened to her?"

Bentleigh stepped forward, forcing himself to speak through the lump in his throat. "Her finger was pricked by a thorn, growing on a vine out in the forest. I would wager anything you like that it wasn't a natural vine. It appeared out of nowhere, and grew aggressively." He swallowed, his voice hitching slightly. "It was like it was coming for her, hunting her down."

"Montgomery's magic," Mortimer said grimly. "It has to be." He cast a shrewd glance at Bentleigh, then stepped forward, putting a firm hand on his shoulder. "Don't blame yourself, Your Highness. I have no doubt you're right that it was coming for her. It would have found her wherever she was. Being outside the wall only meant it reached her early in the morning, instead of having to burrow its way to her throughout the day."

"I should have hacked it to pieces, done anything to stop it touching her," Bentleigh choked, his emotions threatening to get the better of him. "But it happened so fast, I didn't even see it until it was too late." He ran a shaking hand over his face. "Plus I didn't have my sword on me," he added bitterly. "Nothing sharp. Not so much as a belt buckle."

Because I was planning to kiss her, he added silently. *Like a fool I thought she might kiss me back, and I didn't want to take any risks with her so close.*

The thought was agonizing. All the hopes he'd pinned on the morning's conversation were mocking him now.

"This isn't your fault, Bentleigh." Queen Ianthe's gentle voice brought moisture to Bentleigh's eyes, and he turned quickly away. "This course was set almost sixteen years ago."

"The question is, what's wrong with her?" King Victor demanded. "Why won't she wake?"

The physician cleared his throat. "Your Majesty, I've completed an examination of the princess. And from what I can tell, there's nothing physically wrong with her."

"Well, that's good news!" Miranda said, relief heavy in her voice. She glanced doubtfully at the grave faces around her. "Isn't it?"

"What do you mean nothing *physically* wrong with her?" the king asked ominously.

The physician shrugged. "I meant nothing sinister, Your Majesty. Merely that physical ailments are all I am qualified to assess. To all appearances, Princess Azalea is simply asleep."

"She's not, though, is she?" said Melodia grimly. "I can sense the magic hovering around her."

"I am not knowledgeable in such things," the physician said. "But my usual methods for waking an unconscious patient have yielded no result."

"It is an enchanted sleep, without a doubt," Mortimer said, his voice faint. He sank into a chair. "The question is how long it will last."

"Morty?" Miranda knelt at his side, touching his arm gently. "What's wrong? What's happening to you?"

Mortimer shook his head, his eyes screwed shut. "The magic has activated," he said. "I can feel it." He winced. "I used my power to reverse Montgomery's magic. For an ordinary enchantment, one contained and limited to a specific, immediate purpose, our magic would have battled it out on release and been done with the matter. But this…"

"This is different," Melodia finished heavily. "Our gifts weren't that kind of magic. They were highly powered first class enchantments. Beyond anything we've done before or since. They were designed to last Azalea's whole life, mold her experiences constantly."

Mortimer nodded. "Of course, we crafted them carefully, poured all available power into them and then cut off the source. But I had no opportunity to use my crafted gift. I just poured that power into reversing Montgomery's curse."

"What does that mean?" the queen asked, sounding fearful. "What are you saying?" Now that the physician had finished his examination, she had resumed her place by her daughter's side, and was clasping Azalea's hand.

"I'm saying that as Montgomery's magic was activated, so was mine. I can feel the two forces battling even now. I felt it the moment she pricked her finger. That's how we knew something had happened."

Bentleigh stared wide eyed from the enchanter to the sleeping princess. Did that mean Azalea could only last however long Mortimer was able to hold off the dark magic? Was it inching toward her heart, attempting to stop it even now?

"I don't understand it," Mortimer went on. "We're brothers, twins. Our power should be equal. But if it was, mine should be able to sort of…bat his away immediately, and be done with it." He grimaced, his eyes still closed tightly. "But this power that's battering against mine is far stronger than anything I've seen from Montgomery before." He opened his eyes, looking frankly at the king. "I'm sorry to say it, Victor, but it's far stronger than my magic."

"What does that mean?" the king asked frantically. "Will she die after all?"

Mortimer shook his head. "I don't think so. I think the extent of my defense has already been established, and I don't think it will change. If she was going to die, she would have died immediately. My magic softened that death into sleep. It's not unheard of as a counterforce for death curses, when the magic isn't strong enough to provide a true remedy." He shrugged, looking helpless. "But I can't do more. None of us can. The magic was cast a long time ago, and if we wanted to counteract it, we had to do it then."

"So you're saying you have no idea how to wake her?" Bentleigh asked quietly.

Mortimer nodded, his expression regretful. "That's right. I wish I did, Your Highness."

Miranda began to cry quietly, and the queen's face was almost as ashen as her daughter's. "But what are we going to do?" she whispered.

Before anyone could answer, a guard appeared through the doorway, stepping smartly up to King Victor.

"Your Majesty," he said, in a quiet voice that nevertheless carried around the hushed room. "King Rhinehart and Queen Eliza wish to gain entry."

"Tell them they're not wanted," Bentleigh muttered. The guard was clearly well trained, not betraying by so much as a flicker that he'd heard the prince's remark.

"Bring them in," said King Victor calmly. A moment later, Bentleigh's parents entered the suite, their expressions stiff and uncommunicative. Bentleigh saw his mother's eyes flick to Azalea, and then quickly away.

"You have our deepest condolences on this tragedy, Your Majesties," King Rhinehart said.

"She's not dead, Father," Bentleigh snapped. "She's in an enchanted sleep."

"That is a great relief," his father said gravely, with no change in his disapproving expression.

Remembering the battle he had fought to convince his parents to show the proper respect and attend what they termed an "ill-fated occasion", Bentleigh had no doubt what was coming next.

"Given the circumstances, I assume there will be no anointing ceremony," King Rhinehart's eyes flicked to his son, "or betrothal ceremony."

Bentleigh's hands balled into fists at his sides.

"I also imagine you are eager to be free of guests at this inconvenient time," the visiting king continued smoothly.

He was pointedly avoiding looking at all three of King Victor's cousins, and Bentleigh felt embarrassed on his behalf. He wasn't sure what his parents were more uncomfortable with —being in a room with someone under a curse, or being in a room with three actual enchanters. Bentleigh didn't comment on it, of course. His parents knew his views on their drastic reaction to the events of Azalea's christening.

Even Listernia, the true target of Montgomery's curse, hadn't been as offended as the monarchs of Bansford had at being turned into powerless statues by the angry enchanter. Bentleigh's home kingdom had outlawed magic within weeks of the christening, and he knew his parents had entertained doubts ever since about the betrothal they had publicly agreed to. This turn of events must be confirming all their worst fears.

"Certainly," said King Victor, keeping his voice civil with

what looked to Bentleigh like a great effort. "You are of course free to return to Bant, and I look forward to resuming our unfortunately interrupted visit at a later time."

"You are very gracious," said King Rhinehart curtly. Bentleigh was sure he wasn't the only one to notice that his father had given no hint of accepting the invitation. The Bansfordian king turned to his son. "Bentleigh, come. We will depart immediately, give Their Majesties the space they must be desiring."

Bentleigh stared at his father. "What?" he said numbly. "Surely you can't think I'm going to leave?" He gestured at the bed. "I'm not going anywhere with Azalea in this state."

"Bentleigh." His father's voice was as hard as steel, and once upon a time that look would have silenced Bentleigh. Not anymore.

"I'm not leaving," he said stubbornly. "I'm staying with Azalea."

King Rhinehart's eyes narrowed in anger, and Bentleigh tried to gain control of his own emotions. He wouldn't get anywhere with his father like this. He needed to think more strategically.

"Of course everyone understands that you have a duty to our kingdom, Father," he said smoothly. "You must return, and no one will question your early departure. I will be glad to fulfill our responsibilities by staying in your place, to provide our allies with our support, on behalf of Bansford."

King Rhinehart hesitated, measuring his son with his eyes. Bentleigh had given his father a way to agree to let him stay without losing face, but it was possible he had angered him so much with his previous defiance that the king would be unwilling to take it.

"Very well," said King Rhinehart at last, and Bentleigh let out a silent breath. "I trust you will conduct yourself as befits a prince of Bansford."

Without another glance at their son, the visiting monarchs took formal leave of their hosts, and swept from the room. Bentleigh watched them go without regret. He would likely get the scold of his life when he eventually returned to Bant, but it was immaterial. He had no room in his mind for anything but Azalea.

Without waiting to be invited, he walked around to the other side of the bed from where the queen still knelt, and took Azalea's other hand. It was unnaturally cold, and he had to watch the rise and fall of her chest for a full minute before he let his tensed muscles relax.

"Thank you, Bentleigh." Queen Ianthe's soft words brought his head up, and the emotion in the older woman's eyes nearly undid him. "Thank you for standing by her."

"Always," he said simply, and she nodded.

For as long as he could remember, Azalea's mother always seemed just a little uncertain, but Bentleigh had realized before now that when it came to her daughter, she didn't miss much. He was fairly sure she knew what he hadn't said. What he'd tried so clumsily to say in the clearing a short time before.

He stared at Azalea's unresponsive face, a different kind of guilt gnawing away at him. He suspected that Queen Ianthe understood just how significant his defiance of his parents was. He hadn't missed the look King Victor had given him at dinner the night before, when Azalea had commented that he had no choice in their betrothal. Bentleigh was sure the king and queen knew what their daughter clearly didn't—that according to Bansfordian law, a prince had the right to choose his own bride. His parents would have had to reveal that information when agreeing to the betrothal sixteen years ago, since legally they could only form the alliance dependent on his consent.

He fingered the chain around his neck, which he had never taken off since the day it was placed on him as a small child. He was old enough now to give that consent, and had never considered for a moment refusing it. But he hadn't been able to bring himself to confess to Azalea that technically he had the power to end their betrothal. He was too afraid she'd ask him to do it, which was the last thing he wanted. Or that she'd resent him for having a hand in chaining her to a future not of her own choosing.

His conscience had squirmed in the clearing that morning, when she'd talked about him being in chains. But he'd argued with himself that he wasn't really deceiving her by keeping quiet. He might technically have the power to choose his own bride, but practically speaking, that was far from the truth. His parents had always kept him and his brother on a tight rein, and they would never actually let him make that decision. There was no way he could stand up to them in such a matter, so it was a good thing he so heartily approved of their choice.

Of course, none of that mattered if Azalea didn't wake up.

Bentleigh remained at Azalea's bedside for the entire day. No one told him it was improper for him to be in her suite, and no one pressed too hard when he refused every offer of food.

His periodic circuits of the room showed him the bustle outside the window as the preparations for the day's ceremonies were quietly dismantled. There seemed to be a permanent lump in his throat now. This was supposed to be the day that marked Azalea as officially his, and him as officially hers. Instead, she was lifeless and unresponsive, and he was going mad with worry. How long would she be like this? What could he do to wake her? There must be something.

Finally, as the sun neared the horizon, the queen insisted that he join her and King Victor for a meal. Bentleigh just clasped Azalea's hand more tightly, unable to bring himself to let go.

"I'll give you a moment," she said gently. "But then you really must come and eat something."

He nodded mutely, grateful for her understanding. She stepped out into the corridor, chivvying a sentimental maid out in front of her. Azalea's windows faced west, and the last rays of orange light were slanting in, falling on the bed and giving a golden tint to Azalea's dark hair.

Free of witnesses, Bentleigh pressed his lips to her cold hand, his heart full of an ache it could hardly contain. The sun was mostly below the horizon now, the last few seconds of this horrible day counting themselves out. All at once, Bentleigh was overcome with a wave of sleepiness, completely sudden and unexpected.

He blinked stupidly, trying to resist the relentless pull toward sleep. But it was futile. The last thing he knew was the softness of the covers on his cheek, as sleep reached out and enveloped him.

CHAPTER FOUR

Azalea

Azalea opened her eyes slowly, confused and disoriented. She blinked up at the familiar canopy of her four poster bed.

She was in her bed? Was that right? She tried to remember where she had been last, and why it was dark. It was unusual for her to wake in the night.

She shifted slightly, wondering why she seemed to be on top of the covers instead of under them. The movement set off a sharp pain in her finger, and everything came rushing back. She froze, her eyes wide with shock.

She'd pricked her finger. She'd thought she was dying.

But she was alive! The curse hadn't been completely successful, then. Uncle Mortimer's magic must have come to her rescue, bless the dear, wonderful man.

Her heart bounced erratically in her chest as she remembered the terror of those last few moments of consciousness. And Bentleigh! Something inside her squeezed painfully as the image of his horrified, devastated face swam before her mind's eye.

A rush of remorse passed over her. What an utter fool she'd

been, so confident that the curse was broken, that it wouldn't affect her. What Ben must have suffered, not to mention her parents.

Her mind caught up with her senses, and she realized that something was gripping her hand. Turning her head to the side, she let out a gasp.

Bentleigh! He was in her suite? That must be the first time in years. Her heart ached all over again. Had she been unconscious all day? He must have been sick with worry. Her heart was touched by the way he was clutching her hand, even in sleep. She had no idea how he was allowed to be in her room alone, but she'd wager her favorite necklace he'd been at her side all day.

"Ben!" she cried, leaning up on her elbow and shaking his shoulder with her free hand. "Ben, wake up! It's all right. *I'm* all right."

He didn't respond, and she frowned. His hand was strangely cold in hers, and for a panicked moment fear seized her. She extricated her hand with some difficulty, sliding it across his chest to rest over his heart. She let out a long breath as she felt its steady beat, and the way his chest rose and fell.

To her own embarrassment, she was momentarily distracted by the feel of his firm muscles under her fingers. He'd certainly filled out since the days of their childhood antics. She withdrew her hand quickly, frowning at his peaceful face.

"Bentleigh! Wake up!"

Nothing. She hesitated for a moment, then lifted his eyelid with her thumb. His eye didn't move at all, and when she released the eyelid, it drifted gently shut again.

"Well that's...creepy," she said aloud.

She sat up properly, crossing her arms and rubbing her shoulders. She was still in the practical dress she'd thrown on that morning. Even her boots remained on her feet. She slipped to the edge of the bed, sitting for a moment next to Bentleigh. He was seated in a chair, slumped forward so that his torso draped across the coverlet.

She made one more attempt to rouse him, shaking his shoulder roughly, then prodding his cheek, but he remained entirely unresponsive. She pushed herself to her feet, padding quietly to the window. The tiniest hint of light lingered on the western horizon, so darkness had only just fallen.

She walked back over to Ben, pausing next to his motionless form. Something was definitely not right here. She wasn't normally so near Ben when he slept, of course. For all she knew he was a heavy sleeper. But this unconsciousness was something more than that, she was certain.

She hesitated, then leaned down to touch his head. His chestnut hair was more disordered than she'd seen it in years. She ran a hand over it, a surge of emotion twisting her heart as she remembered their encounter in the clearing. Had he really been on the point of kissing her? He'd said it was different for him, but what did he mean by that? Would she ever find out?

Withdrawing her hand, she made her way toward the door with nervous steps. It felt strange to leave Ben lying there, half draped across her bed and unable to be roused. He'd always been so strong, and much less prone to taking foolish risks than her. Never before in her life could she remember feeling concerned for his safety, and she didn't like the sensation at all. Was this how he'd been feeling these last months? And all she'd done was scold him for siding with her overprotective parents.

The door to the suite stood open, and Azalea stepped out into the corridor. An involuntary gasp escaped her at the sight that met her eyes. Two guards were stationed at the doorway, but they were both slumped on the floor, backs against the wall, and heads lolling unnaturally. One of them was still gripping an upright spear, his helmeted head leaning against it. A quick check showed that they were alive, but deeply unconscious, the same as Ben.

Extremely spooked now, Azalea hurried down the corridor, following the familiar morning route to the royal dining hall. She had only gone a few paces, however, when she stumbled over something in the dark.

Righting herself just in time, she peered down at two prone forms splayed on the floor. With a flash of horror, Azalea recognized her mother, and her own maid.

"Mother!" she gasped, kneeling beside the queen. "Mother, what's happening? Please wake up!"

She smoothed her mother's disordered hair from her face, and chafed the older woman's hands between her own. There was absolutely no response, and tears began to well up against Azalea's will.

"Mother, *please* wake up! I'm sorry I wasn't careful enough. Please. I don't want to be alone here, in the dark."

Queen Ianthe's face remained impassive, her breathing even and slow.

Azalea drew a shuddering breath and pulled herself together with an effort. The sight of the queen had made her want to collapse into her mother's arms, to let someone else fix whatever had gone horribly wrong. But her mother was the last one who could make this right—she'd been afraid of it all Azalea's life, and her fear had been proved justified.

And Azalea wasn't a child, to run to her mother to fix everything. She was sixteen, old enough to be anointed as her father's heir. Old enough to take the burden of some of his responsibility.

Old enough to instantly prove herself unworthy of that responsibility by carelessly disregarding everyone's fears and activating the curse. What were the words of that long ago enchantment?

The whole kingdom will suffer with her.

Azalea buried her face in her hands for a moment, struggling with her emotions. What had she done? She hadn't thought Montgomery had intended that part of the curse to be so literal.

But she lowered her hands quickly, pausing only to arrange her mother's limbs more elegantly before pushing herself to her feet. Whatever was happening, it wasn't what Montgomery had intended. If it was, she would be dead.

She hurried on, still moving toward the dining hall. She passed dozens more collapsed servants, and even a couple of courtiers. After the first few, she stopped checking to make sure they were alive, and to attempt to rouse them. It was clear that whatever was happening, it was happening to everyone.

Everyone except her.

Azalea shuddered, the feeling of being alone weighing so heavily on her that she was afraid it would smother her. When she found several sleeping guards splayed across the floor outside the dining hall, she had a fairly good idea of what she would find inside.

Sure enough, her father was seated at the large polished table, his torso lying across his place setting much the same way Ben's had been draped across her bed. A quick glance at his companions showed Azalea the familiar forms of Uncle Mortimer, Aunt Melodia, and Aunt Miranda. Her mother must have been on her way to meet them.

She knew it was hopeless, but she couldn't resist trying to rouse them. Nothing worked, of course, although she did notice one difference. They all looked peaceful in sleep, like Ben had done, with the exception of Uncle Mortimer. His face looked pinched, his expression slightly troubled even in slumber.

She tried especially hard to rouse him, even going so far as to tip water from a pitcher over his face. But it had no effect.

"Sorry, Uncle Morty," she muttered, attempting to sponge off the moisture with a napkin. She ran a hand over her face. "What's happening here?" She glanced at the spread of food on the table, noting that steam still rose from some of the dishes. They hadn't been asleep long, then, and they had been about to eat a late dinner.

The food smelled good, making Azalea's stomach grumble. How long had it been since she'd eaten? Not since the dinner with Ben's parents the night before, but her confused mind was still struggling to figure out what time had passed since then.

She snagged a boiled egg from the table as she passed, figuring that the slumbering diners wouldn't miss it. Then she made her way back out of the room. She headed for the servants' hall next, dodging sleeping bodies all the way.

The normally bustling kitchen was the eeriest sight of all. Bodies were strewn everywhere, looking like they'd all been slain by poison simultaneously. Everyone's faces were placid, but their poses ranged from comfortable to grotesque. Azalea turned away quickly, her heart beating with unpleasant speed. But a singed smell drew her attention back to the room. She realized with a start that one of the cook's assistants had fallen with his arm too close to the fire, and the fabric of his sleeve was starting to smoke. She hurried over, shifting the man's arm and slapping his sleeve to make sure there were no embers. Her pulse raced in her ears as she realized the myriad dangers that could arise from a whole castle's worth of people suddenly collapsing.

After reassuring herself that everyone in the room was safely positioned, she hurried out through the door that led to the kitchen garden. The normally familiar castle was terrifying in its silent stillness, and she couldn't bear to stay there any longer. The moon was full, and she had no difficulty making her way through the rows of vegetables.

When she reached the wall of the garden, she knew a nervous moment. She wasn't accustomed to wandering around the city alone at night. But she needed to find help. She swallowed, pushing the gate open and striding through.

If she'd thought the castle was eerie, it was nothing to the scene that greeted her eyes outside its walls. The street was littered with sleeping people, lying in the road, propped against buildings, leaning back in carriages. Some were on the ground alongside horses, clearly having fallen asleep in the saddle and toppled off. Even the horses themselves were asleep, some standing with drooped heads, others lying on the road. Azalea moved forward, feeling like she was in a trance, and almost tripped over an alley cat, sleeping peacefully in the gutter.

She would have thought she'd be used to the sight of unconscious people by now, but instead, her terror rose the further through the city she traveled. It was all like some horrible dream. She didn't try to explore every corner of Liss, but in the area she covered, not a single person or animal was awake. The terror of her loneliness, and her vulnerability, threatened to overwhelm her.

The creak of a tavern's wooden sign swinging in the breeze made her jump, looking nervously around her. She'd wandered a long way from the castle, and she realized with a flash of grim humor that she was in a part of the city she'd never been allowed to visit. From what she could tell, everyone had collapsed at sunset, so it wasn't as though there were any late night revelers caught in slumber. But still, there was a tawdry feel to the place. She would normally have reason to be afraid to wander this neighborhood alone. It was strange to realize that as terrifying as the situation was, she had no reason to fear being harmed. Anyone who could harm her was fast asleep.

As was anyone who could help her.

"This can't be real," she muttered. "This can't be happening."

She cast her eyes around desperately, her sight falling on the castle's spires rising up at the city's northern edge. She started walking back that way, jumping at shadows, and rubbing her arms for warmth. She wished she'd brought a cloak, but such practical details had been far from her mind when she'd stumbled from her room.

Thoughts of her room brought up the image of Ben, lying unresponsively across her bed. How different this exploration would be if he was with her. She wouldn't be afraid, for one thing. She was never afraid when she was with Ben. They would search for answers together, determined to solve the mystery. Ben had a way of turning everything into an adventure, or at least he used to, before he got so worried about Azalea taking risks.

Not without reason.

Remorse once again seared her heart, red hot and painful. She found her feet hurrying forward, carrying her toward the castle, toward Ben. But before she actually entered the building, a thought grabbed her. She redirected her steps, heading for the forest gate. That was where this had happened. Perhaps she could somehow reverse it if she found the thorn that had pierced her.

But when she pushed on the gate—averting her eyes from the sprawled guards nearby—it wouldn't budge. She frowned. It had given her no trouble when she went to meet Ben. She tried again, grunting with effort as she strained against it, and it gave way the tiniest bit. Peering through the slit, she gasped, springing back in horror.

The familiar clearing just outside the gate was gone, overrun with thick, twisting, thorny vines. She yanked the gate shut, reassured by the click of its latch falling into place. Azalea stared at the gate for another fearful second, then turned, hurrying toward the safety of the castle. She stumbled in her haste, trying to outpace the feeling of phantom vines reaching, twisting, following her, of thorns piercing her fingers, her face.

She ran straight for her own room, although she knew the young man currently occupying it couldn't offer her any protection either from her fear or her loneliness.

"Ben," she sobbed, falling to her knees beside him. "Ben, I need you. Come back to me. I'm sorry I pushed away from you. I'm sorry I didn't let you say what you needed to say. You can say anything you want, just please, talk to me."

Ben was silent, his steady breaths the only indication that he was alive. Azalea moved closer, placing her face right next to his, just to feel the reassuring warmth of his breath on her cheek. She knelt there for a long time, her face pressed into the bed, and Ben's breath warming her cheek.

The night was well advanced now, and the longer she lay there, the less inclination she felt to ever rise. She was ready to surrender, to give up. She had been foolish, and headstrong, and she'd driven her kingdom into disaster before even being anointed as heir. And Ben was suffering for it, which was harder to swallow than all the rest.

"Why am I awake?" she moaned quietly. "If everyone I care about is doomed to sleep forever, why can't I as well?"

Almost as soon as she'd said the words, she felt an irresistible compulsion to climb back onto her bed. She followed it unthinkingly, not even questioning the sensation. A solitary twitter sounded from a bird outside her window, and the thought flashed idly through her mind that dawn must be approaching. She couldn't muster the energy to care. She was too weary, too full of grief and fear.

She laid herself down on the coverlet, a long breath escaping her. The last thing she was aware of was her hand snaking its way back into Ben's, although she had made no conscious decision to place it there.

CHAPTER FIVE

Bentleigh

Bentleigh blinked slowly, trying to make sense of his position. His face was pressed against something soft, but he also seemed to be seated.

He lifted his head with a soft groan, squinting at the dim light filtering through the window. Where was he?

He suddenly became aware of something clasped in his hand, and he started. Azalea! He pushed himself up, leaning over the bed. His hope drained away as he scanned her face. There was no change. She was still unconscious, not a hair having moved since last he'd seen her.

He reluctantly let go of her hand, running his own over his face. Emotionally speaking, he was still drowning in a sea of misery and guilt. But physically, he couldn't remember the last time he'd felt so well rested. He must have fallen asleep by her bedside. He frowned. And slept right through the night? It was hard to imagine the king and queen allowing him to spend the night in their daughter's room, however deeply asleep she was. And he had a vague memory of Queen Ianthe insisting that he come and eat dinner with them. Come to mention it, he was feeling incredibly hungry.

He gave Azalea one more lingering look, smoothing her dark hair with a gentle gesture. Then he made his way quietly to the door. He pushed it open and started in surprise at the sight of the two guards who'd been stationed on either side of the door. They were on the floor, stirring and looking blearily around them. One of them caught sight of Bentleigh and jumped hastily to his feet.

"Your Highness!" he gasped, looking as horrified as if Bentleigh had caught him in the act of murdering someone. "I can't think how…I swear I've never fallen asleep at my post in all my life." He glanced fearfully at the door. "Is the princess—"

"She's the same," Bentleigh said. "No one's done her an injury while you slept."

"Where are our replacements?" the other guard asked, struggling to stand. "We were only supposed to be here until an hour after sunset."

A groan from down the corridor made the three men turn, and Bentleigh's eyes widened at the astonishing sight of Queen Ianthe picking herself up from the floor.

"What's happening?" she asked, looking around groggily. Her eyes fell on Bentleigh, and she started toward the doorway with a gasp. "Azalea?"

"She's fine," Bentleigh assured her. "Or at least, you know," he ran a hand over his face again, "still in an enchanted sleep from which we have no idea how to rouse her."

The queen nodded, tension draining from her form even as anxiety settled once again on her brow. "What's going on, Bentleigh? The last thing I remember, I was walking to the dining hall, to meet my husband, and Mortimer, Melodia, and Miranda." She frowned at him. "You were supposed to join us."

"That's the last I remember too, Your Majesty," Bentleigh said heavily. "Then I woke up, still sitting by Azalea's bed, and it was morning." He cast a glance at the guards, and at the maid who was pushing herself awkwardly to her feet behind the queen. "I think we were all in an enchanted sleep of our own during the night."

Queen Ianthe's brow lowered even further. "I need to find Victor," she said, turning and hurrying down the corridor.

Bentleigh turned to the guards. "The princess must not be left unguarded," he said curtly. "Shall I send replacements?"

The guard who had first spoken shook his head. "Speaking for myself, Your Highness, I've never been more alert."

The other guard nodded his agreement.

"Yes, I feel the same," Bentleigh said dryly. "And it's no wonder. When's the last time any of us slept solidly from sundown to sunup?"

He didn't wait for an answer, just hurried to catch up with Queen Ianthe. They passed at least a dozen servants on the way, all emerging from sleep, wearing identical looks of bemusement. They found the king in the dining hall, blinking in confusion and wiping soup off his sleeve.

"Ianthe!" he cried, when he saw his wife enter. "I've just been...I think I was..."

"Asleep," Bentleigh interjected. "We've all been asleep, Your Majesty."

The king pushed himself to his feet, hope lighting his face. "And Azalea? Has she wakened with the rest of us?"

Bentleigh shook his head, his heart wrenching at the way the light died from King Victor's eyes. The king turned to his cousin, a frown on his face.

"What's happening, Morty? Why were we all asleep?"

Mortimer shrugged helplessly. "I don't know. I didn't anticipate this."

"It makes sense though, doesn't it?" Miranda said slowly.

"The curse said that the whole kingdom would suffer with Azalea."

"It also said," Melodia added grimly, "the princess wouldn't live through the night."

"So..." Bentleigh frowned as he tried to put the pieces together. "So Uncle Mortimer's magic softened death to sleep, meaning that Azalea is in an enchanted sleep rather than being dead, and by extension the whole kingdom suffers with her by not 'living' through the night? As in, we all go into an enchanted sleep at nighttime?"

"The whole kingdom?" Queen Ianthe repeated faintly. Her eyes were on Mortimer. "Can that be true?"

He let out a shaky breath. "It's possible. Montgomery's magic is strong. Very strong."

The king was silent, clearly thinking through the many and complex implications of such a situation. His eyes fell on Bentleigh.

"And clearly it affects anyone physically present in the kingdom, not just those who come from our kingdom." He let out a breath. "Well, that's a relief, I suppose."

Bentleigh nodded fervently, instantly grasping the king's meaning. The idea of the whole kingdom being prone and powerless every night, with anyone from outside free to enter and maraud at will, didn't bear thinking about.

"Well," King Victor said briskly, still looking at Bentleigh. "You have plenty of time to cross the border, Bentleigh. But I would recommend you don't cut it close. In fact, the same goes for any travelers. We must issue an urgent edict, warning people to be in their homes before sunset." He frowned. "We can be grateful the weather is still mild. There must have been countless people caught outside in the elements last night."

"Your Majesty," said Bentleigh, unable to remain silent a

moment longer. "I'm not heading for the border. I'm not leaving."

The king's face softened. "You are a good man, Bentleigh," he said, and a shot of warmth passed through Bentleigh. His own father had certainly never said such a thing to him, and somehow it meant even more coming from Azalea's father.

King Victor sighed. "But there's no reason for you to suffer with us. You should return to your home, while we know you can do so safely. If there are any developments, we will apprise you of them."

"With all due respect, Your Majesty," Bentleigh stood straighter, "I'm not suffering with you, I'm suffering with Azalea."

The king met his eyes. "You are showing great nobility, Bentleigh," he said seriously. "But you are not bound to this curse." His eyes dropped to the chain visible around Bentleigh's neck. Pain flashed across his face, but it was quickly suppressed. "No one would blame you if you chose to remove that ring, in light of the circumstances."

"I will never do that, Your Majesty," said Bentleigh, with unnecessary passion. "Our betrothal may not have been formalized yesterday as planned, but as far as I'm concerned, it is still settled. Azalea is my betrothed, and I have a duty to her. While she's in this fix, I won't leave her."

Mortimer cleared his throat. "Your Highness," he said heavily, "I fear that is a promise you cannot make. Surely you are not at liberty to stay here indefinitely."

"Not indefinitely," Bentleigh said impatiently. "But for however long it takes to break the enchantment." He saw the look exchanged between the enchanter and his sisters, and fear spiked within him. "It can be broken, can't it? There must be a way."

Mortimer didn't answer straight away. "There may be," he said noncommittally. Queen Ianthe seemed to be crying softly again, and King Victor was clenching and unclenching his hand around a goblet. But Bentleigh narrowed his eyes, watching the enchanter shrewdly.

"We must make inquiries," said the king, after a tense moment. "Discover if this affliction truly has affected the whole kingdom. There is a great deal to be done, and only so many hours of daylight in which to do it."

The king barked an order, bringing servants scurrying toward him. The dining hall descended into a bustle of activity, and Bentleigh took the first opportunity to slip away, back to Azalea's room. To his relief, the guards didn't challenge his entry.

Azalea's maid sat beside her, and Bentleigh almost rolled his eyes when he saw that the girl had folded Azalea's hands over her chest, and tucked a blooming azalea into them. Zayla would hate that kind of melodrama.

He had intended to sit beside her again, but somehow the maid's presence made him self-conscious. And the pose she'd put Azalea in made her look like she was stretched out on her deathbed. It was the last thing he wanted to look at.

He made his way back to his own suite, which was naturally also located in the royal wing. He'd come to Liss for at least two visits every year since he could remember, often staying a month at a time. So the suite was permanently his, not used for other important guests. It held many, many memories, the most recent of which was his nervousness as he dressed with special care the morning of the betrothal ceremony, practicing his ill-fated speech as he tried to figure out how to make their romance feel as real to Azalea as it did to him. He distinctly remembered thinking that if they weren't betrothed, he'd probably have more success in sweeping her off her feet.

And he would have done it, too. He'd always been very determined about the things that were important to him. And winning Azalea's love—her actual, real, willing, throw-herself-into-his-arms-and-kiss-him-passionately kind of love—was more important to him than almost anything. She would never know how she tortured him with her flippant complaints about their betrothal, and her insistence on treating him like some kind of favorite brother rather than her future husband.

He paced his room restlessly for several minutes, but he knew he wouldn't take inaction well. His eyes fell on his sword, lying where he'd left it the morning before. A scowl grew on his brow. He always wore his sword. He'd even kept wearing it throughout the period, about a year before, when Zayla had taken every opportunity to steal it from him, trying inexpertly to wield it in the most inappropriate of situations. She'd even pestered him to teach her to fight. He'd known her parents would never allow it, but he'd given in, of course, teaching her the basics in secret. She was just so blasted difficult to say no to, at least for him.

The memories brought the lump back to his throat. What a fool he'd been to think it was safer to be without it on that disastrous outing. The curse was that she'd prick her finger, not slice it open on a blade. Maybe if he'd been armed, he could have protected her from the vine that evil vermin had sent after her.

A surge of pure fury raced through his blood, terrifying in its suddenness and intensity. He'd never met Montgomery, but he hated him. Hated him with a passion that threatened to overwhelm him. How dare that vile, treasonous snake think he could reach into Bentleigh's life, and rip away the person most precious to him in all the world? How could he possibly have wanted to kill Azalea, a girl who lit up every room she entered?

Bentleigh strapped on his sword, desperate to find an outlet for his rage. Three quick strides took him to the door of his suite, and before he could stop and think, he found himself leaving the castle, heading for the forest gate. The four guards clustered nearby were too distracted to challenge him—apparently in the midst of some kind of confused altercation about what day it was and who was on duty.

He pushed the gate open with a grunt, surprised by how much resistance it gave him this time. The moment he stepped through it, the reason was evident. He froze in place, his eyes widening with horror at the ugly, angry vines that crowded the little clearing. They were as thick as saplings, and covered in thorns, each of which had a red tip, red like the single drop of blood that had bloomed on Azalea's finger.

The memory of that moment—easily the worst of his life—woke Bentleigh's rage. With an inhuman cry, he pulled his sword free of its sheath and fell on the vines. He hacked at them mercilessly, venting all his fury on the unnatural plants. They writhed under the onslaught, the severed ends curling up and away from him, like creatures in pain. Bentleigh poured his grief, and his fury at his own powerlessness, into his attack. He kept going until the entire clearing was littered with dead, brown lengths of vine. When there were no more within his reach, he stopped, his brow lined with sweat, and his breaths coming heavily.

After what felt like an eternity, he turned back toward the gate. It stood open, and all four of the guards were staring at him like he'd lost his mind.

Maybe he had.

They didn't comment on his impassioned outburst, merely stepping aside to allow him to pass through. Bentleigh didn't care what they thought. He'd let his blind rage rule him for a brief spell, and he felt the better for it. Now it was time to start looking for a solution.

He strode through the castle, perfectly sure of his purpose.

In the chaos, it took him some time to hunt down his quarry, but eventually, a helpful servant showed him into a sitting room he'd never entered before.

"Prince Bentleigh." Mortimer stood, summoning an unconvincing smile. Bentleigh noticed that, unlike every single other person he'd seen, the enchanter looked weary, as though he would desperately like to sleep.

"Are you still feeling the effects of the battle?" Bentleigh asked, alarmed. "Between your magic and his?"

Mortimer nodded, sinking bank into his seat. "I think I will feel it for as long as the situation continues," he said calmly.

Bentleigh felt a flash of sympathy for the older man. "I'm sorry," he said gravely, taking a seat at a gesture from his host. He cleared his throat. "I wanted to talk to you about breaking the curse."

"I'm sure," sighed Mortimer.

"Before, in the dining hall," Bentleigh pressed. "When I asked if the curse could be broken, you didn't say no. There was something in your mind, I could tell."

Mortimer smiled faintly. "You're very perceptive, Your Highness." He sighed. "There was something in my mind, but I don't know if it will get us anywhere."

"Tell me."

The enchanter met Bentleigh's eyes. "How much do you know about enchantments, Your Highness?"

Bentleigh shrugged. "The basics, I suppose. Clearly not enough." He scowled. It seemed like a glaring oversight given Azalea's situation, now he thought about it. But his parents had certainly not encouraged the study of magic.

"Well, most enchantments can be broken," Mortimer said. "It's usual practice to build in a counterforce, at least for a conscientious enchanter."

Bentleigh couldn't help snorting at the word "conscientious", and Mortimer grimaced.

"Indeed. But even for unscrupulous magic users, it's difficult to get around the natural and inevitable counterforce. Most of the time we try to include a way to break the enchantment on purpose, in order to shape the counterforce to be somewhat in our control." He shook his head. "Whatever the more arrogant of my kind might believe, our magic is not the strongest force in our world. And it is therefore necessarily true that a stronger force exists, and that our magic can be broken."

Bentleigh frowned. "You're talking about the dragons?"

"No." Mortimer shook his head. "The magic of the dragons is the same magic as ours. That's where humans acquired magic, from exposure to dragons. They just have it much more potently than we do. I was talking about an older, more powerful magic. But that's not my point. My point is that, even if Montgomery didn't build in a counterforce, one exists in his magic, whether or not he acknowledges it, or wants it there."

Mortimer sighed. "I think it's safe to say he didn't build one in intentionally." His face darkened. "At least, I hope he didn't. You see, you can tell a lot about an enchanter by the inclusion or exclusion of a counterforce, by whether or not the enchantment itself mentions the remedy, and by the nature of that remedy."

Bentleigh's frown deepened. "What do you mean?"

"I mean that if an enchanter, or enchantress, includes the remedy in their spoken curse, they clearly *want* the target to break the curse, or at least to have a chance at it. Otherwise, why give that information?"

"So if there's a stated way to break the curse, the enchanter is really on the side of the person they've enchanted?" Bentleigh asked, confused.

Mortimer shook his head. "That's not necessarily true. If the way to break the curse involves a for-your-own-good type action, then the enchanter probably has good intentions, whether misguided or not. But with the type of magic Montgomery unleashed, it's more common for there to be a much more vicious remedy."

"What do you mean?" Bentleigh asked again, an ominous feeling coming over him at the enchanter's words.

"Oh, I'm sure you can imagine the kind of thing. A death curse that can only be prevented by someone else agreeing to die in the target's place. A curse of blindness that requires the victim to physically remove one eye in order to regain sight in the other. Anything where the remedy is something tortuous, painful, or makes you betray your deepest principles, is a sure sign that the intentions of the enchanter were always evil."

Bentleigh was silent for a long moment, digesting all of this. "So where does that leave us with Montgomery's curse?"

Mortimer let out a breath. "Well, I hope he hasn't built one in, because if he had, I very much fear that it would be a particularly nasty one. If it wasn't in his control, then it's much more likely to be something we would actually be willing to do."

"But?" Bentleigh prompted, picking up on his tone.

"But, it becomes much more difficult to figure it out, because even he wouldn't know."

"Someone must know!" Bentleigh protested.

Mortimer shrugged. "Not necessarily." He frowned. "It's a matter of understanding Montgomery, of identifying what was in his mind at the time. And," he said frankly, "that's been puzzling me for sixteen years. It's not like he grew up expecting to inherit. Victor was the crown prince. We always assumed he would marry, have children, pass his crown in the natural way. I doubt the thought of being Victor's heir ever even occurred to Montgomery until Victor and Ianthe took so long to have a child."

He frowned. "But even so...Victor is our cousin, and the way we were raised, he was almost like a brother. Montgomery wasn't as close with Victor growing up as I was. But I never realized there was any dislike there until the former king died, and Victor became king himself. It was so sudden and unexpected, with Victor only thirty years of age. And Montgomery became bitterly jealous of him, almost overnight."

He sighed, returning his attention to Bentleigh. "You're probably wondering why I'm telling you all this. My point is that there's something I'm missing, something that turned Montgomery against Victor. By the time he cursed Azalea, he was certainly coveting Victor's crown. But I think there was more to it than that. I think something else had power over him, and he undoubtedly poured that power into his magic. Whether he meant to or not. If we can figure out what it is, we can figure out the counterforce—it will be the natural counterforce to that power."

"That might make sense to you," said Bentleigh frankly, "but I'm just as lost as ever on how we wake Azalea up."

"So am I," admitted Mortimer. "But in theory, I know where we have to start. We have to understand what was behind Montgomery's actions."

Bentleigh was on his feet, although he didn't remember standing. "I don't want to understand him!" he snapped. "I don't want to get in his head. He's a monster!"

"He wasn't always a monster," Mortimer said sadly. "And if we can't understand what made him that way, we may never learn how to wake Azalea."

Bentleigh deflated, his righteous anger subsiding in the face of cold fear. "That's not an option," he said firmly. He groaned. "So if I have this right, my only way forward is to find your insane, murderous brother, and get him to talk about his feelings?"

Mortimer gave a dry chuckle. "More or less, except not you

personally, of course. King Victor has already doubled the efforts to find Montgomery." His face turned serious. "I would be an obvious choice to help, given I might be most likely to reach him. But..."

"But what?" Bentleigh stopped pacing, taking in the look on the older man's face.

Mortimer met his eyes seriously. "This isn't to go beyond this room."

Bentleigh gave a curt nod, and the enchanter continued.

"You were present when I explained that my magic is battling with Montgomery's, even now. What I said was true, that the extent of the defenses is set, and unlikely to change. Although it is exhausting, it doesn't actually require specific thought or effort from me. My magic is simply in use all the time, struggling with Montgomery's in the way defined all those years ago. But it is essential that it continues to do so. Without my enchantment to fight Montgomery's, I suspect his original purpose would be fulfilled."

Bentleigh stared at him in horror. "You mean, if you die, so does Azalea?"

Mortimer nodded. "As you can imagine, my safety has just become one of Victor's highest priorities. I doubt I'll be leaving the castle at all until Azalea wakes."

Bentleigh was silent for a moment, his thoughts whirling. "Do you have any clue where to find him?" he asked abruptly. "He's your twin. Surely you have a guess as to where he's hiding."

Mortimer looked more weary than ever. "If I knew where he was all these years, don't you think I would have told Victor from the start?" He sent Bentleigh a sharp look. "And if I did have any suggestions, I wouldn't be telling them to you, Your Highness. It's not for you to go after Montgomery. You are far too important."

Bentleigh didn't answer. He had plenty to think about, and no need to reveal those thoughts to the man sitting before him. But they were mad, all of them, if they thought he was going to sit around in safety and wait for someone else to figure out how to wake *his* princess from her sleep.

CHAPTER SIX

Azalea

zalea woke with a suddenness that was disconcerting. This time, reality came back quickly. She sat up, trying to make sense of this latest development. Darkness surrounded her again, but she felt absolutely fine. None of the sinking exhaustion that had driven her back onto her bed.

She glanced over to where Bentleigh was seated, and jumped. He was gone. She turned the other way and saw her maid, not in a chair, but asleep on a cot that had been brought into the room.

Azalea's heart raced as she grasped the implications of these changes. Everyone else had been awake since she last saw them! They weren't trapped in an enchanted sleep forever. It had been temporary.

She felt amazingly well rested, but she rubbed her hands over her face anyway, trying to clear her thoughts. She longed for the comforting clarity of daylight, but judging by the smear on the western horizon, she had once again awoken just as night fell.

She slid to the edge of her bed, and a flower fell from her lap. She frowned at it. Why was there an azalea in her bed? It wasn't important. She padded to the hallway. There were two guards by her door again, but they weren't sprawled on the floor. They were lying on simple pallets, stretched protectively across her doorway. A quick glance up the corridor showed no limp bodies this time.

She frowned, pondering these signs. So everyone had expected to be in an enchanted sleep again tonight, had they? Would they be asleep every night, and her asleep every day? The horror of that thought washed over her, as she imagined prowling the city alone night after night. She swallowed, steeling herself. She mustn't allow herself to fall apart.

But what was she to do? She seized a torch from a bracket on the wall and wandered down the corridor. She didn't bother trying to rouse anyone this time.

It was no surprise to find that there wasn't an elaborate spread laid out in the dining hall. No doubt everyone had eaten before dark tonight. But she was able to scrounge up some food in the kitchen, and she ate it greedily. The boiled egg the night before hadn't been nearly enough.

She remembered how Uncle Mortimer had seemed different from the other sleepers the night before, and she directed her steps to his rooms. Curiously, there were four guards stationed outside—the same number usually to be found shadowing her father—but of course they were all asleep. There was no one to stop her from walking straight into Uncle Mortimer's sleeping chamber. He was laid out on the bed, on top of the covers, and just as the night before, his face was pinched with stress.

She felt a rush of affection and gratitude for the man who had saved her life. She ran a hand firmly along his forehead, trying to smooth out the furrows. Of course he gave no response. Azalea glanced around the room, noting the papers piled haphazardly on a desk. She hurried over to them hopefully. Uncle Mortimer would definitely be trying to figure out a way to break through his brother's magic. Was it possible he'd made some progress?

She bent over the papers, holding the torch close enough to read. The scribblings clearly related to her situation—she saw her name repeatedly. Bentleigh's name was there too, with an underlined note: *Careful with information. High risk of putting himself in danger.*

Azalea sighed, moisture rising to her eyes in spite of herself. She had no doubt Uncle Mortimer was right. If Ben caught a hint of a way to break her curse, he'd be sure to rush headlong after it, with total disregard for his own safety. Another entry on the same page caught her eye, and she squinted at it.

Unintentional counterforce. What had power over Montgomery? Jealousy? Counter: selfless kindness. Note: probably not strong enough. Hatred/spite? Counter: love? Note: too general.

None of this made much sense to Azalea, but she got the gist that Uncle Mortimer was working through a theory, looking for an explanation that fit the situation. She could only hope his rumination yielded some result. It was incredibly frustrating to not be able to ask him, or to explain her own experiences. It might be useful in his experiments.

Her name again drew her eye, and she frowned at the entry.

My magic softened Azalea's death into sleep. Death = permanent, constant. Therefore sleep is permanent, unless curse broken. "Kingdom suffers with her" = all the kingdom unable to "live" through the night. In enchanted sleep from sunset to sunrise.

Azalea's eyes widened. The whole kingdom? Everyone in Listernia was in an enchanted sleep right now? She hugged herself in an instinctive gesture. The idea of being the only one in possession of her mind in the entire kingdom was almost more than she could take in. She scanned over the page again. And this situation would continue indefinitely, unless the curse was broken? They had to break the curse. There must be a way.

She frowned at the phrase "sleep is permanent". Obviously the whole kingdom's sleep wasn't permanent, since they'd clearly been awake during the day. But she realized all at once that since she was the only one awake at night, and she'd returned to the same position when she got back into bed, no one knew she'd been awake. They likely thought she was in a permanent, unbreakable sleep.

Well, she thought briskly. That much she could change. She drew a sheaf of blank parchment toward her, and scribbled a quick note to Uncle Mortimer. After a moment's hesitation, she drew more blank pages and wrote messages to her mother, her father, and lastly, to Ben. It read:

Ben,

I'm not asleep all the time. I'm awake at night. I'm the only one, and it's eerie. I wish you were with me, because this adventure might be a little too big for me to undertake on my own.

Thank you for catching me when I collapsed. I'm sorry I was so stupid as to prick my stupid finger. But we'll find a way to break the curse. Don't lose heart.

Azalea

She paused for a moment, then, with a rush of nerves, added a postscript.

· · ·

PS. Don't think these dramatic events have gotten you out of handing over my birthday surprise. I want to know what you were going to say, before that stupid vine stupidly interrupted us.

She tucked the letters into her belt, with the exception of the one for Uncle Mortimer, which she placed on his pillow, next to his head. She made her way through the castle, heading for her parents' adjoining suites.

She found them both in her father's room, lying fully clothed on top of his enormous bed, and clasping hands. Their faces were peaceful, but so were those of everyone else in the castle, excluding Uncle Mortimer. It was the posture that brought tears back to Azalea's eyes. Nothing could more clearly show how desperately they each needed comfort.

She left their letters in a prominent position on a carved side table, and crept back out of the room. Of course, there was really no reason she couldn't make as much noise as she wanted. But their vulnerable embrace made her feel like an intruder.

She kept Ben's letter in her pocket as she again wandered out of the castle. It wasn't that she didn't know where his room was —she did, of course. But she was second-guessing her postscript. *Did* she want to know what he'd been about to say? Was she ready for their relationship to change?

She thought of the feeling of his arms going around her, and the firm strength of his chest under her hand when she'd felt for his heartbeat. She scolded herself for these superficial thoughts, letting the night air cool her heated cheeks as she stepped through the castle's main entrance. The guards were all laid down on simple pallets, clearly ready to spring back to attention once the sun rose.

But why shouldn't she admire Ben's attractiveness? She had to marry him anyway. She might as well enjoy the prospect.

She sighed, silencing this voice. She couldn't get around her complicated emotions by focusing on his physical appeal. Ben meant so much more to her than that. She would never be able to separate their relationship in that way.

She didn't wander far, the silent, empty streets almost as spooky as the strange tableau had been the night before. She knew there was no one to disturb her, human or animal, but she still couldn't shake the instinctive fear that came from wandering around alone at night. Every shadow was menacing, every noise suspicious.

Having satisfied herself that no one nearby was awake, and that the inhabitants of Liss, like those in the castle, had prepared themselves for their enchanted sleep this time, she turned back to the castle. She knew where she was going. She had been steeling herself for it since she awoke. She needed to try harder to examine the magical vine. If she wanted to go after the curse, it was the most logical place to start. The night before, she'd run away in terror after one glance, and she was ashamed of herself. This time she would be braver.

To her dismay, she didn't even reach the forest gate before her resolution was tested. As soon as she caught sight of the small wooden door, she did a double take. For one hopeful moment she thought it was just a trick of the darkness, but when she held her torch high, the sight only came into sharper focus.

The vines, which had crowded the clearing the night before, had begun to breach the wall surrounding the city. Thorny ends poked through the crack around the edge of the gate, and more were crawling over the top of the wall. Not that they were actually moving, or at least, not quickly enough for her to see. But they had certainly advanced since the night before.

Her heart in her throat, Azalea mounted a stone staircase to one side of the gate, bringing her up to the battlements from which she would be able to see the clearing. Her torch didn't cast light far enough, but the moon helpfully sailed out from behind a cloud as she peered down at the forest floor.

She gave a gasp of horror. Just as the night before, the clearing was overrun, but it wasn't untouched. Someone—and her aching heart had a pretty good idea who—had hacked and slashed their way through the monstrous growth. But newer, younger vines were twisting their way over the severed, dead ends of the original vine. It was a many-headed monster, its advancement slow but inexorable.

Azalea sank to her knees on the battlements as the horrible truth suddenly hit her. It was coming for her. The curse knew its purpose had been thwarted, and it wasn't done trying. It was slow and steady, and it would take time to force its way through to her rooms, but it was coming. And while guards surely stood watch over her throughout the hours of daylight, there was no one to protect her, no one to help her once darkness fell. The vines would come, they would choke everything in their path, and they would claim her.

Despair washed over her, and for a mad moment she considered throwing herself into the clearing, letting them find her. If she was to live her whole life alone, in darkness, surrounded by eerily sleeping forms, was it even worth fighting?

All of a sudden, she pushed herself to her feet. No. She wasn't giving up. She took a step back, away from the walls, but stopped, scowling at the vines. More than that, she wasn't going to take this lying down. She wasn't going to mope around the castle while the curse ate its way into the heart of her kingdom.

Her glance fell on the furthest-reaching strand of vine, creeping down the wall near the gate. With wide eyes, she realized it was close to one of the guards, who was sleeping peacefully against the wall. What would happen to him if it touched him while he slept?

She raced down the steps two at a time, forcing down the fear the vines awoke in her. Casting around for a weapon, she focused on the sword worn by the guard. She drew it clumsily from its sheath, trying to remember all the techniques she had pestered Ben into teaching her. Raising it in both hands, she hacked at the exploratory vine. It severed on the second blow, falling to her feet and drying out with unnatural speed, clearly dead. Azalea glanced along the wall, looking for more creepers. She sliced through several more that had advanced further than she liked, and then took out the one that was forcing its way through the crack of the gate.

Panting from the exertion, she returned the sword to the sleeping guard, determination washing over her. She would get a weapon of her own. Her guards might not be able to defend her during the hours of darkness, but she could defend herself. And she would do more than that. She was the crown princess of this kingdom, and from dusk until dawn her people were vulnerable to the curse's attack. She would be their defender. She would come back every night, keep the vine at bay for as long as it took.

She reentered the castle with renewed determination. It was time to be bold. She would give Ben his letter, and stop worrying about losing the friend she'd relied on all her life. Ben was betrothed to her. She gave a grim chuckle. She couldn't lose him, even if either of them wanted that. She would just have to accept that their relationship was going to change. If she stopped fighting it for a few seconds, some part of her that she had been keeping ruthlessly submerged started to feel a jittery excitement about the prospect.

She let herself into his suite, her steps soft. It was strange to be in here. It had been a long time. She lit a candle from the torch, then placed the guttering light in an empty bracket in the corridor. Carrying the candle, she made her way silently to Ben's sleeping chamber, pausing on the threshold.

He was spread out on the bed, his sword leaning against it, and his hand extended in that direction, as if ready to spring into action the moment he awoke. She smiled at the picture. He was a formidable force when he chose to be, and it sent a tingle through her to know she had him fighting in her camp.

"Oh Bentleigh," she scolded aloud. "You really shouldn't be sleeping in your boots. Your blankets will get filthy."

Ben was unperturbed by the rebuke.

Azalea made her way to his side, lowering herself to sit on the bed beside him. Her weight made the mattress tilt, and Ben's head leaned further down toward her. She stared wistfully at him, taking in the disarranged hair and the shade on his chin.

"You are very attractive, after all," she said, as if making a concession. Her eyes softened. "And you have a kind heart. I could do much worse for a husband, couldn't I?"

She touched his chin tentatively, a smile tugging at her lips. She'd never seen him with stubble like this. He was always self-possessed, always in control.

Except for that morning in the clearing, when for that brief, most agonizing of moments between piercing her finger and being claimed by the curse, she'd seen him begin to fall apart. It was a sight she hoped she'd never witness again.

"Oh, Ben," she said unsteadily, her momentary flash of humor deserting her. "I'm so sorry. You can be anything you like, just come back to me. I'll marry you tomorrow if it means you'll be awake, and talking to me."

But there would be no tomorrow, at least not a shared one. Ben would wake up, go about his day, but she'd be completely unaware of it. And when the next night came, he'd be equally unconscious of her strange nocturnal wanderings.

Already she could feel the pull of the enchanted sleep,

making her mind fuzzy and her limbs leaden. She looked around Ben's room for a chair. Perhaps she could fall asleep next to his bedside, like he'd done for her. Then he'd know without doubt that she'd been awake, and moving around.

But something strange was happening. A compulsion was taking hold of her, urging—no forcing—her to move toward the door. She pushed herself up from the bed, fighting it as it seemed to move her feet for her. She retained enough control to slip her letter into Ben's open hand, but she couldn't slow herself down enough to do anything else.

Fear gripped her as her feet carried her out into the corridor. What was happening? Was the curse taking her back toward the vines? Would it force her to surrender herself to them? The thought was horrifying.

She felt a tiny flicker of relief when her feet turned away from the castle's entrance, instead going in the direction of her suite. Still, not being in control of her own body was even more terrifying than everything else that had happened. She tried to resist the strange force, but there was nothing she could do. It carried her back to her rooms, right up to her bed. To her horror, she found herself lying back down, gathering the fallen azalea and clasping it in her hands like she was laid out for a funeral.

The edges of her mind were getting foggy, but she retained enough awareness for the truth to dawn on her. The curse was forcing her to resume the exact position she was in when she woke. She remembered the way her hand had wormed its way into Ben's at the end of the previous night, and her heart seemed to drop. They would have no idea she'd been awake at all. There was nothing to tell them she'd moved.

She suddenly remembered her letters, and a surge of relief went through her. There was something to tell them, of course there was. They would read her words—Ben would read her words. He would leave her a letter too, and together they'd figure out a way to free her. She would just have to hold back the vines and hang on to her sanity for however long it took.

She could do it, she promised herself determinedly, as her mind sank toward slumber. It might be a week, it might be as long as a month. But she could do it.

TWO YEARS LATER...

Bentleigh

"Ben!"

Bentleigh turned, giving his brother a wave to show he'd heard. Rian urged his horse forward, catching up within moments.

"Mother and Father want to speak with you," Rian said, once he was within hearing.

"I'm sure they do," Bentleigh replied calmly, his eyes still on the soldiers training in the valley that spread out before him.

"They're not happy about you leaving again," Rian pressed.

There was no change either in Bentleigh's expression or his tone. "I'm sure they're not."

Rian shook his head. "I have to say, Ben, I'm a little impressed. I never realized you had so much courage."

Bentleigh snorted. "If standing up to Mother and Father is our idea of courage, it's not the best image to project for our kingdom, is it?"

"I don't know," Rian shrugged. "It's hard to imagine anything much more terrifying."

Bentleigh smiled at the light-hearted words. He glanced away from the training exercise still taking place in front of him, back toward the hill rising up behind Rian. The city of Bant, Bansford's capital, covered the gentle slope, with the castle adorning the top.

Bentleigh sighed. "I don't have the patience to have this conversation yet again, Rian. Nothing they say will change my mind. Surely they know that by now. If they want to stop me from visiting Zayla, they're going to have to arrest me."

"Careful what you say," Rian said grimly. "I wouldn't plant the idea if I were you."

Bentleigh sent his brother a look. "We're adults, Rian. Don't you think it's time we started pushing back if we think they're wrong? I'll be twenty in a month. And you'll be king one day. Surely *you* at least are entitled to an opinion on the mess Father is leaving you."

He gestured at the scores of soldiers in the valley, engaged in their training exercises. "We could be sending three times as many soldiers to bolster the desert border if we weren't wasting so many resources on hunting down anyone who has the faintest whiff of magic about them."

Rian's expression was troubled. "You're so sure of your opinions, Ben, but Father is trying to do right by our kingdom. And so am I. I know Bansford has its problems, but I love this kingdom," he said simply. "I care about it."

"And I respect that," Bentleigh said, his words sincere. His gaze was pulled northwest, toward distant Liss. "I care about Bansford too, Rian, you know I do. I want to see our people thrive. But from my earliest memories, I was raised knowing my future was elsewhere. My loyalties lie just as much with Listernia. I can't help it."

"Another thing I wouldn't let Mother and Father hear you say," Rian commented dryly.

Bentleigh snorted at the unnecessary warning. "I'm not completely stupid."

"I know you're not, Ben," Rian said, his voice heavy. "But are you sure they're wrong?"

Bentleigh snapped his head around so quickly, his neck hurt. "Don't tell me you're siding with them! Surely you don't want me to give up on Azalea, too? Think how it would reflect on our kingdom, if you don't care about anything else!"

"I do care, Ben," Rian said patiently. "You know I liked Azalea—*like* Azalea," he corrected hastily, seeing Bentleigh's glower. "But...is there really anything to be gained by you going there? It's not like she'll know you're visiting. It's been two years, with no change at all. Ben, I know you don't want to hear this, but what if she's never waking up? What if it's hopeless?"

"It's not hopeless," Bentleigh said, through gritted teeth.

"How do you know?"

Bentleigh put a hand to the chain around his neck. He twisted it between his fingers, reassured by its solid familiarity.

"Because I still have hope."

Rian was silent for a long moment, his expression once again troubled. "I understand that," he said at last. "But I also understand our parents' view."

"How can you say—"

"By taking emotion out of it," Rian cut across Bentleigh's impassioned protest. "You think it will look bad for Bansford if we pull back from our alliance, but a lot of people think it will weaken us much more to be allied with a cursed kingdom."

"It's not just some alliance, Rian," Bentleigh growled. "It's my life."

"Well, I care about that, too," Rian said frankly. "And I don't blame Mother and Father for not wanting you mixed up with magic and enchantments."

Bentleigh sagged in the saddle, weary of the topic all of a sudden. "Magic isn't evil, Ri," he said.

Rian shook his head incredulously. "I don't understand how

you, of all people, can defend magic still. After everything it's taken from you. After experiencing a curse yourself night after night, every time you're in Liss."

Bentleigh sighed. "I can defend magic because I've seen so much more of it than you have. Listernia was wiser than us, in seeing the potential magic has for good, in spite of what happened. There are so many ways in which magic is useful over there. From harvest protection to healing. Besides, don't forget there were four enchanters present at Azalea's christening. Only one of them used his magic for evil. The others all willingly weakened themselves in order to use it for good."

"So having your girlfriend be attractive and witty is worth an entire kingdom being cursed?" Rian asked dryly.

Bentleigh glared at his brother. "Don't talk about her like that!"

"Like what?" Rian stared at him. "Like she's your girlfriend?"

Bentleigh scowled, not entirely sure himself what it was about Rian's tone that had set his back up. "Like this is all somehow her fault. She's not to blame for any of it."

"Well, it's her curse, isn't it?" Rian said, with a shrug. "And her whole kingdom's been dragged into it. Not to mention ours, a little, thanks to your connection." He spoke without rancor, but the whole conversation still made Bentleigh feel angry.

"She was a baby when she was cursed," he snapped. "It was nothing she'd done. If anyone's to blame, it's me, for letting that blasted vine get to her."

He fell silent, grinding his teeth as a fresh wave of grief and guilt washed over him. He knew that King Victor and Queen Ianthe had never blamed him, but even after two years, he felt sick to his stomach every time he remembered that horrifying moment.

Which was often.

An approaching rider pulled him from his thoughts. He

turned toward the soldier, waiting while the man saluted first to Rian, and then to Bentleigh.

"Your Highness," he said, addressing the younger prince. "As requested, a squadron of six will be ready in two hours to ride with you as far as the border."

"Thank you," Bentleigh said, dismissing the man with a nod.

He rode away at a smart trot, and Bentleigh turned toward his brother.

"Ridiculous, really, since they're not allowed to enter Listernia." He rolled his eyes at the long-standing requirement. "I mean, how much trouble am I going to get into between here and the border?"

"Isn't two hours from now a little late in the day to be starting out?" Rian asked, frowning as he turned his horse back toward the castle. "You surely won't make it to Liss by nightfall."

Bentleigh shrugged, riding beside his brother. "So what? I'll stop at an inn, or camp in a grove."

"Don't let Mother hear you talking about camping in a grove," Rian said flatly.

Bentleigh laughed. "Trust me, I'll be fine. No one in our castle can see anything but the destructive impacts of the curse, but there are some upsides, you know. Listernia is the safest kingdom in Solstice come nightfall. I have absolutely nothing to fear from sleeping in the open, provided the weather is mild. Even wild animals aren't a risk."

"Safe for everyone except those guarding the castle walls," said Rian dryly.

Bentleigh sobered. "Yes, that's true," he acknowledged. He glanced over at Rian. "Still, don't tell Father this, but you should hear the talk from some of our people who live near the border. You'd be surprised by how many want to move into Listernia."

Rian threw him a startled look. "Why would they want that?"

Bentleigh shrugged. "Well, for one thing, people might be

stressed in Listernia, but they're never tired. Everyone gets so much sleep. And crime has dropped drastically since the curse hit, with no darkness to hide misdeeds. Plus, the Listernian crown gives aid to those who simply can't do all the work needed to maintain their farms during daylight hours. The gold allows them to hire extra help, so there are more jobs going. No one even has to worry that the hired hands will rob them while they sleep."

"Sounds like a heavy burden for the crown," Rian said, thinking like the future monarch he was.

"It is," Bentleigh admitted. They had entered the city by this time, and their conversation dwindled as they urged their horses up the cobbled streets.

Bentleigh felt nothing but weariness at the thought of the upcoming conversation with his parents. It was the same every time he went to Liss. He could still hardly believe he'd managed to win that initial argument, when he'd first come home after the curse hit. He'd eventually had to admit he couldn't stay in Listernia forever, not that Azalea's parents had given him much choice. He'd been distressed at the time, hating the thought of leaving Zayla in that state. But he could understand their perspective now. The scene that had met him on his arrival back in Bansford had validated their concern that there would be trouble between the neighboring kingdoms if the Bansfordian prince stayed away from his home for too long.

Fortunately for his future, he'd been able to read the mood in a moment. His parents had been one defiant declaration away from forbidding him to ever set foot in Listernia again. So Bentleigh had shown no defiance whatsoever. He'd just systematically and calmly downplayed the drastic impacts of the curse, and had found a myriad of subtle ways to remind his parents of the benefit to be gained from an alliance with their neighboring kingdom.

He'd prevailed, and in spite of some misgivings, his parents had allowed him to continue the schedule of visits that he'd paid to the Listernian royal family since he was a young child. But the cracks had begun to show a long time ago, and Bentleigh could see them widening with every passing visit. Rian was right: there had been no change at all in two years. Bentleigh wasn't the least surprised that his parents were starting to question letting him keep visiting Listernia.

Usually he'd be grateful for Rian's presence when confronting his parents, but after their conversation, he wasn't entirely sure which side his brother was on. Still, it wasn't like he could tell him not to come. The two brothers entered their mother's receiving room in step, to find Queen Eliza seated gracefully on a settle, and King Rhinehart standing before a handsome writing desk, his gaze focused on the view outside the window.

"Bentleigh," the queen said, her voice calm. "There you are."

"Yes, Mother," Bentleigh said, trying to speak cheerfully. "I've come to take my leave. I'll be off in a couple of hours."

Instead of responding, his mother exchanged a look with her husband, and Bentleigh's heart sank.

"I'm not sure that's a good idea, Bentleigh," King Rhinehart said gravely.

"Father," Bentleigh spoke with studied patience, "we've been over this."

"Many times," his father agreed, irritation lurking behind his regal features. He exchanged another look with the queen. "But things have changed since then."

Bentleigh frowned, his gaze passing between them. "What things?"

"Never mind that at present," his father said dismissively.

Bentleigh glanced at his brother, but Rian just shrugged, looking as bemused as Bentleigh felt.

"Bentleigh, I don't like the idea of you traveling to Liss on your own," his mother started. "The latest report is that the walls are entirely surrounded."

"You could always send some guards with me," Bentleigh suggested with a touch of humor.

"I will not risk my people," his father started sternly, and Bentleigh sighed.

"I know, Father. I wasn't serious. I'm perfectly happy to travel alone, and I know King Victor and Queen Ianthe won't take offense at my lack of escort. They will consider my presence a sufficient demonstration of our commitment to the alliance."

But the gambit that had served him well many times fell flat on this occasion. "You seem very comfortable to speak for them," the king said, with a snap in his voice. "I think sometimes you forget whose son you actually are."

A flash of annoyance passed through Bentleigh at the barb, but he was careful to show no sign of it on his face as he waited silently for his father to continue. He was acutely aware of how thin was the ice on which he stood with regard to this issue. He had no intention of making even the slightest of movements.

"Perhaps I have already indulged you too long," his father said tightly. "Your little stunt with that unsanctioned trip into Albury shows how unworthy you are of our trust."

Outwardly Bentleigh remained impassive, but inside he was entirely unrepentant. He'd known that his parents wouldn't approve of his unplanned trip into Albury. But the rumor he'd heard, that there was a girl there who might have figured out how to break Prince Justin's curse, had been well worth the risk. Not that she'd been able to help him with Zayla's situation, of course. But he didn't regret meeting Felicity, or offering her and Justin the limited aid he'd been able to give. He was glad Justin's curse was broken, and Albury was free. He just hoped Listernia could emerge with equal success.

But his father certainly didn't care about Albury's fate, and Bentleigh was starting to question whether he still cared about Listernia's. The silence stretched out, and a band tightened around Bentleigh's chest. They couldn't stop him going, not now! He had to be there the day after tomorrow. He'd never missed a single one of Azalea's birthdays, not in her entire life. It was on the tip of his tongue to declare that he was going with or without their permission, but he forced the impulse down. Such a declaration would ensure their refusal.

His father watched him from narrowed eyes for a tense moment, before the queen reached up and touched her husband's elbow.

"Rhinehart," she said softly. "We agreed."

The king let out a long breath, the tension slowly easing from his shoulders. He gave his wife a curt nod, then turned back to Bentleigh. "We're willing to give you one more chance."

"One more chance to do what?" Bentleigh asked, nonplussed.

"One more chance to visit Princess Azalea, and discover if any method has been found for waking her."

Bentleigh stared back at his father, panic rising. They were saying he had to break her curse this visit, or they'd never let him return? Did they not realize he'd been trying to do that for two years? How was he supposed to suddenly find a solution?

"We are aware that enchantments," judging by his father's expression, the word tasted sour in his mouth, "sometimes have time limits. Given that this visit will mark two years since the unfortunate crisis began, we feel it is wise to allow you to attend as planned, in case of a change."

"But, Father—"

"If there is no sign of any change," his father continued over the top of his protests, "we believe it is time for you to devote your attention to the future of Bansford."

"But an alliance with Listernia will strengthen the future of Bansford," Bentleigh argued.

"You cannot form a marriage alliance with a princess in an enchanted sleep, Bentleigh," his mother said, with a trace of regret. "And there are..." she glanced at the king, "other ways you can serve our kingdom."

Bentleigh again looked at Rian, but it was clear his brother had no more idea what was behind these hints than he did. His mind whirled, trying to find an argument that would be persuasive in his parents' estimation. But he had no opportunity to convince them.

"Have a safe trip, Bentleigh," his father said, without warmth. "We look forward to your return, and a new chapter in your life, either way."

Bentleigh hesitated for only a moment before turning on his heel and striding from the room. He was no fool. It was clear that further talk was fruitless. If his parents tried to stop him from returning to Liss next time, he would have to cross that bridge when he came to it.

CHAPTER EIGHT

Bentleigh

It was in a subdued frame of mind that Bentleigh completed the trip from Bant to the border. He couldn't even bring himself to initiate the cheerful chatter he would usually employ in an effort to convince his escort that their prince wasn't riding to his doom. The soldiers were all visibly relieved to turn back at the border, and Bentleigh wasn't sorry to see the end of them. It was absurd how jumpy most of Bansford was about Listernia's situation.

As Rian had predicted, he had left too late in the day to make it all the way to Liss, so he camped in a sheltered copse of trees some distance off the road. Even after all his trips, it still felt strange to begin looking for a place to sleep before the sun had even set. He propped himself as comfortably as he could against a moss-covered tree trunk, his sword in his hand and his senses fully alert until the last moment of surrender.

Of course, he had nothing to fear from the hours of darkness. When he awoke in the morning he was a little uncomfortable from sleeping in the unnatural position, but undeniably full of energy. It was something he missed about Listernia when he was at home.

His horse, also unusually refreshed, carried him without complaint the rest of the distance, and they caught their first glimpse of Listernia's capital city a couple of hours after noon.

Bentleigh's hand jerked involuntarily at the reins, causing his horse to falter slightly. He gave the animal a soothing pat, murmuring an apology, without taking his eyes from the sight before him.

His mother had not exaggerated. Even from a distance, Bentleigh could see that the city's walls were totally overrun, the thick angry vines creeping over the stone on all sides. It was a formidable sight, and it sent an involuntary chill down Bentleigh's spine. But immediately following was the flash of hot anger that always filled him at the sight of the vines, and the memory of that morning in the clearing. He would like to put his strong hands around Montgomery's neck and choke the life from him, but since that quarry was denied him, the vines were the closest thing he had to a tangible enemy. He was always ready to pour his anger and bitterness out on them.

Nevertheless, as much as his hand was itching for his sword as he rode through the gates, he resisted the urge to join the team of guards who were methodically hacking away at the creeping vine, slowing its progress as best they could. They were keeping the gate clear, at least.

Several of them called cheerful greetings to him, and he smiled as he waved back. One of the guards was even whistling as he worked. It was easy to forget while he was in Bansford, where everyone was edgy at the mere mention of Listernia, but in the cursed kingdom, the populace had more or less adjusted to their new reality.

Bentleigh directed his horse up the broad carriageway, eager to reach the castle and be at Azalea's side again. A groom hurried forward to take his horse, and Bentleigh thanked him with a warm smile. Everyone in Bansford looked at him like he might be carrying a dangerous disease. It was refreshing to be in Liss again, where the people treated him like some kind of hero.

His smile slid away as he entered the castle, in search of his hosts who he knew would expect a formal greeting before he visited their daughter. He didn't deserve the people's admiration. His carelessness had allowed Azalea to be taken by the curse with embarrassing ease, and he'd done nothing useful to break it in all this time. His body sagged in defeat as he thought of his parents' words. He remembered how determinedly he'd vowed that he would break the curse, that he wouldn't sit around just hoping Azalea would wake up. But none of his inquiries had led anywhere useful, and at the end of the day, that was exactly what he'd done.

A helpful servant showed him into Mortimer's study, where King Victor was deep in conversation with his cousin. The double collection of guards outside would have told Bentleigh who was in there, even without the servant's help.

"Bentleigh, my boy!" King Victor said, greeting him with a warmth that provided a stark contrast to the cold farewell he'd received from his own father. "It's good to see you."

"You too, Your Majesty," Bentleigh said, returning the smile and glancing at the king's companion. "Uncle Mortimer, I hope you're well?"

"Still holding on, Your Highness," Mortimer said with a faint smile. Bentleigh felt a flicker of concern. The older man looked more frail than the last time he'd been here. Alone in all the kingdom, he looked tired, almost to the point of exhaustion. What a toll the constant battle of magic was taking on him.

"Any change?" he asked delicately, and both men's expressions dropped.

"Nothing new, I'm afraid, Bentleigh," the king said, his voice defeated. Bentleigh gave a curt nod, and after a short and awkward silence, the king summoned another smile. "Go on, lad. No need to stand talking with us."

Bentleigh's smile was a little sheepish, but he took the offered release without hesitation. His feet seemed to move of their own accord, carrying him down the familiar route to Azalea's chambers. It was strange to remember how he'd once refused to set foot in there. He spent most of his visits in the suite now.

He'd expected to find Azalea's maid by her bed, but today it was her friend.

"Good afternoon, Lady Winifred," he said, with a smile. Azalea's form on the bed was drawing his eyes irresistibly, but he called on his manners, forcing himself to greet the conscious girl first.

She gave him a look, and his smile became more genuine.

"All right, Lady Winnie."

"Better," she said approvingly. "Good afternoon, Your Highness. Welcome back to Liss."

"I wouldn't miss it."

"No," she agreed sadly. "You've never missed a birthday, have you?"

"Never," he echoed softly. He at last allowed his eyes to go where they wanted to, as he approached the bed. His gaze passed hungrily over Azalea's face, willing there to be some sign of movement, of awareness. But of course there was nothing. A splash of pink drew his eyes to her clasped hands, and he raised an eyebrow at Winnie.

"An azalea? Still?"

"I know, I know," she said, her attention now on the embroidery she was working on. "She would hate it. But it makes the maids happy, and really, what's the harm?"

"None, I suppose," Bentleigh conceded. He lowered himself

onto the bed, sitting beside Azalea and taking her hand. "Always so cold," he muttered, with a frown. He chafed the hand between his own, but it had no effect. He gave a deep sigh, his expression twisted as he remembered his arguments to Rian. They felt like empty words now.

"What's that expression for, Your Highness?" Winnie said suspiciously. "You look like you're blaming yourself again, and you know none of us will stand for that."

Bentleigh summoned a smile for her. "I'm not blaming myself for the curse," he said. *At least not at present.* "I'm just remembering something particularly stupid I said to my brother. About the curse having good effects. I'm struggling to remember them right now."

"You mean like the babies?" Winnie asked brightly.

Bentleigh stared at her, confused. "The babies?"

"Yes, I've heard it from lots of mothers," Winnie explained, her expression placid as she stitched. "All the babies in the kingdom sleep through the night now, every night. Life changing, some call it." She smiled. "Some of the older women grumble about how easy the young ones have it these days, not even tired when they have a newborn in the house."

Bentleigh returned her smile mechanically, not in the mood to see the humor of Winnie's anecdote. He stared softly down into Azalea's lovely, unresponsive face, and a fresh wave of grief washed over him. It was unbearable, exquisite torture, coming here. On his darker days, he was tempted to give in to his parents' pressure and cease his visits. Seeing her like this, having her so close but so agonizingly inaccessible, was almost more than he could handle.

Her appearance had changed since the day she was cursed. The enchanted sleep didn't freeze time. She'd aged, the slight roundness of her sixteen-year-old face gone, replaced by the elegant features of a young woman. Her curves were considerably more noticeable than they had been, and her expression seemed more refined, even in sleep. But the sparkle of mischief in her eyes—the one that had made him lose his heart to her before he was even sixteen—was hidden, shrouded by the enchantment. She was in there somewhere, but he couldn't reach her.

Tomorrow she would be eighteen. They were supposed to marry when she was eighteen.

Bentleigh sighed, tearing himself away and taking his leave of Winnie. He had better settle himself into his own rooms, and prepare for the evening meal. They ate incredibly early in Liss these days—to give the servants time to clean up before darkness fell—and he couldn't sit down to dinner with the king and queen in all his traveling dirt.

He couldn't quite resist stopping by Azalea's room on his way back past, an hour later. The guards at the door nodded him through, and he slipped into the room quietly. He was surprised to find no companion sitting with the princess. Winnie must have stepped out, or perhaps whichever maid had replaced her.

He approached Azalea's bed again, glad of the rare opportunity to be with her alone. Some part of him wanted to laugh at his own absurdity. What was the point of being alone with her? It wasn't like she could hear a word he said. But he found himself talking to her anyway, keeping his voice to a whisper so as not to risk the guards overhearing.

"I miss you, Zayla," he said, running a hand through her dark hair. "Nothing's been right since you fell asleep. Nothing will be right again until you wake up." Glancing around to make sure he really was alone, he leaned down to press a kiss to her forehead. "I'm so sorry I've been such a failure," he whispered, his voice cracking. "I *will* figure out a way to free you. I *will* end this."

Azalea made no response, her face as peaceful as ever, and

her breathing even. Bentleigh's heart ached at her silence. It was just so wrong. She'd always been the brightest spark in any room, whether she tried to be or not. If she could hear his sappiness, she'd make fun of it, or respond with some cheeky quip that would startle a laugh out of him.

He stood, knowing he'd indulged his sentiment too long already. He'd be late for dinner if he didn't hurry. He stepped back out into the corridor, frowning as he turned to the guards.

"Why is no one in there with Princess Azalea?"

"What do you mean?" one of the guards said, looking startled. "Her maid is with her. She relieved Lady Winifred half an hour ago."

Bentleigh raised an eyebrow. "There's no one there."

"That's impossible," said the other guard. "The princess is never alone. The maid must have stepped into the receiving room for a moment."

Bentleigh frowned, unease passing over him. Had the maid been hovering in the other room, listening in on his private moment with Azalea? He'd never known one of Azalea's companions to wander around the suite like that before, instead of sitting by her bed.

"Something's not right," he muttered.

Following his instinct, he pushed back through the door. A cry of rage burst from him at the sight of a man kneeling on the bed, knife raised in the air above the princess's chest. Bentleigh sprang forward, his sword in his hand before the intruder could blink.

The man, whom Bentleigh didn't recognize, made no attempt to flee. He cast one frantic look at the charging prince, then plunged his blade downward, straight for Azalea's heart.

But Bentleigh was faster. Steel rang against steel as his blade intercepted the knife an inch from its target and flung it across the room. He mastered the impulse to run the man through then and there, as his logic barely held his fury and terror at bay. They needed answers.

The guards surged into the room behind him, and a sharp shout from one of them told Bentleigh that more help would be coming. He disregarded all this, clambering straight over the bed to put his body between Azalea and her attacker, who had thrown himself toward his fallen weapon.

He snatched it off the floor and straightened, but Bentleigh's sword was already at his throat. For a moment he hesitated, a battle visible in his eyes, and Bentleigh tightened his arm, allowing his blade to prick the other man's skin. A single drop of red appeared, and the intruder dropped his knife with a clatter, raising his arms in surrender.

"Check the other room," Bentleigh snapped, and one of the guards hastened to comply. There was a shriek, and the guard emerged again, his face grim as he clutched a quivering maid by one arm. Bentleigh recognized her as one of Azalea's regular attendants, although he didn't know her name.

"You will pay the price for your treason," Bentleigh hissed, rage making his muscles tremble.

The maid began to weep, but the man made an inarticulate noise of protest as the other guard detained him. "We ain't treasonous, Your Highness," he said, his voice rough but steady. "We ain't enemies of Listernia. We want to save it."

"By killing the crown princess?" Bentleigh demanded, enraged.

The man's expression was mulish. "She can't inherit the crown if she's sleeping." He cast a glance at the bed, a hint of sadness in his eyes. "She's as good as dead, Your 'ighness, as those of us who're awake can see."

Bentleigh's heart seized at the words, but he didn't let his anguish show. "She would be if you had your way," he growled, taking a menacing step toward Azalea's attacker. Now that the need for sudden action had passed, terror was threatening to pull him apart as he realized just how close it had been.

"We can't go on this way, Your Highness," the maid sobbed. "We lost our father, our mother, our home, everything, and we're not the only ones."

Bentleigh frowned between them, noticing a faint resemblance he'd been too distracted to observe initially. Siblings, most likely. It seemed he had his answer as to how an armed intruder had gained entry to Azalea's bedchamber unnoticed.

"What are you talking about?"

"Our father was a blacksmith," the man said, his expression dark. "It was all 'e could do to hold on these past two years. In summer 'e 'ad a chance, but in winter there simply ain't enough hours in the day to complete the commissions 'e needed to make ends meet."

"The crown gives aid to—"

"It weren't enough," the man interrupted Bentleigh's impatient words. "And 'e always pushed it to the last rays of light, to try to make the most of the day. One day 'e cut it too close. Didn' leave enough time to properly secure things for the night. The fire was still too strong, and it got loose. The whole workshop burned, along with our home." Pain passed over his face. "With our parents inside."

"The fire burned all night," the maid said, sobbing harder than ever. "Of course there was no one to fight it, no one to help stop the spread. No one even knew until the morning..."

Bentleigh stepped back, his anger draining away, replaced by a hollow feeling. For all his defensive words to Rian, he'd heard too many of these stories in the past two years. Too much suffering, too much fear. Too many people feeling trapped and powerless.

"So you wanted revenge?" he said wearily, his eyes drifting to Azalea, beautiful, irrepressible...utterly silent.

"Of course not, Your Highness!" the maid protested. "I never wished the princess harm. But nothing has changed in all this time—she's not coming back to us. We have to break the curse, free the kingdom."

"What makes you think killing her would break the curse?" Bentleigh demanded.

The man shrugged. "It's her curse," he said, unknowingly echoing Bentleigh's brother. "We suffer because she suffers."

Bentleigh turned away from the pair, the ache in his chest unbearable. More guards had arrived by this time, and the pair were led away immediately. Bentleigh was sure the king and queen wouldn't be far behind. He needed to collect himself before he could face them. He sank to his knees beside Azalea's bed, clutching one of her hands and pressing his face against it as he fought the emotion threatening to overwhelm him.

Almost as horrific as all the rest was her unperturbed face, her total stillness. The idea of Azalea lying meekly by while someone defended her against attack was so completely contrary to who she was that for a moment it felt like the intruder had been right. Like he'd already lost her, beyond recovery.

But it wasn't true, he reminded himself fiercely. She was in there, just sleeping. All he needed to do was wake her up.

All thought of dinner was gone. Bentleigh had no intention of leaving Azalea's side. He spoke with an enraged King Victor and a tearful Queen Ianthe when they came, and reassured them that Azalea had been untouched by the attack. He suffered the guards to prowl through the suite, checking for further threats, and securing the window through which the maid had let her brother in.

But when another maid arrived, expecting to occupy the cot

next to Azalea for the somewhat pointless night shift, Bentleigh vehemently opposed her entry. He didn't know her any more than he knew the maid who had shown herself a traitor, and he wasn't ready to trust the task of guarding Azalea to anyone but himself.

With the exception of that very first night, when the enchanted slumber had taken everyone completely by surprise, Azalea's various minders had been fastidious about chivvying Bentleigh out of the princess's rooms before darkness approached. But tonight, no one challenged him. Bentleigh suspected that if there had been time after he expelled the maid, someone he knew and trusted, like Lady Winifred, would have been sent in her place. But the maid had arrived a mere ten minutes before sunset, and Winnie didn't live in the castle. So when the guards laid themselves down on their simple pallets outside the door, Bentleigh remained in sole possession of the suite, except for Azalea's unmoving form.

He could feel the unnatural sleep beginning to tug at him, and he was seized by a sudden impulse to be near Azalea. His emotions were still not under control, the anxiety of the last two hours taking its inevitable toll. With a glance at the door, he shifted off his chair, lowering himself recklessly onto the bed. The mattress was enormous—it wasn't as though even their arms were touching. But he stretched his hand out, taking one of hers and pulling it across the mattress, so that the clasped pair met in the space between them.

A memory flashed painfully through his mind—Azalea's face, eyes wide and uncertain, as she stepped away from him in the clearing the morning of her sixteenth birthday. Would she welcome his closeness now, if she knew of it? Or would she be uncomfortable with him taking such a liberty?

But it was too late to change his mind. His eyelids were too heavy to hold up, and his thoughts had become foggy and sluggish. He was well accustomed to the sensation by now. He made no effort to resist as the enchantment pulled him down, down, and under.

CHAPTER NINE

Azalea

Azalea's eyes sprang open in the darkness, the usual irritation flickering through her at the feel of a flower clasped in her hand.

Of all the irritating, melodramatic...She sighed, unfurling her fist and letting it go, both physically and mentally. It was the least of her concerns. She rolled her neck from side to side, trying to work out the stiffness. She had always preferred to sleep on her side, and it was beyond frustrating that she no longer had control of that simple decision. It was clear that whoever cared for her during the day did things like brushing out her hair. Unfortunately, however they did or didn't shift her, they always saw fit to arrange her back in the same position, like she was on display at a funeral.

Quite apart from being unsettling in its reminder that others could move her around while she slept, it was incredibly annoying. She woke with a stiff neck and an aching back more nights than not. She knew she couldn't afford to dawdle for too long, but she gave herself a brief moment to shake off the fog of sleep. She suddenly became aware that her other hand was being held, and turned her head to the side in confusion.

"Ben!" she gasped, almost tumbling off the bed in her shock.

He was lying on his side, one arm stretched across the empty space between them, clasping her hand in his. Her heart did a strange kind of somersault, and her breath seemed stolen from her throat at the sight of him so near. It had been months since his last visit, and his familiar form was such a beautiful sight it brought tears to her eyes. She'd expected him, of course. As of midnight, she would be eighteen years old, and he'd never once missed her birthday.

But she hadn't expected him to be in her suite at nighttime, let alone lying on her bed. She had no idea how such a thing had been allowed, but she didn't waste time wondering about that. She was too busy soaking in the sight of him, her eyes tracing every line, every familiar feature.

He'd grown a beard since his last visit—something she'd never seen on him before. It suited him, and it made him look older. She reached out tentatively. The wiry brown hair was scratchy under her fingers. His face was peaceful in sleep, but the lines of it had changed. His brow was more serious than it had been two years ago, and there were lines on his face that made him look older than his almost twenty years. It hit her all at once that he was the boy of her childhood antics no longer. He was a man, and a strong and extremely attractive man at that.

Her eyes fell on the chain glistening around his neck, and she reminded herself with a tingling rush that if she could just figure out how to break this stupid curse, he'd be *her* man. Her husband. The plan had been for them to marry when she was eighteen.

She shuffled closer to him, eagerly searching his face for an indication as to how he was. Knowing him as she did, she was guessing he was feeling like a failure for his continued inability to break her curse. But how could he be expected to find the solution? It wasn't as though he'd had any hand in creating the problem.

The temptation to stay there, to shelter in the illusion of safety created by his nearness, was like a powerful ache in her stomach. But as her eyes passed over his form, she saw that the hand not clasping hers was resting on the hilt of his sword. She frowned. The posture looked as tense as she'd seen any of the enchanted slumberers, and she couldn't help but wonder if it related to his presence in her room. Had something happened? And if so, what?

She pulled herself together, sitting up. She didn't have time to lie around mooning over Ben all night. She had things to do, and if she was going to investigate a possible incident as well, she couldn't afford to delay.

She padded silently across the room, heading for her stash of supplies, deep inside a cupboard. Her eyes were drawn to the stack of parchments on her writing desk, but she didn't even consider attempting a message. She thought ruefully of her optimism the second night of her curse, when she'd left parchments with so many people.

Bitter trial and error had taught her the futility of such attempts. The curse didn't just keep her asleep during the day— it kept her fully isolated from the rest of her kingdom. From all she could tell, any written communication simply disappeared with the rising of the sun.

She could move things, like how she'd gathered a collection of useful items, hidden in a place where they were unlikely to be found. But anything that would too clearly demonstrate her activity, the curse forced her to undo before she returned to her bed. As dawn approached, she became a puppet on a string, erasing all signs of her presence. She remembered all too clearly the hours she'd spent replacing items, erasing messages from the dirt, even changing her own clothes, all against her will, and all while tears of fear and loneliness and frustration poured down her face.

But that had been a long time ago. She was much stronger now. She hadn't cried in months, and she certainly hadn't wasted time on pleas for help that were doomed never to reach their targets.

She retrieved her lantern, lighting it from the dying embers in her room's fireplace. The servants no longer bothered to light torches in the corridors, believing that no one was awake after dark to benefit from them. So she had to take her illumination with her. With a self-conscious glance at the catatonic Ben, she changed quickly into a more practical dress and sturdy boots. The flowing lilac gown some maid had slipped her into was lovely and all, but it would only get in her way. Finally, she strapped on the sword she'd pilfered from the castle's armory. It had taken her six attempts to successfully acquire a sword that she hadn't been forced by the magic to return. But apparently the curse was satisfied that no one would miss this one, or at least, that nothing about its absence would point to her.

With one last look at the surreal—and if she was honest, a little swoon-worthy—sight of Ben stretched across her bed, she slipped into the corridor.

"Evening Phil, Martin," she said cheerfully to the two sleeping forms outside her door. "You've been on night duty for a week straight, now. I thought you'd be off tonight. They must have changed the schedule."

There was no response, but that wasn't what brought the frown to Azalea's face. Glancing past the two guards, she realized there were four more stationed along the corridor. Six guards outside her suite? Something had definitely happened. The thought made her jumpy, but none of her fear was for the present moment. She had long ago adjusted to the eeriness of wandering around in constant darkness. She no longer saw sinister shapes in the shadows, or jumped at the sound of the wind.

She made her way first to Uncle Mortimer's suite, as was her habit. A quick scan of his notes showed that he had no new discoveries to share. She paused beside his bed, remorse creeping over her as she noted the lines on his face. He looked older than her father now, although he was ten years younger. His expression was troubled, his face twitching occasionally as if he was suffering in his dreams. She had read his notes extensively, and she understood now the cost he was still paying for his intervening magic. She was kept alive day after day because his magic continued to battle that of his twin brother, even though he knew it could never overcome, never throw off the stronger power.

She turned away, following her usual route to her parents' suites. They were both in her father's chamber, but they weren't in bed. Her mother seemed to have fallen asleep in a large armchair, and her father was laid down on the floor, as if he'd been pacing the room when he'd finally succumbed to the irresistible slumber. Azalea's alarm spiked. Some event had upset them all, Ben, her mother, her father. It was unspeakably frustrating to have no way of finding out what it was.

She walked over to her mother, kneeling beside her chair and searching her face. The queen looked older than she had when Azalea was cursed, like more than two years had passed. Azalea laid her hand over her mother's, remorse washing over her once again for how carelessly she'd dismissed the older woman's fears. She had been frustrated with her mother for not being stronger, but she understood so much better now how hard it was to be strong all the time when your life was ruled by fears you couldn't control.

She turned from her mother, hesitating for a moment before retrieving a blanket from the bed. She laid it over her father, slipping a pillow under his head as well. She usually avoided such gestures—the enforced need to undo them cost her precious time for her other nightly activities. But she felt it was worth it in this instance. She didn't like to think of her father waking cold and sore from a night on the floor. She'd caused him enough pain and worry as it was.

She was heading for the kitchen, to pilfer some food as normal, when she noticed a guard on duty where there normally wasn't one. She frowned to herself, redirecting her steps. That was the corridor to the dungeon, which hadn't been occupied in some time. She followed the winding passageway, a chill pervading the air the deeper she went. Her little lantern seemed especially feeble in the growing blackness of the underground level, but she barely noticed it. Darkness was her reality now. Her eyes had most definitely become stronger in low light, and she no longer felt the fear that had crippled her at first.

Another guard was stationed just inside the dungeon's entry, convincing Azalea that she would find at least one of the cells occupied. What she had never imagined even for a moment, however, was that the prisoner would be one of her own maids. She stared in astonishment at the girl, stretched on a hard cot in one of the cells. What could she have done to land her in there? A quick scout showed Azalea that another cell was also occupied, by a young man she didn't recognize.

What had been their crime? She had little doubt that it had to do with her. Had they tried to do her an injury of some kind? Fear shot through her, knowing how helpless she was in the daylight hours. If they'd attacked her, she didn't even know it had happened, let alone how to prevent it another time.

But then an image flashed across her mind, of Ben lying across her mattress, one hand clasping hers and the other on his sword, and she relaxed. Much as she might hate her own powerlessness, she knew she had nothing to fear while Ben was standing guard over her.

Still, her steps were heavy as she made her way out of the dungeon. That maid had been with her for years, and she hated to think of the girl wishing her harm. Grief stirred deep within her as she realized that there must be plenty in Listernia now who resented her, perhaps even hated her. She hadn't taken her responsibility to her people seriously before the curse hit. Now, not only did she long for their respect, she wanted desperately to protect them from the dark magic that encircled them. And she had no opportunity to show them how much she loved their kingdom, how much she cared about her people.

But at least she had the opportunity to protect them. The thought bolstered her.

The unknown incident made her feel exposed, and reluctant to enter her private battlefield. Not to mention that Ben's presence—however unresponsive—dimmed her enthusiasm for leaving the building. She was tempted to stay in the castle, spend the whole night in the library, rather than just returning there for the last couple of hours as she normally did.

But she had a job to do, and whether they knew it or not, her people were depending on her. It was this purpose that had kept her sane through two truly hellish years of darkness and isolation. She crossed the castle's entranceway swiftly, running across the gardens with nimble steps. Much as she hated returning to the forest gate, it was where she always started.

The area was unrecognizable now, covered as it was with the vines. The walls had done a lot in holding the growth back, and she knew from pilfering through Uncle Mortimer's papers that his sisters had put an enchantment on the wall to make it harder for the vines to grow over the top of it.

But harder didn't mean impossible. The vines had been working away for two years, and in addition to growing all the way around the length of the city's walls, they had crept over the top in many places. One of those places was the forest gate.

Azalea picked up the pace as she drew near the spot and saw how close the vines had crept to the guards who were on duty there. The men had set up their pallets well back from the wall, but she had clearly lingered too long with Ben and in the dungeon, because the reaching tendrils were almost upon the guards. She ran forward with a battle cry that no one could hear, slicing her sword through the air and slashing the closest vine.

The severed stretch shriveled up, and the stub curled back on itself as if in pain. She made short work of the rest of the breaches, then turned, beginning her slow circuit along the wall that surrounded the main part of Liss. The vine was maimed, and would need time to regroup. She knew it would recover, and continue its assault. But by that time, the guards and soldiers would be awake, and could take over the city's defense.

As she hacked and slashed her way around the wall, she thought longingly of how nice it would be to have a whole team fighting this enemy, as must be the case in the daytime. She spent most of every night on the task, and it was still beginning to exceed her ability to control it. Her arms were strong now, muscles standing out where there had been none visible before, and her endurance was easily ten times what it had been when she first started.

"I was never much interested in gardening before," she told the vines conversationally as she sliced her way through them. "But it seems to be all I do now. I can't decide whether I'm going to feel an ongoing affinity for gardening once the curse is broken, or whether I'll never want to tend to another plant again. What do you think?"

Most rudely, the vines made no answer. Azalea chatted on, undeterred. She'd never been the silent type, and two years of isolation hadn't changed her so much. Talking to sleeping people, plants, and inanimate objects was another habit she might have to work hard to shake once the curse was lifted, she thought ruefully.

"Because it will be lifted," she told the vines sternly, as if they'd been following her temporarily internal conversation. "And I'm sorry to have to tell you, I won't miss *you* at all."

A familiar surge of hatred rose up in her at the thought of what the vines represented, but she forced it down. Her muscles weren't the only evidence of her increased endurance. One of the keys to her survival was the discipline of choosing, over and over again, to consider her circumstances with a humorous lightness instead of giving in to despair. She would do what she could to change her situation, and she wouldn't give the things she couldn't change more thought than strictly necessary.

"I might be fonder of you if you weren't so ugly," she told the vines with brutal frankness. She lifted the sword above her head yet again as she spoke. Her breath was coming in pants from the effort, but she continued brightly. "I may not have done much gardening, but I do remember the head gardener explaining pruning to me when I was admiring the rose bushes. Apparently," she grunted as she hacked at a particularly thick branch, "pruning is supposed to make the plant grow even more."

She paused for a moment, laughing as she wiped sweat off her forehead. "If it turns out that my work here is the reason you're growing so profusely, I'm going to feel like an absolute fool." She sighed. "But I don't think so, somehow."

She returned to the attack. "Any chance you'll bloom for me, though? Flowers would be nice. Something pink, or yellow perhaps. Nice and bright." She rolled her eyes. "I suppose they'd have poison nectar or something, though, wouldn't they?"

She'd reached the main gate by this time, and she paused, leaning on a stone pillar as she gathered her strength. She would need it. The sight before her was grim, noticeably worse than it had been the night before. The gates were flung wide—no longer any need to lock them overnight—and the entrance was largely overgrown with the creeping, curling vines.

Azalea drew a deep breath, then charged at the encroaching vines. She didn't immediately start her chatter again. They were more frightening when hanging into space like this, somehow. They weren't crawling along a wall—they had a body, and a life, of their own.

"Beauty," she panted as she swung, "and grace." With a grunt, she lopped off a particularly thick strand. "Sounds nice for a princess, Aunt Miranda, but I could really have used strength. And Aunt Melodia, wit isn't much use when there's no one else in all the kingdom awake to appreciate it." She fell silent for a moment, swinging once, twice, three times against another stubborn stretch of vine. "I suppose health was a good one," she admitted grudgingly. "But Uncle Mortimer, much as I love you and bless the ground you walk on for saving my life, you were going to give me sweetness? And good nature? What's the good of that?"

She paused, wiping away a trickle of sweat that was making its way down her cheek. "Endurance would have been nice. Or prowess with a blade." She grimaced. "Or brilliance with understanding enchantments so I could break this stupid curse."

She returned to her task, encouraged that the open gateway was almost clear. She knew she couldn't just be magically given endurance, really. She had to develop it, like anyone, and she'd been working hard to do just that. The same applied to understanding enchantments. It was one of many topics she researched in the library each night. She'd also read through most of Uncle Mortimer's private tomes. A lot of it was hard to make sense of, not having the basic grasp of magic that he, as an enchanter, had. But she was fairly certain she grasped the concept of a counterforce. It was just unfortunate that she had no way of figuring out what counterforce might have been unconsciously built into Montgomery's enchantment.

And magic wasn't her only area of study, of course. With nothing to distract her, and a desperate need for something to put her energy into, she had focused on her studies in a way her parents had tried unsuccessfully to get her to do all her life. In the two years since the curse, she had learned more about Listernia's history and economy, the cultures of its neighboring kingdoms, its relations with those kingdoms, even about dragon lore, than she had in the sixteen years before it. She'd even studied up on swordsmanship, although she felt she'd reached the limit of what she could learn about such things from books. She usually spent some time each night drilling herself in some of the techniques she'd read.

The gateway was now free, and she moved on, continuing around the wall. She passed casually through a district that had once been considered tawdry. She had long since become used to the cleaner, neater streets, and the intangible but undeniable difference in the feel of the taverns. She supposed that the removal of all nighttime hours had come with pretty drastic effects for the operation of such places.

She paused to read the familiar proclamation attached to a nearby post. Same as usual, reminding people of the curse—as if anyone in Listernia was likely to forget—and warning people to be indoors and in their beds before darkness. Also encouraging everyone to stay back from the wall, and never to lay themselves down to sleep near its shadow. Whatever the day's dramatic incident, it hadn't yet filtered out from the castle, at least not through official channels.

By now she was three quarters of the way around the wall, and the vines were further from the source, and therefore not as bad. She was physically sore and weary, and had begun to relax.

She lopped off a few particularly bold tendrils with a casual air, turning away before they even fell to the ground.

She'd taken only one step when her foot snagged on something in the darkness, and she fell heavily forward. She threw out her hands to catch herself, her sword clattering to the cobblestones, and a grunt of pain escaping her as her forearms connected with the ground. She tried to push herself upright, but her foot was still caught. She turned, confused, and let out an involuntary scream at the sight of a thorny creeper, twisting around her ankle and pulling her back toward the wall.

CHAPTER TEN

Azalea

Acting on blind instinct, Azalea reached toward the vine with her hand, desperate to rip it loose. But her sense broke through her panic, and she pulled her arm back just in time. In two years, despite a number of close calls, she'd never let another thorn pierce her skin. Her thick leather boots were saving her so far, but she needed to get the vine off before it could pierce through to her foot.

She squinted through the darkness, searching frantically for her sword. She saw it lying a few feet away and reached for it. But before her hand could close on the hilt, the vine gave a sudden violent tug, dragging her backward across the cobblestones. She knew she shouldn't look behind her, but she couldn't help herself. The strand of vine in question had pushed its way through the walls, and more shoots were following, enlarging the hole. They were twisting and writhing frantically, reaching toward her across the empty space, as though the contact with their quarry had sent them into an almost sentient frenzy.

She abandoned her sword momentarily, pulling a small dagger from her belt. She slashed at the vine, not slicing through it, but scoring it. With a hissing sound, the vine's momentum paused, its leaves wriggling as if in pain.

It was enough reprieve. Reaching down, Azalea ripped at her laces, yanking her boot off. The moment her foot was free, she sprang back out of the vine's reach, snatching her sword from the ground.

Her instincts screamed at her to run far away, but she ignored them, wading back into battle. Her sock-clad foot slipped a little on the cobblestones as she swung at the vine, hacking it again and again. The various shoots fell before her methodical attack. It took several more minutes, but she destroyed the new growth that had forced its way through the wall.

When the ends were all brown and dead, she strode forward, stepping carefully with her exposed foot. Using the tip of her blade, she flicked the dead vines from her boot, and scooped it up. She retreated to a safe distance before putting it on.

"These," she informed the dead vines, with haughty dignity, "are my best boots."

She laced the boot back up, breathing heavily and telling herself she was absolutely fine. But her shoulders were beginning to shake, the shock of her near miss rising up to belatedly take hold of her. The quip about the boots was one of the many ways she tried to maintain the illusion of some control. The truth was she knew she couldn't abandon the boot, even if she'd wanted to. The curse would have forced her to return for it, because its presence, and her unclad foot, would have been too telling. And who knew what would happen if she'd come that close to the vines when in the clutches of the curse?

She suspected that no one knew for certain what would happen if another thorn pricked her, but she knew from Uncle Mortimer's notes that he at least had grave fears that it might kill her. After all, if the vines couldn't do her any further damage, why were they still trying to grow through the wall to reach her?

She knew that keeping the vines at bay was a serious priority for the city's daytime inhabitants. She also knew that her parents would be absolutely horrified if they were aware Azalea had appointed herself as the nighttime guardian of Liss. But observation had shown her that if the vines were left to grow unhindered through the entire night, they would very quickly overwhelm the defenses. And she couldn't allow that.

Her parents had been right about the curse, and she'd been foolish not to take their fears more seriously. But they'd been wrong about other things. Being important to the kingdom didn't mean she should run from every possible source of danger. It meant she should be the most active in trying to figure out how to overcome that danger. Especially when it threatened her people as well as her.

Once her boot was back on, she hurried away from the wall. This stretch was usually not so bad, and she could afford to leave it for the night. Cold and heat were rushing over her in quick succession, and she could tell that she was close to falling apart. She needed to put some distance between herself and her silent enemy, give herself a chance to regroup. She hurried back toward the castle, but her steps didn't take her to the library. Not tonight. She was too shaken by the night's events—Ben's nearness, the mystery of why her maid was in the dungeon, the fear of the vine's attack. She wouldn't be able to focus on study tonight.

She turned before she reached the castle's main gate, wending her way through the manicured grounds. She had time to spare, and it had been a while since she'd indulged in an hour's relaxation in her favorite garden.

It had been her favorite even before the curse, although for different reasons, she reflected as she sank down onto the soft turf. The grass was growing long here, and fallen pine needles littered the ground from the tall, graceful trees that rose up around the edge of the space, reaching toward a clear, starry sky. The gardeners had done a wonderful job of mimicking a small forest meadow here in the castle's gardens. She had always preferred it to the more landscaped part of the grounds. It was peaceful, far from the building full of sleeping people, and far from the vines.

Although its location wasn't its main charm now. It had something even better that Azalea had never discovered before the last two years. She leaned forward, letting her tension out in a long breath as she ran a hand through the water of a still pond. Mossy rocks lined its edges, and tiny insects scuttled across them, busy about their nighttime doings. Azalea had long since discovered that while animals were captured by the enchanted slumber, insects seemed to be below the curse's notice. They scurried on, unperturbed by the curse, unaware of the kingdom's crisis. It was soothing, somehow.

She couldn't be guaranteed to see what she'd come for, of course—some nights there were hundreds, some none at all. But it seemed luck was with her. A light breeze stirred the tall grass, and suddenly she saw a tiny glow rise up from the branch of a nearby tree. More soon followed, and Azalea let her fear and stress melt away for a moment as she watched the fireflies dance.

They swirled through the air, dozens of them, looking like so many glowing embers. Whether they had always congregated here, and she just hadn't been aware of it before the curse forced her to live nocturnally, or whether they'd only discovered the meadow garden since the area had become so reliably undisturbed at nighttime, she didn't know.

But they were mesmerizing, either way. They lit the clearing with their soft light, and they moved with such an unhurried, graceful rhythm. Simply put, the sight was magical. Slowly, she felt the tension leak from her shoulders, as she gained control over the fear that still lingered after her run in with the vines. It always helped to settle her anxiety when she came here, and watched them go about their business. It reminded her that not all magic was evil and destructive. So many things were beautiful, even in a world of endless night.

And without her endless night, she wouldn't have discovered the fireflies. She'd never been here late enough to see them before. Her parents had never allowed her to wander outside the castle after dark. The curse had taken so much from her, but the fireflies were one of the things she'd gained in her years of struggle. She lay back against the grass, her breathing slowing further as she gazed up at the stars. It was a clear, warm night, without a light to be seen other than her glowing friends, and the stars were as bright as she'd ever seen them. There was a vast world around her, and as all-consuming as her problems seemed to her, much of that world was going on just as before, untroubled and whole.

She drew strength from that thought, reminding herself that her unexpected discoveries thanks to the curse weren't only external. She'd found a strength within herself that she hadn't known was there. Probably never would have known if her old supports hadn't all been ruthlessly stripped away.

Temporarily stripped away, she told herself firmly, as she pushed herself to her feet. She wouldn't be alone forever. Even now her thoughts drifted ahead of her steps, to her suite and its sleeping occupant. He might not be out here with her, but Ben's proximity still gave her spirits a boost.

Her thoughts took on a wistful note as she entered the castle. Reminding herself of the beauty around her might help keep despair at bay, but it would be so much better if she had someone, anyone, with whom she could share her discoveries.

She remembered to stop at her father's rooms on her way back to her own, regretfully replacing both the blanket and the pillow she'd supplied him with. She hated to leave him uncomfortably on the floor, but she didn't want to be forced to leave her room again when dawn approached. Better to replace things now.

She paused on the threshold of her own chambers, feeling unaccountably nervous. Ben was still there, of course, laid out on his side and looking impossibly handsome. She approached the bed, her eyes softening as they searched his well-known features. This was familiar—as creepy as it sounded, she was used to watching him sleep. She visited his rooms to catch a sight of him almost every night of his visits now. She'd long ago accustomed herself to the feeling of being a stalker. She often commented to him on how scandalous her behavior was, although he'd yet to reply to her jokes. Perhaps one day they'd be able to laugh about it together. The thought made her heart ache.

She changed back into the lilac dress and returned her treasures to their place. There was still plenty of time before dawn, but she felt exhausted, worn down by the night's exertions and fears, with no fight left in her.

She slipped back onto her bed, lying on her side and facing Ben. This *wasn't* familiar. She'd never lain beside him like this, and she couldn't help the way her heart picked up speed, even though he was an unresponsive statue. She reached out a hand, unashamedly tracing the shape of his face. He'd always been nice to look at, but there was no denying he'd become more, well, dreamy in the last couple years.

"I'm so glad you're here, Ben," she said, giving his still form a weary smile. "I know it's silly, because it's not like we can actually spend time together." She realized that midnight had long since passed. "But it's my birthday, and it wouldn't be right if you weren't here." For a moment she was silent, her eyes glazing over as she thought about the fact that she was eighteen now. Not that it made the slightest difference to anything.

"Two years," she choked out, her lightness deserting her with painful suddenness. "It's been *two years*, Ben. How long will this nightmare go on? Am I stuck like this forever?"

Tears were trickling down her cheeks now, and she made no effort to check them. The peace of the fireflies' meadow was gone, and the harsh reality of her loneliness refused to be held at bay any longer.

"The vines almost got me tonight. I'm sick of trying to be brave, Ben. The truth is I'm scared." Her voice hitched on the last word, and she shook her head furiously. "I can't believe what a fool I was that morning." A snort escaped her. "I was—what? Scared of our relationship changing?"

She gave a bitter laugh. "As if I even knew what fear was back then. Now I spend my life wandering the darkness, trapped and alone, with magical vines coming for me, and a curse afflicting my whole kingdom." Her eyes, still brimming with tears, searched his face. "I have plenty of fear in my life now. How could I ever have thought I was afraid of you, in any way? You're the last thing I fear. You're my favorite person in the whole world, and I trust you more than anyone else."

She wriggled closer to him, gripping his tunic with both hands and pressing her face into his chest. "I'm lonely, Ben. So, so, unbearably lonely. I miss the *sun*." Her voice, already muffled by the fabric, dropped to a whisper. "And I miss you. I miss you so much it aches. It's like part of me has been torn out."

She pulled back, looking at his face again. "What wouldn't I give to hear you teasing me again, to pull pranks together? Forget that—I'd even take you scolding me, telling me to be careful. All I want is for you to talk to me."

His face was motionless, his voice silenced by the magic. The familiarity of his features, peaceful and relaxed in slumber, brought her tears back. She laid her hand on his chest again, and a spark seemed to race into her from the contact.

It wasn't true, she realized with a rush of honesty. She didn't just want him to talk to her. She wanted more than that, much more. She wanted him to look at her the way he had in the clearing, not just once, but every day. She wanted to be close to him, in a way they hadn't been even before the curse. She wanted to feel his arms around her.

She pressed her face into Ben's tunic again, trying to pull herself together. But what was the point? There would be no one to witness her composure, just as there was no one to judge her for falling apart. She wouldn't be able to fight the force that would draw her back into her funereal pose in all too short a time, so why fight the magnetic pull Ben had on her now?

She rolled toward him, onto her other side, so that her back was against his chest, and she was lying across his outstretched arm. Reaching over her shoulder, she pulled his other hand from his sword hilt, draping it over herself. She clutched at his arm, half of her basking in the security of his nearness, the other half embarrassed by her pathetic pretense.

"I know it doesn't count," she whispered, her eyes closed as she pressed her cheek against his hand. "But it's the closest to real I can get." She breathed in his smell, a surprised laugh escaping her. "You're so warm!"

He was, as well. She'd touched people's skin a number of times in the last two years, usually in taking someone's hand, or in shifting people in the marginal ways the curse would allow, to remove them from harm's way. Everyone had always felt unnaturally cold to the touch, Ben included. But pressed against his chest like this, she could feel the warmth of his core, slowly seeping through the curse's restrictions, reaching into her and making her feel somehow a tiny bit less alone.

She lay there for what felt like forever, and yet not nearly long enough, just listening to him breathe, and soaking in that warmth. She'd never yet fallen asleep in the hours of darkness, but she was close to drifting more than once.

When she began to feel the inexorable tug of the curse, forcing her to return to her usual position, she felt the tears again threatening to come. Telling herself sternly that she'd fallen apart quite enough times that night, she once again pushed the sadness away with humor.

"If you can't break the curse and wake me up, Ben," she said, even as her body shifted unwillingly away from his, "can you at least stop them from lying me out like I'm at a funeral? I really much prefer sleeping on my side."

No smile, no answering quip, greeted her light words. Azalea wouldn't have resisted the urge to place her hand back in Ben's, even if she could. She tried to keep her head to the side, watching his peaceful face until the last moment. But as her eyes began to drift closed, her head swiveled inevitably back into place.

CHAPTER ELEVEN

Bentleigh

Bentleigh felt awareness returning, but he didn't immediately open his eyes. For once, he wished he could remain in the enchanted sleep that normally chafed him. He didn't usually dream when he was in Liss, but last night he was fairly sure he had.

He didn't know how else to explain the sensation that was lingering still—of holding Azalea in his arms, her slim form nestled against him as he held her tightly, safe from the world and close to him. Tantalizing and unbearable. And the best dream he'd ever had.

But the dream was already flitting away from him, and he opened his eyes with a sigh. The sight of Azalea lying a foot away brought him fully awake. In the haze of waking, he'd forgotten his reckless decision the night before, to stretch out on her bed instead of letting himself fall asleep in the chair. She was so agonizingly near. No wonder he'd had such a dream.

He sat up hastily, releasing her hand and slipping back into his seat before anyone else could enter the room. The last thing he needed was for the king and queen to ban him from entering Azalea's suite. With the thought of his decision came the memory of the reason for it. His fists clenched convulsively. Someone had tried to murder Azalea yesterday.

He knew no one could have been moving about the room during the hours of darkness, of course he did. But he still couldn't be easy until he'd searched her suite thoroughly, satisfying himself that no intruders lurked in dark corners. When Lady Winifred arrived, pale faced at having just heard of the attack, he relinquished the duty of Azalea's companion to her, feeling the need for some fresh air.

Just before exiting the room, however, he paused, glancing back at the bed.

"This is ridiculous," he muttered. He strode back across the room, leaning over a surprised Winnie to grasp Azalea's immobile form. He rolled her halfway over, so that she was on her side. And he yanked the flower from her hand.

He turned to find Winnie watching him, mouth open and eyebrows raised.

"She's not on her deathbed," he said curtly. He tossed the flower into the embers of the previous day's fire. "And I think two years is more than long enough to indulge the maids' love of the dramatic." He gestured back at Azalea, now looking like she genuinely was asleep, rather than dead. "Don't you think she looks more comfortable that way? How would you like to lie in one position for two years?"

"I...I don't know," Winnie said, still looking taken aback. She cast a glance over Azalea, her voice doubtful. "I suppose she does look more comfortable."

Bentleigh didn't stay to discuss the matter. He still wasn't entirely sure himself what had made him do it. He left the room quickly, striding down the corridor toward the royal family's private dining hall with agitated steps. Between Azalea's near death experience, and his own parents' ultimatum, anxiety threatened to swallow him. And on top of it all, his somewhat scandalous dream had only served to remind him just what the enchantment had taken from him. He had to find a way to break this curse, and he had to find it fast.

He was so distracted when he rounded the corner at the end of Azalea's corridor, that he walked right into a manservant. The man bowed low, and Bentleigh barely glanced at him as he mumbled a distracted apology. He didn't recognize the servant, and his attention was already elsewhere. He entered the dining hall in time to hear the end of the daily report given to the king each morning.

"And there was a significant breach on the western wall," the guard was saying, "but it seems to be surprisingly well contained."

"Thank you," King Victor said, dismissing the man with a nod. His brow was heavy. "We can be thankful the vine doesn't seem to grow as quickly at night as it does during the day."

The king wasn't talking to him, but Bentleigh still nodded in silent agreement. With no one awake to fight the vine's progress, the city would be overrun if it grew aggressively all night.

"Bentleigh." Queen Ianthe's gentle voice brought his attention to her. "Welcome. Won't you join us?"

Bentleigh took a seat with a word of thanks, not commenting on the queen's red-rimmed eyes, or subdued manner. He knew the reason.

King Victor welcomed him as well, although he was clearly distracted. Bentleigh wondered what was going to be done with the prisoners he knew were in the dungeons at this moment. Remembering the tears pouring down the traitorous maid's face, he decided he didn't want to know.

"It's her birthday today."

The queen's sudden comment startled Bentleigh from his thoughts. Had she thought any of them had forgotten? He looked up to see Queen Ianthe's eyes filling with tears, and suddenly wished he'd dawdled longer before entering the room.

"Two years, Victor," she continued, her voice choked. "There must be more we can do." A fierce note entered her voice. "We can't let Montgomery take her from us forever."

The king reached a hand toward his wife, his voice defeated and weary, despite the many hours of uninterrupted sleep he'd just had. "If we knew anything more we could do, we'd be doing it, Ianthe."

"Well, my maid did say…" The queen trailed off, and King Victor's voice became tight.

"What did she say? Does she know something of the attack by Azalea's maid?"

"No, no, nothing about that," Queen Ianthe said hurriedly.

Bentleigh had been busying himself with his food, trying not to witness the emotional moment, so he was taken completely by surprise when the queen addressed him.

"Bentleigh." Her voice was softer than ever, almost as if she was…embarrassed? That couldn't be right. "Bentleigh, I'm sorry to ask such a personal question, but…"

The door to the dining hall opened, and the king's three cousins entered. Bentleigh wondered for perhaps the twentieth time how they managed to synchronize their arrival so consistently.

They all took their usual seats at the table, greeting the king and queen in subdued tones, clearly all rattled by the previous day's events. Mortimer looked over at Bentleigh, a greeting on his lips, but something in Bentleigh's expression must have made him pause.

"Are we interrupting something?" he asked hesitantly, glancing from Bentleigh to the king.

"That remains to be seen," King Victor said. He spoke lightly, but Bentleigh got the sense that he didn't know where the queen was going, and it made him edgy. "Apparently, Ianthe was just about to ask Bentleigh a personal question." He looked at his wife. "Please continue, my dear."

Queen Ianthe transferred her gaze to Bentleigh, her expression apologetic. Bentleigh felt a crawling sensation moving up his neck. Her demeanor had made him nervous enough before, let alone now there were three additional witnesses.

"I know I shouldn't really ask," she said softly, "but for a long time now I've had the impression that you...that you care greatly for Azalea."

The room went unnaturally still, and Bentleigh could feel his face going red.

"Of course I do, Your Majesty," he said as smoothly as he could.

"No, I mean..." The queen sighed. "There's no point being delicate, Bentleigh. You've always been very gracious about the arrangement we formed with your parents. But I'm asking about your heart."

"You're asking," Bentleigh said, hoping his voice sounded calm, "if I love Azalea."

"You're quite right, Ianthe," King Victor cut in firmly. "You shouldn't ask the poor boy such a question."

"It's all right, Your Majesty," said Bentleigh, with a faint smile. He was painfully aware that he had the unwavering attention of a goggling serving maid, but he wasn't going to give a dishonest answer. Not about this.

"I do, Your Majesty," he said seriously. "I have for a long time." A painful smile tugged at one corner of his lips. "I'm afraid I couldn't help it."

Queen Ianthe returned his smile, looking close to tears again. But at a sentimental sigh from the maid, the queen's gentle face transformed into something quite forbidding. One glance from her was enough to send the girl scuttling from the room. The queen turned back to Bentleigh, her face smoothing out again.

"Thank you for being so honest," she said. "I wouldn't ask if it weren't for..."

"Weren't for what?" her husband prompted as she trailed off, in a rare show of impatience. "What does this have to do with the curse, or with your maid?"

Queen Ianthe was silent for a moment, and to Bentleigh's amazement, she was actually fidgeting.

"It's probably foolish," she said at last, with a glance at the three enchanters. "But my maid said something about the curse. Apparently many people think they know what might break it."

Bentleigh sat up straighter. He had no idea what the queen was getting at, but he couldn't help the bubble of hope that grew inside him. Whatever this suggestion was, how had it not come up before now?

"Well, what is it?" the king asked, sounding as eager as Bentleigh felt.

Queen Ianthe glanced at the siblings again, and following her gaze Bentleigh saw that Mortimer looked rueful. He obviously had a guess as to where this was going.

"The rumor is that enchantments can often be broken by a kiss," the queen said in a rush. She cast a glance at Bentleigh. "By a kiss of true love."

Heat once again rushed up Bentleigh's neck as all five of his companions turned to look at him. The queen's awkward question suddenly made sense. She was trying to figure out whether a kiss from him would count as a kiss of true love. He knew a sudden desire for a hole to open in the floor below him.

"I don't think it would help," he said awkwardly. "I'm fairly certain I kissed her hand the day the curse hit. It didn't make any difference." In fact, he was *very* certain, but there was no need to share the details of his anguish as he'd pressed his lips to her hand, his chest heaving with dry sobs.

"I think you would need to kiss her lips," the queen said, her tone making it clear she felt just how awkward the conversation was. The king made a disapproving noise in his throat, and Bentleigh didn't dare to look at him.

"Surely that wouldn't work," he said instead, clearing his own throat uncomfortably. "For it to be a kiss of...you know, wouldn't the...feeling have to go both ways?" He couldn't bring himself to meet anyone's eyes, but he could hear the sympathy in the queen's voice as she replied.

"Azalea cares for you more than you realize, Bentleigh. More than *she* realizes."

Bentleigh sighed. He wanted to believe that was true, but he could see no way of finding out, not while the curse was in place. For a moment he pictured doing it, unable to help himself. He could barely keep from wrinkling his nose. It wasn't like he'd never thought about kissing her. He'd been thinking about it more days than not, since well before the curse. But the idea of pressing his lips to Azalea's cold, unresponsive ones—possibly in front of a tense, hopeful audience—held no appeal for him.

Still, he could understand why the queen was desperate enough to grasp at any possible solution. He forced himself to push down the discomfort of this conversation and to take her suggestion seriously.

"Even if you're right about the emotion being on both sides, Your Majesty," he said evenly, "I don't think it can be a 'kiss of true love' without the kiss itself being from both sides. That can't be right." *Plus,* he added silently, *what good would it do me to break Zayla's curse if her first act on waking up was to throttle me for kissing her without her wanting it, or even knowing about it?* The image brought a flicker of amusement into his mortified thoughts.

Mortimer cleared his throat, mercifully drawing the attention off Bentleigh. "I'm afraid that's just an old wives' tale, Ianthe," he said sadly. "A persistent one, but one without any foundation in the study of magic."

The queen deflated slightly. "It just sounded like the kind of counterforce you've described, Morty," she persisted. "Surely if Montgomery was motivated by hatred, then love—true love—would be a logical counterforce."

Mortimer sighed. "Hatred and love are too vague for what we're looking for. If it was just that he hated Victor, or even hated Azalea, and love was enough to counter it, you wouldn't need Bentleigh to do anything. *Your* love for Azalea is stronger than any hatred against her, and you're not the only one. All of us love her dearly, and any one of us could do some equivalent act to demonstrate it if that was all it took to wake her."

He paused for a moment, and Bentleigh couldn't help but notice more than one handkerchief being raised to a suddenly moist eye.

"No," Mortimer said, his tone frustrated. "There's something I'm missing, and without that information, I can't figure out the counterforce."

"We must find Montgomery," the king growled. "But even with agents searching every kingdom in Solstice, I can find no sign of him."

"He wouldn't have fled across the desert, would he?" Queen Ianthe asked doubtfully.

"Prince Bentleigh?"

Bentleigh had been too engrossed in the conversation to notice anyone's approach, but he saw now that a servant hovered at his elbow.

"Yes?"

"There's a messenger for you, Your Highness. He arrived at

the castle yesterday evening, but there wasn't time for him to speak to you before dark. He's waiting outside now."

Bentleigh raised an eyebrow. A messenger for him, here? He glanced at King Victor, who gave him a nod of dismissal, then rose from his seat to follow the servant. He felt a surge of unease. Was the messenger from home? Perhaps his father had changed his mind about letting him come. Was he about to discover the reason his parents had decided it was time to end his visits?

But the man waiting for him in the castle's entranceway wasn't wearing the livery of Bansford's royal family, but of Albury's. He was looking around him nervously, and his relief was clear when he saw Bentleigh approaching. Bentleigh could understand why. If the man was hoping to get over the border and into Albury before nightfall, he needed to leave immediately.

"Prince Bentleigh of Bansford?" he asked importantly, and Bentleigh confirmed it. The man gave an officious nod and held out a sealed parchment. "I was instructed by Her Majesty Queen Felicity to put this into no hand but yours."

Bentleigh took it automatically, blinking down at the royal seal of Albury imprinted onto the paper. This was from Felicity? He pictured the cheerful, copper-haired girl he'd met some months before. He'd heard that she and Justin were married now, of course, and that accordingly she'd been crowned as Albury's queen. But why would she be sending him a message?

He muttered his thanks to the messenger, but the man was already trotting toward the castle's open doors. After a moment's hesitation, Bentleigh strode toward his suite, the parchment clutched in his hand. Once in the privacy of his rooms, he ripped it open, smoothing out the first sheet.

Prince Bentleigh

· · ·

I'm sure you're surprised to hear from me, and I hope it's not presump-tuous of me to write to you. But I've given it a great deal of thought, and I just can't be at peace until I at least give you the information, so that you have the option of pursuing it.

I'm not sure how much you've heard about what happened when Justin's curse was broken. But to cut a long story short, we had the assistance of a dragon. As a prince, you are doubtless as astonished by that fact as Justin was, although I barely thought twice about it.

I'm aware that your situation is unchanged, and I have thought about your plight often. It's been in my mind for some time that if Rekavidur (that's the dragon's name) was willing and able to help me break Justin's curse, he might be able to break Princess Azalea's.

Bentleigh tore his eyes from the letter, his breath catching in his throat. A cascade of conflicting emotions chased one another through him, and he lowered his gaze back to the parchment.

I should clarify that this is a personal message from me to you, not a missive from the Alburian crown. Justin has explained it all to me now, and I understand why my suggestion is dangerous. But I didn't feel right about deciding for you that you didn't want to take the risk. The thing is, Rekavidur isn't from Solstice. He told me he came from across the sea, from a distant land, and he doesn't belong to the colony in the south. I think that's why he was willing to help me. I suspect he was as ignorant as I was of the unwritten agreement between humans and dragons regarding the use of magic.

My suggestion may be useless, anyway, as I have no way to contact Rekavidur. But I thought you should know what I know...that there is a dragon out there, somewhere in Solstice, who has shown a willingness to assist humans, even with breaking curses cast by human enchanters.

I hope you're well, and I hope you can wake your sleeping princess.

Ever your friend,
    Felicity.

Bentleigh's eyes glazed over as he reached the end of this message, his thoughts whirling.

A dragon had assisted in breaking Justin's curse? How had he not heard this? He shook his head. No doubt Justin hadn't been eager to advertise it, and no wonder.

Felicity was right—unlike her, Bentleigh was raised a royal, and therefore well trained in dragon lore. He knew exactly how astonishing and dangerous the dragon's involvement had been. It was the most basic principle of the coexistence of dragons and humans on Solstice—dragons didn't use their magic on humans, either to help or hinder, and humans didn't use magic on dragons.

It was a situation that benefited the humans enormously. The dragons were infinitely more powerful than any human enchanter, and they could annihilate all six kingdoms if they chose. The true history of the dragons' arrival in Solstice— hundreds of years before—wasn't known in great detail. But humans had certainly been on the continent first, and the story was that they pestered the new dragons for magical assistance so frequently, the dragons grew tired of it. Apparently, some of the less friendly of the colony began to contemplate wiping the humans out and claiming the continent as their own.

By that time, humans had started to display signs of magic. Before then there had been no enchanters, but it turned out that some humans had a hitherto unrecognized capacity to carry power. Those people began—quite unintentionally—to absorb the magic shed by the dragons as they moved about the land.

Happily, the less aggressive amongst the dragons prevailed, and instead of a mass slaughter, there was an agreement reached between dragons and humans that neither kind would use magic on the other, either to help or hinder.

Or so the story went. No written agreement existed, but every royal in Solstice learned some version of that history, and understood what an offense it would be for a crown to ask the dragons for magical assistance. Bentleigh had always been taught—and had unquestionably accepted—that the loss of any potential help from the dragons was well worth the security of not being vulnerable to their attack.

It was why King Victor and Queen Ianthe would never have even considered going to the dragons to ask for help with Zayla's curse. It was completely unacceptable for humans to break the unwritten treaty in such a way, and could well lead to war with the dragons.

Such a war would be short and decisive.

Bentleigh ran a hand over his face. Felicity's letter had terrified him almost as much as the attack against Azalea the day before. At least on that occasion, he'd known what to do, and been in a position to do it immediately. But now, he'd been handed a possible power that he was petrified to hold. If there was any hope of breaking Azalea's curse, he couldn't just dismiss it. But if he blundered into this, if his actions offended the dragons...well, Azalea would be dead along with the rest of them, so what would he have gained?

He scanned the parchment again. This Rekavidur wasn't from the colony in the south, Felicity said. Bentleigh frowned. So would the dragons of that colony be offended if Bentleigh went to him for help? What did it have to do with them, really?

For a moment the possibilities intoxicated him. Felicity said Rekavidur had broken Justin's curse. The prince—now king—of Albury was free, and the kingdom was once again prospering. Months had passed, with no sign of trouble from the dragons. Could something similar be done for Zayla? Could she be free, and Listernia with her?

They could spread around a different story, so no one would have to know the dragon had helped. A smile tugged at his lips. Perhaps they could tell the populace that the princess had been awakened by a kiss from her betrothed.

He sighed, running his fingers through his hair. He was getting ahead of himself. Azalea was still fast asleep, and he had no idea how to find this Rekavidur, even if he wanted to take the risk.

He pocketed the letter, making his way into the corridor again. Without even realizing he was heading there, he found his feet carrying him to Azalea's room. Winnie was still sitting there, placidly working on her embroidery. The sight brought a smile to Bentleigh's face. Zayla had always said it was the one benefit of the curse, not being forced to learn to embroider. Her parents had never allowed her to handle a needle, of course.

His eyes passed to Azalea, still on her side, looking comfortably asleep for once. But her face remained unnaturally calm, with no hint of the mischief that had always entranced and exasperated him in equal measure. The sight decided him. She wouldn't hesitate to take the risk if their positions were reversed. If she never woke, if those sparkling brown eyes never tormented him again, it wouldn't be because he'd left any stone unturned.

He strode to the bed, ignoring Winnie as he ran a hand over Azalea's hair. "I don't know if it will work," he whispered. "But I swear, if there's any way at all, I'll do whatever it takes." He paused. "And happy birthday, Zayla."

With one last lingering look, he turned for the door, only to be confronted with the sight of King Victor, hovering on the threshold. The king fixed him with a shrewd look.

"Are you leaving, Bentleigh? Not bad news from home, I hope?"

Bentleigh hesitated, wondering what to tell him. He certainly wasn't going to explain where he was going. If he did, King Victor would tell him not to go, and then he'd have to obey.

"No, it's not from home," he said carefully. "But I have received some news. I'm sorry to cut this visit so short, but I need to follow it up. I'll return as soon as I can."

The king frowned, and Bentleigh held his breath. But then King Victor stepped aside, seeming to reach a sudden decision. "Travel safely, Bentleigh," he said, the words an order. "Return to us soon."

With a grateful nod, Bentleigh swept past him. He wasted no time, and before an hour had passed, he was riding back through the gates of Liss. He didn't know where to find this Rekavidur, but there was only one place to start. He was going somewhere he'd never gone before.

He was going to the dragon colony.

CHAPTER TWELVE

Azalea

Azalea blinked slowly as she woke, taking a moment to identify what was different. She felt...comfortable. She realized suddenly that she was lying on her side, rather than laid out formally on her back.

She sat up, marveling at the lack of stiffness. This was different. Had she managed to move while in her enchanted sleep? Or had someone arranged her differently? Either way, it was the first time in two years.

All at once she remembered Ben's nearness the night before, and she searched the room hopefully. But there was no sign of him, just a maid sleeping soundly on the usual cot, next to Azalea's bed.

She sighed. She hadn't really expected him to be there a second time. It was incredible enough that he'd pulled it off once. But her thoughts were still full of him, and after performing her usual routine of preparation, she made her way straight to his suite.

To her alarm, it was empty. And it wasn't just that there was no Ben in the massive four poster. None of his traveling belongings were there. It was clear that he'd departed. But what could have sent him running so quickly? He'd only arrived the day before. She couldn't recall him ever making such a short visit before. A well of loneliness seemed to open up within her at the sight of his untouched bed. Close behind it was the usual frustration, at her inability to communicate with anyone who could answer her questions. She might never know the reason for his hasty departure.

With a sigh, she continued through the castle, checking Uncle Mortimer's suite, and looking in on her parents. It was a blow to lose Ben's presence so soon, but she wouldn't let it cast her down too much. She had her routines to keep her sane, and a tryst of swordplay and one-sided banter to keep with the vines. She also needed to catch up on her study, having avoided the library altogether the night before. Perhaps she'd look for a book on fireflies, see if there was a way to lure more into her little garden.

But first, the vines. She was just heading for the entranceway when she heard a sound that stopped her in her tracks.

"It's this way."

A human voice! The words were soft, and the voice rough, but it was the sweetest sound Azalea had ever heard. In two whole years, she'd heard no voice but her own. Someone was awake!

Her shock had momentarily frozen her, but she forced herself forward, drawing in a shuddering gasp. The voice had come from the direction of the royal wing, and she hurried after it. She rounded a corner, and was confronted with an empty corridor. A thin beam of light, spilling from an open doorway, caught her eye. She opened her mouth to cry out, when she realized with a start that the light was coming from her own room. The speaker had gone into her suite?

Did whoever it was somehow know she was awake at night-time? The excitement of the previous moment melted away, replaced with a feeling of deep unease, right in the pit of her stomach.

"There's no one in the bed!" a voice hissed from inside the room. "Are you sure this is the right suite?"

"Of course I'm sure," snapped the voice Azalea had first heard. "I scouted it out this morning. I was lucky not to get caught, too. The prince walked straight into me."

"The prince is 'ere?" The second speaker sounded nervous, and Azalea felt a stab of pride on Ben's behalf that he was able to inspire such a reaction, even while in an enchanted sleep.

"Of course he's not here," growled the initial voice. "Do you think I'd pick tonight if he was? He took off this morning. Got some message from Albury and split."

Azalea frowned. Albury? Who in Albury would be writing to Ben, and why would that make him leave?

"I don't like this," the nervous man was saying. "Where is she? I thought you said they kept 'er in this room all the time."

The other man grunted. "I thought they did," he admitted.

"So where've they put 'er?"

"No idea."

"It's eerie, i'n it?" the second man said. "With everyone asleep like this, and only us two wandering 'round?"

Azalea gave a silent scoff. They had no idea. But the next words sobered her up instantly.

"This was supposed to be the easiest gold we ever made. Quick job, get in, kill the sleeping princess, get out. No one said anything about 'aving to 'unt down some 'iding place."

The man's companion just grunted, and the nervous one went on, his voice uncertain.

"So what do we do now? Do we kill the maid instead?"

Azalea's eyes widened in horror. She gripped her sword more tightly and took a step forward, on the point of bursting into the room. She wasn't going to stand by and allow them to murder her maid.

But the first man's derisive snort made her pause.

"No, we don't kill the maid, you driveling idiot. We're supposed to be avoiding detection."

"I was just askin'," said the second man, sounding sulky.

The first one sighed, the sound morphing into a yawn. "I suppose we just get out of here."

Azalea started backing silently away, straining her ears to hear the rest as she put some distance between her and her would-be killers.

"We can't go searching the castle for her. The enchanter said the talismans would keep us awake for an hour at most, and we're more than halfway through that time already."

"He ain't gonna be 'appy," said the sulky man, his voice also sounding sleepy now. "He said it took 'im months to put enough power into these talismans."

"Well, it's a good thing he gave us more than one," said the first conspirator impatiently. "No need to tell him we couldn't find her. We'll come back another night, and find her then."

Azalea had backed around a corner by now, and she ran with silent steps until she reached an unused guest suite. Fortunately Aunt Miranda's gift of grace allowed her to move swiftly and noiselessly. She hid herself inside, hands clasped on the hilt of her sword as she listened for the men's footsteps. They didn't linger—she heard them hurry past her hiding place, heading for the entranceway.

She stayed there for a long time, heart pounding. What had just happened? How was any of it possible? She could hardly comprehend the fact that two men had just entered her suite intent on killing her while she slept. The enchanter they'd spoken of must be Montgomery. So he was not only still out there, but still actively trying to kill her. A shiver went down her spine.

And he'd figured out—albeit through months of effort, and with limited effectiveness—a way to counteract the magic that kept everyone asleep at night. What she wouldn't give to get her hands on one of those talismans! She imagined slipping one into Ben's hand while he slept. Then she remembered that Ben wasn't in Liss anymore, and she felt more vulnerable and alone than ever.

Tears threatened to fall as she wrestled with her disappointment. For a tantalizing moment, she'd actually thought the curse was weakening, that she'd get to speak with another human being. But she wouldn't allow herself to cry. She had to be strong, because there was no one but her, no one else to protect herself, or her city.

She waited in the room for a whole hour, wanting to be certain that the magic of the men's talismans had run out. But even so, she was jumpy and anxious as she made her way around the wall. She kept glancing at shadows, sure that she saw movement in every whisper of wind.

What was she going to do? They were gone now, supposedly, but they said they had more talismans. How many more? She returned to her suite well before dawn, but she didn't want to lie on her bed. She felt too vulnerable there. She paced the room until the curse compelled her to move, driving her back to her sleeping position. She curled up on her side, her eyes wide open and alert until the last possible second. But of course, there was nothing she could do to fight the oncoming slumber.

For the next two nights, she was so edgy she could barely function. She had thought she'd been afraid before, but this was a whole new level of fear. It felt like death was constantly hanging over her head, and she never knew when it would fall. She sprang from her bed the moment awareness returned, desperate to be out of the castle and into the sleeping city before the men could get near her suite. She longed to warn whichever companion was sleeping in harm's way beside her bed, but of course she couldn't. She still worked her way around the wall, as stealthily as she could manage, but she didn't read Uncle Mortimer's notes, or study in the library. She didn't return to the building at all until the curse compelled her to do so.

As far as she could tell, there was no sign of the men the first night, or the one after. She had assumed they'd come back straight away, but perhaps they'd decided to leave it for a while. Were they doing reconnaissance during the day, trying to figure out where she was supposedly moved before darkness fell? The thought alarmed her.

She didn't miss the irony—she had spent many hours over the past two years looking for a way to tell someone, anyone, that she was awake during the hours of darkness. Now there were others awake as well, and the last thing she wanted was for them, and through them Montgomery, to find out the truth about her own state.

On the third night, she forced herself to sit on her bed for a few minutes, taking stock of the situation. She couldn't keep running scared. She needed to be alert, to watch over the castle as well as the wall. She pushed away the temptation to find a safe hiding place within the building and stay there all night. She couldn't afford to do that either. The vines would fully breach the wall if she left them unchecked. And who knew how long she'd be hiding? She couldn't live her life that way.

Besides, what if, unable to find her, the men went after someone else Montgomery had reason to target? Her father perhaps, or Uncle Mortimer? It didn't bear thinking about.

Everyone watched over her during the day. She was the only one who could watch over them at night, and she wasn't going to leave them exposed. Not to Montgomery's assassins, and not to the vines.

So, swallowing her instincts, she forced herself up, collecting her lantern and her sword as silently as possible. She tried to recall every detail of the encounter. The men had come to her suite early in the night, so they must have been close by. And they'd said the talismans could only keep them awake for an hour. She realized suddenly that they must have had the talismans on them when darkness fell, otherwise they would have been in an enchanted sleep and unable to retrieve them. So any activity they undertook would have to be completed within the first hour after sunset. She'd been foolish to be so jumpy all night. The first hour was what mattered.

She hid in a shadowed alcove and lay in wait for an hour, but there was no sign of the men approaching her room. Relaxing marginally, she began her usual tasks, deep in thought. They were probably close by, in the city if not in the actual castle. She knew that one of them at least had been in the building the day before their planned attack. He'd said as much. She frowned as she passed the kitchen, looking at the serving boy laid out on a pallet in the corner, ready for breakfast duties. It was a shame she hadn't gotten a look at the men. They could be anyone for all she knew.

Looking in at her parents' rooms, she felt a spike of alarm at their vulnerability. After two years, they had probably all stopped feeling anxious at their inability to guard themselves at night. But the introduction of these talismans changed everything. There was a lot of mischief that two men could do in an hour, with nothing and no one to hinder them. In a perverse, twisted way, it was a relief that they had come with only the specific purpose of killing her.

She scolded herself for her panic that first night. If she'd been smarter, she would have pulled herself together immediately and followed them. Without any idea where they might be hiding while not using the talismans, there wasn't much she could do but wait for them to make another move.

And, curse it all, she was so very sick of waiting.

CHAPTER THIRTEEN

Bentleigh

Bentleigh looked up at the mountain range rising up in the distance to his right, westward. He let out a sigh of relief. He was almost there. He turned his gaze forward again, toward the south, urging his horse back to a canter.

He glanced around as he went, reflecting that Fernedell really was a pleasant kingdom. He was riding through what looked like fertile land, although it was some time since he'd seen any farms. It wasn't an issue in either Bansford or Listernia, but he'd heard that in the southern kingdoms, the crown sometimes had difficulty finding those willing to work the land near the dragon colony. Apparently the beasts had a frustrating habit of pilfering livestock when they fancied a snack. And it wasn't like anyone was going to take them to task for it. Bentleigh couldn't really blame people for wanting to establish their farms in a different part of the kingdom.

Of course, it wasn't as if the area near the colony was abandoned. Far from it. There were plenty of towns, and he'd passed several bustling marketplaces already that morning. He'd even heard of communities consisting entirely of enchanters taking shape in the environs of the colony. Apparently enchantments were easier to cast, and magic was more powerful when closest to the dragons. Everyone knew that to purchase especially potent artifacts, the marketplaces near the colony were the place to go.

And since the dragon colony was situated where the borders of Mistra, Entolia, and Fernedell met, Fernedell must be doing a roaring trade in such talismans. Most people, Bentleigh included, were reluctant to take part in any unnecessary travel to either Mistra or Entolia, not while they were still in the grip of the border skirmish that had started over four years ago.

Bentleigh bypassed a noisy market as he headed for the gap at the eastern edge of the mountain range. He kept thinking about Azalea, lying still and vulnerable with that man raising a dagger above her heart. He was still edgy about his decision to leave Liss so soon after the incident, and it had taken him longer than it should to reach his destination.

He'd made it out of Listernia without incident, with the exception of a run in with a small pack of wolves. The creatures had become something of a nuisance for travelers, since they had no choice now but to hunt during daylight hours, given they slept through the night like the rest of the kingdom. It was just one of many problems the curse had caused for Listernia's wildlife. But Bentleigh had evaded the animals without great difficulty—he even knew a moment of pity for the poor creatures. They were clearly struggling to adapt to a hunting style that wasn't in their nature, and they looked weak and emaciated.

He'd passed from Listernia straight into Fernedell. He'd known better than to pass through Bansford, well aware that if his parents caught any hint of his intentions, he'd be back home and locked in the castle before he could say "dragon fire". That wasn't a problem—going through Fernedell was a fairly direct way to reach the dragon colony. But he'd been eager to avoid being forced to interact with Fernedell's royal family, so he had given the capital city of Fernford a wide berth. Accordingly, he'd been traveling for two days since leaving Listernia, and he was still only just arriving at his destination.

But if this worked, it would be more than worth the delay. The letter from Queen Felicity was rolled up in his pocket, dog-eared from being read and re-read. He hardly dared to hope for an outcome as happy as her own had been, but he had to tell himself such a thing was possible. Otherwise there could be no justification for the risk he was taking in approaching the dragons.

A merchant's wagon rumbled down the road ahead of him, the driver waving a jovial hand. He pulled across the road such that Bentleigh was forced to stop.

"After artifacts, young sir?" the merchant asked, in a wheedling voice. "I have the finest in Solstice here! Ones to make you invisible, ones to make your hair grow. Ones to make you sleep like the dead," he chuckled, "not that a young whippersnapper like you would need help with that."

Bentleigh scowled, the merchant's light words hitting a nerve. Of course the man had no way of knowing who Bentleigh was, or that he'd just come from Listernia, where the princess truly did sleep like the dead. But it still wasn't a joke Bentleigh could find funny.

"No, thank you," he said politely. With great diplomacy, he extricated himself, trying not to think of how much gold he'd thrown away on such talismans in the early months of Azalea's curse. None of them did quite what they claimed to do, or at least not very well, and not for very long. There certainly weren't any strong enough to counteract Montgomery's power.

Bentleigh frowned as he navigated his way around the wagon, once again puzzling over the mystery of Montgomery's impossibly powerful magic. Even Mortimer and his sisters swore they'd had no hint of their brother having such power prior to

Azalea's christening. He must have been honing his craft in secret for many years.

But it didn't matter, Bentleigh reminded himself firmly. However strong a human enchanter could become, it was nothing to the power of the dragons.

"There's naught but the dragon colony that way!" the merchant called out after him, as if reading his thoughts. "They'll not let you in, lad! No point pestering them."

Bentleigh ignored the friendly warning, his thoughts on his destination. Nerves were starting to rise, overwhelming his hopefulness for the moment. What if the dragons were offended that he'd come uninvited? What if they turned on Bansford, or Listernia, as a result? In all of Solstice's recorded history, the dragons had never attacked a human kingdom. But he knew that all the royal families lived in fear of such an event nonetheless. It was inevitable, with a crown on your head, to be wary of another, completely uncontrollable power, much stronger than you.

As soon as the merchant was out of sight, Bentleigh drew off the road into a small copse of trees. Fishing in his satchel, he retrieved a simple golden circlet. It wouldn't do to advertise his royal status to Fernedell's countryside, but it would probably help him win an audience with the dragons.

He had no magic in his blood, so he didn't sense any shift in the air when he reached the boundary of the dragons' realm. He only guessed he'd reached it because he knew of the magic shield, and because he was suddenly unable to see any great distance ahead. It was like a shapeless fog had descended, though the day was clear and the weather mild.

He pulled his horse to a stop and cleared his throat nervously.

"Mighty beasts," he called in a clear, strong voice. "I am Prince Bentleigh, and I humbly seek an audience."

After a moment of silence, a shape shifted in the fog, and a reptilian head emerged, ridged with bearded temples. Bentleigh swallowed nervously, trying to control the frantic pace of his heart as the rest of the creature followed. It was five times as tall as he was, and many times as wide. The dragon had scales of a deep forest green, and its eyes were like glowing yellow orbs. Bentleigh cast a surreptitious glance over it, remembering all he'd been taught of dragon lore. Dragons grew bigger indefinitely as they aged, and their scales grew darker. Judging by this dragon's size, and the relative brightness of its green coloring, it wasn't especially old. No more than two centuries, he'd guess. He supposed the older, more venerable dragons didn't get assigned the duty of gatekeeper.

This wasn't exactly the first dragon he'd ever seen, and he knew it was rude to stare, but it was still hard to keep his eyes off the razor sharp talons on the creature's paws, and the spiky triangular plates running down its back, right to the tip of its tail.

It could rip him to shreds in about five seconds if it chose.

But apparently the beast wasn't inclined to violence, because after regarding him in silence for a moment, it addressed him in the language of men.

"Greetings, human. You are a prince of men?"

"That's right," said Bentleigh evenly.

"From which kingdom do you hail, young prince?"

Bentleigh hesitated for a moment, picturing how his parents would respond to him addressing the dragons on behalf of the Bansfordian crown without their approval.

"I am a prince of two kingdoms," he said carefully, knowing that dragons could recognize falsehood. They would certainly take offense at any lies, so he must say only what he absolutely believed to be true. "I was born of Bansford, but my fate is tied to Listernia."

The dragon watched him unblinkingly, its expression impossible to read. The creature shifted slightly, and the fog seemed to swirl around it. Glancing past the dragon's scaled side, Bentleigh caught a glimpse of a bright landscape beyond. He could see vibrant green hills under a clear sky, groves of deep green, and a vast sparkling lake. The lake disappeared at one end into the darkness of a yawning cavern, cutting into the heart of a lone, stately mountain.

The realm of the dragons.

Bentleigh's eyes snapped back to the creature in front of him. He knew not many humans saw the sight he had just seen, and he wasn't entirely sure whether he'd been supposed to.

"And you come seeking an audience with my kind, Prince Bentleigh of two kingdoms," the dragon said, its eyes still assessing him shrewdly. It wasn't a question, but Bentleigh confirmed it anyway.

"I do. I seek a dragon named Rekavidur." He doubted he'd said the name correctly, but hopefully this dragon would know who he meant. "He is a visitor among your colony, or so I have been told."

The green dragon tilted its head to the side, showing a flicker of interest. "For what purpose do you seek him?"

Bentleigh measured his words carefully. "I received a letter from the queen of Albury," he said. He knew that dragons, while generally not concerning themselves with human affairs overmuch, had a certain level of respect for royalty. Hopefully it would give him some credibility to have now invoked the crowns of three kingdoms. "She made the acquaintance of this Rekavidur, and she wished to make him known to me."

"Did she indeed?" the dragon asked slowly, its tail sliding slowly back and forth across the ground. It fell silent, measuring its response for an unreasonably long time. Bentleigh waited in growing unease. Had he put a foot wrong?

"It is fitting," the dragon said at last, "that your kingdoms would wish to pay their respects to this representative of a new dragon colony."

Bentleigh let out a quiet breath of relief, but the dragon wasn't finished.

"However, Rekavidur is not here."

Bentleigh deflated. "Do you...do you know whether he's coming back? And when that might be?"

"His movements are his own." There was a definite note of finality in the dragon's voice, and Bentleigh sensed that he had approached the line of impertinence. He could only hope he hadn't crossed it.

"Thank you," he said politely, despite the gloom that settled over him as the dragon disappeared back into the fog.

It seemed he'd ridden all this way for nothing. If asking the dragons directly didn't help him find this Rekavidur, he couldn't imagine what else could. The dragon could be anywhere in Solstice, and although the magical beasts could fly from one end of the continent to the other in a matter of hours, Bentleigh couldn't afford to spend weeks roaming throughout the kingdoms looking for him. He was due home in a couple of weeks, and if he returned without a solution, his parents were going to sever his betrothal to Azalea.

A surge of bitter frustration took hold of him as he turned his horse and began plodding back the way he'd come. It was infuriating that, in spite of the law, his parents had so much power over his decision. The irony wasn't lost on him. He'd had no power at all when they informally promised him to Azalea as a small child. But he'd never resented it for a moment. Now, when he was an adult and theoretically had a choice, he felt trapped by his parents' intention to undo the betrothal. Perhaps this was how Azalea had felt about the arrangement all along.

The thought did nothing to cheer him up.

He continued northward for almost an hour, growing gradually more uneasy the further he went. He'd been trying to be inconspicuous as he traveled through Fernedell, not wanting word of his unofficial visit to spread. And on his way toward the dragon colony, he hadn't attracted any especial attention. But as he rode away from it, there was no ignoring the strange looks he received from almost everyone he passed.

He was just contemplating veering off the main road, and picking his way across country for a while, when a rush of wind temporarily flattened the rows of wheat growing alongside the road. Bentleigh glanced up at this telltale sign, and sure enough, the dark shape of a dragon was blotting out the sun.

The beast descended right in front of him, and his horse reared in alarm. For a moment, it took all Bentleigh's focus to calm the frightened animal, but once the horse stopped plunging enough to see what had landed on the road ahead, it stilled. Bentleigh relaxed his grip, turning his attention to the dragon.

"Greetings, Mighty—" he began, but the dragon cut him off.

"Yes, yes, all right, but you can just call me Dannsair."

Bentleigh blinked. "Oh. Well...thank you?" He gave as good a bow as he could manage from the saddle. "I'm Prince Bentleigh."

"Yes, I figured that," the dragon said, eyeing his head. Bentleigh suddenly realized what had drawn the creature's attention, and he could have kicked himself. He'd forgotten to take his golden circlet off again—no wonder half the countryside was staring at him. So much for keeping a low profile.

"Well, you can call me Bentleigh," he offered, feeling that he should respond to the dragon's gesture of informality.

"All right, I will."

The dragon—who seemed to be a female, judging by her voice—sat back on her haunches, curling her tail around herself. Bentleigh looked her over with interest, noting that she was smaller than the first dragon. And the impression she'd given of a dark and forbidding form had been caused only by the sun behind her. She was, in fact, quite a bright purple. Clearly young, and by far the least intimidating dragon he'd ever encountered.

Which wasn't to say she couldn't still kill him any moment she chose, of course.

"I understand that you came to our colony asking for Rekavidur," Dannsair continued. "You wish to speak to him?"

"I do," Bentleigh confirmed, excitement rising. Perhaps this hadn't been a fool's errand after all.

"You are the prince from Bansford who is betrothed to the Listernian princess, are you not? The girl who is locked in an enchanted slumber?"

"That's right," Bentleigh nodded, hiding his surprise that she not only knew of him, but was aware of his situation with Azalea.

"Hm." Dannsair regarded him shrewdly. "And why do you wish to speak to Rekavidur?"

Bentleigh fell silent, wariness returning. Did she know he wanted to ask Rekavidur to help break the curse? Would she expose his intentions to the rest of the dragons, or to his own family? After a moment's hesitation, he decided not to answer at all. He had a feeling that carefully worded vagueness wouldn't serve him this time.

The silence stretched out, and Dannsair's reptilian mouth stretched out also, in a thin smile.

"Well, I appreciate that you are not attempting to lie to me, at any rate," she said, with a touch of humor.

"I wouldn't be foolish enough to think I could get away with it," Bentleigh said frankly.

Dannsair made the strange guttural sound that indicated dragon laughter. "I thought you were going to say that you would never wish to lie to me. Your honesty is refreshingly rare, in a human." She observed him in silence for a moment. "I will honor it with a disclosure of my own. I know where Rekavidur can be found."

"Will you tell me where to go?" Bentleigh asked, eagerness tinging his words.

"No, I will not," said Dannsair calmly. "But I will tell him you are looking for him, if you wish it."

"I do," Bentleigh said quickly. "And you have my eternal gratitude for your assistance."

The dragon chuckled again. "You cannot offer anything eternally, Bentleigh," she said, making full use of his offer to call him by his name. "You will be dust in the earth before the blink of my eye." She watched him in tolerant amusement for another moment, but when she spoke again, her voice was softer, and her words unexpected. "I like Rekavidur. He looks with eyes that see. He has seen something in our colony that most of us would choose not to examine too closely, and he is not afraid to look it in the eye. I know you have been taught to fear us, prince that you are. But when you meet Rekavidur, take note of what a dragon can be. We are not all the same, and perhaps a change is coming in the way our kinds will interact." A strange expression passed over her face. "Perhaps it has already come."

Bentleigh blinked, too astonished to speak.

"I wish you well, Bentleigh," Dannsair added placidly. "May you wake your princess from her sleep."

On those words, she crouched, springing up and into the air in a fluid motion that flattened the stalks of wheat all over again. She turned in a wide and apparently unnecessary somersault before shooting into a bank of clouds. Bentleigh stared up into the suddenly empty sky, trying to make sense of her words. Did she know, then, that he wanted to ask Rekavidur for help with

Azalea's curse? Was she—a dragon of Solstice—actually in support of the attempt?

She'd said she liked Rekavidur—although why she confided such a thing in him was a mystery all its own—but that didn't seem reason enough for her to support the other dragon acting in a way that went against the dragon colony's long-established rules. Her words had been cryptic, as dragons invariably were, but she certainly gave the impression that she would welcome a change in the rules governing dragon-human interaction. She hadn't gone so far as to offer to help Bentleigh herself, of course. But she clearly didn't want him to be afraid of her, and he found that he wasn't. Not in the least.

He shook his head, returning his gaze to the road before him. It seemed he knew a lot less about dragons than he'd thought.

CHAPTER FOURTEEN

Bentleigh

The rest of the day passed uneventfully, as Bentleigh continued moving northward. He realized after Dannsair left that he'd given the dragon no indication of his planned route so she could pass on his location to Rekavidur. But dragons probably had their own ways of finding humans. He put his trust in that fact when he decided to remove his circlet and stash it back in his rucksack before continuing.

The main road was taking him toward the capital, Fernford, and had he been going there, he probably could have made it by nightfall. But he intended to once again skirt around the city, so he continued at a more leisurely pace, and drew off the road as dusk began to fall. He wasn't far from the capital, and he felt no concern at the prospect of sleeping in the open. Not even in light of the three rough-looking individuals who'd been casually trailing him for some time.

He set up camp in a grove, trying to hide his amusement as he lit a fire. They clearly thought he was unaware of their presence, lurking between the trees. He'd chosen a small clearing, with an enormous boulder stretching halfway across it. The men had clearly marked him as a wealthy but naive traveler, and were expecting some easy gold. Their attempts to look nonchalant as they followed him at a consistent distance had been quite entertaining. He wondered whether he should pretend to sleep immediately, get it all over with, or whether he should make them work a little harder.

As it happened, they took the decision out of his hands. He'd taken the opportunity earlier in the day to shoot down a wild pigeon, and he was just roasting it over the fire when one of the men strolled into the circle of his light.

"Good evening, friend," he said cheerfully. "Mind if I share your warmth a minute?"

"The bold approach," said Bentleigh, raising his eyebrows. "Congratulations, you've surprised me."

"Eh?" The man looked confused and wary, and Bentleigh didn't miss the way his hand strayed toward his belt.

"Nothing, nothing," Bentleigh said soothingly. "Of course you can join me. I have no objection."

"Very kind of you," the man said, still looking suspicious as he sat on a fallen log.

"Food?" Bentleigh offered his would-be attacker.

The man shook his head. "Oh, no, I wouldn't trouble you to feed me. Just after warming my hands before I'm on my way again."

"Less convincing," said Bentleigh disapprovingly. "Wandering vagabonds such as we are would never say no to the offer of free food. You should work on your character."

"What you saying about my character?" the man growled.

"Nothing at all, my good fellow," Bentleigh said, stifling a smile. "Just making conversation."

The man watched him in silence for a moment, his eyes narrowed. "Heading for Fernford, are you?" he asked at last.

"No, I don't think so," said Bentleigh vaguely. "Not unless I really can't avoid it."

His visitor slid along his log, moving closer to Bentleigh in what he clearly considered to be a surreptitious gesture.

Bentleigh ignored him, biting into a leg of pigeon. "Cooked to perfection, if I say so myself," he commented. "Sure you won't have some?"

The man shook his head, and Bentleigh shrugged. "Suit yourself." He gave a satisfied sigh, and closed his eyes. "It's days since I had hot food."

As Bentleigh had known he would, the man leaped on the opportunity offered by Bentleigh's closed eyes. The sudden creak of the log alerted Bentleigh to the man's attack, and he had his sword from its sheath in a heartbeat. Spurning the blade, he brought the hilt of it up to connect with the chin of his guest, just as the man was plunging his own dagger toward his host. There was a painful cracking sound, and the man fell like a rock to the forest floor, momentarily stunned.

"Whoops," said Bentleigh amicably. "Sorry about your tooth."

One of the man's teeth was indeed lying on the grass, glinting in the orange light cast out by the flames. But it didn't slow him down. Spitting blood, he snatched up his fallen dagger and scrambled back to his feet. At a shrill whistle, two more forms emerged from the trees, stalking toward the prince.

"Yes, best to get it over with at once," Bentleigh said, nodding approvingly. He moved to put his back against the rock formation for which he'd specifically chosen his site. For all his light words, he was no fool. He had the undeniable advantage in both weapons and training—none of the men were carrying swords —but he knew that he needed to keep that advantage if he didn't want things to take a disastrous turn.

"Wandering vagabond, are you?" the first man sneered, advancing with his dagger once again raised. "Look pretty well dressed for a vagabond."

Bentleigh shrugged. "I try to put my best foot forward."

As he spoke, he did indeed lunge forward with his favored foot, his blade whipping out with lightning speed and flicking the man's dagger from his hand. With a howl of rage, the man lunged after it, but Bentleigh pressed his advantage. Dashing forward, he gave the man a swift kick that sent him crashing onto his face on the bracken. Once again employing the hilt of his sword, Bentleigh dealt the man a blow to the back of the head that he judged would be enough to knock him senseless.

There were now two attackers left, and Bentleigh whipped around in a circle, expecting them to have exploited his advance, and gotten on either side of him. But only one of them was coming his way, the other having apparently decided to rifle through his satchel instead. Perhaps he was considering taking the loot and bolting, leaving his companions to their struggle.

"Oi!" Bentleigh said, feeling genuinely irritated for the first time. It would be highly inconvenient if the man found Queen Felicity's letter. "That's not yours!"

"Is now," the man grinned, shouldering the satchel. He turned toward the trees, but Bentleigh was quicker. Lunging forward, he deflected a thrust from the other attacker and sped past him, risking exposing his back. He tossed his sword from one hand to the other as he ran, pulling a knife from his belt. The fleeing thief had almost reached the tree line, and Bentleigh knew he needed to act now, while he had the light of the fire, and no obstacles.

Taking aim, he threw his knife with a practiced flick. It whizzed through the air, burying itself in the back of one leg. The thief let out a howl of agony and faltered, crashing to the ground.

Bentleigh rushed forward, yanking the satchel back, and retrieving his knife. "I was going for your thigh," he said with a shrug. "But close enough."

The man started to struggle up, and Bentleigh pressed one boot firmly against his leg wound. He let out another cry of pain, his features twisted in anger, and Bentleigh raised an eyebrow.

"Stay down, there's a good fellow," he said casually.

But he'd become distracted, and hadn't realized the remaining attacker had followed him so quickly. The man grabbed him from behind, pinning his arms against his sides.

"Not so full of smooth talk now, are you?" he hissed in Bentleigh's ear, as Bentleigh struggled against his undeniably strong grasp. The man was built like a bear. Bentleigh's knife had fallen from his hand, but he still gripped the hilt of his sword awkwardly. The fallen man dragged himself to his feet, snatching the satchel back from Bentleigh's grip. He flipped it open, his eyes widening as Bentleigh's golden circlet was exposed. His gaze passed up to Bentleigh's face, and his grin widened.

"Who'd you swipe this from, then? Been hitting the fancy folk, have you?"

"It's always good to aim high," Bentleigh grunted. The man holding him leaned forward to have a look at the glinting gold, and Bentleigh sensed his opening. Bringing his head forward to build momentum, he cracked it back into his captor's face. He was rewarded with the dubious satisfaction of a splintering crunch as it connected with the man's nose. The wounded attacker roared, his grip slackening enough for Bentleigh to rip himself free. He whipped around, his arms now able to stretch out to extend his sword in front of him. With a shrewd glance at his two opponents, he charged, running his sword into the arm of the one who once again held his satchel.

The man dropped his stolen prize with a yowl, his injured leg crumpling under him as he brought his good arm around to grip the bleeding gash on his arm.

The bear-like one had charged at Bentleigh, but Bentleigh

sprang nimbly to the side, slashing at the man's ribs as he barreled past. The attacker recovered, turning back toward him, but before they could wage battle, a rushing sound filled Bentleigh's ears, and the tree tops began to whip violently in a sudden wind.

All three conscious men looked up, and two shouts of terror rent the air as the firelight glinted on the yellow scales of a descending dragon. It landed right in the clearing—although Bentleigh would have sworn it couldn't fit there—not seeming to notice that it had touched down with one taloned front foot actually in Bentleigh's campfire.

"It seems my timing is inconvenient," the dragon said mildly, glancing from Bentleigh to the bear-like man now cowering at his feet. "Do I interrupt?"

"Not at all," said Bentleigh, bowing politely. "I believe we were just finishing up."

He raised a questioning eyebrow at the two men, and without so much as a glance at each other, they dropped his belongings and fled into the trees, limping as they went. Their fallen comrade still hadn't stirred, so Bentleigh ignored him, turning back to the dragon. It was about the same size as Dannsair, meaning it was young, and from what he could see in the firelight, its scales were yellow with a tinge of purple.

"Are you Rekavidur?"

The dragon inclined his head. "I am. And you, I assume, are Prince Bentleigh of Bansford, future king of Listernia."

Bentleigh was silent for a moment, unsure how to respond. "I hope so," he said at last, his voice a murmur. "I hope that future isn't lost to me."

"But it will be if you cannot wake your princess," the dragon said, matter-of-factly.

Bentleigh looked at him in surprise, and he stretched his mouth in an unnerving smile. "Dannsair has told me about your plight," he said. "And it seems you have heard of me as well."

"I have," Bentleigh acknowledged. He drew Queen Felicity's letter from his much abused satchel. "From Albury's queen, who you assisted some months ago."

"I did," said Rekavidur gravely. "But my actions were not entirely altruistic. I believe I told Felicity of my interest in concealment magic, but perhaps she did not grasp the import of what I said." His voice was indulgent. "She is, after all, a human."

"Yes, well, so am I," said Bentleigh unnecessarily. "And I'm afraid I'm rather powerless without assistance."

"Interesting choice of words," the dragon said thoughtfully. He leaned forward, sniffing Bentleigh like a dog might sniff a fox. "Given that power lingers about you. Faint, but present."

"There's magic lingering around me?" Bentleigh asked, surprised. He thought about it. "I suppose the curse over Listernia is very strong, and I was there only a few days ago."

The dragon nodded, his orb-like eyes unfocused. "It is certainly strong," he agreed. His eyes sharpened, latching on Bentleigh's. "This curse is cast by a power-wielder? That is, what you call a human enchanter?"

"That's right," Bentleigh nodded.

Rekavidur frowned. "And the purpose of this curse was to kill?"

Bentleigh nodded again.

The dragon's frown only deepened. "No. There is much more to this magic than that. I would almost have called it an enchantment to conceal...but it cannot be. Such was clearly the purpose of the enchantment I broke for Felicity, but how could magic designed to kill, but softened into slumber, savor of conceal-ment?" He seemed to be talking to himself, and Bentleigh made no attempt to answer. "It is familiar," the dragon mused. "So much so that I could almost have missed it altogether. It is like an extension of that magic which lingers..." He broke off, his eyes narrowing. "But it cannot be the same as the concealment magic I know. How would these humans even know of it when..."

He trailed off again, his eyes returning to Bentleigh's face.

"You are to be congratulated, Prince Bentleigh," he said, with that same touch of humor that had surprised Bentleigh in Dannsair. "You have succeeded in catching my interest."

Bentleigh brightened. "Does that mean you will help me?"

The dragon snaked his massive head slowly from side to side, seeming to indicate hesitation rather than outright refusal.

"I have learned a great deal in the months since my encounter with Felicity," he said, instead of answering. "I understand now the complexities that may arise if I assist you with human enchantments."

Bentleigh deflated, and the dragon watched him thoughtfully.

"However," he went on, bringing Bentleigh's head snapping back up, "for...reasons of my own, I am willing to assist in relation to concealment enchantments."

Bentleigh sighed. "I am grateful for your kindness," he said tonelessly. "But the curse afflicting Azalea isn't a concealment one."

The dragon let out a sigh that smelled faintly of smoke. "Humans do not listen well," he said severely. "I have just told you that the magic lingering around you savors of concealment. There is evidently more to your princess's enchantment than you have heretofore discerned."

Bentleigh frowned thoughtfully. "Everyone does say that it seems too strong for just Montgomery's magic," he mused.

The dragon nodded. "Just as with the enchantment afflicting Felicity's prince."

Bentleigh felt a flicker of amusement. He was well pleased to have all the dragons referring to Zayla as his princess, but he wondered how Justin, king of powerful Albury, would feel about the mighty beasts knowing him as "Felicity's prince".

"I will take a look," Rekavidur said decisively. "My interest, as I said, is raised. If there is a magic of concealment, I believe I will identify it."

"What is your interest in concealment magic, if it's not too bold to ask?" Bentleigh said curiously.

The dragon eyed him in what seemed to be amusement. At last he spoke. "It is just bold enough, young prince. I will not tell you all that is in my mind. I would not wish to overwhelm you beyond what your reason can endure."

"You're very kind," said Bentleigh, with a straight face.

"I believe I am," the dragon acknowledged, inclining his head slightly. "To answer your bold question, I must tell you a little about my own land. There, dragons long chose to be completely concealed from the humans, remaining in isolation within their own realms, neither mixing with humans, nor allowing hint of their presence to be seen. They are not so isolated now, but concealment magic is still used to create an impassable ring around their colonies, just as is the case for the dragon colony here."

He turned his head in that direction. "By contrast," he continued, "in this land, dragons have mingled freely with humans for hundreds of years, never—as far as I understand—attempting to hide their presence. And yet, I have sensed since I first arrived here a magic of concealment that lingers across the whole of the land, such as I have never sensed even in my own land, where total concealment was once the way of life of my kind. Do you not find that curious?"

Bentleigh was taken aback at being asked his opinion, but he readily agreed. "Very curious. Are you saying it's the same concealment magic that's used around the dragon colonies?"

Rekavidur sighed. "I am not. In point of fact, I don't know what type of magic it is. I am not yet familiar enough with the nuances of power in this land. It certainly bears similarity to the concealment magic I know. But is not all magic of one kind, at its root?"

"Can you at least tell whether it comes from dragons or human enchanters?" Bentleigh pressed curiously.

The dragon let out a huff of irritation. "As I just said, I have not yet ascertained what type of magic it is. I thought perhaps that it originated from the castle in Albury which was the focus of such a strong enchantment of concealment. But I lifted that enchantment, and it made no difference whatsoever." His eyes looked into the distance for a moment, clearly not focused on what was before him. When he spoke again, he seemed to be talking to himself. "It would be something indeed, if the source was a human enchanter, or even a group of such...For humans to be able to cast magic strong enough to block my farsight..." He shook his head.

"Your farsight?" Bentleigh repeated, fascinated by this glimpse into dragon life. He had never before met a dragon willing to share any of its thoughts with him in this way. "What's that?"

Rekavidur seemed almost equally interested in Bentleigh. Upon the prince's words, the dragon bent a keen eye upon him. "You have never heard of farsight?"

Bentleigh shook his head.

"And yet, as a prince, you are trained in dragon lore, unlike Felicity?"

"That's right," Bentleigh confirmed.

"Interesting," Rekavidur mused.

Before Bentleigh could ask more, a low moan drew his attention to the first attacker. He seemed to be coming round.

"Ready for more?" Bentleigh asked cheerfully. The man's groggy gaze slid past Bentleigh, fastening on Rekavidur. His eyes started, and his mouth fell open in a high-pitched scream.

"You will see me again, prince of men," Rekavidur said calmly. "But for now, farewell." He disregarded the screaming man completely and crouched in readiness to take flight. With a rush of wind, he took to the night sky, his form blotting out the few stars that were visible from the clearing.

The attacker's scream cut off abruptly at the dragon's departure, but another voice immediately filled the silence.

"Over there! I heard a shout!"

Bentleigh barely had time to turn toward the sound before an eager-faced teenage boy burst into the clearing, a patrol of soldiers hard on his heels.

"Prince Amell," Bentleigh said blankly. "What are you doing here?"

The teenage prince squinted at Bentleigh. "Prince Bentleigh?" he asked in tones of astonishment. "Is that you? What are *you* doing here?"

Bentleigh let out a breath, summoning a smile for Fernedell's young prince, and resigning himself to the inevitable. There would be no getting out of a visit to the capital now.

CHAPTER FIFTEEN

Azalea

Azalea crouched, tensed, in her alcove. She judged that she'd been awake for about fifteen minutes. Still plenty of time for the assassins to make an appearance. The thought had barely crossed her mind when she heard a quiet voice.

"She's got to be here this time. I hovered around her suite until ten minutes before sunset. There was no talk of moving her."

Azalea's muscles tightened, and she gripped her sword in her hand. The men were approaching up the corridor, coming for her room. Her blood pounded in her ear, and she told herself to be bold. This was her chance.

"No talk that you 'eard," the second man was muttering. "They obviously do it on the sly." His voice turned nervous. "You don't think they know what we're up to, do you?"

"How could they?" his companion asked dismissively. "But I'm not surprised they're edgy anyway. A couple of servants tried to do her in several days back, after all."

Azalea's eyes widened. So her maid really had tried to kill her. It was hard to take in, but this was no time to dwell on it.

The men had just come into view. She obviously carried no light, not wanting to give her position away, but her eyes were sharp in the darkness now. She could make out their forms, one considerably taller than the other, both thickly muscled. She swallowed. Either one would be much stronger than her. She would have to be smart in how she went about this.

The men disappeared into her suite, and she heard a curse.

"Seems ten minutes was long enough to move her, after all," one of them said grimly.

"Where would they have put 'er?" the other said, clearly frustrated. "The prince's suite?"

For the first time, Azalea was glad that Ben had disappeared so quickly. She shuddered to think of him lying prone and unprotected in his suite while these two prowled through it.

The noncommittal grunt that greeted the suggestion told her that the taller of the two wasn't convinced, but they made their way out of her suite and down the corridor toward Ben's anyway. She waited until they'd entered Ben's receiving room, then slipped silently after them. She positioned herself behind a plinth holding a marble bust, not far down the corridor from Ben's rooms. There was nothing of great interest to hear as they searched the suite, and Azalea ran over her plan in her mind. She'd had plenty of time to think about what she should do if the men came back. She would follow them back to where they slept, identify them if possible, and search for their other talismans once they were sleeping. If she could remove them, perhaps she wouldn't have anything further to worry about.

She was hoping not to be seen, but just in case, she pulled out the shawl she'd draped around her shoulders, and wrapped it around her head and over her face. It was a stifling sensation, but the fabric was light enough that she could breathe through it.

When the men exited Ben's suite, more than half an hour

had passed since darkness fell, which meant they had less time than that left. Azalea followed at a safe distance as they wandered back down the royal wing, discussing their next move. It wasn't difficult to trail them from a long way back. There was no other sound or movement in the castle—even their quiet conversation declared their presence from many halls away.

Azalea questioned her plan of remaining unseen when they entered Uncle Mortimer's rooms. Once she was sure they'd gone through to Uncle Mortimer's sleeping chamber, she took the risk of darting in behind them and hiding herself behind a large armchair in the receiving room. She would be in trouble if they searched both rooms thoroughly.

But they didn't. To her relief, they mostly ignored the man sleeping uneasily in his bed, and made for his writing desk. Azalea couldn't help but notice, as she listened to them rifling through Uncle Mortimer's papers, that it was bizarrely reminiscent of her own routine. First Ben's rooms, then Uncle Mortimer's notes. She was glad that at least they hadn't shown the audacity to stroll through her father's suite.

"Makes no sense to me," one of them said gruffly, with the sound of a book being slammed shut. "You sure 'e said not to take the notes back to 'im?"

"Course I'm sure," grunted the other one. "He said not to remove anything. Didn't want anyone to be able to tell we'd been here."

Azalea smiled grimly at the wistful note in the man's voice. The temptation to rob an undefended castle full of wealthy nobles and royals must be excruciating to resist. She could only assume that Montgomery was paying them very well for them to show such restraint.

"Well, 'e'll be disappointed with just my memory," said the first speaker. "I can't make 'ead nor tail of any of this."

"That's why I'm looking at the notes about magic," the other said derisively. "You try to find if there are any journals about their childhood."

Their childhood? Azalea frowned from her hiding place. Why would Montgomery be after something like that?

"Why does 'e want to read about 'is own childhood?" the dimmer of the intruders asked, voicing Azalea's question for her. "Aren't they twins? Surely 'e knows it all."

"You think he's going to tell us his plans?" snapped the one who seemed to be the leader. "All I know is we're to look for any mention of Rosewood, and find out what's written about it."

Rosewood? Azalea started at the familiar name. It was the city her mother came from, in Listernia's southwest. But Uncle Mortimer, and all his siblings, had grown up in Liss, alongside her father. Why would Uncle Mortimer's childhood journals say anything about Rosewood? And why was Montgomery interested in it?

She waited in tense silence for several long minutes. She could only hope that if the men found anything, they'd declare it aloud. But it seemed they had no success.

"I can't see anything that looks like a personal journal," the henchman said at last. "Maybe 'e never kept one."

His words were punctuated by a large yawn, and his companion's tone turned businesslike. "Time to go. We don't want to end up collapsed in the middle of a room we shouldn't be in."

"But we're no better off than before," the other one protested. "And we've only got one left each."

Azalea let out a breath. Only one more talisman each. That was information worth having. She had optimistically hoped this might be their last night, but it could be much worse than one more.

"I know that," barked the more assertive man. "We're going to have to figure out where they're taking her before we try again. Maybe one of us needs to hide in her other room, so we can see exactly where they take her, and so we're right there as soon as everyone's asleep."

A cold rush passed over Azalea at his words. She would be powerless to hide her presence if the men were in her room. She had to wake and get out of there, whereas they would remain awake throughout the brief in between period when the rest of the kingdom were asleep and she wasn't yet conscious. If they didn't manage to kill her in that undefended time, they would certainly see her waking and getting up.

The thought flashed through her mind that she could attack them now, try to kill them. But even knowing they'd been sent to kill her, she couldn't bring herself to do it. She wondered idly how the curse would get around that. Dead bodies on the floor of Uncle Mortimer's room would certainly give away that someone had been active during the night. But it wasn't exactly an action the curse could make her undo.

It was a moot point, because she wasn't going to try. Quite apart from her reluctance to kill someone, she wasn't confident enough of the outcome. There were two of them, and they were armed.

"We can't do any more tonight, though," the leader was continuing, his voice dopey. "You'd better move if you're going to get back to the stables before this thing wears off."

The stables. The other man must be a groom, or posing as one. He gave a grunt, and Azalea held her breath as he emerged back into the receiving room. He passed out of the room with quick strides, and Azalea let him go. She hadn't banked on them splitting up. But at least she knew his general location, and the other one seemed the more dangerous.

He stayed for a few more minutes, leafing through papers and muttering to himself. He was clearly trying to commit some of Uncle Mortimer's findings to memory. The thought of Montgomery's brazenness in sending these men into the castle, in having them snoop on his own brother—not to mention attempt to kill Azalea—sent a flash of anger through her. No amount of gold should ever be enough for someone to agree to this.

Eventually the man emerged, and Azalea forced herself to count to thirty before she followed him back into the corridor. She crept along in the direction of his shuffling steps, which echoed throughout the otherwise silent castle.

He seemed to be heading for the kitchens, and she frowned. Was he a serving man perhaps? Not one she recognized, but there had probably been lots of new hires in the last two years. She was aware from what she'd read that many Listernians had fled the kingdom to settle somewhere curse-free. There must have been plenty of gaps to fill in the castle's staff.

She was trying to move stealthily, but to her alarm, the man suddenly stopped walking, halfway to the kitchens, and swiveled around.

Azalea dashed behind a suit of armor, hoping the darkness hid her movements. The man squinted up the corridor, his face invisible even to her improved eyesight.

"Who's there?" he called warily. "That you, Ralf?"

So she had a name for one of her attackers. Not that it did her much good.

"Hello?" the man tried again.

After a moment, his footsteps started again, and Azalea realized with horror that they were coming toward her this time. He was obviously suspicious enough to investigate. He passed by her hiding place, and she gripped her sword more tightly. She couldn't help her hands shaking, and the very tip of the blade dinged softly against the suit of armor in front of her.

The man was only a few steps away, and he swung around wildly. Furious with herself for her uncharacteristic clumsiness, Azalea sprang into action. She pushed the suit of armor with all her might, sending it toppling down on the man's head. He went down with a shout, his limbs flailing as he tried to throw off the metal burden. Azalea considered just running, but she didn't know exactly how much longer he had awake, and she couldn't be sure he wouldn't catch her, and see her. As it was, he seemed to still be unaware of who had attacked him. And she hadn't seen where he slept, or had a chance to search for his other talisman.

Acting on the impulse of the moment, she dropped her sword and seized the helmet, now separated from the rest of the suit of armor. Swooping down on the still-struggling man, she swung it into his head with all her might. His head lolled sickeningly to the side, and he stopped moving. Leaning closer, she saw that he was still breathing, but his eyes were closed.

She stepped back, dropping the helmet with a clang, and breathing hard. What to do with him now? He might not have recognized her, but he knew that someone had been awake, someone other than him. And even if she'd known his name, or where he slept, she'd have no way to warn her daytime counterparts of his activities.

A sudden thought came to her, and she sized him up with her eyes. He was large, and it wasn't going to be easy, but she had all night, after all. She backed off further, watching him anxiously for signs of reviving. But after about ten minutes, she was confident that an hour must have passed since sunset. The man's peaceful expression convinced her that he was now in the enchanted sleep, not just unconscious from her blow.

Steeling herself for a true test of her strengthened muscles, she knelt beside him and tried to drag his form up over her shoulder. A very few attempts convinced her this approach was futile. With a sigh, she resigned herself to dragging him. Taking hold of one ankle in each hand, she hauled him across the stone floor, grunting with the effort of sliding his bulk. Foot by foot, she tugged him toward the dungeons.

It took her half an hour to get him there, and by the time she arrived, she was exhausted. Coming down the two flights of stairs had been especially brutal—for him, not her. He was going to have the most ferocious of headaches when he awoke. But after all, he had tried to kill her.

She retrieved a ring of keys from the belt of the sleeping guard, and unlocked an empty cell, averting her eyes from her maid in the next cell over. Dragging the attacker over the one final stretch, she locked him in and returned the keys where she found them.

"Serves you right," she said triumphantly, brushing her hands against each other. "A cell is where you belong, you sneaking little rat."

Feeling much better for the outburst, she made her way back up the stairs with a spring in her step. She had no way to communicate his crimes, of course, and she hadn't had the opportunity to find his nest and search for his last talisman. But it was still satisfying to have confronted him in spite of her fear, and better yet to have bested him on her own and detained him, where he couldn't make any more mischief.

She went about her regular battle with the vines, casting a dark glance at the royal stables as she passed them. Somewhere in there was another would-be killer, and one who had so far gotten away without consequence. But she didn't go searching for him. She hadn't gotten a good enough look at his face to identify him.

She had finished her circuit of the walls—describing her defeat of the assassin to the vines in vindictive triumph all the way along—and was making her way back into the castle's entranceway, when something momentarily blotted out the moon. Glancing up, Azalea stumbled, nearly face-planting on the steps in her shock.

Was that a *dragon*?

What could a dragon possibly be doing wheeling over the city of Liss in the middle of the night? She couldn't make much out in the darkness, but it seemed to be swooping low then returning to the sky, as if looking for—or at—something.

She hesitated for a moment, wracked with indecision. Should she call out? Should she identify herself? A couple of weeks ago, she wouldn't have hesitated. The sight of another living creature awake and moving around would have been too incredible to resist. But the assassins had made her more wary. It seemed like a remarkable coincidence that after two years of nothing, the men and the dragon had appeared within such a short time of each other. Was this dragon somehow connected with their planned attack?

She knew the dragon wasn't there at her parents' request, and not just because she'd read no mention of such a plan in Uncle Mortimer's notes. Her parents would never in a hundred centuries consider going to the dragons for help with a human enchantment. No royal would.

She still hadn't made up her mind on whether she wanted the dragon to see her, when it suddenly dropped several feet, only just catching itself in time to remain in the air. She frowned. She'd never seen a dragon move so clumsily. As she watched, its head began to weave drunkenly from side to side. Just as it crossed the moon, she was able to see it open its mouth in what appeared to be a cavernous yawn.

Azalea's own mouth fell open in astonishment. It was getting drowsy? Montgomery's magic was strong enough to affect even a dragon? A thrill of fear ran over her. How could she ever hope to break an enchantment that powerful?

The dragon seemed to realize what was happening, because

with a shake of its head, it took properly to the sky, disappearing into nothing with the impossible speed of its kind. Most likely it would be able to cross the border of Listernia before being claimed by the enchanted sleep. Azalea stood in the castle's entranceway, blinking. She could almost have believed the whole thing was a dream.

She made her way to the library, thinking she might brush up on dragon lore. Had she made the right call in not attempting to communicate with the creature? She hadn't been given much opportunity to think about it. Due to the run in with the assassins, she had less time than usual for her studies, but she still judged that there was an hour to go before she would be forced to return to her bed.

She was therefore mystified when, having only just opened a book, she felt the tug of the enchantment. Involuntarily, she snapped the book shut, returning it to its shelf and snuffing out the candle she had been reading by. She frowned in confusion as the curse led her away from her own suite, toward the castle's entranceway. Had she left something significant outside when working on the vines?

But it quickly became clear that she wasn't being drawn outside the building. Her heart sank as the compulsion forced her to descend again into the dungeon. She tried with all her might to resist as she took the keys from the guard's belt and began unlocking the cell where she'd deposited her would-be killer. But it was futile. She was so infuriated at being forced to undo her capture of the assassin that she actually screamed aloud in frustration as she hauled him out of the cell. She had so hoped that because knocking him unconscious was an act the curse couldn't make her undo, and because the men were bypassing the curse themselves in their activities, she would be able to move him with impunity. Clearly, it wasn't so.

The curse had not overestimated the time it would take her

to drag the man's limp form back up the steps and along the corridor. It was a full hour before she dropped him next to the fallen suit of armor and collapsed, exhausted, beside him. But the curse wouldn't let her rest. She had no choice but to get to her feet again, and replace the armor on its stand. Apparently the curse had decided that the man should wake there, where he'd fallen.

She ground her teeth as her feet moved of their own accord, taking her back to her suite. After her rush of triumph over defeating the attacker, it was maddening to realize how absolute a failure her plans had actually been. She hadn't seen where either man slept, she hadn't searched for their remaining artifacts, and she hadn't succeeded in imprisoning anyone. They both had one talisman left, and one of them knew without doubt that someone else was awake. They would be more cautious next time. And she had no way of knowing when that time would be, let alone counteracting their next attack. And add onto all of that, a dragon had been circling her undefended home, and she didn't have the slightest idea of its purpose.

She was more vulnerable than ever.

CHAPTER SIXTEEN

Bentleigh

Bentleigh was up with the sun, dressing quickly as he tried to decide how best to extricate himself from his situation. There was no denying that he had slept much better in a guest suite of the castle in Fernford than he would have on the forest floor. But he still couldn't help bemoaning the unlucky chance that had brought Prince Amell's patrol to his little grove. He wanted to get back to Zayla quickly, so he had time to explore any lead Rekavidur might find. The last thing he wanted was to get mired down in an unplanned and unsanctioned state visit to Fernedell.

Deciding that Prince Amell himself was his best bet, Bentleigh went looking for the younger royal as soon as he had strapped his sword on. It was no surprise to discover that Amell had also risen early. Bentleigh had the impression that the fifteen-year-old prince had an endless well of energy.

A helpful servant having directed him, Bentleigh found Amell in the castle's training yard, sparring with his personal guard, who had introduced himself to Bentleigh the night before as Sir Furnis. He seemed a very long-suffering man.

"Prince Bentleigh!" Amell called brightly, the moment he saw him enter. "Join us!"

Bentleigh strode over, greeting Sir Furnis as well.

"Such a stroke of luck that my patrol ran into you last night," Amell said, his voice still eager.

"Yes, incredible luck," Bentleigh said, his voice admirably even. Sir Furnis shot him a shrewd look, but Amell was clearly oblivious.

"I have a feeling Father was hoping that letting me join a patrol would prove to me that it's not nearly as exciting as I think it is," the young prince said with a grin. "It didn't go quite as he planned. First a dragon, then you!"

"I feel compelled to point out," Sir Furnis cut in mildly, "that patrols don't normally run into either dragons or incognito princes."

"So you say," Amell joked. He raised an eyebrow at Bentleigh. "Up for a bout?"

Bentleigh summoned a smile as he shook his head. "Sorry, Your Highness, not this morning. I actually need to be going."

"What, so soon?" The younger prince's face fell. "Don't feel like you need to hurry off just because we weren't expecting you. My parents are delighted to host you. I believe Mother is already composing a letter to your parents assuring them that you're welcome to consider our castle your own any time you might be passing through."

Bentleigh winced. He didn't know Amell's mother well enough to predict whether there would be a reproachful edge to such a letter, but he had a very good idea of how his own parents would receive it. And it wouldn't go well for him.

He glanced at Amell's personal guard, hovering close by, and decided he had little choice but to include the man.

"Amell," he said, lowering his voice. "Do you think there's any way my visit could *not* be mentioned to my parents?"

Amell's eyes widened in horror, and Bentleigh hastened to fix his blunder.

"I don't mean to ask you to do anything underhanded, but—"

"No, no, it's not that," said Amell dismissively. "I'd love nothing more than to have your back, no questions asked. But I'm so sorry, Bentleigh—the cat's already out of the bag. I don't think there's any force on Solstice that could stop my parents telling yours about your visit. And if they found out you didn't want them to, they'd be all the more determined." His voice dropped to a resentful mutter. "They have some pretty set views on the absolute authority of parents."

Bentleigh let out a long breath, trying not to show his dismay. It wasn't Amell's fault, after all.

"I shouldn't have pressed you to come back with me last night," said Amell remorsefully. His expression darkened. "Although I doubt we could've gotten out of it. The rest of the patrol saw you, and they would have reported what they saw to my parents." He sighed. "I can't sneeze without them reporting it back, let alone meet foreign princes sleeping rough in the southern grove."

"They're just doing their job, Your Highness," said Sir Furnis placatingly.

"Well, you manage to do yours without being an insufferable tattletale, Furn," Amell pointed out. He turned back to Bentleigh. "Is there anything I can do to smooth it over?"

Bentleigh frowned. "Do you think your mother would consent to me taking the message to my parents myself? If I explain that I need to leave immediately for Bant?"

"Of course," said Amell. He hesitated. "She would expect an answer, though."

Bentleigh laughed. "Don't worry, I wasn't going to throw the letter in a river. I realize it has to reach my parents. I really will take it to them, by tomorrow if I leave immediately."

Amell gave a curt nod. True to his word, he was eager to help, and shortly after breakfast, Bentleigh found himself riding away from the city of Fernford, a letter bearing the Fernedellian royal seal tucked into his satchel. It was an extremely unlucky chance that would require him to divert all the way to Bant before continuing back to Liss. He grimaced. If his parents would allow him to return to Liss. But they would have to. He straightened in the saddle. He wasn't fifteen, like Prince Amell. Like he'd told Rian, it was time to stand up to his parents. He wasn't going to allow his parents to control his every move. He just had to stand strong.

He had almost reached the border with Bansford when he heard a telltale rush, and felt wind whipping around him. Glancing up, he was rewarded by the sight of a yellow-scaled dragon gliding down from the sky with outstretched wings.

There were a few other travelers on the road, but they all scurried out of earshot, eyes wide as they watched the spectacle. Bentleigh had no concerns that they would listen in. Everyone, royal and peasant alike, had enough respect for dragons not to try to eavesdrop on them.

"Greetings, Prince Bentleigh," Rekavidur said in his gravelly voice.

"Greetings, Rekavidur!" Bentleigh bent in a bow, his gaze springing eagerly back to the dragon's. "Have you visited Liss already?"

"I have," the dragon nodded. Bentleigh waited in barely concealed impatience for him to go on, but Rekavidur appeared deep in thought for a long moment. "What I witnessed—what I experienced—troubled me," he confessed. "I will not share my reflections with you, except to say two things. First, there is most certainly a magic of concealment involved, although it is in a different form from what I know. Secondly..."

He paused for so long that Bentleigh wondered if he would continue. But eventually he let out a huff, a spark flying from his nostrils and igniting a dry leaf on the road near Bentleigh's foot. Bentleigh stamped it out absently, his attention on the dragon's words.

"Secondly, it is strong. Too strong for me to remove." His voice once again dropped to that mutter that made it seem as though he had forgotten his audience. "Surely too strong for an enchanter to achieve." A shudder went over him, as if the idea of a human with that kind of magic didn't bear thinking about.

Bentleigh stared at the beast, startled by his words. "This concealment enchantment, whatever it's for, was too strong for a dragon?"

"I didn't say that, precisely," said Rekavidur with dignity. "There are probably many dragons who could remove the concealment magic. But I am a young dragon, not yet at my full strength. And the enchantment, as you call it, is considerably stronger than that which afflicted Felicity's prince."

Bentleigh rocked back on his heels, trying to process the dragon's words. He hadn't really expected Rekavidur to find a concealing enchantment on the castle, let alone break it. But he felt disappointed nevertheless.

"Well, even if you can't help me," he said politely, "I am very grateful that you were willing to consider it."

"Once again, I did not say that," said Rekavidur, a touch of irritation in his voice. "Humans," he muttered. "I cannot break the enchantment, but I may be able to shield you from it."

"Shield me?" Bentleigh repeated, confused.

"That's right," the dragon responded placidly. "Do you have a shield?"

"Not...not with me," Bentleigh said.

"A pity," mused Rekavidur. "There's something to be said for the object matching the magic. But I suppose we can make do with something else." He eyed Bentleigh's form. How about that garment?"

"My traveling cloak?" Bentleigh asked, pulling it off his shoulders.

Without warning, the dragon's head darted forward. He grasped the fabric in his teeth and flung the cloak high into the air. As it fell, billowing, Rekavidur opened his jaws wide and sort of...breathed on it. No flame came out of his mouth, but the heat of his breath made Bentleigh cover his face with his arms. Rekavidur repeated the exercise several times, before snagging the cloak once more and casting it over Bentleigh.

"There," he said calmly. "If my understanding of the enchantment is correct, that should act as a shield. Make sure you are wearing it when darkness falls."

"Thank you," said Bentleigh, a little dazed. He pulled the cloak back around his shoulders, trying not to wince from the heat of it. Hopefully that would fade.

"I wish you well in your quest," the dragon said, something cryptic about his expression. "Perhaps our paths may cross again."

And without further comment, he launched himself upward in a ferocious gust of wind. Other travelers started to edge back onto the road, casting curious and excited looks in Bentleigh's direction. He didn't linger to speak to any of them, hurrying on to cross the border into Bansford.

He was too recognized in his own kingdom to get away with sleeping in a grove, so he spent the night at one of his family's properties in the west of the kingdom. In spite of the comfortable bed, he used his balled up cloak as a pillow, not wanting to let it out of his sight. Again, he was up at dawn, taking to the road before the housekeeper could fuss over him too much.

He reached Bant just as the sun was setting. He was weary from the many hours in the saddle, and in spite of Rekavidur's gift, his mood was somber. He'd been away from Azalea for almost a week now, and he knew he'd have a battle on his hands to return to her. And once he got there, he had no idea whether the cloak would be any help to him in solving the curse. He didn't know what part of the enchantment could be considered concealment magic, or how being shielded from that would change anything.

A sudden thought—so obvious he should never have missed it—struck him as he rode under the portcullis. Rekavidur had poured magic into his cloak, which meant it was now an artifact. Bentleigh's possession of it was contrary to his kingdom's laws. He suddenly felt like every guard was watching him suspiciously, and he forced himself to sit straight in the saddle. All the more reason to get back to Liss with all possible speed. It wasn't like he *wanted* to sidetrack through Bansford, bringing his contraband with him.

He saw no reason to put off the inevitable, so after completing a quick wash and changing into fresh clothes, he made his way straight to the royal family's private dining hall. He knew dinner would have been served some time before, but he hoped to catch his parents while they were still seated. He was just approaching the room, smiling in his usual friendly way at the various guards and servants who greeted him, when the door opened, and Rian emerged.

"Ben!" he exclaimed, striding forward to grip his brother's arm in greeting. "Back so soon?" He searched Bentleigh's eyes, his expression becoming concerned. "Nothing amiss, I hope?"

"Not more than usual," sighed Bentleigh, trying not to think of the illegal garment he'd hidden in his room. He jerked his head toward the door. "Mother and Father in there?"

Rian nodded, his eyes still fixed on Bentleigh's face. "Something tells me you're going to want backup," he muttered, pushing the door back open.

Bentleigh gave him a grateful look as he walked through into the dining hall. The king and queen of Bansford were sitting at the dining table, finishing their meal in austere silence. For a moment Bentleigh was struck by the difference between the scene and the many meals he'd eaten in Listernia's royal dining hall. His parents looked like a posed portrait of domestic royal life, not like a real family.

His father looked up and spotted him. To Bentleigh's astonishment, his initial surprise gave way to an expression of pleasure.

"Bentleigh," he exclaimed, drawing the queen's attention to her son's arrival as well. "I'm pleased to see you back so soon. Your timing is excellent."

Bentleigh scolded himself for his suspicion, trying to inject some warmth into his words as he greeted his parents.

"I have a letter for you," he added, as casually as he could. "From Queen Pietra of Fernedell."

His father's brow lowered, his friendly tone instantly disappearing. "How do you have a letter from the queen of Fernedell?"

Bentleigh sighed. "I went through Fernedell on...on my way home."

"On your way home?" his father echoed. He was somehow on his feet now. "What were you doing paying an uninvited visit to the Fernedellian crown without our knowledge? What mischief are you up to, Bentleigh?"

"No mischief," Bentleigh said, his conscience squirming. He saw that even Rian looked taken aback at the news of his trip to the neighboring kingdom, and he tried to make his voice reasonable. "I heard...a rumor that there might be someone in Fernedell who could help Azalea."

"And?" His father's voice was as cold as a mountain lake.

"Well, they gave me some information," Bentleigh said carefully. "But I can't be sure whether it will be any help until I return to Liss."

"Return to Liss?" his father repeated in grim amusement. "I don't think so."

"Father," Bentleigh protested, his own anger rising. "Don't be unreasonable!"

"You accuse *me* of being unreasonable?" his father snapped. "Against my better judgment, I have allowed you to continue traveling to Liss, despite the necessity for you to travel alone, a situation not at all befitting for a prince of—"

"Necessity?" interrupted Bentleigh. "There's absolutely *no* reason guards couldn't go with me, if that's what you wish. There's no danger to them from entering Listernia."

"Enough!" his father roared, and Bentleigh fell silent. "If you cannot see the danger that kingdom poses, then the situation is worse than I feared."

His eyes fell on the chain around his son's neck, and narrowed. Bentleigh knew he was on dangerous ground. He had managed to convince his parents that the magic cast long ago on the chain—to prevent it from being lost, or from being forcibly removed—was unfortunate but out of their control, and wasn't sufficient to make the chain an artifact. He wasn't sure his father had ever been fully satisfied by the argument, and it was becoming increasingly common to see the king casting looks of dislike at the item.

"You have allowed your mind to be addled by the Listernians' foolish tolerance of the evil that is magic," the king went on curtly.

Bentleigh was silent, his breath coming fast and his grip on his self-control paper thin.

Satisfied that he wasn't going to retort, his father returned to his initial tirade. "Now I find that you have exploited that freedom to travel all over the continent alone, as if you were some homeless vagabond. And you have humiliated us by arriving in such state at the castle of the Fernedellians?"

"I didn't intend to visit their castle," snapped Bentleigh. "And no one was humiliated."

"That's not for you to judge," said the king smoothly. "But in any event, you will not be returning to Liss. We told you that your last visit was your final chance."

"But I still haven't finished that visit!" Bentleigh argued. "And I have new information, that might help!"

"It won't help, Bentleigh," his mother interjected. "The curse is permanent—everyone accepts that but you."

"Well I *don't* accept it," Bentleigh insisted. "And I never will."

"That's quite enough melodrama," said his father dismissively. "It is time for you to turn your mind to your role as a prince of Bansford."

Bentleigh frowned and glanced at Rian. His brother looked uncomfortable, and wouldn't meet his eye. Whatever their parents had planned for Bentleigh, Rian had discovered it since they last spoke. And he clearly didn't think Bentleigh would like it.

"What do you mean?" he asked cautiously, his gaze flicking between his parents.

"We received a letter from King Thorn of Entolia," his mother said evenly. "He believes he will not survive the coming winter, and he wishes to make certain provisions before he dies."

"And?" said Bentleigh, still waiting for information that would be relevant to him.

He wasn't heartless, but King Thorn had been supposedly dying for several years now, and he felt justified in taking the dire words with a grain of salt. If King Thorn really wanted to ensure the well-being of his kingdom after he was gone, he should focus his attention on ending the war with Mistra. Bentleigh couldn't see how that would involve him.

"Provisions for his daughter," his mother pressed delicately.

Bentleigh frowned, still confused. "Which one? Don't they have a dozen?"

"His oldest one, obviously," Bentleigh's father cut in impatiently. "None of the others are old enough for a marriage alliance."

"Princess Zinnia?" Bentleigh said, before the rest of his father's words filtered through. "Wait, marriage alliance?" He took a step forward, his fist clenching. "With me? That's impossible."

His father raised a quelling eyebrow, but Bentleigh ignored him.

"I'm already betrothed to Azalea! You can't just exchange one alliance for another!"

"Of course we can," the king said coolly. "Such things are done all the time."

"Play those games with your own life, not mine," Bentleigh said passionately. He paused. "Besides, isn't Princess Zinnia only fifteen?"

"She's about to turn sixteen," his father said dismissively.

Bentleigh made no attempt to hide his disgust, and it was his mother's turn to raise her eyebrows.

"You didn't raise any objections to formalizing your betrothal with Princess Azalea when she was about to turn sixteen."

"That's because I wasn't even eighteen yet!" Bentleigh protested. "And it was Zayla!"

"I understand your disappointment, Bentleigh," his mother sighed. "But you simply can't form an alliance with a girl who's in an enchanted sleep. I know Entolia isn't as promising an option, since they have a crown prince. I have found it difficult to let go of our plans myself. Every mother blessed with two such fine sons would wish to see them each as king of their own kingdoms. But we must adapt to circumstances."

Somehow, Bentleigh was unable to take any pleasure in her compliments. "You think I care about being king?" he said incredulously. "I care about Zayla!" He hadn't noticed his voice rising, but somehow he was shouting. "I love her!"

"I thought I told you to stop with the dramatics, Bentleigh," the king cut in impatiently. "A marriage alliance is not about emotion. It's about what's best for the kingdom."

"Come Bentleigh," his mother added, "if you could learn to care for Princess Azalea on the basis of an alliance, I'm sure you can learn to care for Princess Zinnia."

"You can't do this to me," Bentleigh said, his throat dry. "You can't do it to Listernia. The law gives me the choice of who I marry."

"My duty," his father's voice was a deadly hiss, "is not to Listernia. And neither is yours." Menace dripped from his words. "As I trust you will remember."

"Law or not, Bentleigh, you can't choose a bride who can't be woken," his mother reminded him.

Bentleigh's fists were still clenched at his side, his muscles trembling. But before he could say something he would inevitably regret, he felt a grip on his shoulder. Rian had stepped up beside him, his eyes holding a warning.

Bentleigh held his brother's gaze for a tense moment, then gave a barely perceptible nod. He turned back to his parents.

"I will not marry Princess Zinnia," he said curtly, keeping his voice level with an effort. "I still believe that my marriage to Azalea, and an alliance with Listernia, is what is best for Bansford."

Without giving his parents a chance to respond, he turned on his heel and stalked from the room. His blood was pounding in his ears as he strode blindly toward his suite, and it took him a minute to realize Rian had followed. He made no comment on his brother's presence, and Rian also stayed silent until they were in Bentleigh's rooms.

The moment the door closed behind him, Bentleigh started pacing. Rian leaned against the bedpost, watching him with folded arms.

"Breathe, little brother," he said calmly.

"Easy for you to keep your cool," Bentleigh snapped. "It's not your life they're trying to control."

Rian gave a hollow laugh. "You think they don't control my life? You think they'll let me choose who I marry?"

Bentleigh stopped pacing, taking a deep breath. Rian was right, and none of this was his fault.

"What am I going to do, Ri?" he asked. "I can't lose her. I don't care what it takes."

Rian frowned thoughtfully at him. "Do you really have new information? Something that might help?"

"It might. But I can't be sure," Bentleigh admitted. "Not until I get back to Liss."

"I'm guessing I don't want to know the details," Rian said ruefully.

"You really don't."

Rian hesitated only a moment before giving a decisive nod. "Go, Ben. Get out of here. I'll cover for you. No one will miss you until morning. Make sure you're most of the way to the border by then."

Bentleigh stared at his brother. He didn't want to get Rian into trouble, but the older prince was right. If Bentleigh didn't get out of Bant fast, his parents were going to make sure he couldn't do so at all.

"Thanks Rian," he said, gripping his brother's offered arm. Pausing only to retrieve his traveling cloak, he shouldered his still-packed satchel and made for the door.

CHAPTER SEVENTEEN

Azalea

zalea sprang from her bed, her eyes searching the room carefully. The idea of the men hiding in her suite had taken hold, and she woke feeling immediately alert and on edge. What had the man she'd bludgeoned done with his day? She didn't know if he'd figured out who she was, but he was surely out for blood. And she had no way of knowing his movements.

Happily, no enraged assassin lurked in the corners of her room, at least not tonight. She chose a different hiding spot, further from her suite, just in case. But the first tense hour of darkness passed without incident, and Azalea forced herself to go about her usual tasks. Having eaten some of the food no doubt intended for her parents' breakfast, she hurried out of the entranceway, drawing her sword as she made for the forest gate. She skipped the visit to Uncle Mortimer's rooms, at least for now. The vines were getting harder to contain every night, and it didn't help that she had to sacrifice her first hour in waiting for the men to appear.

When she reached the area, she paused in dismay. She had

struggled to make any progress on the vines the previous night, and it was already so much worse than it had been then. No guards had even laid themselves down in the vicinity, so they must have recognized that it wasn't safe.

Azalea swallowed. The guards' decision to abandon this stretch was surely an acknowledgment of defeat. They were surrendering this part of the wall to the vines. It was the first section which had been truly overrun, and it was hard to accept. But she could see that the guards had been right. They couldn't contain the vines' growth during the day, and she couldn't contain it now. If she waded into the mess before her, she wasn't at all sure she would succeed in dismantling it. And she couldn't possibly guarantee that she'd avoid being pierced in the process of trying.

A lump rose in her throat as she hurried along the wall. For two years she'd been fighting, alone and weary. She'd been risking her safety, giving every ounce of strength she had to the task of defending her city against the curse's attack. And it still wasn't going to be enough. If the vines had breached the wall here, they would breach it in many other places soon. And once they were inside the city, they would come for the castle, and for her, with unstoppable persistence. What would happen to everyone in their path?

Of course, if the assassins managed to hide in her room before tomorrow night, the vines would have their job done for them. What would happen then? Would they stop growing, or continue to overwhelm Liss?

With these grim thoughts, Azalea worked her way around the wall, her heart too heavy for one-sided banter. Things were worse than she realized. There were two more breaches that she couldn't contain, and it took her a full hour to hack away at the vines growing thickly over the city's gate.

She knew the problem had been growing steadily more out of control, but surely this escalation was too rapid. Was it connected to the assassins Montgomery had sent? Had he also sent some further magic, to bolster the power that propelled the vines? Or was it some other cause entirely, like the work of that dragon?

Panic threatened to take hold as Azalea worked. It was like a living, growing thing, trying to choke her as surely as the vines would if she let them reach her. She refused to let it latch on, turning it back tendril by tendril, the mental process like an identical extension of her physical work. But keeping the fear at bay didn't alter the reality. She was running out of time, and she was powerless to change her situation.

When she returned to the castle, she was exhausted and hungry. She wandered through the kitchen's enormous storeroom, taking a little bit of this and that, as the curse allowed. She used to dream of a fresh, hot meal, but she no longer thought of such things. Or at least not very often. She was used to her simple fare. The luxurious life she'd once taken for granted seemed a century ago now.

She was about to head toward the library when she paused. Her thoughts had been swirling around the strange task Montgomery had set his henchmen, and she'd been wondering how to investigate it. She supposed Uncle Mortimer's notes were the best place to start. The men hadn't found anything, but they'd had such a limited time to search. She still had a couple of hours before dawn.

She spent over an hour of that time flicking through the various ledgers and parchments stacked on Uncle Mortimer's desk. She even rifled through his drawers, and hunted on his shelves. It wasn't necessary to read the contents of what she found. It was clear at a glance that nothing she came across was in the nature of a personal journal. She was inclined to think the intruder had been right, and Uncle Mortimer didn't keep a journal.

She paused, thinking. Her mother kept a journal, she knew that for a fact. She'd never been tempted to read it during the hours of darkness. She didn't really want to know more detail of her mother's fears and uncertainties. What she'd always seen from the outside was more than enough.

But perhaps she should check to see how far back those records might go. Her mother was a similar age to Uncle Mortimer and his twin. Her childhood would coincide with theirs, and she actually had been in Rosewood. Could her journals contain some clue as to Montgomery's strange interest in the place?

Azalea only had an hour left, so she probably wouldn't be able to search her mother's suite thoroughly. But she figured it was worth making a start. She padded through the corridors with her habitual grace, slipping into her mother's room as silently as a shadow.

The queen wasn't there. She was in her husband's room, as was now the usual situation. How nice, Azalea thought with dry humor, that her curse had produced the happy effect of bringing her parents closer together.

Somehow the absence of her sleeping mother made it easier for Azalea to rifle through her belongings with only a minimum of guilt. She was careful to replace everything as she went, so as to avoid a tedious enforced clean up later. That would be a poor use of her valuable time.

Somewhat to her surprise, she actually succeeded in finding her mother's journal after searching for some time. It was a recent one, with no sign of earlier records in its vicinity. Azalea didn't expect to find anything helpful in it, but she couldn't quite resist flicking the pages open.

She read a sentence or two regarding her mother's emotions on the eighteenth birthday of her slumbering daughter, and pulled her eyes away guiltily. It felt wrong reading this. Her mother hadn't intended it for Azalea's eyes.

But as she went to close the tome, she was amazed to see the word she was looking for. *Rosewood.* Drawing the journal closer to her guttering candle, she squinted at the entry, marked from the day that had just passed.

I had a dream last night. That in itself is notable—I haven't dreamed since the curse hit, from what I can recall. And I have heard others say that dreams don't interrupt their enchanted slumber. But last night one most definitely did, and it was a peculiar one.

I was a child again, and back in Rosewood. It felt in every particular like reality, down to the furniture in our family manor. It was more memory than dream. I was perhaps ten, and my sister and I were teasing the cook for pastries, then sneaking them into the garden to eat them before mother caught us.

But then the dream diverged from reality.

We received a royal visit, which is something I do not recall ever occurring. And had it occurred, I certainly would recall it. The visitor was Victor, of course. He would have been fifteen when I was ten, but in the dream he was my age. We played together, laughing and splashing in the creek with our shoes off. He told me all about the capital, and his castle. It was strange. I didn't see his face much—it was like my dream self was unwilling to look at it.

. . .

It wasn't a short visit, either. He stayed for a month, with his family, although I never saw his parents. Mortimer was there, and Melodia, and Miranda. But Montgomery was not. I suppose my mind was considerate, not wanting to cause my dream to descend into nightmare by bringing that evil vermin into it.

It was a bizarre kind of dream, the way it sped through time. I had the sense of growing steadily older, as though my childhood was occurring in rapid motion. After that early meeting, Victor and I exchanged letters, although I couldn't see their content. By the time I was eighteen, I had stopped responding, though. I can't quite remember why. I think I knew in the dream, but I'm unable to grasp the memory now that I am awake.

A strange dream indeed.

Eighteen is Azalea's age. She used to talk about turning eighteen, about the grand ball we would hold, and the dress she would wear. Such foolish details to dwell on, but I love to remember a time when she was happy. Now she is always still, always unresponsive. Peaceful —much more so than she ever was when awake—but cold. And all wrong. I would give anything to have her fire back again.

Azalea shut the book with a snap, moisture in her eyes. She had plagued her mother with her "fire", as the queen so delicately put it. She wished she could go back, soften her defiance, insert more kindness into her conversations with her mother. She had been impatient so often, had never really tried to understand the reasons for her mother's timidity.

She still didn't understand it, but she no longer felt frustrated. Or at least, only with herself.

She could feel the curse tugging at her, and she replaced the journal carefully. Even if resisting hadn't been futile, she wouldn't have tried. She had no fight left in her, not tonight. She would need all the hours of her enchanted sleep to regain her strength for the following night's hopeless battle with the vines. And although she treasured the cryptic insight into her mother's mind, she was no closer to understanding Montgomery's interest in Rosewood. She frowned. Still, it was interesting that Montgomery had thought Uncle Mortimer might have a childhood journal mentioning Rosewood, and the queen's dream placed Uncle Mortimer in Rosewood, as a child. Surely there was something there, if she could just decipher it.

Her mind ran back over her mother's notes as she walked toward her room. She agreed with her mother, that it was peculiar that she had dreamed. What her mother, and apparently the rest of the kingdom, had experienced was in line with Azalea's own observations. She hadn't dreamed in two years. She wondered what had made the night before different. She frowned, remembering the dragon that had flown over the castle in the darkness. Could there be a connection? Had some magic of the dragon's broken through the curse the tiniest bit? Enough to allow dreams? It would be interesting to know whether others had also dreamed the previous night. Perhaps she should snoop around, try to find more journals. She sighed, her curiosity tempered by her current weariness. Just another task to add to her nightly routine of hopeless battles.

She returned to her bed disheartened and uneasy. The panic of the vines' encroaching growth battled with the fear that the assassins would be waiting for her the following night. She was so sick of being afraid, but there was only so long she could hold the fear at bay by sheer determination.

Her last thought as she drifted into unconsciousness was of her mother, barefoot and giggling as she swiped pastries from the kitchen of her childhood home. Her heart ached for that child, who had been carefree and confident, innocent of the fears and burdens motherhood would bring to her life.

And it ached for another child, carefree to the point of foolishness, headstrong and happy and believing she was invincible.

Neither girl was anywhere to be found in the castle of Liss.

Azalea jerked awake with the usual suddenness the following night, pushing herself upright immediately. She spared a wistful thought for a life when she'd been able to linger in bed upon waking, luxuriating in the warmth of her blankets. But even as the memory ran through her mind, she was already racing across the room to retrieve her sword. She hated how vulnerable she now felt on waking.

She had just strapped it to her side when she heard a shuffling sound in the corridor, signaling someone's approach. She threw a frantic glance around her room, looking for a place to hide. But there was no time. She'd taken no more than a step toward her receiving room when a lantern appeared in the doorway to the corridor. Its yellow light cast an eerie upward glow onto the unpleasantly familiar face of the man she'd tried to lock in the dungeons.

"You!"

The assassin gasped, his eyes wide as he took in the sight of Azalea awake and upright, gripping her sword before her. He said nothing more, but the way his eyes narrowed told Azalea that he'd figured out her role in his misadventure, and that his intended attack had just become personal.

She didn't say a word, dropping into a defensive stance that Ben had taught her in those long-ago lessons. It was heartening to know that the assassin hadn't been able to get past her guards and hide in her receiving room, but he'd clearly been hiding very close by to arrive so quickly. And because he'd come from the corridor, he was blocking her only route of escape.

She would have to fight, and her very life depended on her ability to hold out for an entire hour. The thought sent a cold shot of fear through her, but she pushed it aside as the man advanced. She couldn't afford an attitude of defeat, not even for a moment.

The man didn't rush her straight away, instead treading carefully across the stone floor. His eyes kept flicking to her sword, and Azalea could tell that he was trying to calculate how well she could use it. He was probably wishing he'd brought more than the dagger in his hand, but how could he have expected her to be armed? She hadn't even used her sword when she knocked him out during their previous encounter.

She realized, as he stalked toward her, that she was in danger of being backed into a corner. Following the impulse of the moment, she decided to strike first, lunging out with her blade.

The man dodged out of the way with surprising nimbleness, considering his size. Seizing the opening, Azalea leaped onto her bed, intending to bypass him and make it to the door. But he read her intention immediately, and he sprinted around the foot of her bed, blocking her path. Azalea backed up across the mattress, again dropping to the floor on the far side. It had been worth a try, although she wasn't sure where she would go even if she made it out of her room. He would catch her quickly enough.

The man hovered near the door for another moment, and

Azalea found herself next to the lantern he had set down when he drew his dagger. On a sudden thought, Azalea struck at the lantern, shattering the glass and extinguishing the flame. The room was plunged into darkness, only a thin silvery light filtering in through the window. She heard the man curse and allowed herself a brief smile. She had gained another small advantage. Beyond a doubt, her eyesight in the darkness was far superior to his.

She could see him hesitate, his gaze latched on her form with a focus that suggested he was worried he'd lose her if he took his eyes off her. Reaching out with lightning speed, she seized a cushion from her bed and flung it across the room. Her opponent probably had an imperfect idea of what was flying toward him, but he raised his arms defensively nevertheless.

Making the most of his distraction, Azalea dropped to the floor as the cushion hit him, crawling in frantic haste toward his feet. She seized one of his legs just as he spotted her, and tugged with all her might.

He toppled backward, only half catching himself on a nearby table. Azalea sprang to her feet, again making a dash for the door. But the man had managed to regain his balance, and he snatched at her arm as she passed him, yanking her back across her bed.

He had seized on her sword arm, and Azalea flailed, unable to use the weapon. The moonlight glinted on his dagger as he raised it, and Azalea knew she had to act quickly. Curling her free fist, she slammed it forward with all her might, sinking it into her attacker's stomach. He let out an oomph, and his grip on her arm slackened.

She wrenched herself free, the movement taking her back to the far side of her bed, further from the door. She was no longer in a position to flee, so she brought her sword up wildly, not caring what part of him she sliced. He clearly saw the move coming, because he jumped sideways off her bed, landing at the foot of the bed and trapping her between the mattress and the wall.

He advanced, and in such close proximity Azalea realized his blade wasn't the small hunting knife she'd taken it for, but a lethal dagger, almost half the length of her sword. She swung her sword back around, trying again to break through his guard, but he deflected her attack. One more wild swing, and her sword connected with the post of her bed, sticking into the wood and refusing to budge.

She only had time for one fruitless tug before she had to abandon the weapon, scampering out of the way of the man's blade. He was clearly expecting her to make another dash across the mattress, so she tried a different approach. She dropped to the ground again, sending one foot kicking into his knee with all her might. He staggered backward into a dresser, this time losing his balance and crashing to the floor. Azalea leaped onto the bed, once more making for the door.

She didn't get far. The man scrambled onto his knees, reaching for her across the bed. She felt his meaty hand close over her ankle, bringing her face first onto the mattress. It was all she could do to roll onto her back, the better to see her death leering down at her.

She thought she heard a noise out in the corridor, and realized with a sinking heart that the man's companion was probably on his way, taking longer to arrive from wherever he'd been when darkness fell. She'd had little hope of holding one man off on her own, let alone two.

She struggled to roll away again, but her attacker had the upper hand now. He kneeled painfully on her legs, laying one arm suffocatingly across her neck as he raised his dagger with the other hand. Spots danced before her eyes as the pressure on her throat intensified. Blackness clawed at the edges of her mind, and her scrabbling hands grew still as numbness began to spread.

For two years she'd fought alone, holding on with every ounce of determination she possessed. But Montgomery had gotten her at last. She had no fight left.

It was over.

CHAPTER EIGHTEEN

Bentleigh

Bentleigh was exhausted after his hard day's travel to reach Bant, but he didn't waste a second in lamenting the loss of the expected night's sleep in his own bed. He made his way through the castle swiftly, eager to reach the little used side gate he and his brother had often snuck through in their teenage years. At the moment, no one had any reason to question him as he strode through the corridors, and he didn't want to give his parents time to decide he needed to be watched, and to spread such a message through the guards. Rian could be relied on—he would ensure that the king and queen believed their son was sulking in his room.

Sneaking out of the gate took a little more ingenuity, but it was nothing Bentleigh hadn't done before. He waited until the guard was changing shift, and made the most of the forgiving darkness to make his escape. He sent a silent message of thanks to his brother at sight of the young groom waiting with a saddled horse, and with no awkward questions.

Before long, Bentleigh was out of Bant, riding northwest as quickly as his mount could manage. As Rian had said, he needed to be most of the way to the border before morning. He was hoping he might even cross the border before the sun rose, but that proved too much both for him and his horse. He had to stop from time to time to rest his mount, and despite his best efforts, he found himself dozing on a couple of these occasions.

When the first gray of dawn showed in the sky, however, the border was less than an hour's ride away. Knowing that any guards sent by his parents wouldn't follow him into Listernia, Bentleigh decided to press on and cross over before taking a proper rest. In spite of his utter exhaustion, he felt a weight lift from his shoulders the moment he left Bansford. And it wasn't just that he was no longer breaking the law by carrying an artifact. Curse or not, entering Listernia felt more like coming home with each passing visit.

He rode for another half an hour in the direction of Liss, watching as the countryside woke and went about its day. His traveling cloak was wrapped warmly around him in the chill morning air, and his thoughts kept circling back to it, wondering what, if anything, would be its effect.

When he spotted a ramshackle ruin that had clearly once been a barn, he turned off the road. Even his eagerness to return to Azalea couldn't keep him going forever. If he didn't stop soon, his exhaustion would send him toppling from his horse like some careless traveler who'd failed to reach shelter before dark.

He rubbed his horse down and tied it behind the barn where it could reach the tall grass growing against the building. Then he made himself a rough bed on the abandoned hay and fell quickly into a dreamless sleep.

He'd only intended to doze for an hour or so, but when he woke he was dismayed to see the sun hanging low in the sky. The afternoon was well advanced, and he'd struggle to make it to the capital by nightfall now. He groaned. Sleeping during the hours of sunlight was an unbelievable waste of a day in Listernia. But he couldn't do anything about it now.

He pushed his horse almost as hard as he had done the night before, but as he'd predicted, the sun was dipping toward the horizon before he reached the walls of Liss. He was a stone's throw from the walls, but if he was reading the sun correctly, he had about a minute left. He'd never get to the castle in time. He didn't even have time to find proper shelter.

"Sorry, old boy," he muttered to his horse as he led it to a nearby tree. "Looks like it'll be a cold night for us both."

The horse gave a soft harrumph, already looking sleepy. Bentleigh propped himself against the tree, and, remembering what Rekavidur had said, wrapped his traveling cloak tightly around himself.

There were, of course, no other travelers on the road. All had found shelter by this time. Bentleigh turned his eyes from the castle to face westward, watching the sun disappear. He waited for the familiar tug of the enchanted sleep, but to his amazement it didn't come. Had he misjudged the timing of the sunset? But no—the sun had definitely sunk below the horizon now. The seconds ticked by, and still he sat against the tree, wide awake and alert. A glance at his horse showed the animal peacefully slumbering, having passed too quickly from wakefulness to sleep for it to be natural.

Bentleigh pushed himself to his feet and stared around in amazement. It was dark. It was genuinely dark. He hadn't seen nighttime in Liss for two years. Could this really be happening? He tugged the cloak more tightly around him, silently thanking the dragon. Until that moment, he hadn't dared to actually believe the cloak would do anything, let alone something as substantial as this. He had no idea how the enchanted sleep could be considered concealment magic, but he wasn't complaining. Any progress was cause for celebration.

His breath hitched at a sudden thought. Was it possible that wrapping the cloak around Azalea would wake her? It surely couldn't be that easy...but of course he had to try. Although he'd best wait for morning to do so, as once he took it off himself, he would be once again vulnerable to the curse, unable even to see if it had worked.

He left his horse to its slumber, continuing on foot to the wall. He didn't really know what he hoped to achieve by wandering the castle in the silent hours of darkness, but it seemed the only logical course to take. And he still had the persistent niggle that was always in the back of his mind when he was away from Azalea.

He drew in a breath as he came close to the gate and the moon emerged from behind a cloud. The vines were rustling audibly in the darkness, and he felt a spike of alarm. Weren't the vines supposed to be less active during the night? How were they already reaching out across the open gateway? Surely by morning they'd be completely out of control if they went on like this all night.

He drew his sword, after checking the cloak was tightly clasped. It wouldn't do to have it fall off and pitch him into slumber so close to the cursed vines. He began to hack at the growth, slicing his way through the encroaching plants. In a couple of minutes the way was clear enough for him to pass through. He glanced at the guards sleeping peacefully on pallets set on either side of the gate, some distance back. But he didn't pause, eager to reach the castle.

He passed through the eerily empty streets at a run, his attention on the spires rising up ahead. He was out of breath by the time he arrived, but he went straight through into the entranceway. For reasons he couldn't explain, the desire to be near Azalea had grown the further he came, until it was more like a burning need. He didn't divert to his own suite, making straight for hers.

It was surreal, moving through the dark, silent castle, past guards and servants laid out on pallets. It made his skin crawl somehow, knowing he was the only person awake in the entire kingdom. It occurred to him that if he'd been so inclined, he could do a lot of mischief in the hours before sunrise. He could only be thankful that most people didn't have the resources—or the foolhardiness—to seek help from the dragons.

He had almost reached the royal wing when he heard it— the sound of shuffling feet. For one heartbeat he froze in astonishment, but then he pushed his feet faster. He had thought he was the only person awake in the entire kingdom—who else could have found a way around the curse?

He rounded the corner, and a rush of horror passed over him at the sight of a dark form creeping toward the doorway of Azalea's suite. Moonlight slanted in from a nearby window, and Bentleigh caught a glimpse of silver from the dagger in the man's hand.

He didn't pause to think, or to ask questions. He just raced forward, his sword in his hand before the thought even crossed his mind. He didn't call out, but the sound of his racing steps must have alerted the intruder. The man turned with a gasp, his eyes going wide at the sight of the prince bearing down on him. He faltered back a step, then turned, clearly intending to flee.

White hot anger had Bentleigh in its grip, but he retained enough sense not to run the man through. He would lose all opportunity to get answers from him if he did so. Sword still in hand, he tackled the man from behind. He went down without so much as a cry, his face cracking against the stone floor. Bentleigh grabbed at the man's hair, yanking his head up again, but he must have hit hard, because there was no response. Bentleigh leaned close, ascertaining that the man was breathing. He was unconscious then, but maybe not for long.

A sound from the direction of Azalea's rooms drew Bentleigh's attention, and he abandoned his fallen opponent, hurrying to the doorway as quickly as he could in the darkness. His eyes had adjusted now, and he could make out the corridor fairly well. Azalea's curtains must be open, because her chambers were considerably lighter.

Bentleigh paused on the threshold of the familiar suite, his eyes drawn irresistibly to the bed. His heart seemed to stop at the sight of Azalea, lying in her usual position, with a second man actually kneeling on top of her, raising a vicious looking blade above her chest.

This time Bentleigh wasn't silent—a cry of pure rage burst from him as he leaped across the room. The man's head jerked around, his eyes widening in alarm as they found the source of the shout. Unlike the servant who had tried to murder Azalea, he didn't hasten to finish his job. He jumped backward, abandoning his task as he prepared to defend himself.

But he didn't have a hope. Any vestige of restraint had fled Bentleigh at the realization of how very close he'd come to being too late. He charged the man in a blind rage, and the assassin's dagger may as well have been a bread knife for all the protection it gave. Bentleigh's sword flicked it aside with a clang, barely checking as it thrust past the man's guard and straight into his chest.

The attacker's eyes widened and then drooped, and he toppled silently to the floor. Bentleigh stood for a moment, his chest heaving as he stared at the body. He thought of how Rian had helped him escape from Bant like a prisoner fleeing a dungeon, how he'd slept so much of the day away in that barn, waking only a few hours before sunset, how he'd inexplicably felt the need to run straight through the city instead of exploring.

Change any of those details, and Azalea would be the one lying dead now.

Azalea.

He turned, his heart full of too many emotions to name, hardly able to bring himself to look at her docile, unresponsive, almost lifeless face.

Nothing could have prepared him for what he saw. Azalea was not lying still on her bed, unfazed by her near murder. Her eyes weren't closed, and her face wasn't peaceful.

She was sitting up, her face as frozen in shock as his was, staring at him out of wide brown eyes. Wide *open* eyes.

"Ben?" she whispered, her voice hoarse and disbelieving.

The sound of his name on those lips broke the spell holding Bentleigh frozen. His sword dropped from his hand as he surged forward blindly, his eyes riveted on her face. Azalea pushed herself up from the bed and toward him, and in the next moment she was in his arms.

She buried her face in his chest, her body heaving with dry sobs. Bentleigh could hardly trust the evidence of his own arms, struggling to believe that it really was Azalea, and not some phantom, that was wrapped inside them.

"Zayla," he murmured, his breath catching on the word. "Zayla." He wanted to say something, to say *everything*, but he couldn't find words. All he could do was repeat her name over and over in a choking gasp.

Her hands still clutched his tunic, but she pulled her head back, and he saw in the dim moonlight that she was crying actual tears after all. He placed his hands on her cheeks, wiping the tears away with his thumbs. More followed instantly. Lowering his head impulsively, he kissed them away, pressing his lips first to one cheek, then the other, then drawing her close again, so that her head was against his chest.

She made a sound that was half-laugh, half-sob, but she didn't protest, didn't pull away like she had in the clearing. After a few more shuddering breaths, she slowly gained control of herself. She drew back enough to look up into his face, although she made no attempt to break loose from his arms.

"Is this real?" she asked, her voice hoarse. "Is this actually happening?"

Bentleigh nodded mutely. He understood the question. He felt like he was in a trance himself. He could barely grasp the overwhelming reality of the situation, his mind latching on to the little things instead—the way her slim form trembled in his arms, the tears glistening on her eyelashes, her unwavering gaze as her eyes searched his.

"You're awake," he said numbly. "How are you awake?"

She gave a laugh that sounded slightly hysterical. "How am *I* awake? I'm always awake. How are *you* awake?"

"Always awake?" he spluttered. "You're never awake!"

Azalea passed a shaking hand over her face. "I meant I'm always awake at night," she amended.

Bentleigh was staring at her, trying to make sense of her words, when a low moan from the corridor drew his attention. Azalea's head snapped toward the sound as well, and she sprang forward, tugging at a sword buried into the wood of her bedpost. For a moment Bentleigh could only stare—how had he missed the weapon before?—but her muttered words woke him up.

"The other assassin."

"What?" He grabbed her arm. "You know about them?"

She nodded curtly. "This isn't their first visit."

Bentleigh was still very hazy about what in the blazes was going on, but the image conjured by her grim words made him want to snatch her back into his arms and never let her go.

Azalea had other ideas, clearly. With another big tug, she managed to pull the sword free, and she strode purposefully toward the doorway. Bentleigh wasn't having that. In a few quick steps he overtook her, emerging first into the corridor. The man he'd tackled was still face down, but he was stirring.

"I should kill him where he lies," Bentleigh hissed.

"That would be no use at all," said Azalea in a practical spirit. "He was sent by Montgomery, and he might be able to tell us where to find him."

Bentleigh stared at her, open mouthed. "He was sent by Montgomery?"

Azalea nodded briskly, casting her gaze around the dark corridor. "Quick Ben, he's coming around. What can we bind him with?"

Bentleigh glanced about him, but couldn't immediately see anything. The man had lifted his head, blinking groggily between them, and Bentleigh acted on the impulse of the moment. His fist shot out, connecting with the man's head and sending it once again crashing into the stone floor. He went limp for a second time that night.

"What did you do that for?" Azalea demanded.

"He came here to murder you, Zayla," Bentleigh said darkly. He shrugged. "Besides, it will be easier to tie him up now. He'll come round again." He disappeared back into the bedroom and returned with the decorative ropes that had been holding back Azalea's curtains.

"He might not come round in time," Azalea said, frowning.

Bentleigh glanced up at her from where he knelt as he bound the man's hands and feet. "What do you mean?"

"He can only withstand the curse for an hour before he'll fall back into the enchanted sleep. Montgomery gave him some kind of talisman, but it doesn't last long."

Bentleigh frowned up at her as he rolled the bound man onto his back. He glanced at the guards sleeping peacefully on their pallets on either side of the door, his thoughts flying also to the dead assassin in Azalea's sleeping chamber.

"Come on," he said, holding out his hand.

Azalea took it without hesitation, and he pulled her down

the corridor, toward his own suite. He didn't drop his hold until they were in his receiving room. There was a lot he wanted to say to Azalea, and he didn't want to do it with an unconscious assassin lying nearby.

The king and queen must have taken Bentleigh's promise to return soon to heart, because the remains of a fire could still be seen in the hearth. They must be keeping the suite in constant readiness for him. Bentleigh seized a branch of candles and lit them from the embers. Their orange light danced across the room, casting a warm glow over Azalea's face. Bentleigh realized she was staring at him, and he pushed himself to his feet.

"How do you know that man only has an hour?" he asked.

"Because I heard them talking about it, the first time they came," Azalea said. "They had three talismans each, and they're on their last ones tonight. They used their first ones the night after you left so suddenly."

Bentleigh's eyes widened, horrified by the thought that someone had been prowling through the castle intent on harming Azalea while he'd been riding through Fernedell. Not that he would have been any use if he'd stayed.

Azalea stepped toward him, her expression hesitant.

"What's protecting you from the curse? Do you have a time limit? Are you going to fall asleep at any minute?"

Bentleigh shook his head, his breath catching at her nearness. "I don't think so," he said softly. "My cloak is an artifact now—a powerful one. I think it will work as long as I'm wearing it."

Azalea reached out, running a hand along the thick fabric. "Then don't ever take it off," she said, with an attempt at a smile.

"Azalea." Bentleigh placed his hand over hers, trapping it in place where it rested on a fold of cloak falling over his chest. "I can't tell you how I've missed you."

"You don't have to," she whispered, her other hand creeping

up to touch the overgrown scruff on his cheek, the result of his day and night of constant travel. "I know. Believe me, I know."

A more sensible part of Bentleigh's mind told him to be cautious, not to risk driving her off again. But that voice simply wasn't strong enough to override the intense emotions rocking him. He seized the hand on his cheek as well, sliding it over his face and pressing his lips to her fingers. His eyes were squeezed shut as he struggled to master himself, but he heard Azalea's sharp intake of breath at the contact.

"Some days," he whispered, "I thought I'd never see you—I mean, properly see you—again."

"How did you?" Azalea's voice sounded as breathless as he felt. "How did you find a way around the enchanted sleep?"

Bentleigh opened his eyes, drinking in the sight of her, alert and responsive.

"I went to the dragons."

CHAPTER NINETEEN

Azalea

Bentleigh's words acted like a bucket of cold water, dousing their moment. Azalea pulled her hands free and took a step back.

"Ben, you didn't!" Even as she felt the blood draining from her face, she couldn't help her heart being torn at the anguish in Ben's eyes as she pulled away from him. "It's not that I don't appreciate you trying to break the curse," she said quickly. "But it's not worth war with the dragons."

"There won't be war," Ben said hurriedly. "I'm almost completely certain of it."

"Almost?" she repeated dryly, feeling a flicker of amusement in spite of herself.

"I didn't get help from the dragon colony," Ben explained. "It was a foreign dragon, one from a land far across the sea, or so Felicity told me."

"Felicity?" Azalea arched an eyebrow, trying to show merely curiosity rather than the alarm that was racing through her. He'd never mentioned a Felicity, but she could only imagine how much she must have missed in two years.

"The queen of Albury," Ben clarified.

Azalea blinked. "I thought Albury's queen was named Queen Racquel. And that she died when we were children."

"I'm talking about the new queen," said Ben. "Married to Justin."

Azalea relaxed slightly, although she was more confused than ever. "I guess his curse is broken, then," she said.

Ben nodded. "And this dragon helped break it," he said. "So she wrote to me, suggesting that I ask him to help with our curse."

Our curse. The words unlocked something inside her, and without thinking it through, Azalea stepped back into him. His arms closed around her automatically, and he stopped talking in evident surprise.

"Oh Ben, you can't imagine how alone I've felt," she whispered. "There's been no one to help me carry this."

"Have you really been awake every night, all this time?" he asked, his arms tightening.

She nodded, with her head pressed into his shoulder. "It's been a living nightmare," she said frankly. "I haven't seen the sun for two years."

A shudder went over Ben at her words, and knowing that he sympathized with her plight—even just that he *knew* about it— made her feel infinitely better. She stepped back again. A small thrill went through her at the reluctance on Ben's face as he let her go, but she tried to keep her head clear this time.

"So what did this dragon do?" she asked, her tone businesslike.

"Well, he was only willing to help with any concealment magic," Ben said, frowning slightly. "He had reasons of his own, although he didn't fully explain them. But he could sense the curse still lingering around me, and he claimed there was concealment magic at work. He came here, and—"

"I saw him!" Azalea interrupted. "He flew over the city two nights ago."

Bentleigh stared at her. "He didn't mention you!"

"Oh, he didn't see me," she clarified. "I didn't try to catch his attention—I wasn't sure if he was friend or foe, to be honest. I was worried he was connected with Montgomery's assassins."

A dark look passed over Ben's handsome features, and for a moment he was silent. Then he pulled himself together with evident effort, and continued.

"Well, he confirmed that there was concealment magic at work, but he said it was too strong for him to lift. Instead he put his magic into my cloak, turning it into an artifact which he said would shield me from the concealment magic."

"Interesting," mused Azalea. "That suggests that the sleep which everyone else falls into at nighttime is the result of concealment magic. That, at least to some extent, its purpose is to conceal that I'm still here." She frowned. "That explains a lot, actually."

Ben was looking more confused than ever. "What does it explain?"

Azalea sighed. "Haven't you wondered why I didn't leave you a note, or find some other way to show everyone that I'm awake at night?"

Ben frowned. "Why haven't you, now you mention it?"

"Believe me, I've tried," Azalea said dryly. "I've had two years to experiment, and I've tried *everything*." She sighed. "I left you a note my second night, right in your hand."

"What?" Ben protested. "I never found anything like that!"

"No," scowled Azalea. "From all I can tell, such overt attempts to communicate get destroyed by the curse. But more subtle ones, the magic forces me to undo." She shivered as she remembered the grisly scene in her sleeping chamber, and the time the curse had forced her to drag her attacker up from the dungeons. "I don't even want to know what that will involve tonight."

"Wait." Ben's eyes were fixed on her face. "You left me a note the second night? So you came into my room and watched me sleeping?"

Azalea gave him a look. "Are you seriously going to pretend you haven't watched me sleeping anytime in the last two years?"

"Of course I have," said Ben. "It's just...unnerving to think of you awake when I thought everyone was asleep."

"It was much more unnerving for me," Azalea promised him. She narrowed her eyes at him. "Besides, you're not one to talk. Didn't I find you sleeping actually *on* my bed a week or so ago?" Her accusing look melted into a delighted laugh at the expression on his face. "Ben, you're actually blushing!"

"I'm not," he said defensively, and entirely untruthfully. But a moment later he was the one to look suspicious. "I had a dream that night," he said. "Or not a dream exactly...just an impression. I woke with the lingering feeling that you'd been all curled up against me while I was sleeping."

Now it was Azalea's turn to blush. She opened her mouth to make a snappy retort, but closed it again. This was no time to hide behind humor. "I was," she admitted, her voice dropping. "I'm sorry if I shouldn't have." To her own annoyance, tears were gathering in her eyes, and it was all she could do to keep them back. "There are no words to describe the loneliness, Ben," she whispered. "Some nights I thought I would go mad. I think I would have if I hadn't been needed for such an important job."

Her eyes were lowered, but she could still sense Ben's movement as he stepped forward. He put one hand under her chin, gently lifting her face to his. "I'm so sorry you've been alone," he said, his voice rough. "I wish I'd been there for you." His eyes searched hers. "And don't apologize. I've never had a better dream."

Azalea tried to smile, but she was so overwhelmed by the night's various emotions, she could barely control her features.

"You've definitely made me curious, though," Ben said lightly, perhaps sensing her need for some breathing space. "What was in the letter you wrote me?"

"It was two years ago," said Azalea dismissively. "I don't remember."

Ben pursed his lips. He clearly didn't believe her lie, but he didn't push it. "So what's this important job you're needed for?" he asked instead.

That jolted her out of her stupor. "How long has it been since sunset?" she demanded. "I need to get out there!"

"Out where?"

"To the wall," she said, feeling for her sword. She must have left it in the corridor near the bound assassin.

"You can't go near the wall!" Ben protested. "The vines are growing over it, getting worse every day."

"Are they?" said Azalea, exasperated. "I had no idea." She moved toward the door. "I need my sword."

"Azalea, stop." Ben's hand was suddenly on her arm, and she looked up into his anxious face. "I can't let you go near those vines. I can't lose you, not when I've just got you back."

She met his look seriously, not about to repeat the mistake of dismissing his fears for her safety. "I'm not putting myself in unnecessary danger, Ben. I'm always as careful as I can be. But I have to do this, there's no one else."

"But the vines don't grow much during the night," he said. "They're always surprisingly contained in the morn—"

She saw the moment when understanding hit, and his eyes went wide.

"You've been keeping them at bay all this time?" he whispered. "All by yourself?"

Azalea grimaced. "And it's growing beyond what I can

control," she said. "They've been getting steadily more aggressive." She turned back toward the door, and this time Ben followed her.

"Well, you're not alone tonight," he said forcefully. He gave her a sideways look. "Although don't think you're getting out of answering the rest of my questions. I have about a thousand."

She threw a grateful glance at him. "I have plenty of questions of my own. But first, we need to deal with the mess we left in my rooms. Doing it now is better than doing it later, trust me."

Ben looked confused, but he didn't question her, just grabbed the branch of candles and followed her out of his suite back down the corridor. She could see at a glance that the bound man was now in the enchanted sleep, no hint of care on his brow.

"I hope he wakes with a vicious headache," she muttered.

"He'll have much bigger problems than that," Ben promised darkly. "I intend to see him hanged, once I find out what he knows about Montgomery."

She stopped, staring at him. "Of course! You can actually do something about it! You'll be awake come dawn. That's amazing!" She shook her head. "I can't tell you how frustrating it is to actually manage to fight off an attacker and have no choice but to let them go free."

Ben's scowl grew. "Just how many times have these men come after you?"

Azalea shrugged. "This is the third time." She glanced at the doorway into her room, and wasn't quite able to restrain a shiver. "What do we do with...?" She gestured eloquently.

"Let me handle it," Ben said quickly, and Azalea was only too willing to comply. She busied herself with retrieving her sword from the corridor while Ben dragged the dead assassin's body out. He laid it beside his fellow conspirator and covered it with a blanket from Azalea's room. She'd quite liked that blanket, but she couldn't imagine ever using it again.

"I'm extremely glad that you're going to be awake to explain this mess to the guards," she said in a subdued voice. She wondered apprehensively if the curse would even allow her to leave the men as they were, for Ben to deal with in the morning. Hopefully it would be all right, given Ben was the one who'd actually felled them both.

She noticed that Ben had located his own sword while dealing with the assassin in her room, so she turned for the entranceway without another word. Ben kept stride with her easily, but he also remained silent.

They were just approaching the castle's large front doors when Azalea gave a sudden laugh.

"What is it?" Ben asked.

She shrugged. "I don't know. It's just so surreal, having you here. There's so much I want to tell you, and so much I want to ask you, that I don't know where to start."

Ben smiled. "I know what you mean. I can still hardly believe that you haven't been sleeping all this time. I used to feel like I knew everything about you, and now I don't know the first thing about your life."

"Well, my life is very dark," Azalea offered dryly. She sent him a wry smile to show she meant it light-heartedly. "There are some good things, though. I should take you to the firefly garden if we have time."

"The firefly garden?" Ben asked curiously.

"Better seen than explained," she said with a smile. "But that's only if I have time at the end of the night. Before those assassins showed up, I used to check on everyone first thing. But now I'm often in too much of a hurry."

"Check on everyone?" Ben repeated.

"Well, not everyone," she amended. "But I always look in on

my parents, assure myself they're where they should be, and not in danger. And on Uncle Mortimer, to check his notes and see if he's made any progress." She shot him a sideways glance. "And on you, if you're here."

Ben gave her a look she couldn't interpret, but he didn't comment.

"Then," Azalea continued briskly, "I pilfer some food from the kitchens."

"So why are we going outside?" Ben pressed.

"We've lost too much time already," said Azalea dismissively.

"Nonsense." Ben sounded stern, and he tugged at her arm, pulling her back into the building. "You have to eat something."

She protested, concerned about the time she'd already lost, but when he informed her that he was also starving, she gave in. He watched her gather a meager meal from the kitchen with a crease in his brow, but he didn't speak the thought behind the expression.

"So why are you so hungry?" she asked, as they made short work of some boiled eggs and a couple of thick slices of bread. "Didn't you have dinner with my parents only a few hours ago?"

Ben hesitated, and her suspicions were instantly raised. "No," he said carefully. "I actually came straight from Bant. They don't even know I'm here yet. I was just outside the city wall when the sun set, and as soon as I realized what the cloak was doing, I came straight to the castle." A shudder went over his tall frame. "And I can only be thankful that I did."

Azalea shivered as well, remembering how close to death she'd been when he had appeared, as if by magic, to fight off her attacker.

"You didn't plan your journey very well," she commented, "to be arriving so close to nightfall."

Ben was silent, and Azalea narrowed her eyes at him. "Ben?"

He sighed. "It wasn't a planned trip, exactly. I sort of...escaped."

"Escaped?" Azalea raised her eyebrows. "What do you mean?"

"Well, my parents didn't want me to return so soon," Ben said, clearly hedging. "They're, uh..."

"It's all right, Ben," Azalea cut him off, taking pity on his floundering. "They didn't approve of me before I ignited the curse, so I can only imagine how they feel now that it's active." She rolled her eyes. "I'm sure that once we break it, the lure of my kingdom will once again be strong enough to override their opinion of me personally."

Ben didn't answer, and Azalea frowned. He wasn't meeting her eyes, and she had the distinct impression that he was hiding something. She decided to let it go for the moment. There was so much to say and to ask. They couldn't cover all the ground at once, and she didn't really want to delve into Ben's fraught relationship with his parents as the very first thing.

"Let's go," Ben said at last, breaking the silence. They'd both finished eating their simple meal, and Azalea pushed herself up from the kitchen table she'd been perched on.

"I always start at the forest gate," she said, heading for the door. She felt Ben falter beside her, and she glanced over. Their gazes locked in a moment of wordless communication. The intensity of his expression made it suddenly hard to take in enough air. She knew he was remembering that horrifying moment in the clearing, just as she was, but neither of them put words to it.

"But unless the guards had some unexpected success yesterday," she hurried on, "I doubt there's much we can do there. It was so completely overrun last night that I had to abandon it. I didn't want to risk being pierced by the thorns."

Ben looked troubled, and she could see that he still didn't

like the idea of her battling the vines at all. She appreciated his forbearance in not saying so. Her battle with this physical symbol of the curse was all she had to keep her grounded in reality, and she didn't think she could keep her sanity if it was taken from her.

But when they reached the vicinity of the forest gate, even Azalea was tempted to stay out of the fight tonight. Not only was the area even more overgrown than the night before, but she could actually see the vines crawling across the ground.

"Is it always this bad?" Ben asked, alarmed.

Azalea shook her head, feeling shaken. "Usually they're not growing quickly enough for me to see the movement. This is definitely worse than last night."

"Tell me you're not going into that," Ben said, gesturing at the tangled mess before them.

"Definitely not," Azalea reassured him. "That would be a death wish." She frowned. "That is, I don't know for sure if letting the thorns pierce me would kill me."

"Let's not find out," said Ben darkly, shifting his position. He seemed to think the movement was subtle, but Azalea was perfectly well aware that its sole purpose was to put his body between her and the vines. She found she didn't mind in the least.

She led him along the wall, her dismay growing as she realized how large a stretch the vines had claimed. They walked for several minutes before they found a section of wall that seemed salvageable.

"This is much worse than last night," she said anxiously. "At this rate, I'm not going to be able to hold it for much longer. The walls will be completely overwhelmed."

"It's too much to expect from yourself, Azalea," Ben said, putting a hand on her arm. "The magic is too strong for you to hold it at bay by yourself."

Tears pricked at Azalea's eyes at the gentleness in Ben's voice. She felt like all she could do was cry tonight, but it wasn't really surprising. Two years without human contact, other than the recent visits from the assassins. Every sympathetic glance from Ben's eyes was like a balm to her lonely soul.

But she pushed the emotion down, knowing she had a job to do. "I have to at least try," she said firmly, gripping her sword in both hands as she stepped forward.

"Miss me?" she asked the vines cheerfully. "Sorry I'm late tonight, I hope I haven't inconvenienced you."

Glancing over her shoulder, she saw Ben blinking in surprise. She shrugged. "I talk to unresponsive things a lot these days." She sent him a grin, addressing him this time. "How's my form? And before you criticize, remember that you're the one who taught me how to use a sword."

Without waiting for his reply, she turned, slashing at the closest vine with a sure stroke. She was still a little sore from her fight with the assassin, but she had plenty of strength left for her task. She'd been building her endurance at this kind of exercise for a long time now, after all.

"It's not bad for a beginner," Ben said maddeningly, as the first severed stretch of vine fell, writhing, to the ground.

Azalea hacked off another two before turning to him, her expression indignant. "A beginner? I'll have you know that I—"

"Zayla!" Ben cried in warning, his wide eyes fixed on something over her shoulder.

CHAPTER TWENTY

Azalea

Azalea snapped back around, instinctively bringing her sword up in front of her. She was conscious of Ben lunging toward her, but most of her attention was on the vines. They had begun to writhe and twist, even where she hadn't slashed them. One reached toward her, and she lashed out at it, a familiar panic rising in her. She couldn't let them touch her.

She managed to chop off the first tendril, but three more were shooting toward her, jumping straight out from the wall like living creatures. Before she could react, something closed around her waist, and she let out a cry.

But it was only Ben, tugging her backward, away from the wall. His arm was firm around her, and he'd grabbed her so suddenly that she lost her footing, her boots dragging along the cobblestones.

Just as she thought she was clear, another vine shot out, wrapping around her foot just as the one on the western wall had done not many nights before. She gave a shout as Ben and the vine tugged her in opposite directions. She kicked out with her foot, trying to dislodge the vine's hold, but it was too strong.

And several more vines were snaking toward her across the ground, ready to join their fellow.

With a shout of anger, Ben seemed to see the offending growth. He released her, racing forward with his sword drawn. But the other vines that were coming for Azalea reared up, like deadly snakes, and raced toward him instead. Azalea's horrified cry cut off as the vines reached Ben. Instead of wrapping around him, as she'd expected, they merely buffeted him, shoving him to the side before redirecting back toward Azalea.

Fortunately she still had her sword in her hand this time. She was on the ground now, sitting upright, and she leaned forward. With several awkward slashes, she severed the vine still holding her foot. It fell away, the part around her boot drying up and dying instantly. She scrambled over to Ben, but he was already pushing himself to his feet.

Azalea felt the tendrils of another vine latching on to her skirt, and she whirled, hacking wildly. Again she felt Ben's arm around her, and as soon as she was free, she gave in to his insistent tug, and ran from the wall. They sprinted down a silent, empty street, stopping only once they had put a considerable distance between themselves and the wall. Azalea stared back the way they'd come. The vines were moving more slowly now, but they were definitely still moving, and they seemed to know which way she'd gone. They were piling up on top of one another, like a horrifying nest of snakes, slithering and gathering and coming for her.

"You've been fighting *that* every night for two years?" Ben demanded, sounding angry in his fear. "I thought you said you were always careful!"

"It isn't usually like that," Azalea panted. "The vines aren't normally so...aggressive. Usually I just hack away at them, slowing their progress for a few hours, and move on."

"What's changed then?" Ben asked.

There was still anger in his voice, but Azalea had the sense it wasn't directed at her. She could only imagine that Ben had plenty of bitter thoughts of his own about that day in the clearing, and how powerless they'd both been to stop the vines' attack.

"I don't know," Azalea said helplessly. "I mean, you're here, but how could the vines know that? It might be to do with the assassin, or with the visit from your dragon friend. But something definitely has the magic excited."

Ben frowned back at the vines for another moment. "Come on," he said curtly. "Let's get further away." He shot her a sharp look. "I trust you're not planning to try again tonight?"

Azalea shook her head, her brow furrowed. "I don't see how I can. The whole point of coming out here is to slow the vines' progress. But did you see the way they shoved you out of the way? They were coming for me. I think my presence is going to make them grow faster, if anything." Her frown deepened. "Let's walk around the city, at least. We'll keep our distance, so as not to wake the vines. But I want to see how bad it is."

Ben was anything but eager, but he followed her around the city's perimeter, keeping well back from the wall. Azalea's heart sank deeper the further they went. It was worse than she'd feared. The vines were pushing their way over the top of the wall almost everywhere, and the gate was a tangled mess of thorny twists, with no gaps visible.

"I hacked my way through there only hours ago," Ben said grimly, as they paused near the city's main entrance.

Azalea nodded. "They're growing so much more quickly than last night. And last night was much worse than the night before. Something's changing. It's escalating."

Ben frowned down at her, his concern clear in his eyes. Azalea could tell he wanted to lead her back inside, but she was determined to finish her circuit of the walls first. She tried to redirect Ben's mind as they walked.

"So what should I know? What have I missed?"

Ben gave a hollow laugh. "From the last two years? Where would I even begin?"

"Start with yourself," Azalea suggested. "How are you? I mean, how are you actually?"

Ben was silent for a long moment. She glanced up at him questioningly, and he held her gaze with his own.

"Yesterday? I was a mess. Now that you're awake, I feel like I'm alive again."

The soft intensity of his voice sent a thrill through her, and she looked quickly ahead again.

"And my parents?"

Ben's voice became more natural, but only slightly. "They'll be a hundred times better in the morning, when I tell them that you're still with us."

He sent her a soft smile, but a rush of guilt went through her at his words. "I've really ruined everyone's lives, haven't I?" she murmured sadly.

"What?" Ben stopped walking, turning to face her. "Azalea, what are you talking about? None of this is your fault."

Azalea pressed her lips together firmly, refusing to stop. "What about Uncle Mortimer?" she asked. "Has he discovered anything I don't know about?"

Ben sighed, jogging a few steps to catch up. "Nothing significant. Do you know about the concept of a counterforce in enchantments?"

"I do now," said Azalea humorously. "I've had a lot of time to study, and I know about lots of things I didn't bother with before. I've also seen in Uncle Mortimer's notes that he suspects Montgomery's curse has an unintentional counterforce rather than one he built in. But from what I can gather, he can't figure out what it is without fully understanding what's behind Montgomery's hatred."

"That's right," Ben said. "And as far as I know, he has no new insights on that."

Azalea sighed, glancing at the vine-covered walls. "So I can't fix that either. It seems I'm as useless as if I really were asleep." She frowned. "Maybe I should try again with the vines."

"Azalea!" Ben protested. "That's madness! Getting yourself killed won't help anyone."

"But I can't just do nothing," Azalea cried, her frustration bubbling over. "The city will be overrun."

"Let someone else worry about that," Ben said, his voice harsh.

Azalea raised an eyebrow. "I'm the crown princess of this kingdom, Ben. It's my job to worry about evil magic that's endangering my people."

They had stopped walking again, and Ben stepped toward her, putting a hand on her arm. She tried to ignore the sensation of heat that spread out from his touch.

"I'm not suggesting you should do nothing, Zayla," Ben said seriously. "But you can't expect yourself to achieve on your own every night what squadrons of soldiers can barely do during the day."

Azalea remained silent, still unconvinced.

Ben took a step closer, his eyes searching hers. "This isn't your fault," he said again.

Azalea dropped her gaze, her throat clogging. Of course he would try to shield her feelings, but no amount of kindness could take away the enormity of what she'd brought on her kingdom.

"Azalea." Ben's hand was suddenly on her chin, lifting her face gently. "What did you write in that letter to me?"

Azalea blinked, surprised by the sudden change in topic. She thought for a moment, then realized it wasn't such a change, after all. How did Ben know her so well?

"I said I was sorry," she whispered, not able to meet his eyes. "Ben, there are no words for how terribly sorry I am for all this. For what I put you through, for what everyone is still suffering."

"Stop." The anger in Ben's voice pulled her eyes to his. "This *isn't* your fault! You didn't do anything to earn this curse. You were a baby!"

"I'm talking about that day," she said, her voice a little hoarse. "In the clearing. I knew how significant the day was, and I wasn't even careful."

"We both should have been more careful that day," Ben acknowledged. "We made it way too easy. But the curse would have struck anyway."

Azalea shrugged. "Maybe."

Ben's hand slid from her chin to the back of her neck, his grip firm and reassuring. "Not maybe," he insisted. "Definitely. I've heard Uncle Mortimer say it a dozen times. We've seen without doubt how powerful Montgomery's magic is. The vines would have reached you, sooner or later. There wouldn't have been anything we could have done to stop them, not forever. It's been two years, and they're still trying to reach you, even though they pricked you that first day."

Azalea stared up at him, hardly daring to believe his words. "Is that true?" she whispered. "Uncle Mortimer really thinks that?"

"Absolutely."

She couldn't doubt Ben's earnest words. He wouldn't lie to her. She drew a shuddering breath, feeling an almost crushing weight lift from her shoulders. She had still been foolish, she had still made light of her parents' fears and caused them extra grief. But she hadn't been the one to doom her kingdom.

"It really isn't my fault?" Those frustrating tears were once again in her eyes, and this time she didn't try to keep them in. She let them fall, and just as he had back in her chamber, Ben wiped them away with his thumbs. The emotion in his eyes was almost too much for her to take.

"My poor darling," he whispered, his voice as soft as a caress. "Have you been blaming yourself all this time? As if you haven't had enough to carry."

He'd never called her darling before, or anything like it. The affectionate name on his lips made Azalea's heart bounce erratically in her chest, and she felt herself go still. Ben responded to her sudden change in body language, his own frame freezing. His hand still rested on her neck in an intimate gesture, and it was impossible not to be reminded of that morning in the clearing. Of the conversation that had been interrupted by the vines.

But no, that wasn't right. It hadn't been the vines that had interrupted whatever Ben was trying to say. It had been her. She'd pulled away from him because she'd been afraid. She could remember with perfect clarity the hurt and disappointment in his eyes.

And she'd had two long, lonely years to regret that decision.

The air between them was so tense she could hardly draw breath, but she somehow found enough to whisper, "There was more in that letter I left you."

Ben's eyes searched her face. "What was it?"

She gave a weak smile. "I wanted to know what you were going to say that day. I wanted my birthday surprise."

Ben's face was hard to read. "If it was really a surprise, I was more subtle than I realized."

Azalea pulled her bottom lip between her teeth, noticing the way Ben's eyes were drawn to the movement.

"You said it was different for you," she said softly. "What did you mean by that?"

Ben's gaze didn't falter, although Azalea had the impression he was choosing his words carefully.

"I meant," he said, "even though I had no more choice than you when our betrothal was formed, I felt like a fraud when you complained to me about it, as if you assumed I would agree. It was never a burden to me like it was to you."

"You've never been a burden to me," she cut in quickly, and Ben smiled.

"Even after two years, you're still interrupting this speech," he said, with a flash of humor.

Azalea couldn't help chuckling. "Sorry. You were saying?"

But despite having her attention, Ben was silent for a long moment. "I know you value our friendship," he said finally. "And that you don't see me as a burden, exactly. But our betrothal has been, hasn't it? It's been a frustration for you for as long as I can remember."

Azalea didn't respond, not wanting to be dishonest, but afraid of hurting him. Ben nodded, clearly aware of her feelings. She hadn't exactly tried to hide them all those years.

"It was different for me," he said simply. "Because I can't remember a time when I didn't want the betrothal. You were never just a friend to me. I've been in love with you for years, Zayla, long before the curse hit. I never had any interest in a life without you."

Azalea's breath caught in her throat at his simple, earnest declaration. What had she done to deserve the devotion of this impossibly wonderful man? How had the marriage arranged for her for purely political reasons become so much more real than any romance she could have dreamed of?

"Ben," she whispered, but there were no words. She didn't need them. Not with Ben. She reached out a tentative hand, laying it on his chest. She could feel the links of the chain under his shirt, marking him as hers. His muscles jumped under her touch, and she marveled at the strength there. All of a sudden, she curled her hand into the fabric of his tunic and pulled him toward her.

He didn't need more invitation than that. He stepped forward, closing the last small distance between them. His hand still cupped her head, but he swept his free arm around her waist, tugging her against him. For another blazing moment he held her gaze, but then he leaned down and pressed his lips onto hers, and she couldn't see or hear or feel anything else. There *was* nothing else. There was only Ben. The whole world was reduced to the sensation of his lips moving eagerly against hers, of his arm holding her tight and safe and close, of his fingers sprawling into her hair, sending tingles along her scalp. Both her hands clutched his tunic now, and she pushed up on her toes, the better to reach him as she returned his kiss with everything she had.

She'd thought many times about what it would have felt like if she'd let him kiss her that day in the clearing. She'd imagined it would be gentle, sweet, like Ben himself. And perhaps back then it would have been. But this kiss was born out of two years of desperation and loneliness and the terrible aching fear of losing what you love most in the world. It wasn't sweet—it was intoxicating. It wasn't gentle, but passionate and fierce and insistent. The intensity of the embrace made her head spin, and she threw herself into it without hesitation.

Any fear she'd had about their relationship, any resentment over its dictated nature, had been swept away long ago as the curse forced her to evaluate what really mattered to her. And no fear of any kind could survive through this moment—it was burned up by the searing joy of Ben's nearness, his steadiness, his love for her that she'd done nothing to deserve.

But just as she was wishing for the moment to never end, she felt a horrifyingly familiar pressure, an iron grip that tugged her away from Ben.

"No, no, no, not now," she moaned, even as she broke free of his hold. Could the timing be worse?

But there was no resisting the compulsion. A second later she had stepped away from the warmth of Ben's embrace, into the cold loneliness of her isolation.

CHAPTER TWENTY-ONE

Bentleigh

I ce seemed to shoot through Bentleigh as Azalea pulled back. His every sense had been aflame with the intensity of their kiss—a kiss he'd been waiting two years for—but there was no mistaking her forcefulness as she ripped herself away from him.

Anguish lanced through him as he saw the frustration in her face. Had he really misread what she wanted? Surely not. She'd been as wholehearted in their embrace as she'd always been about every aspect of life. He could still feel her lips on his, the warmth of her hands on his chest. It was everything he'd ever wanted, and he didn't know how he'd survive having it ripped away from him again.

"I'm so sorry, Ben," she gasped, still backing away from him.

"No, I'm sorry," he said gruffly, trying to pull himself together. "You'd think I'd have learned after last time, but I'm still pushing too hard. Still driving you away."

"No, you're not!" Azalea was so far away she was practically shouting by now.

Bentleigh hesitated, beginning to feel a new kind of confusion. Was he supposed to follow her, or did she want some space?

"I can't control it," she called. "It's the curse, it's forcing me back to the castle."

"What?" That snapped Bentleigh out of his internal agony. He hurried after her, catching her hand and attempting to pull her to a stop. "What do you mean?"

She tugged her way out of his grip with an unnatural strength and continued at a brisk walk.

"I mean I've reached my magical curfew," she said dryly. "It kind of makes more sense now that I know about the conceal-ment magic. The curse is forcing me to hide my presence, so in addition to destroying overt messages like letters, it forces me to undo anything that might too clearly point to my activities, and to return to the exact position I was in when I woke."

"Can't you fight it?" Bentleigh protested.

Azalea cast him a look. "What a good idea. Why didn't I think to try that?"

"Sorry," he said, his lips twitching in spite of himself. How many times these last two years had he longed to hear Zayla tease him, to see that look of exasperation in her eyes?

"I've tried everything I could think of," she continued, as he hurried to keep up with her. "I've tried subtle changes that an observant person might figure out, I've tried doing things that I physically can't undo. I've even tried leaving Liss a couple of times. But nothing works. Subtle things are allowed, like swiping some food, but not if they point directly to me. Things I can't undo just get completely erased by the magic. And if I leave the city, I'm compelled to turn around halfway through the night. By the time the sun rises, I always end up back on my bed, just where I started."

Her voice was bitter, and another stab went through

Bentleigh's heart at the thought of the lonely years she'd endured.

"What can I do?" he asked desperately, falling into step beside her. "How can I stop it?"

"You can't stop it," she said, resigned. "I don't expect you to do anything. I just wanted to make sure you know that I wasn't pulling away from you on purpose." Her eyes searched his anxiously. "I can be fairly stupid, but I'm not stupid enough to make the same mistake twice."

"Azalea," said Bentleigh, hesitantly. "It's not a mistake to pull away if this isn't what you want."

"It is what I want," said Azalea, once again sounding endearingly exasperated. "My point is, I liked kissing you. I wasn't trying to end it."

Her words set fire to something inside Bentleigh's heart, but he just hurried on alongside her. It turned out it was just about impossible to have a sentimental moment with someone while both moving at a brisk walk.

"Well, I'll stay with you," he promised. "Until the last moment."

She reached over as she walked, and squeezed his hand. "That's more than enough," she said softly.

Bentleigh returned the pressure with a slight smile, but his thoughts were heavy. It wasn't enough. It wasn't anywhere near enough. When he'd seen Azalea awake, he'd felt like everything had changed. But while he wouldn't trade this night for anything, now that the magic was reasserting itself, he was being reminded that nothing had changed. The curse was still holding Azalea captive, and the rest of the kingdom with her. And the vines had become a hundred times more aggressive.

They were nearing the castle now, their hands still clasped as they walked. Bentleigh knew time was running out, but he couldn't seem to marshal his thoughts. All he could think of was how it had felt to hold Azalea in his arms, pressed against him, and how his need to break the curse was more desperate than ever.

Apparently Azalea's mind was a little more functional.

"Is there anything you need to tell me?" she asked briskly. "Or need to ask?"

Bentleigh let out a breath. "There are so many things I need to tell you," he muttered.

Her expression softened. "I know. Me as well. But I meant practical things. Information that might help us break the curse. Like about this dragon."

Bentleigh shrugged. "There's not much more to tell there. Honestly, I'm not sure whether to confess to your parents that I went to a dragon." His tone turned wry. "I certainly don't intend for my own parents to ever find out."

Azalea sighed. "I have no idea how my parents would react, to be honest." They mounted the stone steps as she spoke, and within moments were crossing the entranceway. "There is one other thing you should know," she said suddenly. "About the assassins."

Bentleigh nodded for her to go on, suppressing the flash of rage that passed over him at mention of the men who had tried to kill her.

"They were looking for something in Uncle Mortimer's notes, the second night they came. They were instructed to look for a childhood journal, specifically one with any mention of Rosewood."

"Rosewood?" Bentleigh repeated, confused. "Isn't that a city?"

Azalea nodded. "It's where my mother grew up," she said. "And she dreamed about her own childhood that same night. It might be coincidence, but..."

Bentleigh nodded. "But definitely worth mentioning. I'll investigate."

"You're going to need to sleep sometime," Azalea reminded him, her eyes lingering on him with concern. "No offense, but you look pretty worn out."

"Trust me," said Bentleigh, as he followed her down the royal wing. "I've never felt more awake."

Azalea's steps had slowed, and the look of frustration on her face told Bentleigh that she was trying to fight the magic, futile as she knew it was.

"It's almost dawn," she said. She cast him a look, her expression suddenly vulnerable. "Can you tell my parents..." She trailed off, then groaned. "Oh, I don't know. There's too much to say for me to say it in a few words. Just tell them that I'm sorry, and that I love them."

"I will," said Bentleigh.

They were passing the unconscious assassin, lying next to the body of his companion, and he saw Azalea avert her eyes from the sight. She stepped into her room, and Bentleigh followed without hesitation. He watched her as she took her sword off, placing it deep in the recesses of a cupboard. Then she turned to the bed. Her defeated demeanor as she climbed onto it awoke his protective instincts, and his restraint suddenly fled.

"I hate this!" The words burst from him passionately. "I don't want to lose you again. I don't want to let the curse take you back, and I hate that there's nothing I can do to fight it!"

Azalea gave him a sleepy smile. "I know the feeling," she said sympathetically. "Sometimes it feels like the magic is a living breathing person. Like I'm a puppet, and Montgomery is pulling the strings."

White hot rage raced through Bentleigh at the name of the

evil enchanter, but he kept it in. Every last second with Azalea awake was too precious to waste on anger.

"That's why battling with the vines helps," she yawned. "It's like I can actually fight back."

She reached out for him, and he hurried forward to take her hand. When she tugged, he didn't stop to think. He just climbed up as well, lying himself down alongside her.

"Will you be here tomorrow night?" she asked softly.

Bentleigh ran the backs of his fingers along her cheek. "Where else could I possibly want to be?" he whispered. "You're here."

She gave a faint smile, her blinks getting longer.

"If I'd known it would be two years before we could be together again," she said sleepily, "I'd never have pushed you away that day in the clearing. I hope you know that."

A frown creased Bentleigh's forehead. "You weren't wrong to pull away, Zayla. I was the one moving too quickly."

Azalea gave a groggy chuckle. "If I wasn't wrong, then my punishment has been outrageously disproportionate to my crime."

Bentleigh's discomfort grew. He thought she'd accepted that none of this was her fault. He didn't like this talk of punishment, as though her lonely years were a direct result of her rejection of him in the clearing. How clouded had her thoughts about him and their relationship become by all she'd been through?

"Zayla," he started hesitantly.

"Mm?" Her eyes were still open, but barely.

"If you could be free of our betrothal, would you want to be?"

"What kind of a question is that?" Azalea's words were punctuated by a yawn. "I'm too asleep to discuss pointless hypotheticals, Ben."

Her eyes did indeed look shrouded by sleep. She obviously

wasn't completely under the curse's effects yet, however, because she leaned forward and pressed the softest of kisses to his lips.

Bentleigh reached for her, but she was already pulling away, her head settling back on the pillow and her hands clasped in front of her. He could tell the moment she succumbed, because the tumultuous emotions of the night were wiped away, replaced with the peaceful, lifeless expression he knew so horribly well.

As if on cue, a rooster crowed somewhere in the castle yard. Glancing at the window, Bentleigh noticed a faint gray light starting to filter into the room. He propped himself up on one elbow and studied Azalea's face. He knew beyond doubt now that she was in there, as spirited and enchanting and perfect as ever. But nothing in her face or posture gave the smallest hint of awareness.

He tried to push aside the discomfort created by her last words. She'd kissed him, hadn't she? Surely he shouldn't place too much importance on the fact that she hadn't actually answered his question. He felt a tiny stab of guilt. He should have told her, when she'd asked why it was different for him, that he had the power to break their betrothal if he chose. He was stronger now than he had been when they were children. He was capable of fighting his parents if he needed to. But breaking the betrothal was the last thing he'd wanted to suggest.

He lifted one of her suddenly cold hands, pressing it against his cheek. "I love you, Azalea," he whispered. "I'll never stop fighting for you."

And he never would. Against the curse, against his parents' latest plans for his life, against anything that threatened to harm her now or in the future.

The sound of stirring in the corridor brought him back to reality, and he gently lowered Azalea's hand onto the coverlet. Pushing himself off the bed, he cast a glance around the room, taking in the still-sleeping maid just beginning to stir on a cot. The assassin's blood was still staining the carpet where Bentleigh had run him through. But there was no sign of the notch in the bedpost where Zayla's sword had been stuck. So it seemed that the results of his own actions remained, but any damage done by Azalea had been erased. He shook his head at this evidence of the curse's work. It was powerful magic, no denying it.

A sudden thought struck him, and he pulled the cloak off with a swirl, spreading it over Azalea. He even tucked it in around her hopefully, but there was no change. The concealment magic that Rekavidur had recognized seemed to be peripheral to the original enchantment. Azalea's unnatural slumber was the heart of the curse, and it wasn't a surprise to find that the cloak had no power over it.

He retrieved it with a sigh, turning to the door just as he heard a shout from one of the guards. They'd clearly woken fully, and discovered the presents Bentleigh had left for them.

He strode purposefully from the room, ignoring both the guards' startled exclamations and the terror that lit the eyes of the now-conscious assassin whose hands and feet he'd bound.

"Your Highness!" one of the guards gasped. "How did you... that is, I didn't realize you were in Liss."

Or in the princess's chambers, was the obvious addition, but no one said it. "I arrived during the night," Bentleigh said curtly. The two guards stared at him in open astonishment, but he didn't intend to explain himself to them. "This man needs to be taken to the dungeons. He attempted to kill Princess Azalea."

The guards just stared, still at a loss for words. Bentleigh didn't wait for them to collect themselves. He strode off down the corridor in search of the king and queen, entrusting the incapacitated assassin to the guards.

He was full of nervous energy, but his sense asserted itself enough to make him realize that the situation wasn't of such urgency that he should burst in on King Victor and Queen Ianthe the moment they awoke. He resigned himself to speaking with them over their breakfast, and spent a restless half an hour pacing the dining hall.

As it happened, Mortimer was the first to enter, looking as weary as ever.

"Prince Bentleigh!" he exclaimed, on sight of his companion. "You've returned so soon! I'm delighted to see you."

"You'll be even more delighted when you hear what I have to say," said Bentleigh, hardly able to contain his news. Mortimer raised his eyebrows, but before he could ask, the door opened again. The queen entered, followed closely by her husband. Neither looked surprised to see Bentleigh, and their expressions were grim as he hurried forward to greet them.

"Bentleigh, my boy," said King Victor tensely. "I'm glad to see you back so soon, but what's this report about you apprehending more assassins?"

"Your Majesties," Bentleigh greeted them with a respectful bow, although he was still bouncing with energy. "It's a little complicated." He drew a deep breath. "I have some news. About..." He was going to say about Azalea, but something stopped him. Better not to give them false hope about her being free of the magic, perhaps. "About the curse."

"Tell us," King Victor said, looking taken aback by Bentleigh's uncharacteristic exuberance. The king gestured to the table, and Bentleigh found himself a place, standing behind the chair. He waited with barely concealed impatience while the monarchs settled themselves, then took his own seat to find them both watching him with piercing expressions.

"What news, Bentleigh?" Queen Ianthe asked. Even in his distraction, Bentleigh noticed that her gaze was sharper than he ever remembered it before.

"I'd better go back a little," he said, his eyes passing over Mortimer as well. "When I left in such a hurry last time, it was because I had received a message with a...suggestion as to someone who might be able to help with Azalea's curse."

"And?" The queen was sitting up painfully straight.

"I pursued the suggestion and met with...them," he said, making a last minute decision not to disclose the involvement of a dragon just yet. "They weren't able to undo Zayla's curse, but they provided me with a powerful artifact designed to counteract concealment magic. They told me to try wearing it at night when I was next in Listernia."

The king sat back, looking disappointed. "That sounds like a valuable talisman, but not relevant to our purposes, I'm afraid. Montgomery's curse has no flavor of concealment. His attack was very much in the open."

"That's what I thought," said Bentleigh eagerly. "But I thought I would try it all the same. I reached the city wall just before sunset last night, and I made sure I was wearing the cloak before dark. And the magic didn't take me!"

"What, you mean...you stayed awake?" Queen Ianthe asked in astonishment.

Bentleigh nodded. "That's right, Your Majesty. I was able to wander the city in the darkness, while everyone else slept." He drew a breath. "Or so I thought. I came straight to the castle, and I made an unbelievable discovery."

The queen's eyes were wide now, and the king had frozen with his hand halfway to his goblet.

"I wasn't the only one awake," Bentleigh said. He opened his mouth to tell them of Azalea's activities, but the words wouldn't come. He swallowed, embarrassed. This was no time to get choked by emotion.

But when he tried again, he still couldn't form the words. He frowned, struggling with himself. The sensation of choking wasn't to do with emotions. It was like he was physically incapable of speaking.

"You mean the assassins were also awake during the night?" the king demanded, his voice laced with alarm.

Bentleigh nodded slowly. "Yes, they were," he said. *And so was Azalea.* The thought formed clearly in his mind, but he simply couldn't transfer it to speech. What was happening?

"But this is disastrous!" Queen Ianthe said, her usual timidity nowhere to be seen. She cast Bentleigh a look that savored slightly of betrayal. He realized that from her perspective, he'd gotten her hopes up with his demeanor only to deliver terrible news. "What are we going to do? How can we protect her when we're all asleep?"

"No, Your Majesty, don't be alarmed," Bentleigh said quickly. "The assassins have been contained. They're not a further threat to Azalea."

"But how did they do it?" Mortimer demanded. "Did they have artifacts, like yours?"

"I believe so," said Bentleigh. *That's what Azalea told me.* The second part of his answer was locked inside, unable to come out. "But less powerful, as they didn't last all night."

He frowned. He'd been able to say that.

"It wasn't the assassins I was trying to tell you about," he said, frustrated.

"Yes, the effects of your artifact are certainly worth investigating," said King Victor, his voice somber. "And I can understand your excitement at any breakthrough, however small. But you must realize that this news is highly concerning to us. The presence of attackers in our kingdom, ones who can withstand the enchanted slumber, changes everything."

There was a scolding note to the king's voice, and Bentleigh realized that he too, was reacting to the clash between Bentleigh's tone and his words.

"There's more," Bentleigh said desperately. "That's not all I found."

"What else did you find?" the king pressed.

AZALEA WAS AWAKE. Shouting the words only made them louder inside Bentleigh's head. It made no difference to the fact that his mouth remained firmly closed. It was a truly horrible feeling, and he felt a fresh wave of sympathy for Azalea as he remembered her comment about being a puppet on a string.

The comparison drove away any lingering doubt as to what was happening. The traveling cloak still wrapped around his shoulders clearly had limits to its power. The concealment magic was strong, and although Bentleigh had been shielded from sleep, he couldn't pass on the truth of Azalea's situation any more than she could.

It was maddening.

"Bentleigh?" the queen prompted, at his prolonged silence. "What else?"

"The vines," said Bentleigh, casting around for what he'd learned. "They were growing last night." He tried to say that they'd been growing at night all along, but the magic morphed his words into the simpler statement. Clearly what he'd wanted to say would have revealed Azalea's activities too much, making it possible to figure out that someone had been fighting the vines at night. He would need to think like Zayla, to be subtle enough in his communication that he didn't trigger the curse's restrictions. "They've become more aggressive," he said, his voice at last matching the somber words he was saying.

"Yes, we've noticed that the last few days," the king said heavily.

Bentleigh shook his head. "Last night was a significant escalation. I think they're coming for Azalea, specifically." He'd been able to get that out, at least. It wasn't quite what he'd wanted to convey—about how the vines had gone into a frenzy at Azalea's proximity, reaching for her like so many thorny hands—but it was a start.

"Of course they are," the queen sighed. "They've been coming after her for two years."

"Mortimer," King Victor said, "I'm hoping you'll be willing to run experiments on Bentleigh's artifact."

"Of course," Mortimer said quickly.

"In the meantime," the king continued, "I need to interrogate these assassins. Find out where they got their artifacts, and why they came. One of the guards said he recognized the surviving assassin as a groom from the stables." He frowned. "My question is, if they really are simply more disgruntled servants, trying to take matters into their own hands to break the curse, how did they get artifacts powerful enough to cut through Montgomery's magic?"

Bentleigh opened his mouth to explain that he knew exactly where they'd gotten talismans powerful enough to counter Montgomery's curse. From the source itself. But the magic wouldn't let him speak. *But why?* he raged internally. How would that information reveal Azalea's presence? It was true that he only knew it because Azalea had told him. But she was also the one to tell him that the assassins' artifacts were weaker than his, and he'd been able to pass that information on.

But after a further moment of reflection, he recognized the difference. Even without Azalea's information, he'd observed for himself the temporary nature of the second assassin's protection.

He curled his hand into a fist involuntarily. Azalea was counting on him to communicate for her, to follow the clues provided by the assassins' presence. And he couldn't even tell anyone he'd spoken with her.

He raised his eyes and saw Mortimer watching him with furrowed brow. Bentleigh met the older man's stare, trying to communicate silently. Mortimer was an enchanter—could he somehow sense the magic that kept Bentleigh silenced? Mortimer's expression was thoughtful, but he said nothing.

Melodia and Miranda entered the room at that moment, full of questions. They quickly jumped into King Victor and Queen Ianthe's conversation regarding the assassins' possible motives and resources, but Bentleigh could barely focus on their words. He was running over his hours with Azalea, trying to think of a way to communicate her various revelations, when a shout from the corridor drew everyone's attention.

The king was already half standing by the time the door burst open and a guard hurried in.

"Your Majesty," the man puffed, clearly having sprinted to get there, "it's the vines. They're coming for the princess. We can't hold them."

CHAPTER TWENTY-TWO

Bentleigh

Bentleigh was halfway to the door before the man finished speaking, his hand feeling for the hilt of his sword. The rest of the group weren't far behind, but Bentleigh ignored them. All he could think of was Zayla, lying prone and powerless, unable to lift a finger to defend herself during the day, despite spending all her nights defending the whole city.

He raced down the corridor that led to the royal wing, reaching Azalea's suite within minutes. She was lying just as he'd left her, one hand clasped on her chest, the other lying along the coverlet. The maid was awake now, of course, and she was hovering anxiously by the window. She gave a quick bow at the sight of Bentleigh, and the king and queen close behind him, but her gaze was quickly drawn back outside.

Bentleigh crossed the room in several quick strides. He drew in a sharp breath at the sight that met him through the glass. The section of the wall that was within his sight was completely overrun by the vines. They had breached the top of the wall and grown right down its side, forming a seething, writhing mass on the cobblestones below. As he watched, he could actually see them growing, twisting and writhing like snakes as they reached toward the wall of the actual castle.

A gasp from beside him announced the presence of the queen. "She must be moved," Queen Ianthe said, her face ashen, but her demeanor more decisive than he ever remembered seeing it before. She turned to her husband. "What's the most secure room, Victor? One of the towers?"

The king nodded, and at a curt order, a guard ran ahead with various instructions. Bentleigh's eyes were still fixed on the vines. They had reached the base of the turret nearest to the city wall. As he watched, two squadrons of soldiers arrived, hacking and slashing their way through the growth. He let out a breath. It would buy them some time, but not enough. The vines were growing too quickly.

"The tower won't be able to protect her for long," he said desperately. "Even with every guard in the place fighting the vines, we'll be lucky to make it to nightfall, and then they'll all be powerless to help."

"We must be grateful the vines don't seem to grow much at night," the king said grimly.

"They do grow at night!" Bentleigh reminded them. "And rapidly." The information was apparently vague enough to be allowed.

King Victor stared at him. "That's impossible. How was the city not overrun months ago?"

Bentleigh tried to tell him exactly how, but of course he couldn't. "All I can tell you is that I saw them, last night," he said through gritted teeth. Again he noticed Mortimer watching him shrewdly, and he focused on the enchanter. "They were growing, almost as quickly as they are now."

"This escalation must have begun during the hours of darkness," said the queen, aghast. She turned to her husband. "What are we going to do, Victor?"

"We have to end this," Bentleigh interjected. "We have to break the curse."

"Maybe you should try the old wives' tale," Miranda said hesitantly, her eyes on Bentleigh. Mortimer shot her a look of exasperation, and she shrugged. "It seems like anything is worth trying."

"If you're talking about the kiss," Bentleigh said, "it won't work." In spite of everything, the smallest of smiles tugged at his lips as he thought about exactly how he knew that kissing Zayla wouldn't break the curse. "I guarantee it."

Mortimer was still watching him closely, and Queen Ianthe was giving him a strange look, so he schooled his features. It wasn't hard. Another glance out the window instantly dispelled the tingling warmth that had spread through him at the memory of Azalea's lips on his. The reality of the dire situation came rushing in to take its place.

"We need to find Montgomery," he said darkly.

"We have no leads on his whereabouts." King Victor's voice was weary.

"Actually..."

Mortimer's voice made every head in the room whip toward him. He swallowed visibly.

"It's not a lead, exactly, but this escalation with the vines is too sudden to be the natural progression of the curse."

"I was thinking the same thing," Melodia said, nodding briskly. "He must be putting more magic into it."

"How can he possibly have more magic?" Miranda protested. She gestured at her brother, her expression angry. "Poor Mortimer can barely function with how much this relentless battle between his magic and Montgomery's is costing him. How could Montgomery have anything more to give?"

"How could he have done any of this?" Melodia countered. She waved a hand toward Azalea, and the vines out the window.

"His magic is much stronger than we ever suspected, we know that by now."

"How does this help us find him?" King Victor cut over his cousins' argument impatiently.

Mortimer frowned. "If he's somehow increasing the magic, he's most likely close by. Not necessarily in the city, but not far away."

The king froze. "You think he's near? I'll double the patrols, and—"

He broke off, and Bentleigh thought he knew what King Victor was thinking. He couldn't afford to double the patrols, not when every available sword was needed to fight the vines' frenetic advance.

"I don't think it would help even if you did," Mortimer cut in. "Montgomery has evaded capture all these years. He wouldn't take a foolish risk. If he's come close, he's been careful. I imagine he's using magical means of concealment. Ordinarily that would be no great barrier. Any one of us," he waved to his siblings, "or in fact any enchanter of similar strength, could identify and dismantle such an enchantment. But with how strong Montgomery's magic is..." He shook his head. "I'm not sure any of us could break through whatever enchantment he's using to conceal him."

Bentleigh frowned, deep in thought. The cloak was a shield against concealment magic, but he didn't see how it could help. If he threw it over Montgomery, maybe, but then he'd have to find him first. He glanced out the window at the battle being waged against the vines. Time was too short for him to go scouring the countryside while wearing the cloak, in the hope that it would enable him to find the concealed enchanter. Not when he had no clue as to where to look for him.

He froze on the thought. But he did have a clue.

At that moment, several more guards entered the suite,

saluting to their monarch. At a nod from the king, two of them leaned down and gently lifted Azalea's limp form. It was all Bentleigh could do to remain by the window. Everything in him wanted to run forward, to insist on being the one to carry her, to hold her close to him, where she'd be safe.

But she wouldn't be safe. He couldn't single-handedly hold back the vines, and he couldn't stop her from being taken by the curse. He had to end it.

"I need to speak to the prisoner," he said abruptly.

The king looked over at him, startled. "The assassin?"

Bentleigh nodded. "I want to see what he knows." He longed to explain fully, to make everyone understand that he had very good reason to think the assassin could lead them to Montgomery. But he couldn't say so. Perhaps he could get the assassin to confess. That shouldn't be prohibited by the curse, surely.

"Very well," King Victor said. "I intend to interrogate him myself, once I have seen Azalea settled, and spoken to those in charge of fighting the vines. But you may see what you can find out in the meantime."

"Thank you, Your Majesty," said Bentleigh gratefully. He hurried for the door, and within minutes was descending into the dungeons. The guard at the entrance let him through with a nod, and he found the prisoner in the furthermost cell.

Bentleigh knew a moment of vicious satisfaction at the fear in the man's eyes when he saw the prince approaching. With incredible restraint, Bentleigh held in the murderous threats he wanted to unleash on the assassin. He wasn't likely to get answers that way.

"If you want to get out with your life, speak," he spat, without preamble. "Who sent you?"

The man just stared back at him, eyes wide. Bentleigh decided that time was too short for subtlety. He opened his mouth to tell the assassin that he knew exactly who sent him, and to demand where Montgomery could be found, but the curse prevented him from speaking. Frustration rose up in him. Surely it didn't activate the concealing magic for him to tell this assassin what the man already knew. But a quick glance around him showed that the guard had followed him in, and was hovering in the doorway. It was most likely the onlooker's presence which was sealing Bentleigh's tongue.

"King Victor has given me leave to interrogate the prisoner," Bentleigh said curtly. "I need to speak to him alone."

It was a sign of Bentleigh's standing in Liss that the guard barely hesitated before obeying. As soon as they were alone in the dungeon, Bentleigh turned back to the assassin.

"I know you were sent by Montgomery," he hissed. "I know about the talisman. Tell me where I can find him."

The assassin's gaze became shrewd. "What's in it for me? I'm bound for the gallows no matter what I say."

Bentleigh took a deep breath in through his nose, fighting the impulse to strike the man down where he stood. He met the prisoner's gaze steadily, trying to project confidence as he thought over his options. He couldn't promise clemency on King Victor's behalf, and the assassin must know that. But it seemed the man was waiting for Bentleigh to suggest a way forward.

"The way I see it," the assassin said quickly, "both our purposes can be served the same way."

Bentleigh snorted. "If you think we have any common purpose—"

"You want to find the enchanter, right?" the prisoner interrupted him. "And I want out of this cell. If you let me out, I'll take you to 'im."

Bentleigh cast him a contemptuous look. "Sure you will."

"I mean it," the man hissed. "I don't know where 'e's living, but I know where to find 'im at noon today."

Bentleigh narrowed his eyes, skeptical about believing a word the man said. "And where is that?"

"I ain't going to tell you for free," the prisoner grunted. "But we was told to report to 'im at noon today. That's why we 'ad to use our final talismans last night, to try to get the job done."

Get the job done? Rage raced over Bentleigh at this casual mention of the man's attempt to kill Azalea in cold blood. He pushed it down, trying to focus on his task.

"Thank you for that information," he said coldly. "I'll pass it on to the king, and something tells me you'll give us the location, whether you want to or not."

"I won't," said the man, with feeling. "I'd rather be 'anged than 'ave that enchanter find out I ratted on 'im. Besides," he shrugged, "I only 'ave to 'old out another couple hours before it'll do you no good at all to find out where the meeting place is."

Bentleigh frowned. "I will speak to the king. Perhaps he will spare your life if you lead him and his squadrons to the meeting place, but I can't guarantee it."

"Squadrons?" the man scoffed. "The enchanter won't reveal 'imself if there're squadrons. And you can be sure 'e'll know if there are soldiers 'iding nearby." He gave a shudder that told Bentleigh that he'd witnessed enough to recognize—and fear—Montgomery's power.

Bentleigh's heart sank at the realization that the man was undoubtedly right, but he didn't let it show. "Then it seems your information isn't especially useful after all," he said coolly.

"It is to you," the assassin insisted. "The king and 'is squadrons will be enough to ensure the enchanter won't show 'imself. But you...that's a different story."

Bentleigh gave a humorless laugh. "I didn't realize he was so eager to make my acquaintance."

"I didn't say that 'e is," the prisoner said. He gave Bentleigh a meaningful look. "But what I do say is that 'e's expecting to meet two of us at noon today, and there're two of us 'ere." He measured Bentleigh with his eyes. "And you're tall, like the other one was tall."

Bentleigh was silent, thinking it over. He didn't trust the man, not in the tiniest measure. But that didn't mean he was wrong. Bentleigh pictured the other assassin, the one he'd killed. They were fairly similar in build. Perhaps if he was cloaked, he could pass for the other man for long enough to get near Montgomery. His mouth formed a grim line. That was all he needed. He cast his glance over the assassin.

"And as soon as we're out of here, you'll pull out another talisman and incapacitate me somehow, I imagine," he said dryly.

The man raised his hands in a gesture of helplessness. "I been searched twice already, but feel free to 'ave another go."

Bentleigh frowned. He didn't like how short time was, and the advantage that gave the prisoner. But he pictured the vines curling their way toward Azalea even now, and he knew that he had to try, even if it was a little desperate. He couldn't stand to do nothing.

At that moment, he heard a familiar voice in the corridor, hailing the guard. Without a word to the prisoner, he slipped through the doorway to greet King Victor. Mortimer was also there, and he nodded a greeting.

"Did you discover anything, Bentleigh?" the king asked, sounding weary.

"I may have, Your Majesty," said Bentleigh. "I know this will sound like I've lost my wits, but..." He drew a breath, steeling himself for the king's reaction as well as looking for words that the curse would allow. "I think I can discover something—something significant, but it requires me to take the prisoner out of the city. Alone."

King Victor's eyebrows were halfway to his hairline before

the end of Bentleigh's speech. "I can't allow you to do that, Bentleigh," he said. "For your own safety as much as for the risk of losing the prisoner."

"You know me, Your Majesty," Bentleigh said seriously. "I wouldn't take such a risk unless I considered it absolutely necessary. I have no concerns about my ability to defend myself against the prisoner himself. And I'm not suggesting that I go completely alone. I know you need as many men here as you can have, but I was going to request that you send a squadron after us. But they would have to follow at a substantial distance."

The king still looked far from convinced, but to Bentleigh's surprise, it was Mortimer who spoke.

"Your Highness," he said, his gaze fixed on Bentleigh's face. "There's more you aren't telling us, isn't there?"

"That is manifestly obvious," the king interjected dryly.

"Yes, but I mean about what you saw in the hours of darkness," Mortimer clarified.

Bentleigh opened his mouth to answer, but any attempt to give details caused his throat to close up. He gave a painful nod.

"Am I right in guessing that you *can't* tell us?" Mortimer pressed. "That you're being prevented from doing so, by means of magic?"

Relief soared in Bentleigh's chest at the older man's astuteness. He couldn't even nod this time, but his silence and his wide eyed stare seemed answer enough.

"I thought so," Mortimer said. He frowned. "That complicates matters."

"I should say it does," the king growled. "I don't like making decisions without all the information."

"I understand, Your Majesty," said Bentleigh remorsefully. "I wish you weren't in that position." He swallowed, meeting the king's gaze. "But all I can tell you is that I'm convinced I need to do this. And that my only aim is to break the curse and free Azalea. I can only ask...do you trust me?"

King Victor searched Bentleigh's face for a long and tense moment. Then he glanced at his cousin. He let out a long breath before he spoke.

"Yes, Bentleigh." His voice was quiet but even. "I do trust you."

He knew he had bigger things to worry about, but Bentleigh couldn't help the way his heart swelled at the words. It was absolutely impossible to even imagine such a response from his own father in an equivalent situation.

"Thank you, Your Majesty," he said. "I will do all in my power not to fail that trust."

Having made his decision, the king didn't waste any time. The arrangements for a squadron to follow a subtle trail to be left by Bentleigh were swiftly made, and Bentleigh was given leave to escort the prisoner outside the city wall.

But he had one task to do first.

He was striding toward Mortimer's suite when a voice hailed him. He turned to see a courier hurrying toward him. To his astonishment, he recognized the man's uniform as belonging to a royal Bansfordian servant. As with the messenger from Albury, this courier hastily excused himself as soon as Bentleigh had taken the missive. No doubt he was eager to return to Bansford before dark.

Bentleigh broke the seal and spread open the single sheet of parchment. It was brief, and to the point.

Bentleigh
You will return home <u>immediately</u>.
We expect a delegation from Entolia next week, at which time we

will formally accept the proposed alliance between you and Princess Zinnia.

You will be in attendance.

There was no name underneath, only the royal seal, as if this personal note was some kind of official missive. Not that Bentleigh needed the proof—he had no difficulty recognizing his father's handwriting. He grimaced. It seemed his parents had been angry enough about his flight to send someone across the border after all. He wondered where along the route the courier had passed the previous night.

Bentleigh scrunched the letter into a ball and shoved it in the pocket of his cloak, dismissing it from his mind. His fingers twisted the chain around his neck in a habitual gesture. His father's menacing words left him unmoved. After the events of the night before, the idea that he would abandon his betrothal with Azalea was laughable. No force in the world could change his mind now, his parents included.

Mortimer had returned to his own suite by the time Bentleigh reached it. The older man was poring over his notes, but he stood hastily on Bentleigh's entry.

"I don't have long," Bentleigh said curtly. "But I want to make sure I properly understand the concept of a counterforce. You said that all enchantments have a counterforce, yes? That the magic we know is not the strongest force in the world, and therefore is inherently defeatable?"

"That's right," Mortimer nodded.

"And you said that an enchanter can intentionally build that counterforce into his enchantment, specifying either aloud or internally the means of undoing the curse."

Mortimer nodded again.

"But if they haven't done so, then the counterforce will be the natural opposite of whatever force had power over the enchanter at the time the enchantment was cast."

"An excellent explanation of the basic concept," said Mortimer, sounding like one of Bentleigh's tutors. Not that he'd ever had a tutor in magic, of course. "And the difficulty in identifying the counterforce that would break Azalea's curse is that we do not know what force had power over Montgomery when he cast it."

Bentleigh nodded. Hopefully he would soon change that.

He drew a breath. "One more question. If Montgomery dies, will the curse be broken?"

"I don't know," Mortimer replied, his voice heavy. "I would have said no, since the curse was cast long ago and should no longer be dependent on its caster. But perhaps it would work, since Montgomery's magic is clearly still active, battling with mine."

Bentleigh frowned, turning away from the grief in the other man's eyes. If he had the chance to take Montgomery down, he had fully intended to do it, and he didn't want to be reminded of the grief it would bring Montgomery's twin. But it sounded like he would be foolish to do anything so irrevocable unless he was sure he had identified the counterforce.

He opened his mouth to pass on Azalea's comment about Rosewood, but the magic prevented him. No matter. There was another way for Mortimer to get that information.

"This is for you," he said, pulling his cloak off and holding it out.

"Ah yes, the artifact," Mortimer said, taking it from him. "I promised Victor I'd examine it."

"No, I mean it's for you to wear," Bentleigh said. He had given it some thought, and he'd decided that Mortimer was the one most likely to be useful to Azalea. "I expect to be back before nightfall, and to reclaim it from you. But in case I'm not, make sure you're wearing it when the sun sets."

He frowned. "In fact, if I haven't returned by an hour before dark, will you wait for me at the northern gate?" His voice turned grim. "Or at least, as near to it as the vines will allow. Make sure you wear the cloak."

"You don't want to wear it yourself, Your Highness, in case you're still traveling back when darkness falls?"

Bentleigh shook his head. He didn't explain himself, but he had realized that as an enchanter, Montgomery would likely be able to sense such a powerful artifact. He would give himself away as an imposter before he ever reached his target.

Mortimer frowned at him. He clearly knew there was more Bentleigh wanted to say, but he didn't press him.

"Very well, Your Highness. I will do as you ask."

Bentleigh gave a curt nod. "Thank you." He hesitated. "And wish me luck."

CHAPTER TWENTY-THREE

Bentleigh

"You said it would take an hour," Bentleigh said, his voice hard. "It's been an hour. You have five more minutes before we're done." He laid a hand on the hilt of his sword meaningfully.

"We're almost there," said the assassin quickly. "That's the grove, up ahead."

Bentleigh glanced at the trees looming in front of them before casting his eyes upward. He judged that they were right on target for the noon rendezvous. It was a relief. He'd been concerned they would miss the deadline, traveling on foot as they were. But it would have been too suspicious if the assassins had left Montgomery on foot and arrived back on horseback.

He spared a guilty thought for the horse he'd brought from Bansford. He hoped the groom he'd sent had succeeded in untying it from outside the city gate, and leading it to the castle. It depended on whether the guards and soldiers had been able to clear the main gate of the vines. Bentleigh and his companion had exited via the smaller northern gate, and it had taken them some time to get through it.

He dismissed the matter from his mind as they drew near

the grove, his senses on full alert. Before they reached the tree line, he fell back a step, eager to keep his eyes on the assassin. He didn't trust the man in the least.

"We met 'im in this clearing," his guide muttered. "But 'e never showed 'is face."

Bentleigh pulled on the hood of his borrowed cloak, making sure his own face was shadowed. He had to hope the deception would be enough for Montgomery to show himself this time.

They shifted forward, just out of the tree line, both of them glancing sharply around the clearing. There was no sign of movement, not even the slightest sound. Bentleigh realized after a moment that the silence was too absolute to be natural. Not a bird chirped, not a creature shifted in the undergrowth. Montgomery must have some kind of concealment charm on the area. It was encouraging that it had let Bentleigh through, although not promising for the chance of back up from the squadron following half an hour behind.

"Well, what is your report?"

Both men's heads whipped toward the sound. The voice came from the shadow of the trees on the other side of the clearing, its words impatient, as though they were halfway through a conversation rather than just greeting.

"Your Lordship, sir," said the assassin, stepping forward quickly. "I'm reporting back as instructed."

"Yes, I can see that," the voice replied, cold and smooth. Bentleigh could see the dark outline of a hooded figure, but it was impossible to discern details from this distance. "Did you succeed in your task?"

"Not in killing the princess," the assassin admitted gruffly. "But I did succeed in your other assignment." He took a swift step to the side, out of Bentleigh's reach, as he gestured to him. "This is the prince from Bansford. I brought 'im to you, like you said."

Bentleigh froze. His first instinct was to draw his sword immediately; his second was to run. But he quashed both impulses. He was here to confront Montgomery. It didn't much matter if the assassin had been leading him into a trap. It had still achieved the intended goal of getting him close to the enchanter.

Bentleigh stepped forward boldly. "Show yourself."

"Gladly, Your Highness." Montgomery emerged from the trees at last, pacing deliberately into the middle of the clearing. His hood was still up, and his face was shadowed.

"You see," the assassin interjected gruffly. "I brought 'im. I tricked 'im into thinking that 'e could pose as the other one."

"You have surprised me," Montgomery congratulated the man smoothly. "You've shown considerably more intelligence than I ever expected from you." Bentleigh couldn't see his eyes, but his head was still turned toward the prince. "Evidently not enough intelligence to predict this, however."

On the words, Montgomery's hand flicked out, and a dagger flashed across the clearing. Bentleigh flinched, reaching instinctively for his sword, but the blade wasn't aimed at him. The assassin had no time to react, crumpling to the floor of the clearing without a cry. Bentleigh couldn't help looking down at him. A look of surprise was frozen on his lifeless face. It was no more than the man deserved, but Bentleigh's stomach still churned at the sight.

"Now then, Prince Bentleigh," said Montgomery calmly. "It seems we are alone." He lowered his hood at last, and Bentleigh found himself staring at the enchanter's face. The twins were not identical, but Montgomery's features were still familiar enough to mark him as Mortimer's brother. The cold and calculating expression, however, gave the face before him an entirely different cast.

"I suppose you came because you wish to break the curse,"

Montgomery said, when Bentleigh failed to speak. He gave a smile so cold it sent a chill down Bentleigh's spine. "Would you believe, that is my desire also?"

"No," Bentleigh said grimly. "I wouldn't believe it."

"Well you should," said Montgomery amicably. "It serves no purpose of mine to see the curse continue as it is. What reason do I have to wish the fair princess harm?"

"That's a question I've been asking myself for eighteen years," said Bentleigh through clenched teeth.

"I can imagine."

Montgomery spoke lightly, and his casual air made Bentleigh's blood boil. He longed to strike at the enchanter, to make him pay for all he'd done, for all he'd put Zayla through, for the way his magic still threatened her life. But he held it in, reminding himself that what he most needed from Montgomery was information.

"It's a sensible question," Montgomery continued, "since the brat was, and still is, nothing to me. What do I care if she lives or dies?"

Bentleigh took a step forward, unable to help himself. One hand was still on the hilt of his sword, but the other was balled into a fist.

"No need to get excited, my dear boy," Montgomery said mildly. "My point is that the princess was never my target."

"Did you curse the wrong baby? How careless of you." Sarcasm dripped from Bentleigh's words, and the enchanter gave a tolerant laugh.

"Of course not. But she was only ever a means to an end. My target was always my delightful cousin."

Bentleigh frowned, his sense reasserting itself over his anger. "The king? So it was hatred of him that drove you all along? Why exactly do you hate him so much? Is it just jealousy? I know you turned on him when his father died, and he was crowned king."

"When he was crowned king?" Montgomery repeated.

Bentleigh thought he saw anger flash across the enchanter's face, but it was gone so quickly he couldn't be sure. Montgomery's features were smooth again as he gave another grating laugh.

"Trying to figure out the counterforce, are you? Is that what my spineless twin told you? That I was so careless as to leave my enchantment open to an unintended counterforce, so that all you have to do is dissect my emotions to find the key to your lovely princess's curse?"

Bentleigh remained silent, his expression hooded.

Montgomery grinned easily at him. "My poor deluded child, do you think there's anything you know about enchantments that I couldn't recite in my sleep?"

"How could you have built a counterforce into your curse?" Bentleigh said bluntly, abandoning the attempt to hide his hand. "You intended for the curse to kill Azalea, plain and simple. Death is irrevocable. What counterforce could you have built into that?"

For a long moment Montgomery regarded him in thoughtful silence. "Is that what Mortimer told you?" he said at last, his voice soft. "I see I was right. My brother truly did get cold feet before ever the curse was activated."

An ominous feeling washed over Bentleigh. "What is that supposed to mean?" he growled.

Montgomery's amusement was once again evident. "The curse did precisely what it was intended to do," he said simply. "It was always meant to kill Victor, certainly, but I wished to punish him first. I flatter myself that sixteen years of fear and anxiety did so effectively."

Bentleigh frowned. "How would the curse kill King Victor?

You mean Azalea was never going to die from pricking her finger?"

"Not thanks to my brother's intervention," Montgomery said pleasantly.

Bentleigh's frown deepened, but he wasn't willing to give the enchanter the satisfaction of admitting that he didn't understand. Montgomery clearly knew it, however, because his smile grew even wider.

"Let me be more clear. Up to and including the moment that the princess pricked her finger, everything proceeded perfectly according to the plan Mortimer and I made together. My dramatic curse at the brat's christening, my dear brother's no less dramatic rescue. The gnawing uncertainty suffered by everyone, as to whether his intervention had been successful. The ease with which the fool child allowed herself to be reached by the thorns."

Bentleigh flushed then paled, the old guilt at his part in that event washing over him. Montgomery's sharp eyes were riveted to his face, and the older man's expression grew a trifle more smug.

"I don't see how any of that would kill King Victor," Bentleigh said, attempting to sound derisive.

"Ah," sighed Montgomery, "that's because things did *not* proceed to plan from there. It wasn't the curse itself that was supposed to claim Victor's life. It was the counterforce."

He obviously saw Bentleigh's startled look, because he raised one expressive eyebrow.

"Oh yes," he said softly, "we built in a counterforce, quite intentionally, I promise you. Mortimer was supposed to tell Victor what it was—having figured it out innocently, and to his own dismay, you understand. He was to explain that since my curse involved taking a life out of hatred, only a life freely given in love could reverse it. And not the life of some convicted criminal, or some such. It would have to be someone who loves the princess more than life itself."

Bentleigh's heart was racing, and his skin prickled uncomfortably.

"Mortimer would whisper it to the king quite confidentially, of course," Montgomery continued. "He would explain, with *such* grief in his eyes, that he had no desire to mention such an abominable solution to someone as gentle as the queen. That way we could be sure it would be Victor who exchanged his life for his child. And we had no doubt he would do it. It would be the final proof of his unfitness to rule—the irrefutable evidence that he cared less for the good of his kingdom than for the brat princess he had the audacity to name as heir in place of the prince he should have had."

Bentleigh's mouth was so dry, he could hardly force his tongue to form words. "You're lying," he said thickly. "Mortimer isn't part of this. He's on our side."

Montgomery chuckled softly. "In a way, you seem to be right, my boy. I have long suspected that he had a change of heart. Not enough to tell the truth, of course. Just enough to fail to fulfill his final task in telling the king of the counterforce. I can only assume he decided it was best to let the curse run its course, to claim the life of the false heir rather than to actually kill the king." He sighed. "Perhaps he is right, but I am still quite attached to our original plan, I must confess."

"Or maybe Mortimer doesn't intend for Azalea to die at all," Bentleigh challenged. "Maybe he's just waiting until the curse expires."

Montgomery laughed. "Expires? With the amount of power we put into that curse, it will last for a hundred years before it expires without intervention." He grinned. "Are you willing to wait that long for your bride?"

Bentleigh's fist was clenching and unclenching in his anger, and he'd never felt more powerless.

"Not that it would come to that, of course," Montgomery said comfortably. "The thorns will claim her long before that. If I'm honest, I'm impressed Victor has managed to hold them back for as long as he has." He wiggled his fingers suggestively. "But I've given them a little something extra since I returned to the area, to meet with my," he cast a careless glance toward the dead assassin, "associates." He looked back at Bentleigh. "If the vines don't claim her today, they will tonight, when Victor's soldiers are unable to defend her." He raised an eyebrow. "Unless Victor can bring himself to pay the price that must be paid, of course."

Bentleigh was silent, waves of horror and anger crashing over him. Against his will, the image of Mortimer's face was dragged up before his sight, innocent and weary and so well-meaning. And all along a snake in their midst. He remembered with perfect clarity that first conversation he'd had with Mortimer about enchantments, the day Azalea pricked her finger. Bentleigh had asked Mortimer what he meant by his prediction that if Montgomery built in a counterforce, it would involve a "vicious remedy".

Oh, I'm sure you can imagine the kind of thing. A death curse that can only be prevented by someone else agreeing to die in the target's place.

Had that been his attempt to give a clue, prompted by his guilty conscience? Anger rose up within Bentleigh. Mortimer was even worse than Montgomery. At least the enchanter before him made no pretense of being anything other than the evil murderer he was.

"Honestly," Montgomery said lazily, his eyes on Bentleigh's face, "I'm surprised no one has figured it out before now. Surely they must have realized I had an ally with magic as strong as my own? The power we put into our enchantment was far too much for me to produce alone."

As the enchanter spoke, Bentleigh realized that for all his bravado, he looked as tired as his brother. His face was prematurely lined, the evidence of what Mortimer had called an ongoing battle etched into his face.

Bentleigh wanted to scream aloud at the thought of Mortimer's guileless confusion when he talked about how impossibly strong Montgomery's enchantment was. Too strong for him to counter, he'd said. When all along, there had been twice the magic fueling the curse, and no magic countering it. How had they all been such fools?

"Why are you telling me all this?" he demanded, his voice shaking.

"Isn't it obvious?" Montgomery said. "I want you to do what Mortimer has failed for two years to do. I want you to tell Victor what he has to do in order to set his mewling child free." His expression darkened. "I want his death to be at his own hand, so that all the kingdom can see how weak he truly is." His face cleared, and he smiled sardonically at Bentleigh. "I imagine you'll be willing to carry that message, after all. With Victor gone, and your princess awake, you'll be king of Listernia within weeks."

Horror crawled up Bentleigh's spine. Did this man truly think everyone was like him? Wanting only power, and not caring who they trampled to get it? But he didn't say as much. Revealing his true feelings on the matter wouldn't serve his purpose at all.

"Tell me," Bentleigh said hoarsely. "Tell me what...the king... has to do."

"At last we see eye to eye," said Montgomery pleasantly. "The remedy is really quite simple. Someone who loves the princess more than life itself must give their own life in her place. They must be touching her at the time they take their life, and it must occur at the exact moment of sunset."

"The exact moment?" Bentleigh said, attempting to sound nonchalant, although his throat was so dry he could barely get the words out. "That's very specific."

Montgomery chuckled. "Well, enchantments always sound best when they're dramatic that way. But you're quite right—the exact moment of sunset isn't actually easy to ascertain. Within five minutes either side would be quite safe, I imagine."

Quite safe, Bentleigh thought numbly. It was good to know there was a way to be *quite safe* when taking your own life to free someone from an evil curse.

"Thank you for being so helpful," he said blandly. As swiftly as he could, he whipped his sword out, lunging for the enchanter.

Montgomery raised a lazy hand, weaving it through the air in front of him.

"Tut tut, that's not polite," he said, as Bentleigh felt his muscles freeze. He was suspended in an uncomfortable position, mid-lunge.

The enchanter strolled forward, leaning down so that his face was inches from Bentleigh's.

"Most rude, in fact," he scolded. "If I didn't need your assistance, I think I would strike you down here and now. Your kingdom deserves its own punishment, you know. Most offensive, the way they've turned my kind into criminals simply for existing."

Rage surged white hot through Bentleigh's every nerve, but he couldn't do more than blink. The freezing enchantment was strong, although he could see in the sudden tension of Montgomery's frame that it was a strain for him to keep it going.

"Did you really think you could just pull out your little sword and run me through?" Montgomery asked mockingly.

"You should have predicted how that would go. Freezing charms are, after all, something of a specialty of mine." He gave an unpleasant smile. "I'm sure your parents can tell you all about it."

Montgomery regarded Bentleigh in silence for a moment. "I'll give you a little while to cool down, I think," he said pensively. "Then you can run along back to the castle, and pass on my message. I imagine Victor will want to act on it this sunset, given the activity of my vines." With that condescending farewell, Montgomery strolled away, and out of Bentleigh's sight.

"A little while" turned out to be several hours. When the enchantment eventually dropped, suddenly and without warning, Bentleigh collapsed painfully to the ground. Every muscle was on fire with agony from the hours of being trapped in position, but even that wasn't his greatest concern. His desperation had grown during the hours of impotence, as he pictured the vines creeping ever closer to Azalea's still form. By the time he was again free to move, he was in a state of near panic.

It had been many many hours since he'd slept, but he couldn't afford to give in to the exhaustion that dragged at both his body and his mind. He forced himself back to his feet, not sparing a glance for his dead companion as he set his path toward the capital. He had hoped to be back long before the sun set, but at this rate, he wouldn't have much time to spare.

His heart raced at the realization that he'd left the artifact with Mortimer, the person in all the castle who he least wanted to be awake when Azalea was. What would happen if Mortimer had access to her when she was unprotected by guards? She'd never think to defend herself against him—she trusted him almost like a parent.

Bentleigh let his fear for her fuel his steps, focusing on his anger at the duplicity and venom of the twin enchanters. It was safer than dwelling on the painful reality of what he knew he had to do. He didn't think he'd lose courage to follow through when the moment came, but it was still something he preferred not to dwell on. Montgomery may have intended his message for King Victor, but Bentleigh had no intention of carrying it to the king.

His legs were burning by the time the wall came into sight, and he drew up in horror. In the few hours he'd been gone, the situation had become so much worse. The stones of the wall weren't visible at all—the whole structure was a tangle of thorns and brambles, cutting the city off from the rest of the kingdom. The vines were growing so profusely they'd even begun to reach outward from the wall, as well as climbing over it. He even had to hack his way through some outlying tendrils that had stretched from the wall to the nearest trees.

He was only able to identify the location of the northern gate by following the path up to it. The actual door wasn't visible. Vines were growing too thickly over it, writhing and stretching and looking more like snakes than ever. By the time he identified it, the sun was hanging dangerously low in the sky. He raised his sword, releasing his fear and anger in a shout as he struck at the vines. They curled back on themselves as they were severed, falling before his relentless advance.

It felt like an eternity, but finally he sliced his way through to the gate itself. He was grappling with it when it swung open from inside, revealing the pale face of Mortimer.

"Your Highness," he said. "I thought I heard you."

Bentleigh froze, for a moment bereft of speech. He had forgotten that he'd asked Mortimer to meet him here. Anger once again swept over him, lanced by the bitter grief of the man's betrayal. It took every ounce of self-control not to lash out, to strike out at the manipulative enchanter, at the very least to confront him.

But he needed to be more careful. He'd seen what Montgomery was capable of, and he had no desire to be similarly incapacitated by Mortimer. He could see his own traveling cloak around Mortimer's shoulders, and he needed to get that back before any confrontation.

"The vines are worse," he said carefully, trying to read how much Mortimer knew, and whether the enchanter intended to show his true colors. Did he know that Montgomery had exposed him? Or had he been unaware of the assassins' true purpose?

"Much worse," Mortimer agreed grimly. "They've moved Azalea, but I'm still not sure it's enough."

"I'd better take my cloak back," Bentleigh said carefully, watching Mortimer's face for signs of defiance.

The enchanter hesitated, running a hand down the fabric. "I confess, I would like to observe the effects of the curse during the hours of darkness. It might be helpful for my research."

Bentleigh tensed, his hand sliding surreptitiously to his sword. He obviously hadn't been as subtle as he intended, because Mortimer's eyes followed the gesture.

"Although," the enchanter amended, his gaze still on Bentleigh's weapon, "I suppose you'll have more success than I will in fighting off the vines during the night. Perhaps you'd better take it after all."

"Good thinking," said Bentleigh, trying not to seem too eager as he seized the cloak. He knew his voice sounded stilted, but he couldn't help it. A small sigh of relief escaped him as the cloak settled around his shoulders. At least Azalea would be safe from Mortimer once darkness fell.

"So what did you find out?" Mortimer pressed, glancing at the sun. By Bentleigh's guess, they had less than fifteen minutes. "Was your...mission...successful?" He cast his eyes behind Bentleigh. "I don't see the other man."

"He's dead." Bentleigh voice was blunt. "I'll tell you all about it in a minute," he lied smoothly. "But first I need to know where they took Azalea."

Mortimer nodded, looking wary as he watched Bentleigh's face. "Of course. I'll show you."

He hurried toward the castle, and Bentleigh followed, keeping his eyes pinned on the enchanter's back. He didn't intend to let the man out of his sight until the sun dropped below the horizon.

As they approached the castle itself, Bentleigh was alarmed to see that vines were growing right up to the building in several places. The streets had cleared by now, and no one was lingering anywhere near the growth. They entered the castle at a jog, nodding to the guards on duty. Bentleigh knew he didn't have time to seek out the king and queen. Everyone they passed was preparing for nightfall, guards laying out pallets, and servants disappearing to their allotted sleeping areas. Mortimer led Bentleigh up a turret on the corner of the building furthest from the forest gate. The light was fading fast as they climbed, and by the time they could see the door up ahead, Bentleigh knew he was running out of time.

"Wait," he said curtly, and Mortimer paused. He glanced inquiringly back at Bentleigh, his brow furrowing in confusion as the prince pushed past him. "Don't come any further. I don't want you in her room."

"What do you mean?" Mortimer asked, looking baffled.

The ring of steel sounded in the close walls as Bentleigh drew his sword. Mortimer fell back a step, his wide eyes fixed on the blade.

"Montgomery told me everything," Bentleigh said in a hiss.

"Montgomery?" Mortimer repeated, his face blanching. "You spoke to Montgomery out there?"

"That's right," growled Bentleigh, his eyes narrowing at the alarm on Mortimer's face. "I know what you've done. I know what you are. And I want you to know that you've failed. Azalea won't pay the price for your treachery, and neither will King Victor."

"Bentleigh, I don't know what you're talking about!" Mortimer protested. But he didn't meet Bentleigh's eye, his gaze still fixed on the blade extended toward him.

Bentleigh made an angry noise in his throat. "It all makes sense now. What fools we've all been. You even told me the counterforce yourself." He shook his head. "The impossible strength of Montgomery's magic should have made it obvious that there were two of you in it from the very beginning."

Mortimer's face was by now drained of all color, but before he could say another word, he sank abruptly to the floor, landing awkwardly on the winding staircase.

Bentleigh, still awake thanks to the cloak, didn't waste a moment. He knew he only had five minutes to act, and he turned and raced up the last steps. The guards by the door were asleep as well, stretched out on their pallets. He pushed the door open, feeling like he was in a trance. His blood pounded in his head, the need for urgent action driving him on. It was impossible to make himself believe that he was racing to his own death.

He stepped into the tower room. It was much less comfortable than Azalea's suite, but someone had carried a simple bed up the stairs. The princess was stretched out on it, looking as peaceful as ever. The aching familiarity of her beautiful features made the breath catch in Bentleigh's throat. Was this really the last time he'd see her?

But there was no time for sentiment. She would wake at any moment, and he had to act quickly. He sat on the side of her bed, taking one cold hand in his. He allowed himself a moment to stare at her face.

"I wish there was another way," he whispered. "But this is the only one I can live with."

He caught himself on the words, a harsh laugh escaping him. He wasn't going to live with it, was he? For a moment his reason tried to reassert itself. How did he know Montgomery was telling the truth? How could he be sure it would work?

Mortimer's own words flashed instantly through his mind. The enchanter had described exactly this counterforce the day Azalea pricked her finger. And, in his subsequent research during the intervening two years, Bentleigh had discovered that a life for a life was the most common remedy for curses of this nature. He'd been relieved that Montgomery hadn't stated such a counterforce in his curse. He'd never guessed that was because it was Mortimer's role to do so.

It was the thought of the vines he'd passed on the way into the castle that steeled him. If he didn't do it now, he wouldn't have another chance until sunset tomorrow. And even with his help, how could he be sure that Azalea would survive the night? The vines were probably inside the walls by now, and no one was currently fighting them. He'd seen the way they came straight for her the night before. At least this way she had a chance.

He pressed a kiss to Azalea's forehead, then straightened. Tightening his grip on her hand, he pulled a knife from his belt and raised it to his own chest. The ring, suspended under his clothes, was in the way. He pushed it aside.

He tried not to think about what a horrible way this was for it all to end. He tried to think only of the truth that drove his desperation—that it was better him than Azalea.

CHAPTER TWENTY-FOUR

Azalea

Azalea's first sensation on waking was the pressure of someone holding her hand. Before her eyes were even open, she felt a smile curve her lips. She knew who it was without having to look. Ben had promised to be there when she woke.

Her eyes sprang open, and she blinked in confusion. Where was the canopy of her bed? She glanced to her left, and realized with a rush of unease that she wasn't in her room. Then she glanced toward where her hand was being squeezed, and all thought of her location fled.

"Ben!" she shrieked. "What are you doing?"

She sat up, trying to extricate her hand, but Ben's grip was like iron. His eyes found hers, agony in their depths, but he made no move to lower the knife he was holding over his own heart.

"I'm so sorry, Zayla," he whispered. "I didn't want you to see this. But it's the only way to free you, and the kingdom. I have to do this."

"Have you gone mad?" she protested, attempting to snatch

the blade from his hand. He angled himself away so that she couldn't reach him, but maintained his hold on her hand.

"I found Montgomery," he said. "This is the counterforce. This is the only way. I wish there was time to explain it to you, but it has to be within five minutes of sunset. I just..." He swallowed. "It has to be someone who loves you more than life itself, and I do, Zayla. I always have."

Terror clouded Azalea's mind, making it hard to think. There was moisture standing in Ben's eyes, and it was only then that she realized tears were pouring down her own cheeks.

"Ben, stop!" she said. "We can figure it out, this is not the way."

"The vines are coming, Zayla," he whispered. "They'll reach you before sunrise. This is my last chance."

He closed his eyes, and she could see he was bracing to do it. She reached forward to try again to wrest the blade from him. At the last moment, she realized she wasn't going to be able to, and she changed course. With an almighty wrench, she ripped the cloak from his shoulders. The enchanted slumber took him instantly, and he crumpled to the floor, the dagger clattering out of his limp hand.

For several long seconds Azalea just sat there, clutching the cloak and trying to slow her frantic breathing. She slid off the bed, careful not to let the cloak touch Ben as she checked to make sure his chest still rose and fell. Hysteria threatened to overwhelm her as she saw the shallow cut along his chest, where the knife had slid from his grip. His clothes were torn, and a glimpse of his thick gold chain showed through.

What was happening? What madness had she awoken to? Terrible things had happened in the sunlit hours since she and Ben had last spoken, that much was clear. A rush of cold horror went over her as she wondered if Ben had been right. Could it be possible that the only counterforce to her curse was for someone who loved her to give their life in place of hers? She couldn't accept that, not ever, but neither could she stop someone making the sacrifice, not when she was rendered unaware by the magic every day.

Her shaking slowly subsided, and she pulled herself together. No use sitting there panicking. She needed to find answers. She laid the cloak carefully out of reach, then knelt down next to Ben. In spite of his peaceful expression, he looked haggard. She would hazard a guess that he hadn't slept since the night before, which meant that he must be exhausted beyond the point of reason.

She knew she needed to leave the tower, but she couldn't bear to leave Ben crumpled on the floor. She pulled one of his arms around her shoulder and, putting her strength to the test, heaved him off the ground. She staggered a step forward, and let his senseless form slump forward onto the bed. With a grunt, she rolled him onto his back, arranging him more comfortably. She would have to come back with plenty of time before dawn to settle him on the floor again, so that the magic didn't force her to dump him painfully off the edge of the bed.

She suddenly remembered his words about the vines. He didn't think she'd make it until dawn. She swallowed, firmly telling herself not to give in to panic. Gathering the cloak, she settled it around her shoulders. It was heavy, and a little too long for convenience, made to fit Ben's tall frame. There were no immediate effects of putting it on—after all, she was already awake—but it made her feel slightly more secure. It had nothing to do with the fact that it smelled faintly like Ben. Of course not. It was just that any magical protection was worth having, even if she didn't initially see how it could help her.

She cast one more uneasy look at Ben's sleeping form, the gash on his chest drawing her eyes even from the doorway. Then she pushed on the door. It swung wide to reveal a staircase, winding down and away. The guards sleeping on either side of the entrance were the only familiar feature of the scene. She must be in a different part of the castle altogether.

A draft of cold air drew her attention, and she peered out a tiny window, set high on the wall. As her eyes adjusted to the moonlight, she recognized the view. If she was in the tower she was picturing, it was about as far from her own suite as she could get. She frowned. Why had she been moved?

But a glance down the outside of the turret showed her the most probable answer. This part of the castle was a fair way from the city wall, but already she could see tendrils of vine in the distance, starting to creep toward the building. She shuddered to think what the scene would be on the wall outside her suite, so close to the forest gate. Hopefully everyone else had the sense to clear out of that wing of the castle before night fell.

She felt a flash of alarm at the thought of her parents' suites, so close to her own. She'd better check on them. She turned and hurried down the steps. In her haste, she almost stumbled over a collapsed figure that was sprawled across the staircase. She knelt down, and gasped as she caught sight of his face. As always, it was pinched and weary, no sign of the peaceful expression that the slumber brought to everyone else.

"Uncle Mortimer! What are you doing here?"

Of course he didn't answer. After only a moment's hesitation, Azalea slid Ben's enchanted cloak from around her shoulders and draped it over Uncle Mortimer's prone form.

Her heart sped with excitement as he began immediately to stir. With a groan, he put a hand to his head. He must have fallen painfully, judging by the awkward posture of his body. He had clearly been unprepared for the descent of the darkness. Had he been chasing Ben, bent on stopping him from his desperate act? A rush of warm affection passed over her.

"Uncle Mortimer!" she said again. "Are you all right?"

Moving at a glacial pace, he opened his eyes and raised his head. She could see his confusion as he squinted at her form in the darkness.

"It's me," she said, giving a laugh that was half sob. "Are you all right?"

"Azalea?" he whispered incredulously. "Azalea, is it truly you?" He pushed himself quickly to his feet, and Azalea followed. "My child! How can this be?" He placed a shaking hand on her shoulder. "You're awake! Is the curse broken, then?"

Azalea's shoulders drooped at the excitement in his voice. "I'm afraid not, Uncle Mortimer," she said softly. "The curse is operating the same as ever."

"The same as..." His voice trailed off, and his eyes widened. "You mean, this is normal? Are you always awake when the rest of us are sleeping?"

She nodded mutely, and if possible, his eyes grew even wider.

"Oh child, what torture that must have been all this time!"

She swallowed, determined not to be as emotional as she'd been the night before. "It has been torture," she acknowledged frankly. "But I don't want to talk about that. Uncle Mortimer, do you know what madness has entered Ben?"

A wary look came into the enchanter's eyes, and she frowned.

"What is it?"

"I don't know what he said to you, Azalea," Uncle Mortimer said, "but I swear to you on my life, I had no part in Montgomery's curse."

She stared at him in astonishment. "Of course you didn't have a part in it! Why would I ever think such a thing?"

He visibly relaxed, although his expression was still strained. "Prince Bentleigh accused me of it moments before I fell under the curse tonight. He said he'd seen Montgomery, and Montgomery told him I was in it from the start, and that was why the magic seemed too powerful for just him." He searched her eyes anxiously in the low light. "But I swear it isn't true. Even if my magic were bolstering his rather than fighting it—which of course isn't the case—Montgomery's power still shouldn't be nearly as strong as it is."

"Of course it's not true," said Azalea dismissively. "Why would you tell me any of this if it was?" She passed a hand over her face. "Oh, Ben. What lies did Montgomery tell you?"

"Where is Prince Bentleigh?" Uncle Mortimer asked with a frown. "Why do you have his cloak?"

"He's in the tower room," said Azalea grimly. "I woke to find him gripping my hand, and on the point of plunging a dagger into his own chest. I ripped the cloak off him when I couldn't persuade him to stop."

"What?" Uncle Mortimer was clearly aghast. It seemed he hadn't known Ben's purpose after all. "Why would he do that?"

Azalea shivered. "He said it was the only way to break the curse."

"A life for a life," Uncle Mortimer breathed, his face ashen.

"Precisely," Azalea nodded. "He said it had to be within minutes of sunset, and…" she felt herself color slightly, "and it had to be someone who loves me more than life itself." She raised a fearful face to the enchanter. "Tell me it's not true, Uncle Morty. Tell me that's not the way to break my curse."

"Of course it isn't," said Uncle Mortimer grimly. "It's Montgomery's lies. A convincing lie, I'll admit. A life for a life is an extremely common counterforce, and those conditions would be entirely realistic. But it would have to have been intentionally established in the curse. I'm confident Montgomery didn't set up a remedy. He intended to kill you outright."

"Why would Ben be so foolish as to believe him?" Azalea demanded. "If Montgomery told Ben he had to give his life to save mine, how could Ben not realize that Montgomery was just trying to kill him?"

"I'm sure Montgomery would have been cleverer than to say anything so obvious," Uncle Mortimer said wearily. "I imagine he found a way to present it that was convincing enough to cloak his true purpose." He shook his head. "I fear I am partly to blame. I told Prince Bentleigh from the outset that if Montgomery had worked in a remedy on purpose, it would be something especially nasty like this. I believe I even named this example specifically."

"Do you think killing Ben was Montgomery's true purpose in whatever he told him?" Azalea asked, more alarmed than ever. It was bad enough knowing that the evil enchanter still had his sights on her—the idea of him targeting Ben as well was horrifying.

"It's hard to guess at that without knowing what precisely Montgomery said to him," Uncle Mortimer said slowly. "But if it was his purpose, you can be sure he had a reason." He frowned. "And I don't think he'd care enough about Bentleigh to want him dead for his own sake. It is possible he knows what could break your curse, and he believes that Bentleigh is the one who could do it. That would be reason enough to want to remove him." He raised his eyes to her face, his voice a little rueful. "Perhaps I shouldn't have dismissed the true love's kiss suggestion so readily."

Azalea felt herself flushing once again. "A kiss from Ben wouldn't break the curse," she said firmly. "Trust me."

To her embarrassment, Uncle Mortimer raised one eyebrow. "He said something similar himself today. I infer that he, uh, saw you last night, when he wore this cloak."

Azalea's cheeks were flaming by now, and to her relief, Uncle Mortimer looked away from her face, giving her a moment to compose herself. He ran a hand over the cloak.

"Speaking of which, this is an impressively strong artifact. It positively leaks power." He frowned back at her. "Bentleigh never said where he acquired it."

Azalea grimaced slightly. "From a dragon, actually." Uncle Mortimer looked startled, but Azalea's thoughts had just caught up with something he'd said. "What do you mean you infer that Ben saw me? Didn't he tell you? Didn't he pass on my messages?"

Uncle Mortimer shook his head slowly. "He told us that the cloak allowed him to escape the enchanted sleep, and he told us about the assassins. But nothing about you being awake. He was incredibly frustrated every time he spoke, and it quickly became clear to me that he was being prevented from speaking freely."

"Blast," muttered Azalea. "The concealment magic is strong." She frowned. "But if he was wearing the cloak, shouldn't he have been immune to it?"

Uncle Mortimer looked thoroughly confused, so she quickly explained to him about the way the curse forced her to remove all signs of her activity, and the way it erased any messages she had left.

"Hm," he said, the interest of a scholar in his tone. "That's impressively sculpted magic. Such power, but such finesse." He shook his head. "I suspect it was irrelevant that he was wearing the cloak. The slumber was imposed on him, as it is on all of us. But the need to remove signs of your activity is magic directed at you. *You* would need to be wearing the cloak for it to counteract that, most likely."

Azalea frowned, trying to wrap her head around the rules of the magic. "It doesn't matter now," she said after a moment. "What matters is figuring out what we're going to do." She cast a glance back up the stairway. "Ben is fine for now," she said decisively. "I need to see the situation in the rest of the castle."

She hurried down the staircase, and Uncle Mortimer

followed, Ben's cloak billowing behind him. She reached the bottom of the turret and hurried down a corridor, heading for the main entranceway. She passed a few side entrances to the castle, but she ignored them. She was only making for the entranceway because it was a central point, not because she wanted to go outside. She knew better than to patrol the wall tonight. The situation had progressed beyond what she could control. Her primary concern was making sure everyone was out of harm's way, as much as was possible. It reassured her to know that Ben was now laid down in what everyone had evidently agreed was the safest part of the entire castle.

Her mind went back over the horrifying encounter with Ben as she ran, and all Uncle Mortimer had subsequently revealed to her. In response to her queries, Uncle Mortimer explained the little he seemed to know about the assassins, and Ben's plan to leave with the surviving one.

"Of course we knew they might have been sent by Montgomery," he said heavily. "I should never have encouraged Victor to consent to Prince Bentleigh's plans. But he was so confident, and the situation had become desperate. We had such high hopes that the squadron following him would be able to report back to us on Montgomery's location. But they returned hours before he did, with nothing to report. They'd somehow lost his trail, and there'd been no sign of Montgomery." His voice was bitter. "I should have known my brother wouldn't be caught so easily, but what choice did we have? We had to try something."

Azalea squeezed his arm. "Don't blame yourself, Uncle Morty. I'm sure there was nothing you could have done to stop Ben if he wanted to go. People think he's much more malleable than he is, because he's so good-natured most of the time. But he's actually incredibly determined when he sets his mind on something." She gave a wistful smile. "Stubborn is the word for it, really."

Stubborn enough to exchange his own life on the slim chance of saving hers. A shudder ran over her, and she picked up her pace.

She emerged into the entranceway at last, and a cry of horror fell from her lips. The vines had forced their way in through the doors, and were creeping across the flagstones. She heard a sharp gasp beside her as Uncle Mortimer caught up.

"Do you have a sword?" she asked him grimly. He shook his head. She felt for her own, and realized that she didn't have it. Obviously whoever had moved her from her suite wouldn't have known to bring along her secret stash of supplies. Her glance fell on the guards sleeping peacefully on either side of the main door.

"Quick, help me," she said to Uncle Mortimer.

She ran forward and dragged one of the guards back into the middle of the entranceway, away from the reaching thorns. If she survived until dawn, she would probably be forced to drag him back, she supposed. And by then she'd be dragging him into the heart of the vines, no doubt. But on the slim possibility that she could keep him free of their reach, she had to try.

Plus she wanted his sword.

Uncle Mortimer had followed her lead and dragged the other guard into open space. He drew his guard's sword gingerly, looking at it like he thought it might bite him.

"Do you know how to use it?" Azalea asked him.

He threw her a sheepish look. "In the most general way, yes."

She gave a tight smile. "Well, I'm no warrior either, but it's not really complicated when you're fighting against plants. You just swing and sever." She demonstrated on the nearest tendril. As soon as she slashed it, several more shot toward her, and she danced back. She was able to hack them all away, but the explosion of growth didn't bode well. It seemed the plant had caught her scent, so to speak. Not that it made much difference this time. The vines were already growing with alarming speed.

Fortunately, they had the advantage tonight of trying to reclaim a doorway, rather than a seemingly endless stretch of wall. The two of them hacked and slashed their way across the entranceway, their boots crunching over dead thorns as they advanced. The vines kept coming steadily, but with two of them fighting, they were able to force them back to the door. It made Azalea nervous to have to discard her sword when she reached the threshold, but she couldn't shove the door properly closed with only one hand. Uncle Mortimer copied her, and together, they slammed it to.

The wood trembled against the onslaught of the vines on the other side. Glancing around, Azalea's eyes fell on a thick metal tapestry stand. She ripped the tapestry off, and lifted the stand. Grunting with effort, she lowered it into the latch, holding the door closed.

"It's not going to last for long," said Uncle Mortimer quietly, as the door rattled. The words had barely left his mouth when the wood splintered in one point, a thorn poking through. Azalea jumped back.

"It's better than when we found it," she said curtly. She turned away, hurrying toward the next entrance. "But you're right. We can't hold these vines at bay all night." The sound of breaking glass made her jump, and she slashed at a vine that was poking through the window she'd just run past. "Our best hope is to try to figure out the real counterforce from the lies Montgomery told Ben."

"That's a slim hope," Uncle Mortimer said grimly.

"Well, what *do* we know?" she asked. "Montgomery told Ben that you helped him build in a counterforce. Namely, that I can be saved from death by someone who loves me, if they give their life in place of mine within a certain time from sunset."

She made a frustrated noise as she lopped off another vine, growing over the doorway of her father's suite. She glanced inside and drew a sigh of relief when she saw it was empty. The guards must have led her parents to a safer location. One of the other towers, perhaps. As she scanned the room, a vine forced its way through the window and snaked toward her. She retreated into the corridor, slamming the door of the suite shut in case it helped slow down the vines that would surely come.

"Why didn't Ben tell anyone?" she demanded, as they hurried back toward the entranceway. "Surely he knew my parents were to be trusted, even if he doubted you."

"There wasn't time," Uncle Mortimer said. "He arrived barely in time to reach you before sunset. But in any event, can't you think of a reason why he wouldn't tell your parents? Knowing him as you do? When he accused me, he told me that neither you nor your father would pay the price for my treachery."

Azalea drew in a sharp breath as she grasped his meaning. "He didn't want my father to decide to give his life." Tears pricked at her eyes. "Ben wouldn't let that happen. He'd be determined to make the sacrifice himself rather than letting anyone else do it." She frowned at Uncle Mortimer. "So do you think my father was actually Montgomery's target? Or my mother, perhaps?"

"Not Ianthe, surely," said Uncle Mortimer, sounding shocked. "Montgomery wouldn't want to kill her."

Azalea shot him a strange look. "What do you mean?"

"Well, he was always so fond of her when we were children," said Uncle Mortimer reasonably. "She's the same age as us, you know. She and Montgomery were the first to be friends. Montgomery was the one who introduced her to Victor, in fact."

CHAPTER TWENTY-FIVE

Azalea

Azalea had stopped walking, and stood staring in abject astonishment at her father's cousin. "What are you talking about?" she asked incredulously. "You knew my mother when you were children? *Montgomery* introduced her to my father?"

Uncle Mortimer had stopped as well, and he looked incredibly confused. "You didn't know that?" He put a hand to his head. "Why do I have the feeling that *I* didn't know that? It's not like I would forget my own childhood. I had a dream about it just the other night." His voice was more than just uncertain—it was unsettled. His demeanor tugged at something in Azalea's memory, but she couldn't place it.

"A dream?" she repeated hollowly. "What dream?"

Uncle Mortimer shook his head, as if trying to clear his vision. "I had a dream about my childhood recently," he explained. "About the time my siblings and I visited your mother, in Rosewood. We kept in touch from that time. We were...good friends." He looked more confused than ever, and he pulled the cloak tightly around himself. "I *had* forgotten," he said in bemusement. "How is that possible?"

"Are you sure it happened?" Azalea pressed. "Are you sure the memory is real?"

Uncle Mortimer nodded, still clutching Ben's cloak around him. A shudder passed over him. "Something unnatural is at work here," he said uneasily. "I'm sure the memory is real, but it was...missing. Until I had that dream. Even the dream I'd almost forgotten, until we started talking about it just now." He shook his head slowly. "It's the most unsettling feeling, not knowing what is and isn't real from my own history. It makes me feel..."

"Adrift," Azalea finished for him, in a whisper. She'd suddenly placed his strange manner. It was unnervingly reminiscent of the timidity that had characterized her mother for as long as Azalea could remember. Uncle Mortimer met her eyes and nodded, still looking uneasy. "You say this dream was recent?" Azalea demanded. "What night did you have it?"

Uncle Mortimer frowned. "I don't know, exactly. It was within the last week or two. A few days after Bentleigh came and left again, I think."

"The same night as my mother had her dream," Azalea whispered. "About a strange memory of something that didn't happen, when she received a visit from your family to her childhood home."

Uncle Mortimer was staring at her. "How do you know?"

"I read her journal," said Azalea without embarrassment. "It was the night of the assassins' second attack. They'd been instructed by Montgomery to search your room for childhood journals, and specifically any mention of Rosewood." She swallowed. "It was also the night the dragon flew over."

Uncle Mortimer's jaw dropped. "A dragon flew over here during the night?"

Azalea nodded, giving him a significant look. "A dragon who agreed to help Ben, but only with any concealment magic that might be at work."

"And that same night, both your mother and I had dreams that were actually memories. Memories of a childhood visit that had somehow been obscured from our minds before then." He gave another shudder, and his voice dropped to a mutter. "What power have you been dabbling in, Montgomery? And *why*?"

"In my mother's dream," Azalea said slowly, "Montgomery wasn't even present. It was my father, but he was the same age as her, and as you. And they exchanged letters from that point on, until she was eighteen."

She did her best to describe what she'd read in her mother's journal.

"No, Montgomery was definitely there," said Uncle Mortimer confidently. "And your father wasn't." He drew a breath. "What you've described sounds like your mother's mind replaced Montgomery with Victor. Like whatever has kept the memory of Montgomery hidden was still trying to remove him from her mind." He frowned. "But I don't understand that, because *I* remember it with perfect clarity now."

A thorny bramble shoved its way through a nearby window, jolting them both back into motion. They hurried back into the entranceway, chased by a chill breeze that had come through the smashed window with the vine. Uncle Mortimer drew Ben's cloak around him as he jogged, and sudden understanding blazed in Azalea's mind.

"The cloak!" she cried. "That's why you can remember it all now! The cloak is counteracting whatever magic has been concealing your memories from you."

Uncle Mortimer stared at her, and she could see the realization in his eyes. He gave a slow nod.

"I wasn't wearing the cloak when I had the dream, of course. I suppose it must have been the dragon on that occasion."

"Will you forget again once you take the cloak off?" Azalea asked anxiously.

Uncle Mortimer shook his head. "I don't think so. It feels like Montgomery stole my memories somehow, and concealed them from me. But I've rediscovered them now. For them to disappear, I think he would need the chance to remove them again." His expression was grim. "Naturally I don't intend to give him that chance."

He frowned. "He must have used even greater power to conceal your mother's memories. Why else would her dream have been incomplete?"

Azalea nodded, a thrill of strange excitement coursing through her. She felt like they were right on the edge of something, although she wasn't entirely sure what.

"We need to figure out what this means," she said with determination. "But not here." They were passing another entranceway, this one also crowded with vines. Azalea fell on them with renewed vigor, excitement coursing through her. Once they'd closed the door, she turned to Uncle Mortimer. "Let's go back to the tower. We can't talk it through so close to the vines."

Uncle Mortimer didn't immediately answer, bending to retrieve the sword he'd dropped in order to help her close the door against the vines' assault.

"My mother's dream wasn't just incomplete, was it?" Azalea mused, as she waited for him. "It was changed. Why would the dream replace Montgomery with my father?" She frowned. "And her journal said that she stopped responding to his letters when she was eighteen. What happened when you were all eighteen?"

Uncle Mortimer joined her, closing his eyes and clutching the cloak in an effort of memory. His eyes slowly opened, fixing on hers. "She came to the capital," he said meaningfully. "Where she met Victor."

Azalea set off for the tower at a brisk pace, her serious gaze fixed on Uncle Mortimer as he hurried beside her.

"Are you saying you think there was some romance between my mother and Montgomery? Before she met Father?"

Uncle Mortimer looked shaken. "I don't just think it," he said, the cloak so tightly wrapped around him now that his arms crossed over one another as he walked. "I remember it. I suppose you could say they were childhood sweethearts." There was a pained look on his face. "He told me he was going to propose to her." He shook his head. "I can see it all once again, as if the memories had never been taken."

"So did he actually propose?" Azalea asked, her eyes wide.

Uncle Mortimer shrugged again. "If he did, he didn't tell me. He had planned it for her visit to Liss. But that was when she met Victor. And one memory I never lost is the moment she and Victor first laid eyes on one another." He let out a sigh. "It was love at first sight, plain and simple." Pain passed across his face. "But I can see it afresh now. How had I forgotten the look in Monty's eyes when he saw?"

Somewhat against her will, Azalea felt a flash of sympathy for Montgomery herself. It must have been incredibly difficult, to watch the girl you'd secretly loved since childhood fall head over heels for someone else. And not just anyone else, but your own cousin.

"So Montgomery was in love with my mother, and she chose Father instead," she said softly. "And he was so humiliated, he somehow used his magic to remove everyone else's memories of their romance." She let out a breath. "No wonder he was jealous of Father. It was never about only the crown."

Uncle Mortimer nodded sadly. They were halfway toward the tower now, their progress occasionally impeded by incursions by the vines. Once or twice Azalea dragged servants or guards away from windows, cutting back any nearby growth. Those moments of hacking and lopping felt surreal. Azalea was so engrossed in their discovery that she felt strangely detached from the terrible reality that the vines had reached her stronghold at last. And she didn't think she and Uncle Mortimer could hold off the vines until morning.

Not far from the base of the tower, Azalea saw with alarm that a servant, lying prone in the doorway of a small dining hall, had thorny growth crawling over the top of him.

She slashed at the vines until they fell away from the man's face, and saw with relief that the thorns didn't seem to have pierced him. He looked unharmed, still peacefully sleeping.

"It's not him they want," said Uncle Mortimer grimly, tugging on her arm. "Come on."

Azalea followed, pausing with her foot on the bottom step of the staircase up to the tower. "Do you think they'll be all right while we're up here?" she asked, glancing back at the castle at large.

"I don't know," said Uncle Mortimer seriously, and Azalea appreciated his honesty.

"Is there any magic you could use, to repel them somehow?" Azalea asked hopefully.

He looked at her sadly. "I'm sorry, Azalea. I haven't been able to do additional magic for two years."

Guilt lanced through her as she looked at his careworn face, and took in his weary demeanor. All his power was being constantly used in battling Montgomery's continued assault.

"Should I take the cloak off you?" she asked apologetically. "Put it on Aunt Melodia, or Aunt Miranda?"

Uncle Mortimer considered the question thoughtfully. "I don't think so," he said at last. "They've been doing their best to slow the vines' advance for the last two years. If they had any dramatic counter to it, they would have used it long ago."

Azalea nodded, not commenting further on the hopeless

circumstances. She was familiar with this fight—the constant refusal to embrace the sense of defeat that was rising up within her, ready to claim her. She had fought this battle for two years, and the bitter struggle had gained her an endurance that stood her in good stead now.

They hurried up the stairs, not stopping until they reached the top of the turret. Uncle Mortimer sank, exhausted, into a chair, and Azalea dropped onto the bed beside Ben's slumbering form.

"What are you thinking, Uncle Mortimer?" she asked.

"Even if I don't know how, I now understand *why* Montgomery took our memories," he said. He ran a hand over his face. "He was always very proud. He wouldn't be able to bear having it known that he'd been rejected by the woman he loved. It's possible that only Ianthe and I ever knew." He frowned, shaking his head. "But lots of people knew of our visit to Rosewood. It must have taken unbelievable power to wipe it out of living memory. His magic was clearly much stronger than we realized, long before he cursed you."

"Did it change my mother?" Azalea asked suddenly. "Father told me once that she was different when she was younger. More sure of herself."

Uncle Mortimer thought about it, and a shadow crossed his brow. "Yes. She *was* different before she became engaged to your father. It was a subtle but still significant change—I used to think it was anxiety over becoming queen." He shook his head. "It's not natural, to be robbed of your memories like that. I wonder how much of her recollection he took in order to impact her so substantially."

"Robbed is the right word," said Azalea furiously. "What gave him the right?"

"He certainly didn't have the right," Uncle Mortimer said mildly. "What I'm more interested in, is what gave him the power? Like I said, that's potent magic. Much more potent than he should have ever had access to."

He looked troubled, and Azalea could understand why. But her immediate concern wasn't where Montgomery had gotten the power for his curse.

"It's all very interesting, Uncle Mortimer, but will it help us break the curse?" she asked anxiously. "I don't think you need me to tell you that we're almost out of time to do it." She glanced at Ben's still form. The state of the vines made his desperation a little easier to understand, not that she was any more willing to let him sacrifice himself. She cast the enchanter a nervous look. "What will happen if the thorns get me?"

He looked as anxious as she did. "I don't know," he said quietly. "But I fear it would kill you."

"And then what?" she pressed. "Would the curse be over?"

He gave her a searching look, but didn't chastise her for the question. "I don't know. I think it highly likely that the vines would stop growing, at least. It seems clear you are their target, and if they reached you, their purpose would be fulfilled. Without the magical impetus to continue growing, they could probably be permanently destroyed."

"But you think the enchanted slumber on the rest of the kingdom wouldn't necessarily lift?" Azalea asked anxiously.

Uncle Mortimer sighed. "I don't think even Montgomery could tell us that."

"What do you mean?" Azalea asked, startled.

He grimaced. "Montgomery said you would die—or, more poetically, you wouldn't live through the night—and the whole kingdom would suffer with you. I then put all the power at my disposal into reversing his enchantment, but without time to use the finesse I would have liked. When you pricked your finger, I assumed that my efforts had softened death into sleep, and that the whole kingdom slept at night because they were sharing your suffering to the extent that they did not 'live' through the night." He pursed his lips thoughtfully. "Now that I know the truth about your situation, it casts a different light on the matter."

"How so?" Azalea frowned.

"Well, it's still true that my intervention softened death to sleep. But it did more than that. If I'm guessing correctly, I 'reversed' the enchantment, so that instead of not living through the night, you *only* live through the night, in a manner of speaking."

"So why does everyone else sleep at night?" Azalea pressed.

"Again, my fault, I suspect," Uncle Mortimer said ruefully. "My power must have latched on to the statement that everyone would suffer with you, and attempted to reverse it. With the result that the rest of the kingdom doesn't suffer *with* you, so much as..."

"They suffer separately from me," Azalea finished dryly. "They suffer during the night, when I'm not suffering, and I suffer all alone during the day." She let out an exasperated breath, the air pushing a strand of hair from her forehead. "As if the time when I'm asleep is the actual suffering," she muttered sarcastically.

After a moment's thought, she met his eyes. "So you don't think Montgomery ever intended for the rest of the kingdom to be in an enchanted sleep at night?"

"No. Why would he have intended that?" Uncle Mortimer said simply. "You were supposed to die. The introduction of an enchanted sleep was my doing, although it wasn't exactly my intention either."

"So no one intended it, and no one can quite predict whether my death would satisfy it," she said grimly.

Uncle Mortimer nodded slowly. "The enchantment has become incredibly complicated," he said softly. "It has multiple elements, and in one way, what Montgomery told Bentleigh is true. My power *is* contributing to it. I can't be certain whether the counterforce to Montgomery's original curse would even fully break my own magic."

Azalea groaned internally. Complicated was the right word, and it made her head hurt trying to understand it all. But she didn't let her dismay show.

"Well, we won't know until we try," she said briskly. "So what *is* the counterforce? We finally have some idea of what drove Montgomery's hatred. Surely that must help us figure out how to counteract it."

"Surely," Uncle Mortimer agreed. "I am almost certain that the connection with Ianthe is the key. Otherwise why would Montgomery have told his assassins to look for mention of Rosewood in my journals? If he was concerned about me remembering the truth, it is likely because that truth might enable us to break the curse."

"That's true," said Azalea, encouraged. "I like the idea that he was getting nervous." She frowned. "And if he was trying to get Ben killed, he may have thought Ben could help break it, as you said." She cast a look of distress at Uncle Mortimer. "It may not be a life for a life, but I have a bad feeling the curse can only be broken by some kind of sacrifice. Am I right?"

"Most likely," he agreed heavily.

She shook her head. "I don't want Ben to carry that cost. Surely there's a way I can break it myself."

"I doubt it," said Uncle Mortimer gently. "That's not usually how such things work. You can't make a sacrifice to save yourself. That would be no sacrifice at all."

Azalea frowned, her thoughts starting to take shape. But she didn't speak them aloud. "What could Ben do, then?" she asked instead.

Uncle Mortimer's breathing was slow in his weariness, and

his brow was furrowed in thought. "I don't exactly know. The opposite, perhaps, of what Montgomery did." He seemed to sense her confusion, and he hurried on. "It's clear that Montgomery's bitterness went beyond mere jealousy. It warped him, perhaps assisted by whatever dark power he accessed." His voice was heavy with sadness, and he let out a sigh. "There have always been whispers about dark ways to increase power, but such things are unnatural. It's said they can drive an enchanter to the point of madness."

"That certainly sounds like Montgomery," said Azalea darkly.

Uncle Mortimer shrugged. "Madness, or just bitterness left to grow unchecked, who can say? But one thing is clear—his love for Ianthe may have been what caused him to begin hating Victor, but that love didn't survive the hatred it created. If he really loved her, he would want her to be happy, at least on some level. He might not be happy about it himself, he might not be able to bring himself to stick around and watch her being happy with someone else. But genuine love wouldn't lead him to do all in his considerable power to ensure that she could never be happy without him. Which is exactly what he did—he wanted her choice of a future without him to be filled with misery. He couldn't let her go."

Azalea was silent for a moment, thinking this over. "Yes, he should have let her go," she agreed. "So the opposite of what he did would be...what? Releasing the person you love to be happy in their chosen path? Even if it's without you, even if it makes you unhappy?" She raised her hands helplessly. "How do you concentrate that impulse into a specific, curse-breaking act?"

"I don't know," acknowledged Uncle Mortimer ruefully. "To tell you the truth, harnessing the power of an unintentional counterforce isn't an exact science. There's a reason conscientious enchanters usually shape that counterforce into a remedy they can control."

Azalea sighed. "A kiss of true love would be much simpler," she muttered. "Or, you know, stabbing yourself in the heart."

Uncle Mortimer gave a weak chuckle and cast a glance at Ben. "Let's not try that."

"Certainly not," shuddered Azalea. "I can see what you mean, though, about how I can hardly perform such a service for myself." She mused for a moment. "And if the vines caught up with me while I was sleeping, there wouldn't be any sacrifice involved that would satisfy the curse, would there?"

Uncle Mortimer shook his head. "No one would be letting anyone go, as such, would they?" he sighed.

"But it would stop the vines at least," Azalea said thoughtfully. "And if I could find a way to let the kingdom go, to have a future that was prosperous..."

"How could you do that?" Uncle Mortimer asked, with a weak chuckle that sounded a little uneasy. "How would anyone let a kingdom go?"

Azalea was silent for a moment, and when she spoke, her voice was brisk. "How indeed?" She drew a deep breath, meeting Uncle Mortimer's eyes and hoping he couldn't read her as well as Ben surely would have. "I hope you won't be offended, Uncle Mortimer, but I think I should take the cloak back."

He nodded, a hint of relief on his face. "I don't wish to desert you, but I have been wondering for some time if someone else would be more effective in helping to hold the thorns at bay."

Azalea didn't miss the way his eyes flicked to Ben, and she nodded, allowing him to believe she intended to wake Ben again.

"Thank you, Uncle Mortimer," she said softly. "For everything."

He nodded, looking so unspeakably weary that she wasn't

surprised at his readiness to hand over the cloak and surrender to slumber again. He slipped it from his shoulders, clearly intending to hold it out to her. But the moment it was no longer around him, he slumped back in his chair, the cloak falling from his limp hand and settling into a pool of fabric on the floor.

CHAPTER TWENTY-SIX

Azalea

For a long time Azalea just stared at the cloak, lying innocently in a patch of moonlight. Unable to help herself, she briefly imagined doing what Uncle Mortimer expected, and putting it back around Ben. But it wouldn't be a good idea. If he was awake, he'd never let her go through with what she was contemplating. And he'd be wise to her tactics after the last time, and wouldn't make it so easy for her to pull the cloak back off him.

She toyed with the idea of finding her parents, and waking them in turn, so she could speak to them again. Her eyes pricked at the thought of feeling her mother's arms around her. And with the cloak on, the queen would reclaim all her memories. Perhaps her timidity would fall away as she became once again certain in her own history. If time hadn't been so short, perhaps they could have finally developed the closeness that had always seemed just out of reach.

But she didn't know where her parents were, and she couldn't afford the time it would take to search the castle for them. Dawn was creeping ever closer, and wherever she went within the castle, the vines would follow. Finding her parents would just put them in danger.

With a sigh, she lifted the cloak from the floor. As she draped it over her arm, a crinkling sound caught her attention. With a frown, she fished in the pockets of the garment, and drew out a crumpled piece of parchment. The candle that had been placed by her bedside was unused, so had clearly been intended for the darkness of early morning. She lit it in the embers that were all that remained in the grate, and held the single flickering flame up to the parchment.

She didn't immediately recognize the handwriting, but there could be little doubt who it was from, even without the royal seal at the bottom. The letter from Ben's parents was short and sharp.

Bentleigh

You will return home <u>immediately</u>.

We expect a delegation from Entolia next week, at which time we will formally accept the proposed alliance between you and Princess Zinnia.

You will be in attendance.

Something squeezed painfully at Azalea's heart, and it was suddenly difficult to draw breath. Ben had told her the night before that he'd escaped from Bant to come to her. She hadn't realized he meant it so literally. It had been clear that he wasn't telling her everything, but she'd never imagined the extent of it. It had never, in eighteen years, occurred to her that the king and queen of Bansford might pull out of the alliance. Perhaps she had been foolish—after all, their views on magic in general and her curse in particular were no secret.

But how many monarchs could see two of their sons become kings?

She scanned the terse note again. She could almost hear King Rhinehart's deep voice, dripping with menace, as she read the last line.

"Oh Ben," she whispered, her eyes traveling to his face. "How many battles are you fighting?"

She sat on the edge of the bed, the paper still in one hand. With the other, she smoothed his tousled hair back from his forehead. The realization that she was going to lose him, no matter what route she took, seared across her consciousness with agonizing clarity. She again felt a flicker of unwilling sympathy for Montgomery, for the devastation of the moment when he realized the woman he loved would marry someone else.

But hard on the heels of that thought came another. Uncle Mortimer was right—Montgomery's love for her mother hadn't been a true, selfless love. The very idea of Ben—*her* Ben— marrying Princess Zinnia of Entolia made Azalea want to smash something. But never, in her wildest imaginings, could she see herself trying to sabotage Ben's happiness in that hypothetical future life. She might feel resentment toward Zinnia, even hatred in her deepest, most shameful thoughts. But trying to remove all Ben's memories of their time together? Cursing —*murdering*—Ben's child because she herself wasn't the mother?

She shook her head. Such blackness of the heart was unfathomable.

Montgomery had been too selfish to let her mother go, but Azalea wasn't like him. She would let Ben go if that was what it took to see him free and safe.

"You deserve to be happy, Ben," she whispered, picking up his hand. She laid her cheek against his palm and closed her eyes. "I wish you could be happy with *me*, of course, but if you can't, well...I hope you'll give a different future a chance, at least."

She set his hand back down, wiping at her eyes. She felt impatient. She had so little time left, and she didn't want to waste it on tears. In the stillness she could hear a horrifying rustling sound that echoed faintly up the dark stairway. There could be no doubt that the vines were coming for her.

"I'm so sorry, Ben," she sighed. "You're going to be very upset with me. I wish I could explain it all." Her eyes fell on the parchment crumpled in her hand, and she had an idea. The curse had always erased written messages before, but this time she had a shield against the concealment magic.

She pulled the cloak around her shoulders, and cast about for something to write with. The tower room didn't have a writing desk like her own rooms did, and for a moment she thought she'd have to give up the search. But on a sudden inspiration she checked Uncle Mortimer's pockets, and came out triumphant. She smiled to herself. It shouldn't be a surprise—he was more scholar than fighter, after all.

She turned the hateful letter over and scribbled on the back of it.

Ben

Yet again, I have to write to you to say I'm sorry. Not that I think I'm doing the wrong thing this time. Just that I'm desperately sorry for how it will hurt you.

Uncle Mortimer can explain the reasoning, although he has no idea what I'm about to do. Ben, if you trust me at all, please believe me that he is NOT our enemy. He had no hand in Montgomery's curse. I'm absolutely confident of that. Montgomery lied to you.

She paused. It was time to get to the point. She was running out of space on the page.

It's very important to me that you know I'm not doing this because I'm giving up. I would fight, for you, and for the kingdom, forever. But I really believe that this is the way. I'm so sick of being powerless against this curse, Ben. Don't begrudge me the chance to do something to defeat it. Uncle Mortimer was right that I can't make a sacrifice to save myself, but I can make a sacrifice to save the rest of the kingdom. I think this is the best chance of breaking the curse that's over everyone else. I really believe it will work, because Uncle Mortimer said that someone needs to let the kingdom go, and that's what I'm doing. Letting it go to thrive without me. He doesn't realize that I have the capacity to let it go in that way, because he doesn't understand how much I love Listernia, how much I want the role of crown princess now. It's a sacrifice I can make, because I've learned to value my status as I never did before.

And even if I'm wrong, and my sacrifice doesn't break the curse, it will stop the thorns. Uncle Mortimer agrees. If I give them what they're seeking, they'll stop going after everyone else. With the vines gone, the kingdom can function, even if the sleeping curse is still active. But if I do nothing, they'll overrun us all completely.

Besides, it might not be hopeless. We don't know that the thorns will kill me. It's not like I'm intentionally killing myself (like you tried to do, you absolute buffoon).

. . .

The blank page was now full. She turned it over, scribbling underneath the curt message from Ben's father.

Listernia deserves to be free and prosperous again. This is my kingdom. And I'm more than willing to do what I can to make its future happy, even if that means it's a future without me.

You deserve to be happy too, Ben. I know you wanted your future to be with me, which is more than I ever deserved. But you can have a happy future without me, if you give yourself a chance. I don't just want that to be true. I genuinely believe it.

If it helps, know that you have all my love, now and forever,
Azalea

She read it back over, trying to hold her emotions at bay. She could imagine his feelings on finding it, but the whole kingdom was at stake. This went beyond what either of them wanted.

She prized open his fingers, placing the letter in his palm and curling the hand closed again. As long as the magic didn't erase it, he couldn't miss it. After one more lingering look at his face, she leaned down and pressed a kiss to his forehead.

Azalea turned to the doorway, steeling herself. She still had work to do. It wasn't just Ben who needed to be set free. It was the whole kingdom. She didn't miss the irony—before the curse she'd chafed at her role as crown princess. She hadn't valued her position as she should have. Over the last two years, she'd learned through lonely bitter sacrifice to care about the well-being of her kingdom and her subjects. And now that she actually wanted to serve Listernia, she had to let the kingdom go. Release it to have a prosperous future, one that didn't involve her.

She pushed the door open, and a gasp caught in her throat.

The vines were already in sight, creeping up the stairway. She hoped she would be able to get through them.

She drew the cloak tightly around herself for a moment, then raised her sword. There was no joking banter this time. With a battle cry, she charged forward, slashing and hacking. She severed the tendrils that had begun to reach into the air, crunching over those on the ground with her boots. Fortunately the vines hadn't been growing up the stairway for long enough to be layering the floor or climbing up the walls. Her boots did most of the work of protecting her, with her sword only needed to beat back any adventurous shoots.

She reached the bottom of the staircase without incident, and breathed a sigh of relief. The vines would have no reason to climb the tower now. Ben and Uncle Mortimer should be safe. When she slashed her way into the entranceway, however, her relief disappeared. It was a grim sight. The vines had overgrown everything. The corridor leading up to the main entrance looked more like a forest than a castle, and the entranceway itself was an impassable tangle of briars.

She swallowed in determination. Not impassable. She would get through it. She needed to if she was going to draw the direction of the growth away from the castle and all its inhabitants.

Raising her sword, she stepped purposefully into the mess of thorns. Within moments, she was surrounded by them, above, below, on all sides. She'd never run into the heart of the vines like this before, and for a second panic threatened to overwhelm her. But she pushed it ruthlessly down. She wasn't a frightened sixteen-year-old. And she wasn't running in fear.

"I want you to know," she panted aloud as she hacked at the plants, "that you haven't won. You haven't beaten me." A creeper tangled itself in her skirt, and she slashed ferociously at it. It fell, dry and dead, onto the tangle of shoots below it. "I'm still fighting, and when I stop fighting, even that will be my way of fighting you."

With a final vicious slash, she broke through to the doorway. Some of the plants were visibly writhing back on themselves as they changed direction, coming after her. In spite of everything, her spirits lifted a little. It was working—she was drawing them away from the castle, and everyone she loved. She knew that many people within the castle must have already been overrun by the vines as they slept. But what she'd seen when she pulled that servant free gave her hope. Perhaps the thorns wouldn't pierce anyone else. Perhaps they only targeted her.

Outside, moonlight illuminated a horrible scene. The castle was surrounded, breached on all sides by thick, ugly growth. Vines had forced their way into every doorway. They grew up the walls and disappeared into windows, they circled the base, looking for a way through cracks in the stonework.

Azalea spared it no more than a glance, knowing that if she stopped moving, the vines would claim her. She had no idea whether it would make a difference where she succumbed, but she knew where she intended to go. Back where it all began.

But she quickly discovered that she couldn't get near the forest gate, let alone through it. It was too overgrown, too tangled and choked. As soon as it was in sight, she stopped walking and laid her sword on the ground. It felt important, and not just because she would otherwise be tempted to keep fighting. She wanted the magic to know—wanted Montgomery to know—that she hadn't been overcome by the vines' aggression. She had chosen to give in to it, for the sake of her kingdom.

It made all the difference to her, and she could only hope it would make a difference to the magic as well.

With a deep breath, she walked deliberately forward, into the heart of the nest. She felt a vine curl up around one foot, then a second one claimed her other foot. She repulsed the urge to fight it. She couldn't help drawing Ben's cloak around her, clinging to the sense of security it gave her, but she made no attempt to shelter. She closed her eyes as the vines wrapped around her, moving rapidly up her body. It was a horrible feeling, and it took all she had not to cry out.

Within seconds, the growth had reached her arms, which were clasped at her throat as she held the cloak. A single thorn stretched out, piercing her finger with a familiar pang.

It was different from the first time. She didn't sink immediately into blackness. Pain—hot and fierce—radiated from her finger and spread into every inch of her body. She let out an involuntary cry of agony, all strength leaving her. She would have collapsed, but the vines held her up, trapping her in place. Her very bones seemed on fire with the pain, and her senses mercifully began to swim.

After a minute that felt like an eternity, the blackness reached out to embrace her at last. Azalea's last thought was of the strength of Ben's arms around her, and the warmth of his nearness.

CHAPTER TWENTY-SEVEN

Bentleigh

Bentleigh awoke with a groan, his muscles feeling strangely sore. He turned his head to the side, blinking at the unfamiliar room. Where was he? It was dark, so he must be in Bant. But this wasn't his room.

He pushed himself into a sitting position. He suddenly recognized the room as the tower where Azalea had been lying, and memory returned. He'd been on the point of trading his life for hers, but she'd awoken. He ran a hand over a shallow cut that stretched across his chest. She must have pulled the cloak from him and sent him into slumber. But where was she? And how was he awake when it was still dark?

A faint moan drew his attention to the man stirring feebly in a nearby chair, and he let out a growl. Mortimer! Bentleigh hadn't had time to tell anyone that the enchanter was a traitor. He felt his hand curl into a fist, and realized that something was clutched in it.

With a frown, he flattened the parchment. A lit candle was sitting on a chest next to the bed, and he seized it. An ominous feeling spread over him at sight of Azalea's familiar handwriting, and he scanned the page frantically.

"No!" he cried aloud, when he reached her mention of the thorns. He flipped the page over in horror, his heart seeming to stop as he took in the rest of her message. Dimly he realized that she'd written her note on the parchment containing his father's imperious summons, and a fresh wave of agony went over him. He'd never intended for her to see that letter. Had that contributed to her hopelessness?

But no, her message was clear. She wasn't giving herself up to the vines because she was hopeless. She was doing it because she had hope that it would free her kingdom. He loved her all the more fiercely for her selflessness, but he couldn't let her go through with it. His gaze moved to Mortimer, who was blinking in a dazed way. Was Azalea right? Had Montgomery lied to him about Mortimer's involvement?

He passed a shaking hand over his face. Perhaps he had been a buffoon—but there was no time to chastise himself.

"Your Highness," Mortimer gasped, apparently fully awake now. He sounded wary, and remembering their last interaction, Bentleigh didn't blame him. He was vaguely aware that he should either be suspicious or offer an apology, but he didn't have time for either.

"Explain this," he demanded. He thrust the letter and the candle into Mortimer's hands, and watched as the enchanter's eyes widened in horror.

"Azalea," he whispered. "My poor, brave child. I wondered if that would work...I hoped she wouldn't figure it out."

He held the letter out with a shaking hand, and Bentleigh snatched it back. He was tempted to throw it into the dying fire, but he shoved it in a pocket instead.

"I don't want her to be brave," he snapped. "I want her to be alive. What was she thinking?"

Mortimer raised his eyes to Bentleigh's face. Succinctly, he explained the astonishing discovery about Montgomery's romance with Ianthe, and what Mortimer and Azalea had deduced about the likely counterforce.

"She found a way to let the kingdom go, as Montgomery couldn't let Ianthe go," Mortimer finished softly.

Bentleigh was on his feet before the words were out of Mortimer's mouth, striding toward the door.

"I have to go after her," he said curtly. "I have to stop her."

"Bentleigh." Mortimer's gentle voice filled him with foreboding. "I don't think you can."

"Of course I can," he snapped. "I'll find her, and I'll protect her from the vines. I can't let her sacrifice herself."

"I think she already has," said Mortimer, his face reflecting a whisper of the anguish Bentleigh was feeling. He gestured around him. "How else are we awake during the hours of darkness? She must have been right that it would break the curse holding the kingdom captive."

Bentleigh felt frozen to the spot. "No," he said harshly. "You're wrong."

He yanked the door open and sprinted down the stairs. One of the guards called to him in confusion, still sounding sleepy, but he ignored the man. Halfway down the stairwell, he realized he was running over vines. They weren't dead and dry like they'd been severed—or at least, only a few of them were—but they were no longer growing, either. They looked almost innocuous.

He refused to believe they'd stopped growing because the curse was broken. That couldn't be it. The whole point of breaking the curse was to free Zayla. Without her, there could be no victory over Montgomery's magic. Not as far as he was concerned.

He was aware of Mortimer following behind him, but he didn't pause as he raced through the corridors of the castle. The place was a mess of vines, hanging limply from doorposts, and stretched motionless across the flagstones. All around him people were emerging, and he was greeted by a confused jumble of fearful exclamations as they caught sight of the plants, and joyful cries at being awake during the night.

He ignored it all, sure of his destination. If Azalea intended to surrender herself to the curse, there was one obvious place she would go. The first hint of dawn still hadn't reached the horizon when he burst from the castle, heading for the forest gate. He didn't make it all the way there—he didn't need to. Some distance away from it, in the castle gardens, was a gruesome sculpture.

A tangle of vines rose up in a solid, cage-like shape. And in the middle, slumped limply against the thick strands, was a form he knew achingly well.

"AZALEA!" he roared, charging at the shape. Afraid of hurting her, he threw his sword aside and ripped at the strands with his bare hands. It was only as he yanked rope after rope away without injury that he realized the difference. The vines no longer had thorns.

This change did nothing to reassure him, and he tore the restraints away more frantically than ever. Within moments, he pulled the structure apart, and caught Azalea's motionless form as she collapsed onto him. She felt unnaturally cold, and she gave no response to her change in position.

"No, Zayla, no," he whispered, lowering her gently to the ground as he searched her face. "Wake up. Talk to me."

He glanced at the sky. It was still nighttime. She should be awake.

"Don't do this," he begged, as if he could retrospectively change her mind. It was unbearable to think that while she'd wrestled with her decision, he'd been totally unaware, powerless to prevent her sacrifice.

He could feel someone's presence behind him, but he didn't

turn to look at Mortimer. He didn't even care that there was a sob in his voice as he cradled Azalea's form in his arms. "I can't lose you forever," he said brokenly. "I can't."

He squeezed her against him, afraid of what he'd find if he looked too closely. But with his face pressed into her hair, he heard her soft labored intake of breath. He almost cried with relief, drawing back and searching her face again. Her features were twisted slightly, as if in pain, but she was definitely breathing.

He glanced down her form and gave a gasp. He clutched at her hand, lifting it up for a better look. There was an ugly gash on one finger, and blood still dripped from it onto Bentleigh's tunic. But the wound itself wasn't what alarmed him. There was a ribbon of black leaking out from it, turning the warm brown of Azalea's skin into a lifeless, shriveled black. It had claimed almost the whole hand, and it was clearly still spreading.

"What's happening?" he demanded, turning to Mortimer at last. Even as he spoke, the first glint of dawn appeared on the horizon. The enchanter stepped forward, his face pale and his eyes fixed on Azalea's hand.

"The curse is claiming her," he said hollowly.

"NO!" Bentleigh's shout was fierce. "I won't let that happen."

"It's happening, whether you'll let it or not," said Mortimer. Something about his voice was different, and Bentleigh looked up at him with narrowed eyes. The enchanter's posture was upright, and although his tone was sad, it had lost the weariness that Bentleigh had come to expect.

"But she's not dead," Bentleigh insisted. "She's breathing, look!"

As if to prove his point, Azalea gave a grunt, her expression twisting. Bentleigh gripped her more tightly, hating these signs of pain, but hoping desperately that they meant she was coming around. But she showed no awareness, her eyes remaining closed.

"She's not dead, but she's dying," Mortimer said, his voice catching a little. "The magic is spreading like a poison, look at it. I think we're seeing what Montgomery intended would happen the first time she pricked her finger. That must be why he didn't just say she'd die, but that she wouldn't live through the night. He intended for it to be drawn out." He grimaced. "Painful. Not just for her, but for Victor and Ianthe."

"I don't care what he intended!" The words felt ripped from Bentleigh's throat. "I'm not going to let her die! If it's poison, there must be a way to stop it spreading."

"Look at it, Bentleigh," repeated Mortimer grimly. "It's not normal poison. It's magic, and it's killing her."

The sky was light enough now that Bentleigh could see the castle's inhabitants pushing their way out through the overgrown entrance. He caught sight of the king and queen, emerging into the dim light.

"Won't your magic keep her alive, like last time?" he pleaded, turning back to Mortimer. He knew his answer before the enchanter spoke. The black growth had spread up Azalea's arm, reaching almost to her elbow now. This was nothing like last time.

"My magic is no longer fighting Montgomery's." Mortimer's voice was soft. "I can't feel it anymore. Azalea's sacrifice must have broken my enchantment. It freed the rest of the kingdom, but it left her unprotected against Montgomery's original assault."

A cry reached Bentleigh's ears, and a moment later the queen was at his side, her eyes wide and horrified.

"What's happening to her?" she demanded, reaching for her daughter. "Why is she out here?"

Bentleigh hardly heard the words as Mortimer explained to

Queen Ianthe what he'd already explained in the tower room. He was too focused on Azalea's tense but unresponsive face. He had to be asked twice to release her before he understood what the enchanter was doing. Mortimer slipped the cloak from Azalea's shoulders and wrapped it instead around the queen.

Bentleigh heard Queen Ianthe's sharp intake of breath as her memories came rushing back, Mortimer's soft voice helping her put the pieces together. He could only imagine how unsettling the sensation must be, but this was no time to dwell on memories.

"How do we stop the poison from spreading?" he repeated curtly.

"We can't," said Mortimer frankly. "The only way to save her is to break the curse."

"But I thought you said Azalea already did that," King Victor demanded, his face ashen as his eyes rested on his daughter.

Mortimer sighed. "She broke my enchantment, that was inadvertently keeping the kingdom in its grip. But she can't break her own curse. Not if we're right about the counterforce. She can't let herself go. That doesn't make sense."

The king continued to argue, trying, as Bentleigh had done, to understand the nature of the magic. But Bentleigh was distracted, his mind running back over what Mortimer had told him earlier. They knew now the type of jealousy and hatred that had held Montgomery in its grip when he cast the curse. They needed to find the natural opposite to Montgomery's evil act.

"It really was because of me, wasn't it?"

The queen's dazed voice cut into the conversation. It seemed she also hadn't been following the argument. They all looked at her, and she shuddered.

"There's so much I'd forgotten. So much more than you know, Mortimer." Her eyes darkened. "And to think that I once felt sorry that I'd wounded him with my rejection. He blamed you, Victor," her gaze shot to her husband, "but it wasn't your doing. I wouldn't have married him even if I'd never set eyes on you." She shook her head. "I won't deny that I cared for him, once. But as he grew older, his magic grew as well, and it changed him. Before ever I came to Liss, I had stopped caring for him the way he cared for me. Even then he was doing things he shouldn't have been, taking risks in his attempts to increase his power. It frightened me."

Mortimer looked as shaken as her. "I never knew any of this," he whispered. "I never imagined how many secrets he kept from me."

The queen's eyes passed to her daughter, and tears glistened in them. "But how could he be such a monster as to take it out on Azalea?" She squared her shoulders. "If I was the cause, surely I can be the remedy. There must be some sacrifice I can make to break her curse."

"Ianthe," King Victor began uneasily.

But Bentleigh tuned him out. It was suddenly clear to him what he had to do. Montgomery might have been angry with the queen, and her chosen husband. But neither of them was the target of the curse. Azalea was. And Bentleigh was the only one in a position to do for Azalea what Montgomery had been unwilling to do for Queen Ianthe. To let her go.

For a moment he argued with himself, telling himself it wasn't the same. It wasn't just that he didn't want to let Azalea go —that wasn't what she wanted either, not anymore. She'd made that clear when he kissed her.

But doubt gnawed at him. He couldn't help but remember her parting words, before she'd fallen asleep the previous morning. She spoke of her isolation as though it had been the result of rejecting him, as though she could have avoided her fate by accepting his declaration. That was nonsense, of course, but had she come to believe it, in her hour upon hour of frustrated loneliness? She hadn't actually answered him when he'd asked whether she wished to be free of their betrothal.

But that kiss, and what she'd said in her letter...

His thoughts went around the same tortured cycle again. Of course she'd fallen into his arms—she hadn't interacted with a living soul, other than those assassins, in two years. He couldn't hold her to an expression of love made out of paralyzing loneliness. He doubted that even she could really tell how she would feel if she was free of the curse. If she had any real choice, he couldn't be sure she would choose him.

And that was all the more reason he should set her free.

He laid Azalea down, and pushed himself to his feet. Everyone stopped talking at the abrupt movement, and turned to look at him.

"Your Majesty," he said, looking King Victor in the eye. "There's something I need to ask of you. I'm afraid it won't be a welcome request at such a time, but I must insist."

"What is it, Bentleigh?" King Victor asked, looking taken aback.

Bentleigh drew a deep breath. "I want you to release me from the betrothal."

There was a long moment of shocked silence. The queen stepped forward, laying a hand on Bentleigh's arm. Gone was the look of perpetual uncertainty on her face. She looked more determined than Bentleigh could ever recall seeing her.

"Don't lose heart, Bentleigh," she said firmly. "We're not done fighting yet."

"I haven't lost heart," Bentleigh assured her earnestly. "But even if Azalea can be freed from the curse, she deserves the right to choose her own husband."

"But Bentleigh, I thought..." King Victor trailed off, his eyes searching Bentleigh's face.

Bentleigh met his gaze seriously. "I think you know that

according to Bansfordian law, I can choose who I marry. And this is my choice."

The king's expression grew hard, and Bentleigh could tell that King Victor believed he was running from the dangerous connection at last. But he didn't disillusion him. He was concerned that if the king understood his motivations, the sacrifice wouldn't be genuine enough to satisfy the curse. He saw Mortimer watching him through narrowed eyes, but if the enchanter understood what he was doing, he didn't say so.

"You're right, I do know the law of your kingdom," said King Victor with something of a snap. "And I have no interest in holding you to an alliance that you—and unless I'm mistaken, your parents—no longer consider desirable."

It hurt to see the disappointment in the older man's eyes, but Bentleigh promised himself the king would understand in time.

"Thank you for being so understanding," he said, his voice stilted. He stepped up to Azalea's side. The black growth had reached her shoulder. Despite being still unconscious, every now and then she let out a whimper. It was all he could do not to snatch her back into his arms.

He drew a deep breath as he grasped hold of the chain that had remained around his neck for eighteen years. Then he did what no one else alive could do, and drew it over his head. He felt strangely empty without it, like he had lost not only the ring, but the future it represented.

He saw that the king had his hand held out, clearly expecting Bentleigh to put the ring into it. But instead Bentleigh knelt, placing the chain around Azalea's neck. He'd meant what he said—she deserved to make her own choice. He could only hope her parents would honor that. It was out of his hands now.

Once the deed was done, he stumbled back several paces, prey to a tumult of emotions. Breaking his betrothal with Azalea was the last thing he'd ever wanted to do, but it was a small price to pay if it worked.

Had it worked, though?

In backing away from Azalea, he had been subsumed into the growing group of onlookers. Melodia and Miranda had arrived, hurrying to join their brother, and he caught sight of Lady Winnie hovering anxiously at the front of the crowd.

But he only had eyes for Azalea.

Queen Ianthe was kneeling on the ground, her daughter's head on her lap. For a long moment nothing seemed to happen, and hope began to die in Bentleigh's heart. But then he heard Miranda give a gasp. A moment later, he realized what she was looking at. The black was receding visibly from Azalea's arm, already down below the elbow. His legs almost gave out the sight. Even as he watched, the blackness reached the tips of her fingers and was drawn all the way out.

She pulled in a shuddering breath and opened her eyes, blinking in confusion. Bentleigh fell to his knees where he stood, still some paces away. His own breath was coming in gasps, and he realized that tears were pouring down his cheeks. He didn't care. He could hardly believe it was over. Everything in him urged him to run forward and pull her into his arms, but he remained in place. His limbs didn't seem to want to respond, and in any event, he no longer had that right. The pain of the thought was barely a pinprick when compared to the over-whelming relief of seeing Azalea not only free of the dark magic, but awake under the light of the sun.

Azalea had barely regained consciousness when she disap-peared completely into her mother's embrace.

"You did it, Bentleigh." Mortimer's relieved voice drew Bentleigh's head up. He hadn't even noticed the enchanter approach. "I must confess, I wasn't at all sure it would work, but it seems you understood the counterforce."

King Victor looked sharply over at the words. His piercing gaze passed between Bentleigh, still on his knees, and Azalea. Bentleigh could see the moment comprehension dawned.

"You did it to free her," the king said slowly.

Bentleigh nodded, wiping quickly at the moisture on his cheeks. "In more ways than one."

King Victor drew a long breath. "Why didn't you just tell me?"

Bentleigh shrugged. "I thought maybe it had to be real to work. I wasn't sure what the magic would require." His eyes fixed on Azalea, and his voice dropped to a soft murmur. "Besides, I meant what I said. She deserves to make her own choice. She doesn't need an alliance, or a king, to make her a strong monarch."

The king's eyes rested on his daughter as well. "I believe you're right." There was a slight smile on his face as he looked back at Bentleigh. "I think I know who she'll choose, nevertheless."

Bentleigh tried to smile, but he couldn't quite manage it. He was too overwhelmed by the various emotions of the last few hours. He was as determined as ever to win Azalea's heart. But his uncertainty as to whether his parents would now allow him to form an alliance with Listernia was the least of his obstacles.

Azalea was free now, in every way. And he had no idea how she would look at him without their betrothal standing between them. Especially once she discovered what he'd selfishly hidden from her—that he'd had the power to free her from it all along.

CHAPTER TWENTY-EIGHT

Azalea

Azalea returned the pressure of her mother's embrace. She could barely make out the queen's jumbled exclamations, but she got the general idea. She laughed and cried at the same time as she laid her head on the older woman's shoulder.

"It's so bright!" she said, delight in her voice. "My eyes actually hurt!"

Her mother pulled back slightly, searching Azalea's face in concern. "I imagine they just need time to adjust. Is there pain anywhere else?"

"Nothing I can't handle," said Azalea cheerfully. "I didn't mean that anything is wrong with my eyes. They're just so used to darkness. You'd be amazed by my night vision now."

"Night vision?" The queen was understandably confused, but Azalea shook her head.

"There's an unbelievable amount to explain," she said, extricating herself gently from her mother's arms, "but we can do all that later." She was still fairly vague on what had happened. The curse was broken, that much was clear. But how had it happened? One face was conspicuously missing from the small group huddled around her, and alarm leaked into her as she remembered Montgomery's claim about the counterforce.

Where was Ben?

Her eyes searched the gathered crowd, and fell on his familiar form, some distance away. Relief swelled inside her. He was on his knees, and tears were glistening on his cheeks. The sight made her breath catch in her throat. She couldn't remember ever seeing him cry before.

She pushed herself to her feet, wincing slightly at the weakness in her limbs. Despite her airy words to her mother, she was in considerable pain. One arm in particular ached sharply, and she could still feel the sting of the thorn that had pierced her finger. Plus, her whole body was sore, as if she was still recovering from a beating.

But it seemed to have worked, so it was worth every ounce of pain. A slight shudder went over her frame. It was even worth the horrifying dream she'd been trapped in since the vines claimed her. She'd been drowning in a sea of thorns. Her kingdom had been burning around her, dragons circling overhead as everything succumbed to total destruction, and everyone she loved fell one by one. And through it all, she'd been trapped, powerless, in a cage of vines that seemed to rip the very flesh from her bones. She didn't understand the strange vision—just more of Montgomery's evil malice, she supposed— but she did know one thing. The hand that had reached into the prison of suffering and pulled her free had been Ben's. She knew its grip as well as she knew her own face. He had somehow broken her free. But how?

She stumbled forward on shaky legs, and her father intercepted her. He wrapped her in his arms, murmuring a barely comprehensible string of exclamations. She returned the hug, only too happy to lay her head against his strong chest for a moment. But Ben's absence still tugged at her mind, making it impossible to be fully at ease.

By the time she pulled back from the king and approached Ben, he had pushed himself to his feet. She expected him to take her in his arms, witnesses be hanged, but he didn't. He just placed a tentative hand on her shoulder, his eyes searching hers.

"You're awake," he whispered. "Are you all right?"

She nodded, smiling mistily. "I am now."

His eyes narrowed. "Good. Then I can afford to be angry with you for surrendering yourself to the vines on purpose."

"Did it work?" she challenged, raising an eyebrow. "Did it free the rest of the kingdom from their share in the curse? *And* stop the vines from growing?"

"Well, yes," he admitted begrudgingly. "But I still don't approve."

Her eyebrow went up still further. "Do I need to remind you what you were attempting to do when last we spoke?"

He grimaced.

"I assume you found my note?" Azalea pressed. When Ben nodded, a pained look in his eyes, she added, "I'm sorry I called you a buffoon."

Ben's eyes narrowed. "Are you, though?"

She grinned. "No, not really."

At that he gave a low laugh and drew her against him for a hug. But it was nothing like his embrace a couple nights before. He was cautious, withdrawn. Something had changed, and she got the sense that it was more than just the presence of an audience.

She pulled back, searching his eyes anxiously. "Ben, what's wrong?"

"Nothing in the world," he said, his eyes smiling down into hers. "You're free, Zayla. What more could I possibly want?"

She frowned, still feeling like she was missing something. If she was honest, the whole reunion was a little disappointing in its flatness.

"Ben," she started, feeling strangely shy. She'd never felt that way around him before. "I was in a dark place after the thorn pierced me again." She shivered, and Ben's grip tightened on her arm. "You pulled me out somehow." Her eyes searched his face again. "How did you do it? How did you break my curse?"

He smiled, but the expression wasn't quite natural. "Never mind that. It turns out it was quite simple. And not as drastic as plunging a dagger into my own heart, I'm happy to say."

Something twitched in his face as he said the words. Azalea would almost have guessed that he was lying, but clearly he wasn't. After all, she could see for herself that he was alive and well, with no injury beyond that shallow cut across his chest.

She reached up tentatively to touch it. Not for the first time, the muscles of his chest tightened under her hand. Something was different though—what was it? Her gaze passed again to his face, trying to find words for the confused jumble of emotions whirling through her mind.

But before she could speak, a cry of rage cut through the early morning air, bringing everyone's heads whipping around to Queen Ianthe.

"You!"

Azalea followed the direction of her mother's pointing finger, and frowned in confusion. A peasant, whom she didn't recognize, was staring back at the queen in horror, his jaw slack and his eyes panicked. Azalea blinked at him. Why was her mother shouting accusingly at this random man?

"You dare to show your face here?" The queen was basically shrieking now. She turned to the group gathered around them. "Guards, seize him! Don't let him get away!"

The peasant was indeed backing away, sheer terror on his face.

"Victor!" the queen appealed to her husband. "We can't let Montgomery go free!"

Ben hissed at the name of the enchanter, and Azalea stared at her mother in total astonishment. Had she lost her mind that she thought this stranger was Montgomery? Surely he was at least ten years too young.

"The cloak!" Ben gasped, and all at once it hit Azalea as well. Her mother was wearing the artifact that counteracted concealment magic. She could see something the rest of them couldn't.

Mortimer obviously reached the realization the same moment she did, because before she could blink, he had surged forward. Gone was the weariness that had hung about him mere hours before. His eyes were clear, and his face was set in grim lines as he called forth power. Azalea couldn't sense magic, but there was still a palpable tension to the air as Mortimer held one hand out toward the cloak. Almost she could imagine she saw the power leaking from the artifact as Mortimer drew it out. Then he cast his arm in a wide motion, like throwing a net into a river.

Seemingly of its own accord, the cloak flared out and then fell flat, its folds hanging limply. Meanwhile the air seemed to shimmer in the wake of Mortimer's arm, as if he was casting the magic from the cloak across the crowd. The shimmering concentrated into one point, right in front of the bewildered peasant, and the form of a man emerged. A man Azalea had never seen before, but who looked familiar nonetheless.

"Montgomery," she breathed, gripping Ben's arm convulsively. She felt him stiffen, and a moment later he swept her behind him.

She wasn't having that, of course. She pushed her way forward again, her eyes narrowed as they focused on the enchanter. This man had put her through misery for two years, out of sheer spite. If he'd come to finish what he started, she had no intention of running away like a frightened child.

For a moment after Montgomery's appearance, everyone stood frozen, even the man himself seeming stunned by his sudden unmasking.

"Seize him!" roared King Victor, and the stupefied guards sprang into action.

Montgomery also shook off his surprise, slashing his hand in front of him in a swift motion. The vines that were lying limp all over the area suddenly reared up like so many disturbed snakes. Screams rent the air, and people began to run in all directions. Vines caught at their ankles, tripping up the slower victims and trapping them in place. Azalea dove toward the nearest trapped resident, intending to cut the man free, but Bentleigh's hand shot out, restraining her.

"Let me go, Ben," she said seriously. "If you think I'm going to sit this fight out, you don't know me at all."

Ben's eyes were troubled as they met hers. She understood the battle waging inside him. He didn't want to cage her, but neither did he want to see her risk her safety. She felt the same about him, after all.

There was no time to argue about it. A thick rope-like plant erupted from the ground at their feet, shoving up between them. It was once again covered in thorns, and they were forced to spring apart or risk being skewered. Azalea cast her eyes around, frantically searching for her parents.

They stood in the middle of a huddle of determined looking guards, but the human barrier was of little use. She could see plants sprouting out of the ground inside the circle, and she darted forward.

"I'll help protect them," she called over her shoulder. "You go after Montgomery."

Ben made no more attempt to hold her back. A glance

showed that he was making his way forward with grim determination, and Azalea's heart lurched unpleasantly. If she'd just sent him to his death, she'd never forgive herself. But she thought he had a better chance than she did of bringing the enchanter down.

Stooping, she seized the sword she'd dropped when she walked into the vines a couple of hours before. She slashed her way through the tangle of thorny vines now shooting out of the ground in every direction.

She looked again toward Montgomery, and her attention was caught by Uncle Mortimer. His eyes were fixed on his twin, and sweat was running down his forehead as he moved, step by painful step, toward Montgomery. She guessed he was fighting some kind of magical shield Montgomery had erected around himself. She could only hope he managed to bring it down before Ben reached the evil enchanter.

She turned her attention back to her parents. Her father had drawn his own sword, and was trying to hack his way toward Montgomery. He wasn't making much headway. Her mother wasn't armed, but she was glaring in fury at her former sweetheart and friend, no sign of fear on her face. Azalea felt a surge of pride. They'd all been through so much in the last two years, but it hadn't weakened them. It had made them stronger.

Her eyes were drawn to Montgomery, and anger rose up inside her. How dare he think, after everything he'd done, and everything it had cost to break his curse, that he could just walk in and attack them so brazenly?

She redirected from her path toward her parents. She couldn't do anything for them that their guards couldn't. She made for Montgomery instead, fighting her way step by step through the tangling growth. It no longer raced for her like it had when she was under the curse. It twisted in all directions, tangling indiscriminately around courtiers and servants alike.

With a vicious slash, she severed a vine that was shooting at random toward her. She felt a strange thrill as it fell to the ground, and a realization hit her with blinding force. Her banter, her jokes, her determined clinging to her routine, had all been a front for the truth. She had been afraid of these vines since the moment the first thorn pierced her. It wasn't that she'd given in to her fear. On the contrary, for two years she'd pushed back against it, fighting the vines in a defiant effort to resist Montgomery and his attack. Being able to physically grapple with the vines had given her a sense of purpose, a way to fight back. Never had that been clearer than now, when the vines seemed like a physical extension of the man standing only feet away from her.

And only now did she realize the incredible truth—she was no longer afraid of them. No longer afraid of Montgomery. Because her fear had been wound up with her guilt. Guilt over her failure toward her parents and her kingdom. Guilt over her childishness in not taking the curse seriously, and her selfish desire to be free of the restrictions and responsibilities of her royal role.

But not anymore. She'd faced her demons, and she'd overcome. The realization that she was truly willing to lay down not just her desire but her very life for the sake of her kingdom, freed her not only from her guilt, but from her fear as well.

Montgomery had no hold on her now, and the vines were nothing more than so many strings held in the hand of a powerless former puppet master. She slashed through them more and more eagerly, almost able to feel the tug of fear falling from her as the brambles fell to the ground.

As if able to sense her sudden defiance, Montgomery's eyes flicked to her.

"The sleeping princess," he purred. "Awake at last." His

voice, dripping with malice, somehow cut through the din. A momentary hush seemed to fall over the space.

His gaze passed scornfully over her, before his eyes flicked to his cousin, still trapped in a ring of writhing, twisting briars. "And this is who you would set up as our ruler, Victor?" he taunted.

In the wake of her bolstering revelation, his words held no sting for Azalea.

"Well, I can't be worse than you would be," she pointed out cheerfully.

Montgomery narrowed his eyes at her, and with a wave of his hand, vines shot from the ground in a perfect circle around her. She froze in place, not wanting to come into contact with the thorns through any careless movement. The shoots grew with impossible speed, meeting together in seconds, so that they formed a dome above her head.

"You will never rule over Listernia," Montgomery hissed.

Azalea heard a furious cry. Turning, she saw through the bars of her prison that Ben had broken free of the general tangle of vines and was rushing Montgomery with his sword raised. Montgomery turned as well, and at a sharp motion from his hand, a similar cage sprung up around the charging prince. Azalea narrowed her eyes in fury and raised her sword.

"Careful now," Montgomery mocked her.

He strolled up to her prison. She could see her father struggling furiously to reach her, and the guards attempting to advance on Montgomery from all sides, but everyone was locked in their own battles with the vines. Uncle Mortimer was only a few feet away, but his eyes were closed, and his hands were clenching and unclenching in front of him, still locked in a fight with magic she couldn't see. Aunt Melodia and Aunt Miranda stood on either side of him, their postures similar to his. A chill went over her. They were standing together, combining their powers against their brother's.

And it still wasn't enough.

Azalea brought her eyes back to Montgomery, who had paused a foot away from her. He rolled his fingers, and the vines began to close in on her, the inch-long thorns glistening evilly.

"You wouldn't want to prick your finger again, would you?" he taunted. "Just stay still like a good little girl, Princess."

"Your mistake," Azalea said coldly. "You may think I'm useless, but it just so happens that slashing vines is the one thing I'm *extremely* good at."

On the words, she brought her sword up in a powerful stroke, slicing through the nearest strand with a grunt of effort. She spared no thought for the advancing thorns, falling into a familiar stance that gave her the full range of movement required to hack her way through the cage. Montgomery's eyes widened and then narrowed, and he began to move his hands more quickly, causing layer after layer of vines to grow on top of the existing dome.

Azalea slashed on, unconcerned. The rhythm was as familiar as breathing, and her muscles made no protest at the accustomed activity. Out of the corner of her eye, she could see Ben making similar progress on his own cage, and it was clearly costing Montgomery some effort to reinforce their prisons simultaneously. She moved faster and faster, and he began to retreat as he added new layers. She gave a grim smile.

With a final spurt of energy, she slashed through the outermost strands of the cage, and burst into the open again. In a sudden movement, Montgomery raised his hands to the level of his head, palms outward, and gave a guttural shout of exertion.

Instantly, everyone in the vicinity froze. Azalea's own limbs locked stiffly, her sword still raised above her head. She couldn't so much as turn her head to check on Ben's status. Out of the corner of her eye, she could see the vines curling back toward her, extra thorns sprouting from them as they came. Were her parents at the same risk, and Ben? So this was what it had felt like for her mother and father the day of her christening, seeing her in danger and unable to lift a finger to help her.

No wonder they'd always been a little overprotective.

"Now I have your attention," Montgomery spat, his tone of fury at odds with the light words, "there are some things I'd like to say." He alone of the gathered crowd was able to move. He walked up to Ben with an angry stride, and vines followed him, like an escort of loyal snakes. Straining her eyes, Azalea could just make Ben out. He seemed to have also freed himself from his cage, although vines were once again crawling toward him.

"You couldn't follow simple instructions, could you?" growled the enraged enchanter. "I made it painfully easy for you to show your devotion by sacrificing yourself for your betrothed. And instead you had to go and figure out how to break the curse, did you? Well if you thought you'd won, then you had no idea of the power at my disposal. As if I would let a Bansfordian imposter set himself up as king in Liss! Your kingdom is even more pathetic than Listernia has become under Victor's rule. Your parents saw raw power, and instead of seeking to attain it, they outlawed it! Their very fear demonstrates their weakness."

He turned to Azalea's parents, his fury becoming even more evident. "You think you can take everything that's mine, Victor? You think you can take Ianthe, and the crown, and blindly run this kingdom into disaster for love of your brat?"

He stalked toward the king, pushing vines aside so as to actually jab him in the chest. "*I* should have been king, not you! You think that because your father was older than mine by some accident of birth, it makes you a better king than me? The moment my father married my mother—the most powerful enchantress in our kingdom—it ensured that our line would be

stronger than yours. *We* are what Listernia needs. *You* are weak."
He drew a breath, his voice shaking with fury. "For years I tried
to accept the lie my witless siblings still believe—that we owe
you some kind of loyalty purely because of your birth. If you
hadn't taken Ianthe from me—as though your status gave you
the right to take whatever you wanted—I would probably never
have challenged it. But my eyes were opened that day."

Montgomery drew a deep breath before ranting on. "Your
failure to conceive a child seemed a fitting punishment, without
me needing to lift a finger." He glanced at Azalea, a sneer on his
face. "And then came the princess." His eyes traveled back to the
king. "When I saw how you were willing to throw the good of
Listernia away for a drooling infant who could never be a strong
monarch, I realized my loyalty should never have been to you."
His hard gaze encompassed the queen. "I gave you a chance to
be part of something beyond your imagination, Ianthe. And you
threw it away for a crown."

He turned his back on the pair, striding over to Azalea,
where she was still frozen, her sword raised in the air.

"You will never wear the crown of Listernia's monarch," he
hissed. "And neither will any Bansfordian."

Despite her earlier certainty, fear curled in Azalea's stomach
as Montgomery raised his hands, his eyes passing between her
and Bentleigh. But at that moment, someone lunged across her
vision. Montgomery, taken completely by surprise, was tackled
to the ground by the flying form of Uncle Mortimer.

"I've had...eighteen years..." Uncle Mortimer panted, "to
work on...fighting off...freezing charms." His face was strained
with his efforts. "I won't let you do this again!"

He was obviously doing more than just resisting the magic
on his own behalf. As he gave a final grunt of effort, Azalea felt
the pressure keeping her frozen drop. She surged back into
motion, gasping as feeling returned to her limbs. All around her,

others were doing the same. Uncle Mortimer, bless him, had pitched his magic against his brother, and this time he'd won.

The brothers were still grappling, and for a moment Azalea thought Uncle Mortimer would subdue Montgomery, and it would all be over. But Uncle Mortimer's movements lacked force, and all at once she realized that even after everything, he couldn't bring himself to really harm his twin.

Montgomery, evidently, had no such qualms. With a sudden wrench, he brought a fist around to connect with Uncle Mortimer's head. Uncle Mortimer fell back, dazed, and Montgomery leaped to his feet just as guards converged on him. With a labored wave of his hands, he brought previously limp vines once again surging up from all over the ground, tangling and tripping the guards.

Azalea raced forward, slashing expertly at the creeping growth, dodging its weaving ends, and leaping nimbly toward Montgomery. She could sense rather than see Ben at her side, the two of them almost close enough now to strike the enchanter.

Montgomery narrowed his eyes at their approach, furious that they were getting past his defenses. He kept waking more and more of the vines, but beads of sweat stood out on his forehead, and he was clearly reaching the end of his capacity.

Azalea was within reach of him when he addressed her, malice in his eyes. "*I am the future,*" his words were a hiss, "not you."

With the words, something thicker than a vine, more like a sapling, shot out of the earth behind Montgomery. Azalea could see Ben lunging toward the enchanter, his sword raised, as the sapling split into two. All in the same instant, Montgomery flourished his hands, and the wood formed into two shafts. They separated from their roots and flew, like sharpened spears, toward Azalea and Ben.

Azalea disregarded hers altogether, leaping with a cry toward the weapon targeted on Ben. He was too far into his lunge to withdraw. Azalea's sword, brought wildly up in an arc, sliced through the wooden shaft when it was an inch from Ben's chest. It shattered into pieces and Ben's lunge continued unchecked. His sword slid into Montgomery's unprotected chest, and the enchanter's eyes widened in shock.

Then he crumpled to the ground, like a Listernian felled by the setting of the sun. Azalea stood frozen, her eyes riveted on the wound in his chest until a guttural hiss drew her gaze to his face.

"You think you can save your kingdom from what's coming?" he panted. "You've seen it—you can do nothing to stop it from falling."

Azalea could think of no response, and there wasn't time for one. He let out a breath that was more like a sigh, and his eyes drifted closed. The vines all went suddenly limp, collapsing to the ground and beginning to dry out, as they did when severed. The magic had left them. They were dead, just like the enchanter whose power had cultivated them.

CHAPTER TWENTY-NINE

Azalea

Dimly, Azalea was aware of a dry sob from her left, and she turned to see Uncle Mortimer being mobbed by his two sisters, all three of them racked by silent tears as they stared at the unmoving form of their brother. Azalea's eyes passed slowly across to her other side, where Ben stood panting. Their gazes locked for an endless moment.

Then Ben's sword clattered to the ground, and he took one fierce step toward her. She mirrored the movement, and the next instant he had swept her up, crushing her against him with his strong arms. The hesitance of their previous embrace was gone, swept away in the intensity of fear and relief, but still he didn't kiss her, still he didn't say a word. He just held her in a trembling grip. She laid her head against his shoulder, drawing deep steadying breaths.

"It's over," she whispered. "It's really done."

"Yes." Ben's voice was deep and familiar and the sound of utter security. "You're really free."

Something in his voice made her pull back. "You said that before," she said, frowning. "Ben, how did you break the curse? What did you have to sacrifice?"

"It's no sacrifice to give up something that was never rightfully mine," Ben said softly, tucking a strand of her hair behind her ear.

She closed her eyes at the gentle touch, wanting nothing more than to sink into his warmth and safety and stay there forever. But as she leaned against his strong chest, she suddenly realized what was different.

"What did you do?" she demanded, touching a hand to his neck, where the chain was conspicuously missing. She followed his eyes to her own neck. How had she failed to notice the ring dangling on its chain around her neck?

"I freed you," said Ben simply. "You're not tied to any betrothal now. You're free to choose your own future."

"What?" She pulled back slightly, startled.

His eyes met hers seriously. "I was too afraid—and too selfish—to tell you before. But according to the laws of Bansford, I *do* get a choice. If I'd had the backbone to stand up to my parents, I could have broken the betrothal the first time you complained to me. And I should have."

Azalea's eyes searched his, as understanding dawned. "So the betrothal was in your hands after all. And you did for me what I did for the kingdom. You let me go."

He nodded, then drew a deep breath. "I'm sorry I didn't tell you before. I never wanted to bind you, Zayla, or to force anything on you."

"I don't want to be free of our betrothal," she protested. "I need you, Ben."

"No you don't," Ben said, his voice fierce. "You're strong, and you're brave, and you care for your people even when it costs you everything. You don't need an alliance, or a king, to legitimize your future rule."

"I'm not talking about my rule," said Azalea, exasperated.

"I'm talking about me." She laid a hand over her heart. "I need you, Ben. *I* need you."

Ben hesitated, searching her face. "But when I asked you if you would choose to be free, you didn't answer."

"I was sinking into an enchanted slumber!" Azalea protested. "You should've realized we didn't have time for a heartfelt conversation."

He gave a weak smile. "I did, of course," he said. "But you made it sound like you thought the curse was some kind of punishment for you not loving me, Zayla, and—"

"That's ridiculous," Azalea laughed. "The curse had nothing to do with my feelings about you, and I know that as well as you do. The punishment I was referring to was the two years of bitter regret when I realized how I really did feel, and had no way to tell you."

Ben frowned, still looking unconvinced. "Zayla, you've never had a choice, and you deserve to. It's your future, and you should have some control over it. I don't want you to feel like a puppet on a string."

Azalea shook her head, her own voice becoming serious. "Believe me, Ben, I've learned in the most brutal of ways that there will always be things in my life that I can't control. I know what it means to be a puppet on a string, and I hated it. But even there, I learned that I had some choice. I could choose how to respond, whether to give in to resentment, or I could look for purpose in it." She sighed. "I wish I'd understood before the curse what I've learned now. I can't believe my childishness in resenting the restrictions of my role instead of appreciating the privilege it is to serve my kingdom as its crown princess. It's an honor no other princess has had in all Listernia's history."

She looked up at him, and saw his eyes fixed unblinkingly on her face. His expression was so earnest, she couldn't help but smile. For all she'd missed their jokes these last two years, she'd always loved it when he looked at her like that. He had a way of making her feel like he was really listening when she spoke, like he took her seriously, even back when she'd been an impetuous child.

"But none of that has to do with you and me, Ben," she said softly. She stepped closer, so they were only a couple of inches apart, and she heard his breath hitch. "I mean, I could tell you that I realize now what a fool I was to resent not having a choice instead of to appreciate my good fortune in having you chosen for me, and it would be true. But it's completely beside the point."

"And..." Ben cleared his throat, seeming to struggle to get the words out. "And what is the point?"

She smiled at this uncharacteristic faltering from her self-possessed Ben.

"The point," she said steadily, "is that if I could choose any man in Solstice, I would choose you, Ben. I love you. I've loved you all my life, I just didn't know what type of love that was when I was sixteen. I wasn't ready for things to change." She met his eyes, her own dancing. "But I'm very much ready now, I promise."

She lifted the chain over her head, draping it around Ben's neck once again.

He reached up a hand, his movements still tentative as his fingers grazed her cheek. "Are you sure, Zayla?" he whispered. "If you need time, I can wait."

She almost rolled her eyes, but she thought she'd better spare his feelings. "Maybe you can, but I think I've had enough of waiting." The dry note in her voice softened, and she leaned against him. "Two years apart is two years too many, Ben. I don't want to add another day more than is necessary."

A sudden fire glowed in Ben's eyes, and before she knew what was happening, he'd pulled her flush against him, and his lips were on hers. Heedless of her surroundings, she snaked her hands around his neck and kissed him with everything she had. It wasn't a kiss of desperation, clinging to a moment which would melt away with the advent of the sun. It was an embrace with no fear and with nothing held back. Ben kissed her under the full light of day, the crunch of dry, defeated vines underfoot, and the giggling gossip of a castle full of servants surrounding them.

But one thing was the same as their first kiss. Nothing around her mattered—there was only Ben.

At least until a cleared throat brought Azalea back to earth, and she pulled away from Ben to see her father watching them with a long-suffering expression.

"Father," she cried, impulsive in her happiness and relief. She pulled away from Ben and threw her arms around her father. "I've missed you so much. There's so much to say, I don't know where to begin."

He squeezed her gently, his voice softer than she'd ever heard it. "I know precisely what you mean. Let me start with saying this—Bentleigh is right. You don't need an alliance to make your rule valid. You are my legitimate heir, and you are the future of Listernia. And I wouldn't have it any other way." He gave her one final squeeze. "And you deserve to choose who you will marry, as I was free to do." One arm disappeared from around Azalea, and she realized that he was pulling his wife close.

She looked up into her mother's face, giving the queen an almost tearful smile. Even more than her daughter, Queen Ianthe looked like someone who had just woken from a long and deep slumber. There would be many hours of conversation to come, but for now, the look they exchanged was enough.

"Thanks, Father," said Azalea, turning back to the king and

speaking lightly. "But I think I'll take Bentleigh all the same. I've grown used to the idea."

Ben gave a light chuckle, his presence suddenly warm and close against her back.

"What did Montgomery say to you, Azalea?" her father asked suddenly. "As he was dying, I mean?"

Azalea shivered. "I didn't understand it. He said I could do nothing to stop the kingdom from falling."

"Do you think it was just more of his malice?" Ben asked, frowning down at her.

"I'm not sure what to think," she said slowly, remembering her horrifying vision of destruction after the thorns had pierced her for the second time. She turned troubled eyes to her father. "Did Uncle Mortimer ever figure out where Montgomery got his extra power?"

The king shook his head. "I'm afraid not. He says it felt like the strength of a dozen enchanters. We're afraid there may be an organized group of magic-users, operating from the shadows."

"Hm." Azalea's frown deepened. It sounded plausible, but she wasn't convinced. If there was a whole conspiracy of evil enchanters, then where had Montgomery's magical allies been when he fell, such a short time before?

"We can worry about that later," said Ben firmly, drawing her against him.

Azalea turned to smile up at him, but all at once she remembered another worry. She drew back, her stomach dropping.

"I'd forgotten about Princess Zinnia!" She pressed herself back against Ben's side, refusing to be dislodged. "Surely your parents will change their minds now that the curse is lifted, though. Surely they'll want an alliance with Listernia again, and want to see you as a future king."

Ben's expression was set in determined lines. "Whether they want it or not, they'll have to accept it." He looked down into

Azalea's eyes. "Now that you've actually chosen me, I'm not going to let you go, Zayla, not ever."

"Works for me," she said contentedly. If she could trust anyone, it was Ben. He would find a way. "Maybe we can get married tomorrow," she suggested idly. "Seal the deal before they can interfere. We were always supposed to get married when I was eighteen, you know."

Ben's eyes lit up with a combination of eagerness and laughter, but King Victor quickly quashed the idea.

"Absolutely not," he said steadily. "If we are to form an alliance with Bansford, it will be done properly. And the wedding of Listernia's princess and heir will be an affair of magnificence, not a clandestine scramble as if we were ashamed."

The king's chief guard claimed his attention at that moment, to discuss what measures must be taken in relation both to Montgomery's remains, and to the vines still choking most of the castle. The queen joined the quiet discussion, and the young couple were given a semblance of privacy.

"I can't deny that I like the idea of a magnificent affair," admitted Azalea, meditatively. Ben's chuckle shook his strong frame, against which Azalea was still pressed. She grinned up at him. "You especially must be resplendent, Ben. You should wear some kind of royal sash, and your best dress sword."

"I'll wear whatever you like," he offered agreeably. "As long as I get to choose the location."

Azalea raised an inquiring eyebrow. "The location?" she asked in surprise. Surely he didn't want to get married in Bansford. Half her family wouldn't even be allowed to attend, being magic users. "What location is that?"

He cocked an eyebrow and gave her a grin that was both heart-stopping and wicked.

"The royal fishpond, of course."

Azalea let out a groan, although she couldn't quite keep the laughter from her eyes. "Fine, but I warn you, I'm going to have so many hair pins in my hair, you won't be able to come within a foot of me without being poked."

"Deal," Ben said promptly, then pulled her into his arms once more. Azalea decided, as he pressed his lips onto hers again, that the details could probably wait until later.

Bentleigh

"They're going to be awful to her, aren't they?" Bentleigh asked, his voice more resigned than angry.

Rian shrugged. "Probably. But I wouldn't worry if I were you. Azalea is tough enough to take it."

Bentleigh sighed. "I know she is, but I can't help but wish she didn't have to be. If you saw how kind King Victor and Queen Ianthe are to me, you would understand why it's so painful that Mother and Father can barely keep from grimacing when they look at Zayla."

"If you ask me," Rian said frankly, straightening his sword belt, "you should just be thankful they let the proposed alliance with Entolia drop."

"Oh, I am thankful," Bentleigh clarified. "And relieved." He shook his head. "You have no idea how hard it was to leave Zayla so soon after the curse had lifted, but it's a good thing I did. Another day and I wouldn't have beaten the Entolian delegation here." He shuddered. "If they had their way, I'd be formally marking my betrothal to Princess Zinnia tomorrow instead of to Zayla."

"Most likely," his brother agreed placidly. "Although, even

though Mother and Father aren't likely to admit it, I think they were actually relieved. An alliance with a kingdom still at war wouldn't exactly be ideal. Entolia was only ever a back up plan. At least until you enraged them by running off like you did."

Bentleigh was silent for a long moment, studying his brother's face. "You've downplayed your role, Ri, but I know I have you to thank for their change of heart. What did you promise them, to get them to back off like they did?"

"Oh, I wouldn't say I promised them anything," said Rian evasively. "I just helped them see the benefits."

Bentleigh frowned thoughtfully, wondering what his brother wasn't saying. "They're not trying to bully you into marrying Princess Zinnia, are they?"

"What?" Rian's laugh sounded genuinely incredulous, and Bentleigh relaxed. "I'm twenty-two, Ben. I'm not about to marry a girl who's only just turned sixteen." He shook his head, and shot his brother a grin. "Besides, you forget, marriage alliances are for the spare. The future king of Bansford is to marry within our fair kingdom, to prove that we have all the strength we need inside our own borders."

"Ah yes," Bentleigh said lightly. "How could I have forgotten?" He threw his brother a sideways look. "Got your eye on any lovely young ladies from Father's court?"

"Not so far," said Rian with a cheerful unconcern that convinced Bentleigh that his heart truly was untouched. "But perhaps I'll meet someone at this betrothal ball of yours tomorrow."

Bentleigh grinned easily. He twisted the thick gold ring he was wearing on his finger, glancing at the royal crest of Listernia emblazoned on it. His mind flew instantly to Zayla's delegation. They should be arriving in Bant within the hour, if their travel had been smooth. Caught up in his own thoughts, he didn't notice his brother's change in demeanor until Rian spoke again.

"I hope I don't, if I'm honest."

Bentleigh looked inquiringly at him, and Rian gave him a wry smile.

"I'm happy for you, Ben, truly I am. You and Azalea have something most people wish for. But you're just fortunate that you fell in love with the girl who Mother and Father chose for you. We both know that law or not, I'll have even less freedom when it comes to choosing Bansford's future queen. I won't have the luxury of acting on my heart, so I think I'd be wisest to try *not* to fall in love, don't you?"

"I don't know," said Bentleigh, troubled on his brother's behalf. "I suppose that's wise, but somehow I can't wish it for you."

Rian gave a sudden laugh, and clapped him on the shoulder. "Why are we talking about me? This is your time, little brother. Your princess is finally awake, and you somehow convinced her to choose you even when she had the option of sending you packing. That's something worth celebrating, if anything is."

Bentleigh grinned, unable to disagree. And an hour later, when Azalea finally arrived, swinging from her saddle and into his arms with a delightful disregard for her dignity, he was even more struck by his incredible good fortune.

He set her on her feet, and she raised her face to his. Her eyes were alight with the laughter that he'd fallen hopelessly in love with from the start, and her lips held a smile that was just for him.

Yes, she was awake, her warm brown skin almost glowing in the sunshine, and she was his by choice as well as by promise.

What more could he possibly want?

NOTE FROM THE AUTHOR

Thank you for reading *Kingdom of Slumber*. I hope you enjoyed this second trip into the continent of Solstice! I would be so grateful if you would consider leaving a review on Amazon—it would really make a difference!

If you want to find out what becomes of Prince Rian, check out *Kingdom of Cinders*, the next installment of the series. As always, more adventure, fantasy, mystery, and romance await.

Join up to my mailing list at deborah-gracewhite.com to be kept up to date on new releases, specials, and giveaways, such as bonus chapters. You will also receive *Dragon's Sight*, an 8,000 word prequel to my first series *The Kyona Chronicles*, told from the perspective of the dragon Elddreki (who just happens to be Rekavidur's father).

Again, thanks for entering the world of *The Kingdom Tales*! I hope to see you back again.

Captive's Return (novella)
Legacy of the Curse
Downfall of the Curse
Downfall's Echo

The Kingdom Tales

Kingdom of Beauty: A Retelling of Beauty and the Beast
Kingdom of Slumber: A Retelling of Sleeping Beauty
Kingdom of Cinders: A Retelling of Cinderella (coming soon)

ACKNOWLEDGMENTS

I really enjoyed writing Bentleigh and Azalea's story! But there's so much more to publishing a book than the first fun sprint (or crawl, depending on the day) of getting words onto the page. I'm so very grateful for my amazing team, and all they do to help turn my daydreams into a book you can actually read.

Huge thank you to Ray, alpha listener and encourager extraordinaire. You're the absolute best, in so many ways.

Thanks as always to my beta readers: Tamara, Mel W, Mum, Dad, and Steph. Your feedback was invaluable.

Extra thanks to Dad for developmental and copy editing, and assistance with publication and release.

To Karri for another spectacular cover (I love this one even more than the last one). And to Becca, for the fabulous map.

To you, the reader, thank you for giving me the privilege of being an author.

And most importantly, to God, who shows me hope when I'm gripped by despair.

ABOUT THE AUTHOR

I've been a reader since I can remember, growing up on a wide range of books, from classic literature to light-hearted romps. The love of reading has traveled with me unchanged across multiple continents, and carried me from my own childhood all the way to having children of my own.

But if reading is like looking through a window into a magical and beautiful world, beginning to write my own stories was like discovering that I could open that window and climb right out into fantasyland.

I cannot believe how privileged I am to actually be living that childhood dream and publishing my own novels. I do so from my hometown of Adelaide, Australia, where I live with my husband and our three little ones.

I've never outgrown my love of young adult stories, so the genre of young adult fantasy was always going to be my niche. If you enjoy *The Kingdom Tales*, don't miss my finished YA fantasy series *The Kyona Chronicles*.

Feel free to email me at deborah@deborahgracewhite.com and introduce yourself! Or subscribe to my mailing list at deborahgracewhite.com for free giveaways, sales, and updates.

www.ingramcontent.com/pod-product-compliance
Lightning Source LLC
Chambersburg PA
CBHW060737190726
48285CB00001B/247